HOW TO FIND A MAN IN FIVE DATES

BY
TINA BECKETT

BREAKING HER NO-DATING RULE

BY
AMALIE BERLIN

BOON

NEW YEAR'S RESOLUTIONS!

Resolutions are made to be broken…!

Childhood friends Mira and Ellory
each make a New Year's Resolution to
stay away from love. Little do they know that
fate has other things in mind…

When two hunky doctors hit the slopes, escaping their
past in the deep snowy mountains, the last thing they
expect to find is two wonderful women who can heal
minds, bodies and souls…and maybe these
brooding doctors' hearts!

This New Year, lose yourself in these
magical snowy romances from
Mills & Boon® Medical Romance™ authors

Tina Beckett and Amalie Berlin

Read Jack and Mira's story in
HOW TO FIND A MAN IN FIVE DATES

Read Anson and Ellory's story in
BREAKING HER NO-DATING RULE

HOW TO FIND A MAN
IN FIVE DATES

BY
TINA BECKETT

MILLS &
BOON

Published in Great Britain 2015
by Mills & Boon, an imprint of Harlequin (UK) Limited,
Eton House, 18-24 Paradise Road, Richmond, Surrey, TW9 1SR

© 2015 Tina Beckett

ISBN: 978-0-263-24681-0

Harlequin (UK) Limited's policy is to use papers that are natural,
renewable and recyclable products and made from wood grown in
sustainable forests. The logging and manufacturing processes conform
to the legal environmental regulations of the country of origin.

Printed and bound in Spain
by CPI, Barcelona

Dear Reader

I seem to have a love/hate relationship with New Year's resolutions. I love making them. Keeping them? Hmm… not so much.

When the heroine of HOW TO FIND A MAN IN FIVE DATES makes a crazy resolution one snowy New Year's Eve she has every intention of keeping it. After all, she's fresh out of a disastrous relationship and not looking to start anything new. What she *doesn't* count on, however, is coming to the rescue of a surfer-dude-turned-newbie-skier when he wipes out on his first run down the slopes. What starts off as one date turns into two, and soon she is doing some slipping and sliding of her own… emotionally.

Thank you for joining Mira and Jack as they make their way down a treacherous slope where trust and self-forgiveness become rules to live by—and hopefully find love along the way. I hope you enjoy reading their story as much as I loved writing it!

Have fun on those ski slopes of life—and maybe even break a resolution or two of your own!

Love

Tina Beckett

Born to a family that was always on the move, **Tina Beckett** learned to pack a suitcase almost before she knew how to tie her shoes. Fortunately she met a man who also loved to travel, and she snapped him right up. Married for over twenty years, Tina has three wonderful children and has lived in gorgeous places such as Portugal and Brazil.

Living where English reading material is difficult to find has its drawbacks, however. Tina had to come up with creative ways to satisfy her love for romance novels, so she picked up her pen and tried writing one. After her tenth book she realised she was hooked. She was officially a writer.

A three-time Golden Heart finalist, and fluent in Portuguese, Tina now divides her time between the United States and Brazil. She loves to use exotic locales as the backdrop for many of her stories. When she's not writing you can find her either on horseback or soldering stained glass panels for her home.

Tina loves to hear from readers. You can contact her through her website or 'friend' her on Facebook.

**These books are also available in eBook format
from www.millsandboon.co.uk**

PROLOGUE

HERE'S TO A brand-new year.

Dr. Miranda Dupris clutched her empty champagne flute and waited for the dreaded annual countdown to begin. The huge gathering area of her father's lodge—with its vaulted ceilings and blazing fireplace—was packed, the free food and drinks drawing in legions of guests and employees, all hoping the year ahead would be kinder than the one they were leaving behind.

Or maybe that was just her.

A fresh glass of glittery amber liquid was pressed into her hand, while the empty one was plucked free and deposited onto the tray of one of the serving staff. The smell of champagne clogged her senses, its sharp bite a welcome diversion.

"Mira, we totally forgot to make our resolutions!" Her best friend grinned at her, long blonde curls bouncing as she swirled the contents of her own glass. "Let's do them now. That way you can dump Robert into the universe's nearest black hole and start over."

At the mention of her ex-fiancé, Mira curled her toes into the ankle-slaying red stilettos while the familiar sting of betrayal lanced through her gut.

Never again. Never, *ever* again.

If anyone was jumping into the nearest black hole, it was going to be her.

She was done with relationships. For good this time. Three failed engagements in the last seven years should tell her something.

"I'm all for that." She forced her lips to tilt upward, trying not to ruin their New Year's Eve tradition, something she and Ellory had done for the last ten years in this very room. She lifted her glass. "I'll even go first. I hereby swear off committed relationships for the next twelve months."

Her friend laughed. "What about uncommitted ones?"

What about them?

Oh! Her foggy brain finally put two and two together. Ellory was asking if she was swearing off men altogether. Was she?

Maybe that was a bit too extreme. She did *like* men. Some of them, anyway. Just not certain bastardly ski instructors.

"Uncommitted is good. More than good, actually." She raised her glass even higher. "Okay, how about this, then? I resolve to date twenty-five men over the next year with no emotional involvement whatsoever. Zip. *Nada*."

Her friend blinked. "Whoa." Ellory now had to yell over the crowd as the clock hands on the huge screen across from them shifted closer and closer to the witching hour. "Are you serious? Miss Monogamy Dupris is going to serial date?"

Um...yes. Why not?

The idea sounded more and more attractive. Or maybe that was the three glasses of champagne she'd had. Whatever. She took another bracing sip. "That's exactly what I'm going to do. Serial date. Twenty-five men...one year."

"This I've got to see. Bet you a hundred bucks you

either back out or you don't make it past man number five without getting attached to him."

Ha! Unless the fifth guy was a puppy hiding in a man suit, she didn't see that happening.

"Make it *ten* men. No, wait…all twenty-five. And backing out is not an option." She waggled her shoulders back and forth, her courage growing with each passing moment. "Tell you what. Next New Year's Eve we'll see who pays whom. Your turn. What's your resolution? And it'd better be good!"

"Well, if you can swear off serious relationships, I can swear off men altogether—maybe work on myself for a change, take on a project. And I'll bet the same amount of money that I *will* follow through." Ellory's expression had taken on a serious note, totally out of character for her fun-loving friend.

But with the hands almost at the top of the dial, she didn't have time to question her. "Okay, so we each have a hundred dollars riding on our resolutions, right?"

"Right."

She'd just gotten the words out when a cacophony of voices began chanting backwards from ten. Ellory clinked her glass against Mira's and they downed the last of their drinks.

Confetti rained all around her, the cheers and laughter of the crowd forming a frothy wave of mirth that carried her up and out of her funk. Mira caught her friend up in a tight hug, so glad Ellory had come to stay with her for a while.

She stepped back, about to say something, when a masculine voice came from behind her. "Well, well, well. Looks like I'm not the only one without a date tonight. Or are you two together?"

Mira's eyes widened when she realized the slightly

slurred tones were far too close to her ear for comfort. Still holding onto one of Ellory's hands, she raised her brows in question. Surely not.

"Turn around," her friend mouthed. "He's talking to you."

Knees quivering, Mira released her hand and pivoted on the spiked heel of her shoe until she was face to face with a beefy hunk who could have stepped straight out of an ad for a gym membership. He was tall and buff, and his too-tanned-to-be-real neck rose from a pressed white shirt and black tux. His blue eyes gleamed with something that looked like...interest. Or boredom. She couldn't decide which.

"I—I..." Her mind went blank, and she scrabbled for the nearest coherent sentence. "Er...hello."

How the hell did one serial date, anyway? She'd have to ask Ellory for some pointers later.

The man's smile grew. "I waited a whole ten minutes to make sure no irate boyfriend was going to bust my jaw for coming over here. I noticed you as soon as you walked through the door. Are you alone?"

Oh, no. Not this fast.

She glanced back at her friend, who opened her beaded purse and tipped it toward her with a knowing jiggle. "You want to pay up now, honey?"

Egads. The woman knew right where to hit.

Straightening her spine, she turned back to the man in question. "Yep. I'm alone."

"What say I buy you a drink, then?"

Since the booze was free, that was hardly an enticing offer. But if her job was to stay unattached, this guy seemed like the obvious choice.

"What say you do?" Mira tried for a purr, but it came off sounding like an asthmatic wheeze.

Before she could chicken out, she handed her empty champagne glass to Ellory, who stared at her with undisguised shock. Mira leaned forward and whispered two words, drawing them out for emphasis. "Game. On."

CHAPTER ONE

JACKSON PERRY WAS going to fall.

No matter how many times he tried to stab his ski poles into the snow, they ended up flailing around like twin javelins about to be launched by a drunken athlete.

Make your skis into a wedge to slow your rate of descent.

The instructor's mandatory lesson played through his skull, but actually obeying that advice was almost impossible, since he was too busy trying to find his center of gravity as his body continued to pick up speed down the slope. He tried to ride it out like a surfer on a killer wave. Only skis were nothing like the smooth, wide surface of his well-waxed board. And the ground looked a whole lot harder than the soft embrace of the ocean.

Wobble.

Correct.

Wobble.

Correct.

Not. Gonna. Freakin'. Work…

A brilliant plume of white spray rose up as Jack belly-flopped onto the snow, his skis detaching from his boots—*thank God*. He bounced his way over some moguls, instinctively tightening his abs to absorb as much of the impact as possible. Fifty yards later he slid to an ignominious halt, still facing the bottom of the hill. He had one pole in his hand, the other was long gone, probably back there with his skis.

Good thing he hadn't tried a tougher slope.

Sucking down breaths into lungs that felt like they were on fire, he assessed his body bone by bone, tendon by tendon. Knees? Undamaged. Wrists? Still there. Ego? He'd come back to that one later. Skull? Intact, although he wondered about his sanity in agreeing to this damned vacation.

He raised a hand to wipe away some of the snow on his face, only to find his gloves were also covered in the stuff.

Hell!

Take a vacation. Have some fun. You need a break.
Or else.

His coach may not have added those last two words, but Jack had seen them written in the tight lines of the man's face when he'd been late to yet another early morning meeting. The product of a recurring nightmare followed up by a sleeping pill. He hadn't even heard the alarm the next morning.

Go skiing, Jack...or I'm afraid we'll have to find ourselves a new doctor.

So, was the plan working?

Oh, yeah. So far, he was having a blast.

And every damn memory he'd been trying to forget had followed him right down that hill, crashing into the snow beside him.

Several more skiers sailed by, none of them seeming to have any trouble with the so-called "bunny slope." Nothing like wiping out on your very first run.

A pair of skis came into view. Angled just like the

instructor had described. *Perfect.* He glanced up, squinting to see past the blinding midmorning sun.

"Need some help there?"

A vision in a white ski jacket and matching snow pants stood before him, the light seeming to halo around the figure's shoulders and head.

Maybe he'd hit the ground harder than he'd thought.

He shook his head and then struggled into a sitting position, but the slick fabric of his own suit caused him to slide down the hill a few more feet. The person matched his downward trajectory inch for inch, again coming to a halt right as he did. Still on her feet.

A quick feminine laugh met his ears. "Here, take my hand. Your boots should help you gain some traction. I've already picked up your skis and pole."

He glanced up again and saw that the woman—and she was definitely a woman—did indeed have his errant equipment caged in the crook of her arm. A white-gloved hand stretched down toward him.

Definitely not a beginner. At least, he hoped not, otherwise he might as well throw in the towel and stick to football and watersports.

"I'm good." The last thing he wanted was to bring her down with him. He struggled to his feet, somehow succeeding on the first try. She was right, though, about the boots giving him traction.

"Think you can make it to the bottom?" She flipped her goggles up over her head, causing the fur-trimmed hood of her jacket to fall back, revealing a pink knit aviator hat. Soft brown eyes that were alight with humor regarded him.

She'd probably get a lot of mileage out of this story over drinks with her friends later on.

She was exactly what he pictured when he thought of

snow bunnies, from her matchy-matchy suit to her obvious ease in the frigid environment. Even her complexion was pale and frosty, with just a touch of pink warming her lips and cheeks. Cool and untouchable. All except for the flaming locks now visible from beneath her hat.

Just like Paula's hair had been. His teeth clenched.

"Are you okay?" she asked.

Right. She was still waiting for him to tell her if he could make it down the hill.

"I'll be fine from here. Thanks again for the help. If you'll just hand me my gear…"

"First time on the slopes?"

Wasn't it obvious? A spark of male pride urged him to tell her that he'd once competed in some of the biggest surfing competitions California had to offer. But that had been before he'd gotten his medical license and changed his focus to football. Before the accident that had changed his life forever.

Coach was right. He'd let himself go over the last four years.

"Yep." His eyes tracked a little girl zipping down the course with ease. "They make it look so easy."

The woman glanced over her shoulder with a smile. "Yes, they do." She turned back and held out her hand again. "Miranda Dupris."

"Jack Perry." He took her hand and gave it a quick squeeze, suddenly glad they both had on gloves. Even so, something in his gut twisted at the brief contact.

A voice came from the side. "Hey, Florence Nightingale, do you mind clearing the slope? I don't want a pile-up on my watch." His instructor from a few minutes ago pushed his poles into the snow and surged past them, heading on down the hill. He didn't glance their way, but something about the wry twist to his voice said he knew Miranda. Quite well, in fact.

Of course the guy knew her. She was a snow bunny. She probably knew all the instructors by name.

Then a strange thing happened. Instead of waving to the man with a laugh, her brown eyes went from smiling and carefree to cool and irritated in the space of a few seconds.

A woman scorned? Or something else?

"Come on," she said. "I'll buy you a hot chocolate once we get to the bottom."

He almost groaned. He'd been hoping to clomp his way down the hill and head straight to his room, where he could lick his wounded ego in private. The last thing he wanted to do was hang around the bar with a woman who'd seen him at his worst.

He swallowed and retracted that last thought. She hadn't seen him at his worst, but his coach had. Including the twenty pounds he'd shed over the past six months as the dreams had swallowed more and more of his nights and haunted his days. It's what had made the man book this vacation in a frozen wasteland. Why couldn't he have chosen Hawaii instead?

Maybe he could refuse her offer with grace. "No need, but thanks." He held out his hands for the equipment she still held.

"Maybe not, but standing here without working my muscles has made me realize I'm freezing my tushie off, and I could sure use something to warm it back up."

Those words finally yanked him free of his morose thoughts and put them right on...

No, you don't, Perry. Don't you dare look.

Too late. His eyes had already skated over her hips

and mentally guessed what lay beneath all those layers of clothing. And it was good.

Wow. If she knew what you were thinking, she'd dump your gear in the snow and march her oh-so-cold tushie right back down the hill.

Damn. Time to renew his gentleman card. Paula would have given him a single raised eyebrow if she could hear him now.

But she couldn't. Thanks to him. And the coach. And the team.

No. That was no one's fault but his.

Suddenly the last thing he wanted was to be alone. Even if it meant spending a half-hour with a woman who'd probably made the rounds more than he had during his entire internship. "Hot chocolate sounds good. Thanks."

She gave him a quick grin and handed him his equipment. "Don't hurry, unless you enjoy sliding down the hill. I'll meet you at the bottom."

With that, she turned around and pushed off, her skis flashing as she leaned forward and took the slope like an expert.

Sighing, Jack juggled his poles and his skis and took his first shaky step.

Did forcing someone to drink hot chocolate count as date number five? Mira scrunched her nose as she waited for her next victim to finish trudging his way down the hill. She wouldn't have pushed so hard if it hadn't been for that Florence Nightingale crack Robert had made as he'd sailed past her.

Yes, it was spiteful to head for the bar with another man when she knew her ex was there on his break, but she wanted to make it as plain as the icicles hanging from the man's heart that she was done. No amount of sweet-talking would get her to take him back. Seducing your female students was not part of a ski instructor's job description, no matter what most people thought.

Ellory was right. She needed to move on. Not getting emotionally attached was something that came hard for her, but if she kept choosing men who were not her type, it should be a breeze.

Jack Perry was definitely on the "not" side of the equation. Her newly written "not" side, anyway.

With his chiseled, clean-shaven jaw and refusal to let her help him up, he was evidently a man's man, something she was now avoiding like the plague as far as relationships went. She'd been there, done that—three times, in fact—and had the heartbreak to prove it. The next guy she got serious with was going to be a poet. Or an artist. Someone who was in touch with his feminine side.

There was nothing feminine about the man she'd met on the slopes. She'd bet he was an athlete—from the easy way his wiry muscles had pushed him up off the ground. Yeah, he might have crashed and burned on that slope, but that was from lack of experience, not lack of strength. Those glutes had some power behind them.

Something she was better off not thinking about.

Hot chocolate. Nothing else. She might have joked with Ellory about bedding a man or two during the next year, but she wasn't planning on actually doing that. Too dangerous. For her, anyway. The words sex and casual? An oxymoron. It always became personal.

So far she'd racked up three losers. Three men who couldn't resist the thrill of the chase, even when that chase involved someone other than their fiancée.

No more bad boys for her.

Surely after a year of empty dates she'd be able to tell

the difference between a player and a guy who was capable of monogamy. Until then, she had to stick to the plan.

But, man, oh, man, as Jack sidled the last twenty feet, making short work of each step in those heavy boots, he was making her little heart go pitter-patter.

Reaching down to undo her skis when she realized she'd been watching him instead of attending to her own business, she stepped out of them and hefted them upright. "Ready?" she asked, when he reached her.

"Yes." His voice was a little tighter than it had been up the hill, although she didn't see how that could be, since he hadn't been jumping for joy at the thought of spending some time with her. She'd had the opposite problem with man number three. He hadn't exactly been happy when she'd closed the door to her room with him on the wrong side of it.

Well, from Jack's guarded expression, getting rid of him should be a snap.

They turned in their skis and poles at the equipment center next to the ski lodge and then Mira led the way into the foyer of the main building. The familiar honeyed tones of wood-covered floors and walls welcomed her like a snug, warm cocoon, especially when compared to the vast snow-covered surfaces outside its doors. The crackle of the fire in the huge stone fireplace in the middle of the room only added to that sense of welcome.

Moving over to the long hallway lined with pegs and cubbies, she shimmied out of her jacket and hung it up along with her hat. As she ran her fingers through her hair to fluff it up a bit, she was far too aware of the man next to her shuffling out of his own coat and snow pants. She smiled at the snug black jeans he had on beneath his clothes. And, man, she was so right about those glutes.

Damn!

He swung back around, catching her in the act. One brow lifted, and his lips tightened just a touch. So he didn't like her looking. Well, it wasn't as if he hadn't checked her out on the slope. She'd seen those dark eyes skim over her in quick appraisal. Right after her ex had zoomed past, like the jerk he was.

Forget about Robert. He was not on her current shopping list. Jack was.

She refreshed her memory about the goals of this particular encounter: have a quick cup of cocoa and then she was free to move on.

To man number six.

CHAPTER TWO

JACK'S SKI INSTRUCTOR was currently staring at his rescuer. And not a subtle kind of stare, either. This was a full-on, you-*will*-look-at-me kind of unwavering attention.

And yet as Miranda set their drinks down, she was chatting away as if she had no idea.

He gave himself a mental palm to the head. Of course. She had to be a ski instructor as well. No wonder she'd helped him up and made sure he got down the hill. It also explained why the other guy had told her to clear him off the slope.

What it didn't explain was why the man was now staring at them.

Best to settle this right here and now, in case this was a pity drink. Surely he didn't look that badly off. He'd have to work on his cheerful see-ya-later grin. "You don't have to sit with me. I'm fine, really."

She frowned. "Never thought you weren't. I'm sitting here because I'm cold and tired and wanted some hot chocolate."

"I didn't see you up at the top when I was having my lesson."

"That's because I wasn't there. I was skiing one of the harder slopes. I decided to finish up on the bunny. As a cool down."

Cool down. No wonder she was in such great shape. And she was. He might deny it until he was blue in the face, but he'd glanced at her a time or two. Enough to know that her slender legs were strong. So were her arms. If he'd met her anywhere else, he might think she was a distance runner. But she wasn't. She was a skier.

"I bet you have to rescue lots of guys like me." The second the words were out of his mouth he wished he could retract them. He hadn't needed rescuing. Not on the slopes, and certainly not anywhere else, despite what his coach might think.

He could have handled things himself, given a little more time.

Yeah? Like he'd handled those dreams? Popping sleeping pills like they were candy was not the best prescription—as he'd soon discovered. The good thing was he'd almost weaned himself from them. The nightmares were back, but maybe they were just something he'd have to live with. Like his guilt.

"Not too many rescues. Just the occasional stray."

She picked up her chocolate and took a long sip. "Ah. Just what I needed. Something to keep me warm and happy." Before he could dwell too long on those words, she continued. "So where are you from?"

Four years ago that would have been an easy question to answer. He would have asked whether she meant originally or at the moment. As it was, he wasn't sure of his actual location. Halfway between anger and grief, if he had to guess, a place he'd been stuck at for far too long. "California, originally, but I live in Texas now. And you?"

"Silver Pass. Born and raised right here on the mountain." She raised her mug and took another drink.

So why didn't she seem thrilled to live in a gorgeous place like this? He took a gulp of his own hot chocolate and then sputtered when an unexpected burn slid down his throat.

"Hot?" She gave him a grin that could only be described as mischievous.

"No. Spiked." His brows drew together. "How do you know I'm not an alcoholic?"

"Are you?"

He could have been, but a couple of years ago he'd realized drinking was not only *not* helping him but it could get someone hurt. His team relied on him to make good decisions. One wrong move and a career could be finished forever. Much like his had almost been.

It's why he'd agreed with the coach about this vacation spot. The cold climate kind of fostered isolation. At least in his head it did. With all that gear on, it wasn't very easy to talk to strangers. It wasn't the same as lying on a beach or surfing. Because the waves always carried you back in to shore. With skiing, you could simply race away from strangers who were a little too anxious to start a conversation.

Like this one?

"No, I'm not an alcoholic," he admitted, although the steamy brew slid down his throat in a way that was a little too comforting. He took one more long pull and then set it aside. He wasn't going to switch one habit for another.

Miranda studied him for a few seconds. She started to say something then the instructor who'd been watching her from across the room appeared beside the table. "You headed back for the slopes, Mira? If so, I'll ride up the lift with you."

The guy pointedly ignored Jack, which was fine. He had no intention of stepping in between these two.

"I think I'll go back to my room and read instead.

And I can catch up on some reports, while I'm there."
The chill in her voice was unmistakable.

"Mira—"

She held up her hand. "I'd rather not do this right now."

The man's lips thinned. "You can't avoid me forever, you know. We both live here. Eventually, we're going to have to sit down and talk."

Jack's glance went to where her left hand gripped her mug. No ring. But there was a definite indentation there.

That's why he'd been staring at her. These two had been involved at some point. Married? An affair, maybe?

Whatever it was, it was none of his business. In fact, maybe it was time for him to take his pity party somewhere else and let these two go at it in private.

Mira beat him to it, standing up, her chin angled at a dangerous height. "I don't see what we have to talk about."

"How happy do you think your father is going to be once he hears about all this?"

She gave a hard smile. "You're right, Robert. I imagine he won't be very happy at all."

Jack was surprised to see the other man's face drain of color.

So that's how it was. The jerk had done something. Something bad enough to make her want to avoid any contact with him. A dark thought came over him.

When the guy reached out to take hold of her arm Jack rose to his feet, no longer trying to remain impassive. He held the man's gaze for ten long seconds before "Robert" backed down.

"I'll catch you later," he said to Mira.

"Don't think so. Let's just stick to our own sides of the slopes."

With an irritated roll of his shoulders the man spun away from them and stalked toward the nearest exit.

Mira dropped back into her seat. "Well, it looks like we're even. I rescued you. You rescued me. Thanks." She sighed. "Sorry you had to witness that, though."

"No problem. Ex…" He had no idea why he gave that leading sentence.

"Fiancé. But that's neither here nor there." She pursed her lips. "You shouldn't go up on that slope again without another lesson or two. Next time you could really get hurt."

If she was worried about her ex pulling something, she needn't bother. He could take care of himself. "I'll do that."

She must have sensed he was just handing her a line. "No, I'm serious. Robert's not going to be a happy camper, so I wouldn't count on him playing nice." She eyed him. "I could give you some pointers if you want. Make sure you stay out of trouble."

That was pretty much impossible. He'd stayed in trouble in one form or another for the last four years. Maybe he should have asked for the beachfront condo vacation despite his earlier thoughts. At least surfing was something he was actually proficient at.

"I don't want to put you to any trouble. I think I can manage."

"Like you did today? Come on. I really do want to show my appreciation."

It was either accept graciously or be a jerk about it. "Did I look that bad out there?"

She laughed. "You want honesty or a gentle lie?"

He found himself smiling back. "Hmm…I'd take the lie, but I think it's already too late for that. Okay, I'll accept the pointers, but I don't guarantee I'll show much improvement. I'm a beachside kind of guy."

"So you're better on the surf than on the turf?"

His smile grew. "No, the turf I can handle. It's cold, slippery surfaces that I struggle with."

"Interesting. So, are we on?"

Why did that seem like a loaded question all of a sudden? But unless he wanted to make a big deal out of what was probably an innocent offer, it was better to let it slide on by. "Yep."

"Great!" She paused to wave at someone across the room. A blonde grinned and held up five fingers.

Mira nodded.

They must be meeting up in a few minutes or something. That was his cue to leave. "What time were you thinking tomorrow?"

"Does tennish work for you?"

"Sounds perfect." He stood. "Thanks for the hot chocolate."

"No problem. I'll see you tomorrow." With one last smile she picked up her cup and headed over to where the other woman was standing. And heaven help him if he didn't watch her hips bump and sway for a couple of beats before forcing himself to turn away.

It's not a date. She hadn't even used that word.

Why he needed to explain that to himself he had no idea. All he knew was that his heart rate had just kicked up a notch and a zing of anticipation was edging through his veins, picking up momentum as it went.

This could be bad.

Very, very bad.

Unless he nipped it in the bud right here. Right now.

The only question…was how.

* * *

"Where did you get your goggles?"

Mira peered into her patient's red, streaming eyes as he sat on the exam table in her tiny clinic. Around twenty-two years old, he was here for a week with several buddies. Yesterday evening, after coming off the slopes, his eyes had begun burning. When he'd looked into the mirror that morning, he'd been shocked to see his lids were swollen and his eyes looked terrible.

"I picked up all my gear at a second-hand store right before coming. It was a bargain."

And like any other bargain, sometimes you paid the price later on. Mira had found that out the hard way when it came to relationships.

She clicked off her penlight and leaned back to check out the eyewear lying beside him. They had the customary reflective surface, but there were no markings that indicated the UV protection the lenses offered. "Your goggles and skis are two pieces of equipment you really shouldn't skimp on. This is why."

"What do you mean?"

"Ever hear of snow blindness?"

Her patient scrubbed moisture from his cheeks. "Snow blindness. Doesn't that only happen to people who are stranded in the snow?"

"Nope. I see it fairly often up here. It's basically a sunburn of your corneas."

He blinked, squinting one eye to look at her. "Can you treat it?"

Swiveling around to her desk, she pulled her prescription pad forward and started writing. "I'm going to give you a prescription for some eyedrops, but you need to stay off the slopes for the next couple of days. Believe me, your eyes aren't going to want to face any light, much less what you'll find up there on the mountain."

"But we're only here for a week."

She felt for him, really she did. "I know. I wish there were a quick treatment, but it's just like any other sunburn. You have to stay out of the sun for a while." She glanced up. "Oh, and make sure you see an eye doctor when you get home."

The man swore a couple of times before finally nodding and taking the slip of paper. He then took his goggles and dumped them in the trash. "I guess I won't be needing those any more."

She smiled. "We have some regulation eyewear at the rental kiosk. Make sure your friends are covered, so they don't wind up in the same boat."

"I will. Thanks, Doc."

"You're welcome."

Once he left, she locked up the clinic and headed up the mountain to meet Jack. It was still a little early, but she wanted to make sure she arrived before he did so she could prepare herself.

Man number five.

Okay, so the guy was cuter than the other men she'd met for drinks or a quick trip down the slopes. In fact, she'd been with one such guy yesterday on the advanced slopes. She had finished on the bunny slope in order to cool down—like she'd told Jack—but only because guy number four had seemed to have hands that never stopped finding excuses to touch her in little ways. Add him to the guy she'd been with two nights ago, and she began to wonder about the wisdom of her resolution. How did serial daters go about avoiding the creeps...and worse?

She needed to be a little more careful about picking these guys. She certainly didn't want to get in over her head. Ellory had forced her to put her cellphone number on speed dial, so Mira could reach out with the touch of a button in case she got into trouble.

She didn't plan on that happening. So far it had just been the two weirdos. Of course, since she'd only been out with four guys in all over the last several weeks, that wasn't much of a track record.

And what about Jack? She'd never been out with a surfer dude before. Although the serious guy who'd sat across from her at the table yesterday did not match her image of a California beach bum.

Just look at the way he'd stood up to Robert.

Yeah, that had been a little heady. She hoped seeing her with Jack had drilled it into her ex's brain that she was moving on—whether it was true or not. Robert had blown it. She'd learned the hard way not to give people second chances.

That included him, and it included her father.

This might be her dad's resort, and he technically might be her boss, but that didn't mean she was going to fall all over him. He'd hurt her mother badly. And even though her mom had been the one to convince her to come back to the lodge and work after she graduated from medical school, she didn't forgive him for his transgressions any more than she'd forgive Robert or her two other exes.

It was exactly why she'd sworn off men. And if she could just get past man number five and move on to the next guy, she'd officially win her bet with Ellory.

Should be a snap.

She leaned on the rail and surveyed the line of chairs on the ski lift.

Speaking of bets, she spied Jack about halfway up

the mountain. His safety bar had not been pulled down, making her frown. She'd have to add that to the lesson.

She sucked down a deep breath as he drew closer. She'd just about convinced herself that he wasn't as good looking as she'd thought he was yesterday. But he was. Even from this distance. With streaky brown hair that was in need of a cut and those broad shoulders, he pretty much filled the chair. She'd have to tuck herself under his arm to fit on there with him if they ever rode up together.

The image made her swallow. Silly. *You're here to teach him to ski and put a notch in your...* Hmm, what should she notch, since she had no intentions of sleeping with him or any other of her dates?

Her skis, that's what. Okay, so he'd be one more notch in her skis.

He slid off the chair with lithe grace that had been lacking yesterday when he'd smacked the ground and slid to a halt. How that must have cost him in the ego department. Except he just stood there.

"Slide over here."

He glanced over and saw her then eased down the hill to meet her, a little less shaky than he'd been yesterday.

She had a feeling he'd be a quick study when it came to skiing. Well, whether he was or wasn't, it didn't matter. This would be his one and only lesson with her—a favor for saving her from Robert's pestering. Tomorrow he'd be on his own.

"Hi." He pulled a hat down over his head, juggling his poles as he did so.

At least he'd remembered to put his skis on before getting on the lift. She checked out his eyewear, nodding at the item in his hand. "Did you get those here at the resort?"

He glanced down at them. "Yes, why?"

"Just wondering. Don't want you to get snow blindness."

His brows went up, but he didn't question her comment.

"You ready?" she asked.

"I have to admit I thought about standing you up."

Interesting. He had seemed a little skittish at the bar yesterday.

"Yeah? Well, I'd have had to come and track you down." Ellory had spied Jack from across the room yesterday after her encounter with Robert and claimed that this time she was going down hard. This one was just too yummy for her to resist.

Oh, she could resist him all right. He was just one more guy. In fact, it was quite liberating to be with a man and know there was no future in it. She didn't have to worry about whether or not she'd have to watch her words or get all prettied up.

The time she'd spent in front of the mirror this morning had been strictly about personal grooming. She'd do that for anyone. No need to send people scurrying for the nearest exit with her morning rat's nest and dark under-eye circles. And her lips were chapped from the cold, so of course she'd had to put on something to soothe and protect them. The fact that it had a little dab of shine was just a coincidence.

He smiled. "I guess it's a good thing I showed up, then."

"Absolutely." Luckily, Robert was off this morning, so one of the other instructors was working with a small group of newbies. She could have sent Jack to the class, since her professed reason for meeting him was because her ex might do or say something she would end up feeling badly about. But since she'd told Ellory he was man number five...

Really, who would know she didn't meet him?

Ellory, for one.

Yeah, and why was that? Because she couldn't tell a lie worth a damn.

"So, let's start with your skis. You got them on, but it'll help if you know how to click in and out of them quickly."

She gave him a quick lesson on doing just that. Once they were back on, she had him face the bottom of the hill, but with the fronts of his skis pointed toward each other.

"I'm sure Robert showed you, but once you start out, you're going to want to stay like this. Think of it like a wedge of pizza, only made with skis instead of food. If you keep your skis completely parallel to each other, you'll pick up too much speed, as you found out yesterday. So wedge them just a bit until you get the feel of your angle and speed." She pulled her goggles down over her eyes. "Let's do a practice run. I'll go first and you follow me down, trying to imitate my movements."

He muttered something that she couldn't quite catch before she used her poles to push off. A hard swish behind her said that he'd done the same thing. She concentrated on going as slowly as possible, not an easy task when you were used to zipping down difficult slopes at top speed. Her father had had big plans for her after she'd won several competitions, plans she'd thwarted when she'd decided to become a doctor. What father in his right mind was disappointed when his child decided to become something other than a professional athlete?

Hers.

Then again, he'd disappointed her as well.

She'd changed courses right after her parents had

divorced, and, yes, maybe it had been partly to get back at him. But she loved being a doctor, even more than she loved the slopes and the snow. Jack had talked about surfing. The ocean didn't appeal to her at all. She was a mountain girl through and through. She didn't think she even owned a bikini other than the underwear kind.

Jack came up beside her, showing a pretty good sense of balance. And every time she changed the angle of her wedge, he imitated her. Out of nowhere came the thought that it might be worth a trip to the ocean just to see him up on a surfboard, that streaky hair of his catching rays of sunlight.

He hit a mogul and wavered for a second or two, the tips of his skis wiggling back and forth, but he caught himself. His speed increased fractionally and Mira let off her brake and matched him. "Good job!"

His face was a mask of concentration, so she wasn't even sure whether he'd heard her or not. At that moment someone passed them on the left at a much quicker pace—which wasn't all that difficult, considering she and Jack were creeping along.

Two more people went by.

Mira was concentrating so much on the man beside her that she almost missed the screams from the pair of teens who'd just passed them. They'd gotten too close, and the left ski of the girl closest to them had overlapped the other girl's. Both were struggling to remain upright.

"Move away from each other!" Her training kicked in, knowing if they didn't get their skis apart one or both of them would fall.

They either didn't hear her or were too panicked to do what she said, because they were still tangled. Then one of the girls shoved the other one, maybe to try to push off her and get away. Instead of working, the girl who'd been shoved careened sideways, taking her friend with her. They fell down hard, landing in a heap in the middle of the slope. The girl who'd pushed the other one sat up laughing, but her giggles soon faded when she saw the other teenager lay still in the snow.

Every muscle in Mira's body went on high alert as she drew closer and saw the girl's right arm sticking out at an odd angle.

The uninjured teen must have seen it as well, because she suddenly leaned back and gave out an unearthly shriek.

CHAPTER THREE

"You go down the hill," Mira said. "I need to stay here."

"I can help."

"Just do as I say." Her tone was a little more impatient this time.

He didn't care. "No can do. I'm a doctor."

Mira gave him a sharp look. "Yeah, well, so am I. I'm the concierge doctor for the lodge."

His heart stalled for a second, and he stared, fumbling a bit as he tried to remain upright. "I thought you were a ski instructor."

"Pizza it, Jack, if you want to stop."

He forced his mind back to what she was saying, using his skis to form a barricade and coming to a halt beside the still-screaming girl.

"What's your specialty?" She nudged him aside so she could get to their patients, sinking to her knees in the snow to look at the unconscious teen. She laid a hand on the panicked girl's shoulder, and like magic she quieted.

He was still struggling to process the fact that he was up on the slopes with a doctor, of all things. "I'm in sports medicine."

Mira's eyes widened when he mentioned the name of the team.

"The Hawks? Are you kidding me?" She gave him

another quick glance. "What are you doing skiing, then? Isn't this your busiest time of year?"

No way was he going to tell her he'd been sent off to recuperate. Especially not knowing what he did now. "I'm taking a short break."

Speaking of breaks, they might have a bad one on their hands here. The teen hadn't seemed to fall hard enough to do any real damage, at least it hadn't looked that way, but the human body was a strange animal.

"Let me check her arm." Carefully unzipping the girl's jacket enough that he could slide his hand down the limb, he found the fracture immediately. Although the bone wasn't protruding from her skin—a good thing—it was pressed right against it. A little more force and it would have come through. The edge felt jagged, though, so it could still break through, if they weren't careful.

The girl was also out cold.

Mira spoke softly to the uninjured girl, while Jack focused on the friend.

"She's still breathing," he said. "Can you get her vitals, while I check her head?" He clicked his boots out of his skis, just like Mira had shown him, and then slid around until he was kneeling beside her shoulder.

Mira nodded, pressing her fingers against the girl's right wrist, while Jack carefully undid the strap to her helmet. He checked it for cracks before running his fingers over her hair, looking for obvious signs of trauma. Her white beanie cap, which had probably been pulled down to hide the unfashionable headgear, lay a short distance away, knocked off by the impact. He couldn't feel any bumps, but he knew that didn't necessarily mean anything. Peeling apart her eyelids one at a time and wishing he had his medical kit, he peered at them to judge pupil size. Equal, and they reacted to light in a way that appeared normal.

Two guys who were evidently with the ski patrol slid to a halt beside them, asking Mira what she had.

"Broken arm at least." She glanced at Jack.

"No contusions on her head that I can see, but I want to stabilize her neck and back just in case."

Her friend stifled a sob. "Is she going to be okay? I wasn't trying to knock her down. I was trying to get my ski loose before I fell. Instead, I made us both fall."

Mira reached over and squeezed her hand, giving the two men a warning look when one of them started to say something. "Of course you didn't. Where are your parents?"

"At—at the lodge. They said we could come ski, but that we had to stick to the easy slopes."

Smart parents.

"And you did what they asked," Mira said. "What's your name?"

"Sandy. And that's Marilyn."

"Okay, Sandy, if you'll go with Hans and help him locate your parents, we'll take care of your friend." Mira stood and helped the girl to her feet, waiting until she'd stopped swaying before saying anything. "Does anything hurt?"

"No. I'm okay."

"Do you feel well enough to ski to the bottom?"

"I—I think so."

The man she'd called Hans patted the terrified girl on the shoulder and gave her an encouraging nod. Then they slowly made their way down the slope, while the other guy went in search of a stretcher and called in the accident, telling the instructors and employees at the top to hold everyone right where they were.

Jack glanced at her. "At least they were wearing helmets. Let's hope she's out because of the pain and not anything else."

"My da...er...the lodge requires all minors to use helmets on the slopes. Her pulse is steady. If we're lucky, she just fainted." She reached her fingers out and smoothed back her hair. "The EMS guys are pretty familiar with the routine up here, they should have something to stabilize her arm."

"I'm beginning to think surfing is a hell of a lot safer."

One curved brow went up. "I can think of a few things that make me think differently. At least you can't drown on a ski slope."

Maybe not, but when her brown eyes met his, looking all soft and warm as she kept her hand protectively on the injured girl's head, he thought it was possible to drown in something other than the ocean.

He shook away the thought.

She's a doctor, Jack. Not someone you want to play around with.

He was glad when a pair of emergency service guys came clomping down the hill, heavy-duty boots making easy work out of the packed snow.

After a quick rundown of her vitals and injuries and explaining what they'd seen, one of the paramedics asked where the girl's parents were.

"We sent her friend and a member of the ski patrol to find them."

In short order, the pair had immobilized the teen's injured arm and done their own assessment of her injuries, coming to the same conclusions as he and Mira had. Then they stabilized her neck and removed her skis before loading her onto a blue stretcher with a metal pull bar attached to it. The girl started to come to, moaning as her eyes fluttered open.

Mira leaned close and whispered to her.

The sight made a pang go through his chest. If he and Paula had had any kids, is that how she would've looked as she comforted them?

Not the time, Jack.

He cleared his throat. "They're going to pull her down the hill?"

"That's the safest way. It's hard to keep your balance on the snow, if you haven't noticed." The right side of her mouth curved slightly, as if she was fighting a smile.

"Oh, I noticed all right." In fact, he was having a little trouble keeping his balance right now, and it had nothing to do with skiing. He felt like the wind had been knocked from his lungs the second he'd realized she was a doctor. He was still struggling to catch his breath fifteen minutes later.

She stood and went over to retrieve the girl's hat and skis. "I'll bring these down with me," she told the men. "Hopefully they've located her folks. I want to be on hand if something changes."

"Sure thing, Mira." One of the medical workers threw her a quick smile.

It seemed everyone knew her around these parts.

The paramedics started down the hill, leaving them to follow.

"Do you want to walk down or ski?"

"At the rate I go, it's probably faster to walk." He took the girl's skis from her and lumped them together with his, tucking them under his arm with his poles.

Together, they trudged down the bunny slope, staying a few yards behind the rescue team. His mind couldn't help wandering back to her instructions on how to maneuver with his skis and how her words had yielded much better results than the lessons her ex—the professional—had given him.

Wanting to show off for the pretty doctor, Jack?

Self-preservation was more like it. Something he should probably remember. Because the fact that she was a doctor was all the more reason he should avoid her for the rest of his stay. If his coach were here, he'd be calling for a time-out and hauling Jack's ass off the playing field.

And the man would be right. Injured players should remain on the sidelines until they had time to heal.

Yeah? Well, he'd had four damn years. How much longer would it take?

Some players never recovered. Maybe he was one of them. He could just throw in the towel right now.

His body gave a quick tug of irritation, one that grew when Mira glanced back at him with a smile. "Keeping up okay?"

Oh, he could keep up just fine. He balled his hands into fists when his mind immediately headed into more dangerous territory. Of Mira saying those words under very different circumstances.

Sidelines, Jack, remember?

Thankfully, they reached the bottom of the slope, and he had other things to occupy his mind, like the small crowd that had gathered near the door of the lodge, and the woman in a pink parka rushing forward to meet the EMS guys as they headed for the pick-up site where their truck was probably parked. Forced to stop, the guys lifted the stretcher just as he and Mira arrived.

Habit made him start toward the group to brief the girl's parents, but Mira beat him to it, smoothly maneuvering right into the center of the gathering. Besides, he wasn't here with his football team. This was her gig, not his.

He could see her gesturing as she explained the situation, but he couldn't hear the words. Whatever she said, it seemed to have the right effect. People started to move away until all that was left were a man and a woman who looked like they were in their early fifties—Marilyn's parent's probably—standing near the stretcher. Jack debated slipping through the glass doors of the lodge and escaping while he could, while Mira's attention was fixed on something else.

Coward's way out. He'd decided four years ago that he wasn't going that route ever again. He'd lost his head in a bottle for a while after his wife's death. Once he'd picked himself up off the bathroom floor after a particularly bad hangover, he'd decided to live a life Paula would be proud of rather than throwing it away in a booze-filled haze. He obviously wasn't there yet—this temporary exile and the sleep aids were proof of that.

What he needed was something to take his mind off himself for a few hours.

His eyes slid back to Mira, whose glossy hair showed beneath her cap as she leaned over the stretcher to talk to the injured girl once more.

Nope. No matter how tempting that might be, it wasn't smart. He needed something light and easy. Something other than skiing with pretty women.

Large black letters from a flyer taped to the door of the lodge caught his attention:

Not a Ski Fan?

Ha, you could say that. He continued reading.

Check out Silver Pass's other exciting offerings.

The bullet points proceeded to list things like evening sleigh rides, trips down the mountains on inner tubes, gondola lifts that boasted spectacular views, and even snowmobile rentals.

The snowmobiles sounded interesting. Maybe even a little bit like jet skis.

He pulled out his smartphone to store the number in his address book.

"The gondola ride is a lot of fun. And there's only room for two in each car."

A sultry voice came from just over his left shoulder. Not Mira's, since she was still over by the stretcher.

He turned around and found a brunette with darkly penciled brows that matched the carefully modulated tones of her voice. Overdone. Whispering of desperation. And when the woman smiled, nothing happened to the skin around her eyes.

Botox.

He'd thought of Mira as a professional snow bunny when he'd first met her, but her sparkling eyes and sunny disposition had dashed his suspicions away. This woman, however...

Swallowing, he nodded. "I'll keep that in mind, thank you."

She took a step closer, her jacket pulling tight across her breasts. "Did I overhear someone say that you're a doctor?"

Oh, Lord. Not what he wanted to deal with right now.

Why was it that a quick fling with Mira appealed to him, despite its dangers, while the thought of spending the night with this woman just left him cold? He didn't want to hurt her feelings—if they hadn't already been paralyzed by the overzealous needle of her surgeon.

"I am. Just here for a couple of days' R&R." Okay, a couple of days was on the verge of being a lie, since he still had three weeks left of his vacation.

"That's enough time to squeeze in a fun activity or two, isn't it? It'll be a tight fit, but it would be well worth the effort."

She said the words with a completely straight face, but she had to know how they sounded.

Hell. He was surprised *she* wasn't listed on that flier as one of the lodge's alternate activities, along with her name, phone number, and measurements. And that she promised a tight fit.

"Well—"

Mira suddenly appeared beside them, looking from one to the other. "I wondered where you went." She glanced at the advertisement and then the phone in his hand. "Planning something fun?"

"Thinking about it. Did Marilyn get off okay?"

"She's on her way to the hospital right now."

The brunette quirked a brow. Wow, maybe there wasn't as much happy juice in her face as he'd thought. "Girlfriend?" she asked, her voice not quite as sultry as it had been.

He wanted to say yes, just to get rid of her without having to be rude. Would Mira kill him? He could always explain later.

"She's—"

"Definitely a girlfriend. And you are?" Mira wrapped her hands around his right bicep, giving it a quick squeeze as if to say she knew he was in a tight spot.

Squeeze. Tight spot. Well the woman might not have done anything for him with those words, but Mira's touch was definitely doing something to his gut. It clenched, one muscle group at a time, until his whole abdomen was a mass of tension.

"Well, why didn't you say so?" The brunette tossed her head.

Mira's hand ventured from his arm, sliding low across his back until it curved around his left side. She left a trail of heat in her wake that he felt even through his coat. "He's too nice. Women get the wrong idea all the time."

Evidently she didn't have any of the same reservations about hurting the woman's feelings as he did, because she continued. "So did you get the number for that sleigh-ride company, Jack, or what?"

"I was just doing that."

"Good." Her glance shot to the brunette. "Thanks for keeping him company for me. I've got it from here."

With a strangled sound the woman wheeled around and then jerked open the door to the lodge before disappearing inside.

The breath he hadn't realized he'd been holding whistled out through his teeth as relief swept over him. "How did you know?"

She let go of his side and lifted her hand to pat his cheek. "Your face is about as red as the walls in the dining hall." She laughed. "And she's a regular. She comes on to all the men."

There was a bitter edge to her words.

So much for thinking she'd singled him out. Ouch. The punch to his ego stung.

"So I wasn't in any real danger."

"I didn't say that. She's dangerous all right."

As much as he tried to school his face into a blank slate, a smile crept up from somewhere inside him. "How do you know I don't thrive on danger?"

"Do you? I didn't take you for the type."

There it was again. That quick one-two to his pride. "I might surprise you."

"Really? In that case, I think you owe me a sleigh ride.

For bailing you out of what could have been an awkward situation. Especially if her husband had found out."

"She's married?" Maybe he did owe her something.

"Aren't they all?"

He wouldn't know. He hadn't been on the dating circuit since he'd met Paula. "I guess you wouldn't accept a simple thank-you."

"I would, but I couldn't promise I'd bail you out a second time. If her being married doesn't stop her, do you really think me saying I'm your girlfriend is going to scare her off? But if she knows you not only *have* a girlfriend but that you're *happy* with that girlfriend, she'll probably leave you alone."

Jack's head was spinning, partly at the audacity of married women propositioning men who were taken and partly just because of the clean crisp scent of the woman at his side. It reminded him of frosty days and mocha-filled nights. He leaned in closer. "Did you just have coffee?"

Why he asked that he had no idea.

She blinked at him in surprise. She could match that look and raise it. His face heated again.

"I just ate a coffee-flavored candy."

"Sorry. I think my brain is misfiring over what just happened."

"You've never been propositioned by a married woman before?" Her voice was shocked, like it was something that happened all the time.

"Never. If you were married, would you do it? Proposition someone who wasn't your husband?"

"Oh, but I'm not married." Although light and delivered with a smile, her words contained a hint of darkness. Because of her ex? Had he slept with Mrs. Botox or something?

He decided to change the subject entirely. "So this sleigh ride. Is it worth going on alone?"

"Um, yeah, but if she finds out you're planning on going solo, she's going to show up and invite herself along for the ride."

He glanced through the glass to see that the brunette in question was indeed eyeing them while sipping on something boozy that looked like it had a tiny plastic ski sticking out of it. He guessed ski resorts didn't want little umbrellas reminding people they could be in a tropical paradise instead. "As much as I never thought I'd say it, would you mind going with me? To ward off trouble…" He wasn't sure that "warding off" trouble was the right way to put it. Because it sure felt like he was busy cultivating it at the moment.

"No problem. I haven't been on a sleigh ride in ages, actually."

So her ex hadn't taken her on one? Maybe they'd had fun in other ways.

Something that made his jaw tense.

She grabbed his hand. "And now for my last good deed until our sleigh ride." She hauled him through the door and paraded him right in front of Mrs. Botox, their hands firmly joined. They were about halfway to the receptionist's desk when she turned to grin at him and then promptly plowed into an older man who stepped into her path.

"Oh, I'm sorry." She turned around. "I didn't see…"

Her voice died away, and her face drained of all its color as she looked up at the man she'd just run into. She let go of Jack's hand in a rush.

The stranger's brows came together, and his eyes narrowed as he studied Jack and then Mira. Then he addressed her, saying, "I think you have some explaining to do."

Her arms went around her waist, and she drew in a shaky breath. "Daddy, what are you doing here?"

CHAPTER FOUR

MIRA TRIED TO give off an appearance of calm.

But her heart was ticking at an alarming pace, and she was aware of Jack standing just behind her. He had to be wondering what the hell was going on.

He wasn't the only one. She was pretty much wondering the same thing.

Why was her father here? He rarely put in an appearance at the lodge these days. And he wasn't exactly what she would call "involved" in her life any more. Although much of that was her own fault. Even when he'd tried to get close over the past several years while she'd been at med school, she'd tended to pull away. Her mom had let his infidelity go, why couldn't she?

"Well?" he said, evidently waiting for that explanation he'd asked for.

She lifted her chin, refusing to act the part of the meek little girl he'd once carried around on his shoulders. "You want an explanation? Maybe you should ask Robert for one."

"Robert, what's he got to do with this?" He looked genuinely puzzled.

Gulping, she scrambled to figure out what else he could be talking about. She figured her ex had called her father—like he'd hinted he would do—to cry on his

shoulder or ask him to intervene on his behalf. And that
her dad had hightailed it up to Silver Pass to give her hell.
Okay, so if that wasn't the case, it could only mean he
was asking for an explanation about why she was holding hands with a strange man. She glanced back at Jack
and blew out a breath at the grim expression on his face.
Her dad wasn't the only one asking some mental questions. Better get the introductions out of the way.

"Sorry. I'll talk to you about Robert later." She motioned Jack closer. "Daddy, this is Jack Perry. He's the
team doctor for the Texas Hawks. He helped out with an
accident on the slopes a few minutes ago."

"The Hawks? I'm impressed." He stuck out a hand.
"Nice to meet you."

He proceeded to grill Jack on his opinion of this team
or that and what he thought of Texas and Colorado's
chances for making it to the playoffs next year.

She felt bad about throwing Jack to Papa Wolf, but if
anything could distract her dad it was football. It would
at least give her time to think before the subject eventually swung back to her and what she feared would be the
subject *du jour*: why she was holding hands with a man
who wasn't her fiancé, team doctor or no team doctor.

Not that she owed him any explanations after the way
he'd treated her mom. But, still, it would be awkward to
tell him to mind his own business in front of Jack.

So, what could she tell him?

How about: Jack was blind, and she was helping him
find the reception desk.

*Nope, that wouldn't work, since the Hawks probably
wouldn't hire a blind physician.*

That left… Yeah. She was drawing a complete blank.

"Mira?" Her dad's voice dragged her from her thoughts.
Her head came up. "Sorry?"

"I invited Jack to have dinner with us tonight at eight. Hope that was okay?"

She couldn't have been any more shocked if her dad had suddenly started doing the chicken dance in front of everyone in the crowded lobby. She'd expected a scene and had gotten a dinner invitation instead. Although with her dad, it normally came out sounding more like an ultimatum. "No, of course I don't mind, if it's all right with him."

Jack glanced at the lobby, and Mira noted that Predator in Pink was still watching them closely. "It's fine with me," he said.

Did this make two or three dates with guy number five? She was supposed to be moving on to the next eligible bachelor and then the next. Her gaze slid back to the woman across the room. Yeah, she so did not want to become that. Maybe she should stop being so anxious to zip from man to man.

Besides, she and Jack hadn't actually had their first date yet. Right? Because the hot chocolate didn't count, and the ski lesson had been interrupted by the rescue on the slope, so that didn't count either.

And the sleigh ride?

Hmm, that could definitely be classified as a date. Which would officially mark the end of their association.

Her father gave her a quick hug. "Do you want to ask Robert to come as well?"

"Robert?" Nothing like her emotions swinging from relief to panic. She was going to have to break the news to her father. But not now. Not in front of Jack. "I'm sure he's busy with lessons."

"Okay, if you're sure." He smiled as he released her. "You know, that boy's future father-in-law is the owner of this joint. I could probably pull a few strings and have him let off early."

Jack visibly stiffened beside her. "It was nice meeting you," he said to her father. "But I need to turn in my equipment and get cleaned up. Thank you for the dinner invitation."

The last thing she wanted was to be left alone with her father. "I can go with you to the rental kiosk, if you don't remember where it is."

"I remember. Thanks for your…help earlier. I think I've got it from here."

That must be one of the man's favorite phrases. How many times did that make now? Three?

About as many times as she'd been with him. Well, that was just great.

Waiting until Jack was three or four strides away, she raised her voice just enough for the woman across the room to hear. "Don't forget about making the reservation for the sleigh ride. Believe me, you won't want to miss it."

Now, why had she said that? Maybe because it stung that he couldn't seem to get away from her fast enough.

Jack stopped in his tracks for a second or two before throwing her a look that was filled with lazy amusement totally at odds with his abrupt departure. And when his voice came back, it was much lower than hers had been. "Believe me, I haven't forgotten."

A shiver went over her at the dark intensity of his words. She glanced sharply up at her father to see if he'd noticed, but he seemed lost in his own world at the moment. Once Jack had gone through the door she turned her attention back to her father, bracing herself for a confrontation. Better to just tell him the truth and get it over with.

"Dad, I have something to tell you," she began.

"I have something to tell you as well. Actually, I wanted to ask you for a favor. It's why I came up here today."

She gulped. A favor? "Is it about Robert?"

If he was going to ask her to give her ex a second chance, she might just blow her top. One cheater asking her to forgive and forget the transgressions of another cheater? Not hardly. Especially when one of the women Robert had cheated with was standing on the other side of the room.

"It's not about Robert, it's about…" He focused on her face. "Is everything okay between the two of you?"

She frowned, trying to figure out exactly what was going on.

"Things are a little complicated." *A little, Mira? Really?* "Anyway, what's this about a favor?"

A sliver of worry went through her as she noticed for the first time the taut lines of his face. If he hadn't come here because of her breakup, then why had he come?

"Not here. Let's go back to my office, Mirry."

She hadn't heard that nickname in forever. The sliver grew to the size of a stake. "Dad, is something wrong? Oh God, is it Mom?"

"No, your mother's fine. I spoke with her this morning."

Mira's eyes widened. He had? More alarm bells went off as he crossed the honey-planked flooring and headed for the door that led to a different wing of the lodge, one that wasn't open to the public. She followed him, winding through the narrow corridors until they reached the small annex where his office and the business areas were housed. Once the door shut behind them, he motioned her to one of the leather wingback chairs across from his desk.

She dropped into it, the creak of leather matching that of her nerves. "Daddy?"

All the differences of the past several years seemed to vanish as her unease continued to grow.

Instead of going behind the desk to face her, he went to the bar on the left and got down a tumbler from the open wooden shelves above the liquor bottles and dumped a few cubes of ice into it. He stared at the selection of alcohol for a long time—as if he'd never seen it before—and finally grabbed a decanter, uncapping it and pouring himself a healthy amount. He rarely drank, and only kept the liquor here for VIP meetings and gatherings.

He took a good-sized swig then sighed and added another splash of whatever was in the decanter. "I know I haven't done right by you and your mother. I've often wished I could go back and change some things, but I can't."

He turned around to face her, leaning against the counter and taking another sip from his glass. As if realizing his oversight, he frowned. "Do you want something?"

It was probably better if she didn't have anything this early, but she suddenly felt the need to brace herself for whatever he was about to say. "Maybe a little red wine?"

He fixed her a glass then brought it over and handed it to her before dragging the other chair around so it faced her.

She clenched her glass. Something was definitely wrong. "Are you ill?"

"No, Mirry, but it might be better if I were."

Her heart squeezed. "Don't say that," she whispered. Suddenly the years she'd wasted being angry with him flew by at an alarming rate, dropping her into the here and now. She set her untouched drink onto the marble-topped table next to her.

He smiled and took another drink, the ice clinking against his glass. "That comment surprises me, to be honest."

"We might have our differences, but you're still my father."

"Yes, I am. And something has come up that's made me aware of all the mistakes I made with you. With your mom. It has made me want to do all I can to make things right and to not…" he gave a visible swallow "…repeat those mistakes with anyone else."

"What is it?"

"Stella's pregnant."

Stella. It took her a minute to put a face with a name. Paramour number six? Or was it seven? Pregnant?

Mira would have asked if he was sure, but from the redness in his eyes and the unsteadiness of the hand holding the drink she'd say he was dead certain. Instead, she ventured, "Are you happy about that?"

He held her gaze for a long time before nodding. "I screwed up with you. With your mother. Maybe I can learn from those mistakes and do a better job this time around."

He wasn't dying. Her mom wasn't dying. That's all that mattered. She stood and went over to him, taking his drink and setting it on the table behind him. Kneeling beside the chair, she put her arms around him and laid her head on his chest, feeling a love and affection she hadn't felt in a very long time. "I'm happy for you, Daddy. Really happy. If I know Mom, she is too."

His hand came up to stroke her hair. "I plan to marry Stella. I came to ask you for your blessing."

She leaned back to look at him. He'd surprised her yet again. Her father of old would have simply declared his intentions and dared her to say a word against it. It was one of the reasons they hadn't reconciled over the years. He'd acted like the world was his to own...to possess at will.

And yet now he wanted her blessing. If she wanted to blast him with accusations, now was the time. Only she didn't want to.

"You have it, Daddy. Of course you do."

"I know I haven't even walked you down the aisle yet, but I want to ask if you'd do me the honor of standing beside me as I take my vows."

A wave of emotion rolled over her, bringing with it a prickling at the backs of her eyelids. She blinked it away as best she could. "Is that okay with Stella?"

"Yes. She wants to meet you. I called your mom as well, to ask her permission. She told me to ask you, and that she'd support your decision whatever it was." He paused. "Stella's a wonderful woman, Mirry. I want to do right by her. And by you this time. This is the only way I know how."

"Then, of course, I'll stand beside you. I'd be happy to."

A ragged sigh went past her ear. "Thank you. It means the world to me."

She squeezed him tight before leaning over to kiss his grizzled cheek. She stood and took a step back, noticing for the first time the heavy streaks of gray in his still thick hair. When had that happened? When she'd been too busy with her anger to look directly at him?

"I love you, Daddy."

"I love you too, princess." The man who'd always seemed larger than life to Mira dragged his fist across his eyes then stood as well. "Now, what's this about you and Robert?"

It was tempting to just put it off, to pretend that things

were fine, but her dad had been honest and real with her for the first time in years. She could do no less.

"I broke our engagement."

He stood there silent for a long time before saying anything. "What happened?"

Honesty, Mira.

Although maybe she could put a little spin on that honesty so she wouldn't mar his moment of happiness or endanger the tentative bridge they'd just built between them.

"It just wasn't working."

"I'm sorry. Is there anything I can do?"

"About that? Not a thing." She nodded toward her untouched glass. "But I think I've changed my mind about my drink. If you have something festive in that wine cooler of yours, like champagne, I vote we pop the cork and toast to your good fortune. And to my new baby brother or sister."

The first snowfall since his arrival met Jack as he stepped into the lobby for his "date."

Why he'd booked that sleigh ride he had no idea. Maybe because Mira had reminded him again at dinner two nights ago with her father—which he'd found he couldn't get out of, no matter how badly he'd wanted to. He'd had no idea Mira was a doctor, let alone that her father owned the whole damn resort. Neither of them had mentioned her ex fiancé. In fact, they'd both seemed pretty set on avoiding that whole subject during their meal.

Did her father even know?

He'd gotten very little sleep last night. His bottle of pills had whispered to him from the drawer of the nightstand, but he'd ignored it. And the dreams had come back with a vengeance.

As tired as he was, the last thing Jack wanted was to get involved in some huge family drama. He'd had enough of that to last him a lifetime. The blame game had made the rounds after his wife's death with every finger in her family—including his own—pointed directly at his chest, where there was still a gaping hole that no amount of shoveling could fill.

Jabbing his fists into the pockets of his dark slacks, he stared out the window at the whisper-soft flakes dancing in the night breeze, the outside lights making them glimmer and sparkle as they made their way to earth. There were a few footprints across the snow, but for the most part the new layer stretched across the acreage of the resort like a blanket. The walkways had yet to be shoveled. Mira said the sleigh would pull up at the far edge of the drive, a hundred yards or so from the front entrance of the main building. There was no sign of the sleigh, or of Mira, for that matter.

Maybe he could just go back to his room and try to get some rest.

As if hearing his thoughts, the far door opened, and the woman herself appeared. His breath caught in his chest. Unlike her puffy white ski jacket, which did a good job of concealing her figure, tonight she wore a long wool coat that skimmed her body and almost reached her ankles. Open at the front, it gave a tantalizing glimpse of a shiny green top tucked into slim black pants that hugged her hips and legs. A belt of silver metallic links encircled her waist, the ends trailing down her left thigh. She made her way over to him, shrugging her way out of the coat as she did and draping it over her left arm.

"I wasn't sure if you'd be outside yet or not," she said.

"Our ride isn't here, so I thought I'd wait by the door

and watch for it." No reason to tell her he'd been about to make his escape.

Her subtle scent drifted up, a melding of vanilla and pine, a combination that wound around him. His exhaustion suddenly vanished.

"You should have worn boots," she said, glancing down at where his loafers peeked from beneath the bottom edge of his pants legs.

"I didn't bring any. Just the rental snow boots."

Her brows went up. "Really? You live in Texas, and you didn't at least bring some cowboy boots?"

"I don't own any."

"Wow, no boots. At all."

"My recreational choices normally involve water. No need for boots. Or even shoes."

Her lips twisted in a wry smile that made her eyes sparkle. "A man who prefers to go shoeless, huh? You wouldn't survive long up here. Not if you wanted to keep those toes."

He peered down at her feet and noted that, unlike him, she did own boots, but these had a tall chunky heel to them. "And those don't look any more practical than my own footwear."

That got a laugh out of her. "I know, aren't they great? I don't get much of a chance to wear them in my profession."

He came back to earth with a bump. That's right. She worked here. *Dr.* Miranda Dupris. "You don't have to entertain me, you know. I'm sure that's not part of your job description."

"Oh, it's the best part. Fraternize with all the handsome bachelors and make sure they're happy."

He shot her a look, only to have her grin again. "I'm kidding. I'll leave that to your buddy from the other day."

Mrs. Botox. Thankfully he hadn't seen her since they'd parted ways in the lobby, despite Mira's warning. Even in the dining room over the last two evenings there'd been no sign of her. But during his dinner with Mira and her father the blonde who had waved to Mira several days ago had made her way over to their table and given Mira a quick squeeze. Then she'd hugged Mira's dad.

As she'd said goodbye a few minutes later, she'd thrown one last wink Mira's way. "Still five, I see."

"It's not quite five. Ask me again in a couple of days," Mira had replied.

It was the same number they'd tossed back and forth the other day, when he'd wondered if they were meeting up for a drink or something. Neither of them expanded on the comment and after that cryptic exchange the blonde had flounced away, waving off attempts to get her to stay and eat dinner with them. "I'm going on a quick hike to work on my own resolution."

Only afterwards did he notice that Mira had made no effort to introduce her to him.

Mira touched his arm, drawing him back to the present. "Do you want to head down the path to wait?"

"Are you going to be okay in those boots?"

"As okay as you'll be okay in your shoes." Her gaze slanted over him. "You look good, by the way."

"So do you." It was true. For once she was hatless, her red hair flowing over her shoulders where it complemented the green of her blouse. Her warm brown eyes seemed darker than usual, although that could be the result of make-up or something. Whatever the cause, the woman was a knockout. And with her heels on, those legs of hers looked endless, her chin coming right to his shoulder level. Unusual for him. At five feet five, the top of Paula's head, even in her tallest shoes, had barely come to the middle of his chest.

Why was he suddenly comparing the two? Turning away, he picked up his leather jacket from across a nearby chair and shrugged into it, zipping it halfway up his chest. Putting on his armor? He forced a lightness to his voice that he didn't feel. "You sure the sleigh company is going to send someone in this snow?"

"They usually do. If not, we can go for a walk instead."

"With your boots and my shoes."

She tossed her head. "Why not? It's just a little snow." When she went to put her own coat on, he took it from her and held it out so she could slide her arms inside. His fingers brushed the warmth of her neck as he set it on her shoulders, the sensation of smooth silky skin branding itself on his senses.

He forced his hands back into his pockets. "Shall we?"

They strolled out the door and started down the pathway as the snow fell around them. It wasn't deep on the sidewalk, more like a dusting, but Mira pulled the collar of her coat up around her neck anyway.

"Are you going to be cold without a hat?"

"I have one in my pocket. Besides, they have blankets in the sleigh that we can hunker down under."

Images of the two of them snuggled together beneath a pile of blankets came out of nowhere. And hell if they weren't followed up by other images of what the parts hidden beneath the blankets could do.

This was *so* not a good idea. He'd known if from the second she suggested they go together. Maybe he should start hoping that sleigh didn't come after all.

He zipped his jacket even higher, though it wasn't in reaction to the cold that was trickling down his spine but because of a wave of warmth he couldn't fight off.

It had been far too long since he'd been with someone. Maybe he should have taken Mrs. Botox up on her offer. Except he wouldn't hit on *Mrs.* Anything. As messed up as he was these days, he still didn't believe in that.

"How long is this ride, anyway?" A question he should have asked at the reception desk when he'd booked this little excursion. But he'd been too relieved at having survived dinner with Mira and her dad and too busy wondering if she'd told her father that the infamous future son-in-law was now an ex. How many of those did she have, anyway? He'd seen her with a couple of different guys when he'd arrived. Since he and Paula had been childhood sweethearts, he'd never been down the date-'em-and-leave-'em path. He'd had a couple of one-night stands since his wife's death, but that was the extent of it. And it had been over a year since his last rendezvous.

One of Mira's feet slid for a second, and Jack put his hand out to steady her.

"Sorry," she said. "Guess I laughed at your choice of footwear a little too soon, since you're doing better in yours than I am in mine."

"Here." Holding out his elbow to her, he wasn't sure if he was elated or disturbed when she took him up on the offer and looped her arm through his and hugged close. It was too much like what she'd done when rescuing him from Mrs. Botox's advances.

And he liked the feel of her next to him a little too much. It felt warm and companionable. Just like Mira herself.

The woman didn't talk nonstop, like he'd been expecting. And he found himself wishing she did. He liked the sound of her voice.

How the hell did he even know what her voice sounded like?

He did, though. He could hear it in his head. Hear the words they'd exchanged since their first meeting less than a week ago.

Was that all it had been?

"We should be good here," she murmured.

"Good?"

She nodded at something next to them. A signpost with rustic hand-painted arrows pointed in various directions. The top arrow said, "Sleigh Ride Pick-up Point Here."

"How long has your dad owned this place?"

"He built it. He inherited the land from his grandfather and decided to do something with it. He and my mom lived in a little cabin a mile or two down the road before he decided to build the resort. He's tried to preserve the natural beauty and disturb the surrounding area as little as possible." She let go of his arm and stuffed her hands in the pockets of her long coat, shifting her weight slightly away from him.

"I'd say he succeeded. It's a restful place. Did you spend your childhood here?"

"Until I got out of high school."

She didn't offer any other explanation than that, but her voice had hardened slightly. Better not to press her for anything more on that subject.

A musical *chink-chink-chink-chink* sounded in the distance, growing closer. A minute or two later a large cream-colored horse came into view, pulling a sleigh that looked like it had come straight out of a Christmas song, complete with sleigh bells. With shiny black side panels, the sled sat atop gracefully curved silver runners. The interior was lined in red velvet and the whole vehicle gave the impression of an "S" that had been tilted onto its side—the driver sitting up front on a high plush bench, while a second seat sat further back and much lower to the ground. The passenger area had a very private appearance that didn't do anything for his already taut nerves. And true to Mira's words, a pile of folded blankets sat next to the driver.

The horse snorted and shook its head, making the bells attached to his harness jingle again. Mira moved over to the animal and stroked its neck. "How are you doing, Patsy?"

Patsy? The huge animal looked nothing like its name.

The driver tied the reins to a bar on the front of the sleigh and clambered down from his seat. "Hello, Mira. It's been a while since you've ridden with us. Patsy's missed you."

"I know. I've missed her too. And you." She glanced back at Jack. "This is Norman, our driver. Norm, this is Jack Perry, one of the resort's guests. He's never ridden on a sleigh before. In fact, there are quite a few things he hasn't done before."

Jack's neck and face grew hot at the way she'd said it, as if he were an inexperienced teenager being let out into the world for the first time.

Actually, that might not be too far from the truth. It had been a while since he'd let *himself* out into the world. And that hadn't even been his idea. He had his coach to thank for this awkward little mountaintop excursion.

"Nice to meet you." Norm—an older man with a close-cropped silver beard and matching hair—reached out to shake his hand. His top hat and black wool coat gave him a formal air that went well with the sleigh. "If you two are ready...? Patsy's glad to be out of that barn and is raring to go."

The man then reached up to his seat, snagged two thick plaid blankets and handed them to Jack. "It gets chilly back there—better bundle up." He smiled. "Mira used to look like a baby polar bear when she was young, she'd wrap up in so many layers. She'd fall asleep in the back and let us pull her and Ellory all over the place."

Perfect. He'd been hoping to ignore the whole hunker-beneath-the-blanket thing. He covered it up by asking, "Ellory?"

Mira came over to stand beside them. "The woman who stopped by our table at dinner. She's a good friend of mine."

That's why her name sounded familiar.

Giving the harness a quick check, Norm said, "Ellory came out to say hello to me a few days ago. I didn't realize she was back in town."

"She's here for a visit. I'm trying to talk her into staying."

Jack shifted the blankets to the other hand. "She's also the one who gestured she'd meet you in five minutes when we were in the bar, right?"

"Five...?"

Jack couldn't be sure if it was just a trick of the old-fashioned gas streetlamp, but her face seemed to grow pink, the tip of her nose taking on a warm glow. "Yes, that was her."

Before he had a chance to wonder if something was wrong, the driver gestured to the back seat. "Climb aboard." He tweaked Mira on the nose. "You want me to take the scenic route up by the silver mines?"

"Would you? I'm sure Jack'll want to see them."

"For you? Anything. I'll let you point out the sights, since you know them as well as I do by now."

The scenic route. He had no idea what that meant, but had a feeling it was a whole lot longer than the traditional route.

The snow had let up as he climbed into the back of the sleigh and then held out a hand to Mira and helped her up. The velvet seats were warm and inviting against the chill of the air. "Are these heated?"

Mira took the blankets from him and shook them out, placing them over their laps. "Mmm-hmm. Norm installed them. They're powered with a rechargeable battery pack beneath the seat." She snuggled deep, pulling one of the blankets up to her chin. "Comfortable?"

With the seats or with the company? At the moment he couldn't really answer that. Despite his misgivings about coming on this little outing, he felt himself relax in a way he hadn't in quite a while. It could be the lack of sleep, or it could just be from having a pretty woman sitting next to him. He could just glimpse a patch of stars through a break in the heavy cloud cover, and although the little pinpoints didn't throw off much light, the streetlamps made up for them, providing a nice glow that ran down the path as far as he could see.

Norm clucked to the horse and turned her around in the small cul-de-sac, and then they were on their way, the metal runners making a slicing sound as they cut across the frozen earth.

The back of the vehicle was clearly built for romance and late nights under the stars. The walls surrounding them forced them close enough together that their shoulders touched.

Mira rested her head against the back of the seat with a sigh. "It's been ages since I've been out on the sleigh. It always used to put me to sleep."

Funny, because, despite his earlier thoughts, the last thing Jack felt like doing right now was sleeping. "How's he going to find his way in the dark?"

"The paths are all lit, even the back ones, and the

resort has its own plow to keep the snow from getting too deep on these throughways." She angled her head to the side so she was facing him. "Thanks for letting me tag along."

A smile tugged at one corner of his mouth. "I should be thanking you again for bailing me out of an awkward situation."

Not that the one he was in now was any less awkward.

"Mmm, well, you saved me from dining alone with my dad. Once you get him talking about football, that's all he wants to discuss. That lets me off the hook."

That surprised him. The two of them had seemed close. "Do you not get along?"

"We haven't for a long time, but things are changing." She sighed and turned toward the front again. "I'm hoping we can make a fresh start."

He shifted to his right so he could see her better in the shadows. "You didn't tell him about your breakup that night at dinner. Did you let him know later?"

The sleigh rounded a corner, pressing him against her for a second or two, before heading down a slightly darker path. He didn't try to move away. With their heads close together, as well as the shared space beneath the heavy blankets, they could have been children whispering in the dark. Only Mira was no child. The rise and fall of her breasts as she gave another sigh reinforced that fact. "I told him that first night, although I just shared the bare essentials. Daddy always liked Robert, so I didn't want to disillusion him."

"About your ex?"

She nodded. "And the reasons we broke up. I'm afraid telling my father about that will reopen some old wounds between us."

Had she cheated on her fiancé? Somehow he didn't

think so. From the way she'd talked about Mrs. Botox and the men the woman targeted, Jack couldn't help but think Mira was cut from very different cloth.

"Your ex was an idiot for not wanting to work things out."

That got a laugh out of her. "I agree with the idiot part, but it was actually me who didn't want to work it out. Why bother when you obviously don't have what it takes to make someone happy."

Have what it took. Was she kidding? He was sitting here trying to think of anything but the warm, soft body hidden beneath those blankets and how easy it would be to simply lean forward and kiss her.

He swallowed, trying to rein in his wayward thoughts, but it wasn't easy. "I had no idea there were silver mines up here. Is that where the town gets its name?"

"Yes. This whole area is riddled with them. It was a big industry once upon a time. The best thing my grandfather ever did was make sure he held onto the mineral rights, even though my dad has no interest in mining the mountain."

Another turn had the wind blowing right at them. Mira shivered and gripped the covers tighter.

"Cold?"

"I'm okay. The breeze is just chilly."

Before he could stop himself, Jack slipped his arm around her shoulders and tugged her against his body, pulling the blankets up around both of them. "Better?"

"Mmm. Much." She laid her head on his shoulder, her arm going across his abdomen and making him all too aware that if she shifted it four inches lower, an uncomfortable reality was going to meet her.

He closed his eyes and let the cold of the outside air flow deep into his lungs in an effort to cool himself from the inside out. Instead, he found himself absorbing the feel of her, and thinking about how long it had been since he'd felt a woman against him in anything other than a quick round of sex.

This felt a whole lot more intimate than that because he was aware of Mira on more than just a physical level.

She surrounded him. Her scent. Her touch. The sound of her breathing. It was all right there. Coaxing him closer. A siren's song that was growing harder and harder to resist, even though he knew he should.

The snow-covered path helped muffled the clip-clop of Patsy's hooves, but the jingling of the bells on her harness sounded with each footfall.

And Mira was right. The whole experience was hypnotic. Soothing.

"Jack?"

"Yep?" He laid his cheek against the top of her head. To keep the wind from hitting it.

Sure, buddy. Keep on telling yourself that.

"I think I'm supposed to be giving you Norm's tourist spiel. What do you want to know?"

He chuckled. "I'm too comfortable right now to really care." As soon as he said the words he knew it was true. He also knew it was the last thing he should have admitted.

Instead of kicking him away from her in horror, she murmured, "That's good. Because I'm too comfortable to play tour guide."

"We're even, then."

He reached up to smooth a strand of her hair that tickled his nose. Then, instead of dropping his hand back to his side, he allowed it to trail down the side of her face, touching the cool softness of her flesh for the first time. Not really, but it was the first time he'd purposely touched her for a reason other than being hauled up off his ass or letting her pretend to be something she wasn't.

She could be, though. The insidious thought whispered through his mind just as his fingers reached her chin, his thumb strumming across the little indentation he found there. And hell if she didn't have the silkiest skin known to mankind.

Her sigh let him know she wasn't unhappy with what he was doing. If anything, she nestled closer, her hand splaying over his abs and sending a heady wave of warmth rolling down to his groin. This was a dangerous game to be playing in the back of a sleigh. A literal one-horse open sleigh.

His lips twisted. Scratch that. This was a dangerous game to be playing anywhere...with anyone...although, since the vehicle was in motion, there was almost no likelihood of having a police officer flash his spotlight on them, warning them to move along.

He explored the line of her jaw, his eyes traveling up to the seat in front of them for a second, but Norm and the horse had their attention focused on where they were going rather than on what was happening behind them. And there was no rear-view mirror that he could see.

No one would ever know.

No one would see if he... He slid his palm across the side of her throat, allowing it to rest there for a moment to gauge her response.

She didn't move. He swallowed, the need to do something crazy growing by the second.

It had to be sleep deprivation.

Still, he raised his head to look down at her. Her eyes were closed, her lips barely parted as she breathed. If not for the frantic beat of her pulse against his skin he might think she was asleep. But she wasn't. His thumb went to the bottom of her chin and exerted a slight upward pressure. As if she knew what was coming, her head tilted back to the perfect angle. Her eyelids parted, warm brown irises meeting his gaze. In their depths he saw the answer to his unspoken question.

She wouldn't stop him.

He murmured her name into the cold night. Softly, so that only she could hear. Then he lowered his head and covered her lips with his.

CHAPTER FIVE

UNEXPECTED.

That was the only word she could come up with to describe the moment his mouth slid over hers. Oh, she'd wanted him to. Her heart had been screaming for him to do this ever since she'd curled into his side and let him pull her close.

She leaned her head a little further back so she could feel the full effect of his firm warm lips as they moved over hers.

A tiny sound exited her throat, and her mouth opened.

He hesitated. For a brief heart-stopping second he paused as if unsure whether to stop or continue.

Please, Jack. I just want this for a minute. Maybe two. Then I'll let you get back to your nice shiny life with your fancy football team. I just need to know that someone, somewhere wants me.

Even if it's just for a moment.

His hand went from her neck to the back of her head, his fingers sliding deep into her hair as he remained poised over her mouth, lips just barely touching.

Then he did it. His tongue slid home with a smooth stroke that had her closing her eyes half in triumph, half in the heady luxury of the moment.

Norm wouldn't look back. He was used to giving his

customers their privacy. And surely he'd had people make out in the back of his sleigh many times in the past. Not her, but generic people. She and Robert had certainly never done anything like this. She slid her hands beneath his coat, seeking the warmth between it and his shirt and debating whether or not she dared to duck beneath a second layer until she encountered bare skin.

Jack's fingers tightened in her hair, and he tugged her head back so their lips came apart. "What are you doing?"

Maybe he'd read her mind.

"I could ask you the same thing," she whispered. "What are you doing?"

"Right now, I'm wondering how long this ride is."

"At least an hour. But it can be as long as we want it to be."

Wow, had she really just said that? Evidently, because he gave a low groan that only she could hear and plastered his lips back to hers.

This time there was no question or hesitation, just a hard demand that she was more than happy to answer. Beneath the blanket, she worked his shirt free of his slacks until she had access to that smooth, firm skin she'd been thinking about. She allowed her fingers to slide to mid-abdomen.

Did he work out with the football players he took care of? Because there was some defined musculature beneath all these clothes. The sleigh turned another corner and her hand slipped further up, running over a hard masculine nipple.

Oops. She hadn't meant to do that, but now that she was here…

He moved from her mouth to her ear. "Don't."

Oh, but she already had. Her fingers circled again,

testing, bumping and finally giving a little squeeze that had him hissing in a breath. "Mira."

And, oh, if she didn't love hearing her name muttered in that rough, sexy way.

Never had she gone out of her way to drive a man wild, but this one was different. He seemed so uptight. So...*unexpected*.

There was that word again.

Any other guy would have been happy to oblige by returning the favor. But not this one. He was acting like a stick of dynamite with a very short fuse.

He bit her earlobe once, twice, sending a desperate shiver over her. Deep down inside her, things were changing. Moistening. Transforming want into need at an alarming pace.

As if sensing the shift in her, he turned his body into hers, using his broad back to shield her from any prying eyes. Then one hand splayed low on her abdomen, taking her breath away as he held it there with firm pressure.

Yes. Please, Jack.

She wasn't sure what she was asking for—it wasn't like they could just have sex in the back of Norm's sleigh. But she wanted something. Wanted to feel him in her hand, wanted to drive him over the edge into insanity. Even if she got nothing more out of it than that. She squeezed his nipple between her fingertips again to see if he felt the same way.

"You're playing with fire."

She blinked up at him. "Fire is the best known antidote to freezing temperatures, didn't you know?"

His hand skimmed up her hip and ducked beneath the hem of her shirt. His skin wasn't icy, like she'd expected, but yummy and warm with slight callusing on the pads of his fingers. He glanced back as if making sure their driver was still facing the front. "This is not a smart idea, you know."

"Never said it was." She squeezed again.

"Hell, woman." Just like that his hand swept up her side and cupped her breast, his thumb stroking across her bra-covered nipple and sending a shot of pure pleasure straight to her center.

Okay, maybe she hadn't been playing fair. But neither was he, sitting beside her looking good enough to eat. And she was a little hungry. She could nibble, even if she couldn't get a full meal, right?

But the second she started to trail her fingers back down his stomach, she found her wrist gripped in a steel band. "No."

All playfulness was gone from his voice, and when she glanced at his face his eyes were dark, intense, a muscle working in his jaw. He slid his hand free of her shirt and tugged her clothing down. Pulled her coat back into place and buttoned it.

Her breath caught. Was he angry? Maybe she had carried this game a little too far. She started to withdraw, only to have his grip tighten, and he jerked her closer. His mouth moved back to her ear. "If we ever do this—and I'm not saying we will—it's not going to be some furtive little quickie, Mira. I want time, lots of it, and room to maneuver. Got it?"

She gulped. "Yes."

Whether she was acknowledging what he'd said or giving him permission she had no idea. But what else could she say? He'd taken her pass and intercepted it. The next play was with him.

With one last heart-stopping nip to her earlobe, he sat back and calmly straightened the blankets, while her pulse pounded madly in her ears.

"Now," he said as the first flakes of snow began falling again, "tell me about the local silver mines."

Jack wasn't sure where he'd gathered the willpower to stop her. It had been pretty obvious where she'd been headed once her hand had left his chest and traveled south. He could have let her continue…a few pumps and he'd have been done. Sated. But that's not what he wanted. If he was going to have her, he'd told the truth. He wanted hours. And he wanted to be able to use his hands. His mouth. He wanted to see her red hair spread out on a pillow and breathe in that purely feminine scent of her body.

Yes, he'd thought of having a fast encounter with some generic woman in his hotel room. But there was nothing generic about Mira. And he wasn't interested in a few brief seconds of pleasure.

Compared to what he really wanted from her, a hand job was like settling for a grilled cheese sandwich when what you craved was a sixteen-ounce rib eye.

She'd seemed a little glassy-eyed when he'd asked her about the mines, but he'd needed to get his own mind off of what he'd wanted to do and put it on something a little less explosive. Between that and the snow that had started to fall more freely he'd been able to cool his body down enough to keep from snatching her up and laying her down on that heated red velvet bench, driver or no driver.

By the end, she'd giggled as he'd reached into the pocket of his leather bomber and pulled out a beanie cap, pulling the black headwear down over her head to protect her from the white, powdery precipitation.

"I have my own, you know."

He couldn't resist a little shrug. "You look good in mine."

Once the ride was over, Mira thanked Norm and gave

him a quick hug before moving to Patsy and rubbing her thickly furred neck. "Thanks for that, you guys. It was great."

She promised to visit the stables more often, and the man tipped his hat and gave a courtly bow before climbing back on his sleigh and heading off again with another round of jingling bells and clip-clopping of hooves.

Then Jack—still in the throes of shaky reasoning and even shakier impulse control issues—had done the unthinkable. He'd asked Mira out again. Up on the slopes this time and ending with dinner in the restaurant.

And she'd done something just as unthinkable. She'd accepted.

"You have another date with him?" Ellory took a sip from her glass of Merlot and leaned a hip against the bar.

Mira squirmed. There was no way of avoiding it this time. Number Five might have become a problem. "Yes. But it's not like it's a big deal or anything. And the sleigh ride kind of got snowed out." But not before they'd done some necking in the back seat…and not before Jack had hinted he wanted to do darker things that involved time and lots of space.

She gulped a mouthful of her own wine.

How could she turn her back on something like that? Besides, it wasn't as if she was looking for a long-term relationship. This might even work in her favor. If they did have sex, she could prove to herself that she could have a one-night stand without it necessarily evolving into something permanent. Wasn't that what she was trying to avoid? Jack didn't live in the area. He'd soon be heading home to Texas. Back to his team.

No strings. No unexpected visits. No occasional sightings, like she had with her ex.

But did she want a one-night stand? Was she built that way?

If not, she'd better figure out how to change her personal blueprint because unless she never wanted to have sex again she was going to have to play by a new set of rules. One that involved a quick roll in the sheets and kicking the man in question out on the other side of the bed the next morning.

No regrets. No heart involvement.

It was the perfect solution, which was why she'd made that toast on New Year's Eve.

She glanced at her friend and took another—smaller—sip of her wine. "Don't worry, Elle, I'm sticking with the program. I'm not getting hung up on him. I'm following the spirit of the bet. You said that I wouldn't make it *past* Number Five. I never said I wouldn't go out with any of them more than once."

"Hmm…really? I understood that you would go out on a single date with twenty-five different men over the course of the year."

Mira tried to think back to the exact wording of that resolution. Had she said only one date apiece? She decided to play dumb. "So are you suddenly going to go all legalistic on me? The queen of all things loose and free?"

"*Touché.* You know me way too well." She sent Mira a grin and lifted her glass in salute before taking another drink of the dark red wine.

Relaxing onto one of the tall leather seats that surrounded the kidney-shaped bar, Mira swiveled around to face her friend. "Okay, so we'll say *intent*, then." She lifted her own glass. "Here's to intent. That I intend to steer clear of serious male-female relationships."

They clinked their glasses together. Ellory set her wine down on the polished wooden surface of the bar. "So let

me get this straight. You're going to have no serious relationships with males or females? Well, that's a damn
shame."

Mira swatted her arm. "Very funny. You know what
I mean."

She laughed again. "Rats. Of course, I've sworn off
men, too." She sighed. "So you're going to let man number five have another shot at getting this date thing right."

"Yep, although there's nothing to get right. We're just
going to hit the slopes one more time tomorrow and get a
bite to eat afterwards. Then it's done." Maybe. That was
if she didn't fall into bed with the man right afterwards.
A tingle of anticipation ran through her.

"Uh-oh. Speaking of hitting the slopes, ex-beau jerk-
wad at oh-three-hundred."

Mira blinked before she realized what her friend
meant. She glanced to the right and saw Robert nursing
a beer far closer to them than she'd like. Their eyes met,
and her ex lifted his glass to her. She just barely refrained
from rolling her eyes. Was he worried she was going
to run to Daddy and tattle about what he'd done? She
should. Really she should, but she wanted nothing more
to do with him. She was willing to let Robert save face
to make that happen, although the creep didn't deserve it.

She turned away and met her friend's worried eyes.

"Did you take a good look at him?" Ellory asked.

"What?"

"Robert. I want you to memorize every last flaw that
man has and imprint it on your memory." She leaned
over and squeezed her hand. "Don't let someone do that
to you again."

"I won't."

Ellory was right. She needed to use Robert as a cau-
tionary tale and not toss away one bad apple only to im-

mediately pick up a second one. Even if at least one part of that apple tasted as sweet as honey. Because who knew what she'd find when she turned it around and looked at the other side?

Although she suspected the back side of Number Five would look just as crisp and tasty as the front. And that was the biggest problem of all.

CHAPTER SIX

SHE WAS LATE.

Jack wasn't sure if he was happy about that or ticked. They'd agreed to ride up to the slopes together for another couple of lessons and then have dinner afterwards.

Propping his skis and poles against one of the heavy pillars that held up the wraparound porch, he inspected his snow boots for the fifth time. Yeah, yeah, yeah, all the laces were well tied and nothing dangled where it could trip him up. He'd leave that to the infuriating woman he'd almost mauled in the sleigh.

He hadn't been able to get her out of his head all weekend, which had seemed to drag. It had been made worse by a phone call from his coach making sure he was resting and having plenty of "fun."

As far as the resting went, it was hit and miss. He'd slept fairly well one night, only to wake up in a cold sweat the next.

But was he having fun?

A little too much, if you asked him. He'd had no business letting things get so out of hand on that ride through the snow. His only excuse was the same pathetic one he'd given himself each time he'd been around the woman. It had been far too long since he'd gotten any.

And how crude did that sound? Paula would be so proud of what he'd become.

Except he remembered her having a little bit of naughty wrapped up in her nice. Maybe that's why Mira's outrageous behavior had bothered him so much. It struck too close to those memories he'd done his best to bury.

Bury. Not a good word to use. Since he'd literally buried the woman he'd loved since high school. The woman he'd gone through medical school with.

Maybe he should just do what he'd said and go to bed with Mira. Be done with it. Except she hadn't shown up yet, and she was now—he glanced at his watch—over a half-hour late. Even knowing she wasn't coming didn't stop him from waiting here like a pathetic loser, going over the thousand and one excuses she might have for standing him up.

None of them, except maybe her father becoming ill, held up. Especially since he'd just seen Mr. Dupris a few minutes earlier and had given him a half-wave as he'd strode through the entrance.

Well, nothing to do but go ahead on up and ski back down. He might as well get some use out of his rental fee. But somehow doing it alone held no appeal any more.

He grabbed his skis and poles and started toward the chairlifts that lay about fifty yards to his left.

"Jack, wait!"

A familiar voice sounded behind him. If he were smart, he'd just keep going and pretend he hadn't heard her. But, of course, he didn't. He turned around and all thoughts of leaving disappeared.

Mira, in the same all-white snow outfit she'd worn the other day, hurried toward him, equipment slung over her left shoulder, her hair streaming around her shoulders. "Sorry. I thought you'd be gone by now."

Thought...or hoped?

"Sorry to disappoint you." The words were more difficult to force out than they should be.

She frowned, falling in step beside him. "Disappoint me? I had a patient this morning and didn't have your cell number. I tried calling your room, but you'd already left, evidently."

His cell number. It hadn't even dawned on him to give it to her. And he had left early that morning, deciding to go for a walk in the crisp air to clear his head and to try to talk himself out of actually sleeping with the woman. When she hadn't shown up, he'd thought she'd regretted that terrible—or was it amazing?—kiss they'd shared.

Now she was here. And he was just as torn over what to do as ever.

Catching the next flight out of Silver Pass would be the smart thing. But his coach would probably not welcome him back with open arms at this point. In fact, he might not welcome him back at all.

Maybe that wasn't such a bad thing, although what would he do with his life then? Allow it to spiral back down to dark places he'd rather not revisit? And if he sat around at home, that's exactly what would happen.

Regrets, he'd discovered, were a poison that didn't quite kill.

Two and a half more weeks.

He could always find Mrs. Botox and be done with it. He could guarantee there'd be no emotional entanglements on his part after spending a night with her.

So why did sleeping with Mira have to be any different?

It shouldn't, but he had a feeling it would be.

"Sorry about the cell number. I didn't even think to give it to you last night."

She grinned up at him. "I don't think either one of us was doing much thinking."

His own smile took him by surprise. "Probably not. How is your patient, by the way?"

"A child with an upset stomach. Judging from the stack of crumbled candy wrappers on her nightstand, I think I found the culprit."

"Such an exciting practice you have here, Doctor."

She gave a slight grimace as they arrived at the chair lifts. "I'm sure it's not as action packed as yours, but it has its moments." She gestured at the line of running seats that swooped by before starting their ascent. "Do you know how to use one of these?"

"I've somehow gotten on them during both of my other outings, but I have to admit it wasn't pretty." He eyed the chairs. Mastering them certainly hadn't been as easy as it had looked. At least with surfing he simply lay on his board and paddled out from shore. Everything was done under his own power, which was how he preferred it.

She moved over to the bench and snapped her boots down onto her skis. "Put on your skis, and I'll talk you through the process."

Once they both had their skis situated, she had him stand and move over to the line with her, handing their passes to one of the attendants. While various people got on the two-man lifts, she explained what they were doing. "We're next. Move to the mark."

He shuffled with her over to a blue line painted on the ground, and they waited for the couple ahead of them to sit on a chair and be carried up the mountain. Then they moved to the second line. "Look behind you," she said, "and keep the chair in sight. Once it gets to us, the attendant will hold it long enough for us to sit."

And just like that they were on, the lift swaying as it

moved up over the snow. Mira snapped a protective bar down over them. He'd been so worried about his balance the last time he'd ridden up that he hadn't even realized the safety feature.

"Have you ever fallen off one of these?" he asked.

"Yes, as a child." She shifted her poles. "Did you fall the last time?"

"Off the ski-lift itself? No. But the first time I tried to move away from the chair? Yes." That had not been one of his better moments, and probably what had contributed to his fall down the slope itself little a while later. The one Mira had rescued him from.

The lift continued up the long ascent, and Jack tried to settle back and enjoy the view. It was beautiful, the range of white mountains stretching out, skiers looking much smaller than they actually were, even though the lift wasn't carrying them all that high.

But more than the view, or the worries about getting on or off the lift, was his concern about how aware he was of the woman next to him. Like the other times they'd skied, she was decked out all in white, but her helmet wasn't on her head yet, just the pink beanie she'd worn during their last outing on the slopes. The chair was small enough that their shoulders and arms touched, whether he wanted them to or not. And along with each bump or wobble came the memories of what they'd done in the sleigh. The way the motions of that vehicle had shifted them together until he hadn't been able to resist her.

This woman ramped him up, almost to the point of not caring who saw them. The truth was he hadn't wanted to stop during that ride, and he wasn't all that sure what had made him grab her hand just before she reached the belt on his slacks.

Maybe the realization that once she touched him

there'd be no turning back. Or was it really as simple as what he'd said, that he wanted more time? More space?

Her fingers slid across the top of his hand, and he jerked his mind back from those chaotic thoughts to listen to what she was saying.

"There's the entrance to the silver mine I told you about." She pointed to something off in the distance about a half-mile away from the lodge. He could just make out brown wooden boards, but it appeared tiny from here. "It's closed to the public?" For some reason he thought maybe they'd made some of the mines into tourist attractions.

"Oh, yes. Not a safe place at all. There's a risk of avalanches out that way as well. We've had some snow, so the safety teams are monitoring the area. There are some off-piste skiing areas not far from there that could be affected."

"Off-what?"

"Off-piste. It means off the trail. Areas between the groomed runs. Some of them are open for skiing and some of them aren't. But here in Silver Pass those sections are reserved for advanced skiers, since there can be rocks and debris hidden beneath the snow—although we try to keep things marked well enough that people are aware of what's there."

"I don't think I'll be tackling any of those this trip."

"Chicken," she said with a smile. "We're almost at the end of the line." She nodded at the sign on the pole to the left that warned skiers to put the tips of their skis up.

Somehow, once they got to the offloading area, Jack managed to keep his skis pointed skyward and slide his ass off the chair, where he then glided down the little slope that led away from the circling chairs. And this time he didn't fall or careen into any other people who were exiting the lifts.

Grabbing onto a rope that was on the far side of the space, Mira slid smoothly beside him. "Good job!"

"Mira!" Her name came from across the way, and when she glanced over with a roll of her eyes he couldn't help but try to figure out who it was.

Ah, his former ski instructor and her ex. Standing at the top of the bunny slope, he was with a group of about twelve novice skiers. Even from here, though, he could sense the man's frown when Mira didn't answer him.

"You ready?" she said, her tight voice indicating she wanted to get away from there.

Judging from the steam he sensed gathering behind the other man's eyes, he nodded. "Why don't you go on? Unfortunately, I'm going to need to start with that beginner's hill again."

Mira gave him a cool glance. "Do you think I'm going to scamper off like a frightened rabbit?"

Hardly. He'd just thought she might want to avoid the guy.

They made their way over to the gentle slope, using poles and sidesteps until they were at the top. Although the instructor kept on teaching his charges how to slow their speed going down the hill, the man's eyes were obviously on them, probably wondering what the hell Jack was doing with her again.

Deciding to play by the other man's rules, Jack stared him down for a few seconds. Once the guy looked away and began to actively teach again, he noticed that Mira's attention wasn't on them but on the abandoned mine she'd pointed out from the ski lift. "What is it?" he asked.

"I don't know. Probably nothing." She gave a quick shrug then pulled one of her gloves off with her teeth before reaching in her pocket. She pulled out her phone and scrolled through something, glancing at the gray cloud cover a time or two. "Weird," she muttered, half to herself.

She put the phone in her pocket and then shoved her glove back on. "Do you want to lead or follow?"

"I always believe in letting ladies go first."

"Perfect. Because I like going first. That way, I can concentrate on getting to the good stuff."

Before he could decide if she was purposely being suggestive or not she'd used her poles to shove off the flat surface and start down the hill. He followed her, watching in awe as she expertly picked up speed and maneuvered from side to side. His balance felt pretty good today, but even so he couldn't match her speed, even using his poles to give himself some additional impetus from time to time. She was halfway to the bottom by the time he'd made it fifty yards.

Out of the corner of his eye he caught sight of another skier, coming just as fast as Mira had gone. Only this person sliced to the right just as he passed Jack, his skis sending out a large burst of snow that pelted him right in the chest. "Sorry about that, Number Five."

What the hell? Struggling not to lose his balance or his temper, he watched as the jerk proceeded on down the hill and did a quick zigzag as he came to Mira and then pulled in front of her, forcing her to come to a quick halt.

Jack frowned. That damn instructor again. He pushed his ski poles into the snow and forced himself to go faster, making sure his skis were aimed straight down the hill to speed his progress. By the time he reached her, though, the idiot had already left, heading toward the bottom in a series of moves geared to show off his skills to their best advantage. Well, that was all the man had going for him, from what Jack could tell.

"What was that all about?"

Mira's jaw was tight. "Nothing I can't handle."

"What is a number five? Is it some kind of skiers' code for 'make way' or something?"

"What?" Her face went very still.

"He skidded in the snow, hitting me with the stuff, then threw me an apology and said 'number five'."

"I…" She took a deep breath and then tried again. "It doesn't mean anything."

Somehow he didn't believe her, because she hadn't given him a blank stare or said she had no idea what it meant. She'd said it didn't mean anything, as if she knew what the guy was talking about but was discounting it.

She scooted closer and brushed some snow off his jacket. "Sorry he's such an ass."

What Jack couldn't understand was what Mira could have seen in a man like this. But he did like the way she'd sidled closer and the touch of her hands on his chest, even if there were ten tons of clothing between them.

"Did he get you too?"

"No. He was just trying to show off for his students."

It was more than that, but if she didn't want to get into it, who was he to try to force the issue?

She again pulled out her phone and glanced at it. "Do you mind if we head toward the mine? We won't go all the way or anything. There's another easy slope or two that we'll need to cover, but they're not much harder than this one. I just want to get a closer look at something."

"That's fine." The further away they got from her ex, the better Jack liked it. He wasn't worried about himself, he was pretty sure he could take the guy on solid, non-snow-covered ground, but he didn't want the bastard bothering Mira. "What do you want to look at?"

"I'm not sure. One of the snowdrifts looks a little iffy from here, but it could just be the angle. I'm not seeing any alerts on the weather site." She nodded at the sky. "But I think we might see another inch or two before the day's out."

Jack had noticed the thick cloud cover as well. He'd been glad for the shade, actually, as the sun glinted off the snow in a way that made his eyes burn, even with his goggles. "Will that be a problem for the resort?"

"It shouldn't be. I'll let you know when we get closer." She glanced back at him. "Follow me, okay, and don't go off the trails."

As if he would.

Slowly, Mira guided him down one slope, taking it slow and easy before sidestepping across a plateau and arriving at another well-groomed slope. No one seemed to take any notice of them, but Mira had checked her phone several more times. Jack had no idea what she was looking at, or even for.

A flick of ice hit his cheek and then another. He reached out to touch her jacket before they started down the next hill. "Do you feel that? I think the snow's started."

"That's what I was afraid of." She put her hand over her brow and seemed to scan the area.

Jack followed her line of sight, but all he saw were skiers going down various slopes, as well as another ski lift on the far side of the resort carrying people up the hills.

Jamming her poles into the snow, she scrolled through her phone, her finger sliding up the screen repeatedly as the occasional flake turned into a light snow shower.

Then she bit her lip. "Jack, do you think you can make it back to the lodge on your own?"

"Why?" Was she texting her ex, getting ready to hook up with him or something?

No, she seemed genuinely worried about something. "I'm not sure."

Jack heard a low rumble then it stopped. He cocked his head, listening. "Does it normally thunder during snowstorms?"

She didn't answer, just shoved her goggles on top of her head and jabbed her finger at her phone. Then she put it up to her ear. She waited and waited then someone evidently answered. She stared off into the distance. "It looks like some snow may have shifted over by the Vendry Mine." She waited and then continued. "No, I'm not positive, but I don't remember seeing it that far down on Friday evening."

Friday evening. When they'd been kissing in the back of the sleigh? She'd paid attention to the snow cover by the mine? That's the last thing he'd been thinking about on that crazy ride. It stung his pride a bit that she'd been able to concentrate on things other than his mouth on hers.

She paused again. "And in case you haven't noticed, it's snowing again, and we got a couple of inches last night. I'd like you to let my dad know. He's not answering his cell." Her brows went up. "What do you mean, he went into town?"

Jack pulled his goggles up over his head as well when the snow kept hitting them and then melting, leaving behind droplets of water. Another roll of thunder came and went.

"I think you should call him and ask him to come back. I'm telling you, you need to be ready, just in case.

Something's going on. Do you want me to have them clear the slopes?"

She waited for the other party to respond. "Are you sure?"

A puff of something that looked like a lazy roll of smoke sifted into the air over by the mine. A fire? There weren't many trees in that particular area, so he didn't think so. And Jack hadn't caught sight of any lightning, neither could he imagine anyone smoking while skiing.

"Okay. I'm going to stay up here for a while. I'll call you in a half-hour or so." She scrubbed her cheek against her shoulder. "Will do. Yeah, me too. Bye."

She hung up and scrolled again, then dropped the phone back into her pocket.

"Problem?" he asked, when her jaw remained tense. Had she been talking to the instructor?

As if realizing for the first time that he was still there, she slowly turned toward him. "Not really." She hesitated and then lifted her chin. "I don't want you to take this the wrong way, but maybe it would best if you headed back to the lodge."

Suspicion immediately flared in the back of his head. "Conversing with the ex?"

Why he'd said that, he wasn't sure. Even if she'd called him, it was pretty obvious it hadn't been to meet up with him or anything. She was worried about something over on that hill. Enough to want whoever was on the other end of that line to call her father and ask him to come back to the resort.

But his veiled accusation didn't go unnoticed. Her eyes chilled. "What I do or don't do is none of your business."

Okay, that had backfired. He'd hoped she'd give him a hint as to why she'd suddenly changed course, going from flirty to worried to angry in the space of a few minutes.

He touched her hand. "Sorry. I didn't mean it that way. I was digging for information, actually."

A thin layer of snow now covered the cute pink cap on her head and dotted her lashes. She smiled. "Okay, in case you're wondering—or even if you're not—I'm not going to get back together with my ex. Not now. Not ever. But I need to check something out, and I don't really want an inexperienced skier on any of those harder slopes."

"The ones closer to the mine."

She nodded. "The snow looks like it's moved, to me, shifted downward since our ride the other night."

"I heard you mention that, but what does it mean?"

"We got some snow last night. And we're due for more tonight. Not a ton, but enough to add more weight to the already thick layer. If it slides any further there could be trouble."

He brushed a couple of flakes of snow off her nose with a gloved fingertip. Her cheeks were pink with cold, as was her nose, and she looked pretty damned adorable right now. In spite of her worried frown.

The thunder rolled again, and Mira immediately jerked around to the side and stared at the mine, where, sure enough, another puff of white erupted into the air. Not smoke. Snow. Just like when Mira's ex had sent a burst of it shooting toward him. Once disturbed, the finer stuff drifted into the air, while the heavier stuff had hit him and then fallen to the ski slope, where it had slipped downhill a few feet. Then it had rolled to a stop.

So if the puffs he saw over by the mine were snow vapor, then something was disturbing it. But what?

At that second the rumbling started up again, this time growing in volume. He vaguely heard Mira's "Oh, my God!" before what seemed like half the mountain began to move, sliding downward, giant plumes of vapor rising into the air. And below the action—on another set of slopes—was a group of about twenty skiers.

He finally understood what Mira was panicking about, his own chest tightening and his breathing shooting through the roof in response to what he was currently witnessing.

Because, like a tsunami that churned its way toward shore, an avalanche was slowly building up momentum. And it was headed right for that unsuspecting group.

CHAPTER SEVEN

"STAY HERE." MIRA'S only thought, once the rumbling stopped, was getting over to the site and helping get those people out.

One second skiers had been whizzing down the side of the mountain, and the next about seven people had been flattened by a crush of snow. The rest of the group had successfully outraced the front edge of the avalanche, joining those near the bottom of the slope who'd escaped unharmed. A few of them were trying to climb back up the steep hill to get to their companions. But who knew if or when the snow would shift again?

"I'm going with you."

"Jack, those slopes are very different from the one we're on now. I don't want to have to worry about you too."

"You won't have to." He motioned to the bottom of the hill. "I'll ski the rest of the way down and walk over. I've done some rock-climbing. I'll make my way back up. You can't handle that many injuries on your own."

He was right. Until help arrived, she was going to have her hands full.

"Okay, go."

He started down the hill, while Mira made the call to the office. They would already know about the avalanche, but she wanted to make sure they knew the numbers. When Chuck Miller answered, she was brief and to the point. "About seven skiers buried. Call in search and rescue. Tell them to get Anson Graves and his dog up here, just in case."

She'd worked with the search and rescue expert before. He was the best there was. She only hoped he could get here in time.

Pushing off with her poles, she began to quickly make her way across the slope in sweeping lateral motions—like a sailboat that had to go against the wind. She used the downward momentum to drive her to the side. The off-piste areas were more challenging, but Mira had been on the slopes all her life. They were nothing she hadn't done before. It wasn't normally under these kinds of circumstances, though.

One of her skis skated over a buried rock, and she lurched sideways before correcting herself, her heart loping across her chest for a few seconds. In the silence that followed the avalanche she could now hear muffled screams of those on the affected slope, as well as cries of dismay from other nearby skiers. Her ex caught up with her halfway to the site.

"What can I do?"

This wasn't the time for a war of words or anything else, and they both knew it. She needed as much help right now as she could get. "Gather up some of the other instructors and send them over to the slope. We have to see if we can get those people out, and fast." If the avalanche victims weren't rescued almost immediately, they'd die.

"On it." He didn't question her authority, just thumbed his phone and spoke to someone, before starting back down the slope with a quick salute.

Her glance went back to Jack. He was already at the bottom and had his skis off, leaving them where they were while he sprinted toward the other slope in his heavy boots.

Mira skied faster, taking a group of moguls in her stride as she stayed the course.

She glanced at her watch, keeping track of time as she knew oxygen deprivation caused by suffocation was a very real concern for avalanche victims, although the cold was one thing in their favor in that respect.

Two minutes. One more off-piste and she'd be there.

She took a deep breath as she ventured off the groomed slopes and onto the rugged terrain that separated her from her patients. This was one of the most challenging off-piste sections on the resort, and she'd only attempted it a couple of times. It was also one of the reasons she'd insisted that Jack not follow her across. She couldn't concentrate on getting to where she needed to be if she had to rescue Jack from a bad spill or crash.

She bypassed one tree, only to whizz past another so close that a branch caught at the sleeve of her jacket. She had to jerk her arm free to avoid being dragged sideways and off her feet. The sound of ripping fabric told her it had worked.

A few more yards of bumps and swerves as she made her way across, and then she came out of it, sailing onto the much smoother section to her left. The slope was steep and slick and it still took most of her concentration to navigate around unstable clumps of snow. Keeping her gaze focused on where she'd seen the small group of people go down, she sliced to a halt when her skis bogged down in a thicker drift. A few skiers had made it back up and were out of their skis, poking their poles into the snow. One person was digging about ten yards away.

"Found someone here," said the man closest to her.

Mira clicked out of her skis and slogged several yards in snow up to her thighs before dropping to her knees beside the man.

"Try to uncover the face first," she directed.

She immediately joined in scooping snow, hitting a jacket a few inches down. A black zipper ran down the middle of it. Thank God the person wasn't face down. They quickly worked their way up and found a young woman. Mira leaned down to feel her pulse and listen for signs of breathing.

There! A gasped breath and the flicker of eyelids.

"Can you stay here and uncover her as much as possible? Don't move her at all, though. I'm going to see if I can help some of the others."

Robert and Jack arrived within seconds of each other, and while Robert sent the other man an angry glare he didn't question his right to be there. He'd probably already heard that Jack was a doctor. And judging from the snide comment he'd lobbed at him on the way down the slope, her ex had overheard her and Ellory's conversation in the bar and knew about that stupid resolution of hers.

No time to worry about any of that right now. They had to get these people out of the snow. And fast. "Robert, I saw at least two others go down about twenty yards to your left."

"Right." Her ex headed toward to the spot.

"Help!" yelled someone to her right. "I found someone, but he's not breathing."

Suffocation and crush injuries were their biggest worries right now, although the last person she'd found had been closer to the surface than she'd expected.

Jack motioned to her. "I'll get it, you keep looking."

Waiting to make sure he successfully navigated to

the location, she paused and her cellphone went off. She mashed the button. "Can't talk now."

"Anson's five minutes out." Chuck's voice came through.

"Got it."

She dumped her phone back into her jacket pocket while she fought her way through snow that was now almost hip deep as she joined in the search. No one that she'd seen had been much higher up on the slope than she was now, and even if they had been they'd have been knocked downhill some way from the force of the snow.

"Any idea how many are missing?" she yelled into the general melee. She'd counted seven, but it had been hard to tell how many had actually gone down.

"I don't know, but my brother is in here somewhere," a woman called back to her from ten yards down the hill.

Thank God this was a more advanced slope. She'd seen no children on it when that thing had come thundering down the mountain.

She pushed toward the woman, whose black tracks of mascara bore witness to her distress. "Where was he when you last saw him?"

"Right here." The woman pointed her pole in an arc.

"Okay, let's start there and work our way down, okay?" She came alongside the distraught woman. "Side by side." Glancing again at her watch, she saw that five minutes had now passed. Time was running out.

She turned her ski pole upside down so she didn't hurt whoever was down there.

Chop, chop, chop. She pushed the metal end into the ground repeatedly, hoping to hit something that was obviously not snow.

Chop, chop, chop.

In the background, she heard others as they shouted

that they'd also found someone, but she couldn't worry about that right now. All of her father's ski instructors were certified in CPR, and they knew the drill about not moving anyone. Her biggest worry right now was finding everyone who was missing before they suffocated.

Chop, chop, thunk. There!

About two feet beneath the white surface, she'd hit something soft. "Here!"

The woman beside her immediately joined her in digging as fast as they could.

They uncovered a hand. Pale and still.

Move up. Hurry, Mira!

The angle of the arm told her the victim was pointed down the slope, but the snow had buoyed the back part of him up, so that his head was buried deeper than the rest of him. It seemed like forever before they'd dug down far enough to reach him. Hair. Hell. He was face down. Mira frantically scooped deeper, digging around his face, until she could reach beneath him.

No breath. She felt the side of his neck. No pulse.

She swore under her breath.

"We need to turn him over." And pray he didn't have a fracture along his spine or neck. If they couldn't get him breathing, that wasn't going to matter, though. He'd die.

It took an additional fifteen seconds before they'd uncovered enough of his body to try to shift him. He was a big guy. And heavy.

"Get on this side with me."

They both tried to lift him to turn him over, but there was so much snow packed tightly around him. Tears of frustration came to her eyes. Then Jack was there beside them.

She threw him a look of utter gratitude.

Getting between her and the victim's sister, he said,

"Grab hold of whatever you can on his far side. We need to pull him up sideways first, in order to flip him. There's not enough room to turn him where he is. On three."

"One, two...*three*!" They all pulled as hard as they could. The man budged, started to turn, and then Mira slipped, losing her grip on the man's jacket. She swore, louder this time.

"Again," she said.

Robert evidently saw their struggles, because he came up beside her. "Anson's just gotten here. Let me help."

He urged the man's sister to move so he could take her place.

Jack didn't even spare her ex a glance. "On three."

This time, when he hit three, they pulled and the victim flipped onto his side as the trio used the momentum to haul him up out of the hole.

Mira glanced over the surface of the snow long enough to see that Anson and his dog were indeed on the scene, the rescue animal already with his nose to the snow.

Jack did what she'd done a moment ago and checked for a pulse. "Nothing. You start chest compressions."

In the background, the man's sister started crying.

"Robert."

That was all she needed to say. Her ex moved toward the woman to keep her back, while she and Jack worked. She ripped open the guy's jacket, no longer worried about hypothermia or anything that didn't relate to his heart or lungs.

Quickly finding the sweet spot on his chest, she lapped one hand over the other, her palms thrusting downward in quick bursts as she counted aloud. His body sank in the snow a few inches from the force of her compressions, but the weight helped pack it down to form a solid enough surface to do some good. "One, two, three..."

No liquid came out of the man's lungs as she continued compressions, so his airway wasn't blocked by melted snow. Jack had evidently known to wait a few seconds to make sure of that fact, because by the fifth beat he'd tilted the man's head back and leaned over him to give mouth-to-mouth between her measured pulses. He lifted his head long enough to say, "Tell me when you need me to spell you."

She couldn't think about that or anything else right now, except what she was doing. With each push of her joined palms she chanted, "Breathe, breathe, breathe," willing the victim to fight. To live.

About a minute later she heard the most beautiful sound in the world. A gasp. Then a cough. Mira stopped what she was doing and reached for his neck, only to find that Jack's fingers were already there. Icy cold without his gloves, but real and alive. Just like their victim, whose eyes now moved beneath his eyelids.

Mira glanced at Jack. Without his quick thinking they might still have been trying to figure out how to turn the man in that hole. A few minutes longer and this scene might have ended very differently.

Jack's gaze met hers, and he gave a quick nod of triumph. She couldn't hold back her smile or her mouthed, "Thank you."

Her fingers were still over his, and he turned his hand and captured them, giving a quick squeeze. The backs of her eyelids prickled, before she forced herself to pull back. Robert still stood over them, his arm around the victim's sister.

"Thanks," she said to her ex. "Can you go find out who else needs help? Check with Anson and see what he wants us to do."

Robert's jaw tightened, and he eyed her for a second before giving a stiff nod and moving away.

Motioning to the woman, who was staring down, both hands over her mouth, Mira said, "He's breathing. Why don't you sit next to him and talk to him while we check him for other injuries?"

The woman dropped to her knees, her hands reaching into the depression in the snow and cupping her brother's cheeks. "Marty, I'm right here."

The man's eyes finally opened, focusing on the woman. He tried to say something but his sister stopped him, tears streaming down her face. "Let them make sure you're okay."

Mira worked on one side of the victim while Jack stayed on the other. No obvious broken bones, and by the way the man's limbs were starting to move around, his spinal cord was intact. Thank God, after the way they'd had to haul him up. They still had to be careful, though. Just because he could move it didn't mean he was out of the woods.

"Your other resus? Did you get him breathing?"

"Yes." He glanced at her. "They've accounted for everyone we know of. All doing okay."

Mira lifted her head so she could look over the snow. The woman she'd dug up at the beginning was now on her feet, someone braced beneath one arm as they watched the rest of the rescues. Anson and his dog were further to the right, far away from the rest of them. Could someone have been carried that far away?

It was as if Jack had heard her thoughts. "It reminds me of an undertow. It just drags you down and carries you with it."

She nodded. She'd never been around the ocean very much but she could see how the two might be similar in nature. Whether you suffocated in the snow or drowned, it was the same death. The same terror.

The man beneath them began struggling in earnest. "You need to lie still. You might have injuries we can't see."

His sister shushed him and gave him a fierce frown. Whether he was just exhausted or had realized what he was doing, he did as they asked.

"Can you zip his jacket back up?" Mira asked. "I don't want him to get any colder than he already is."

EMS arrived on the scene—several squads of men from the looks of it—swarming toward them, stretchers either in tow or folded into packs that were strapped to their backs. It was slow going, though, because this section of the ski resort boasted steep inclines geared toward the most experienced of their guests. But the rescue workers were prepared, the snow cleats attached to their boots grabbing at the surface, whether snowy or slick, with each step they took.

Jack climbed to his feet and made his way over to one of the workers, probably giving him an abbreviated version of what had happened.

A moment later a megaphone sounded through the group. "If you're with an avalanche victim, please raise your hand, and one of us will make our way to you."

Seven hands went up in all, including hers. Everyone was alive, from what she could tell.

Mira glanced anxiously at Anson to see if they were having any luck. She'd assumed there were only seven victims. Had she missed one somehow?

One of the emergency workers reached her. She recognized him. "Hi, Mike. Thanks."

"No problem. What've you got?"

She quickly went through the rescue and then helped

get a fresh set of vitals and stabilize the patient's neck. Mike took the pack off his back and unfolded it into a kind of stretcher-sled combo that could be eased down the hill.

Jack helped with another victim, while a handful of ski instructors helped with some of the others.

From around a hundred yards away Anson's dog gave a quick set of plaintive barks that sent a shiver through her. He'd found someone. She glanced down at her watch then closed her eyes and said a short prayer. Twenty minutes.

It had seemed like no time at all, they'd all been working so hard, and yet for whoever was buried it had been an eternity.

Jack reached Anson first and they went to work, shoveling snow. Mira cleared her current patient and got to her feet, giving the victim's sister a quick smile of encouragement to hide her own anxious heart. She made her way toward the pair, who'd now stopped digging. They'd located whoever it was.

Jack hopped down into the depression in the snow and did some quick maneuvering before his head disappeared as he knelt. In less than a minute he climbed back out again. Even from there she could see his tight jaw. The way he shook his head at Anson.

Oh, no!

She stopped where she was, her eyes shutting for a second or two. Then she wrenched her lids apart. There was still time. The snow could slow body processes down for a while. Jack knew nothing about the mountains, he could assume things that weren't necessarily true.

Surely Anson wouldn't give up that easily. Anger unfurled within her and she moved quicker, her boots slipping a time or two as she tried to run through the drifts.

They were wasting time!

When she reached the pair, she snarled at them, "Help me get the victim up."

"It's too late." Jack grabbed her arm.

"It's not. The snow sometimes lowers the body temperature so that…" She glanced down at the victim and her words caught in her throat.

Snow-clouded eyes stared up at them from about three feet beneath the surface. And his neck…

She swallowed. Jack was right. There was nothing they could do.

The dog whined a time or two and pawed at the snow as if he didn't understand what they were waiting for. Anson dropped a hand onto the animal's head and gave him a quick scratch behind the ears, although when his eyes met hers they were grim. How often had the rescuer gone in search of a live person and come back with a body instead?

"Damn." She scrubbed her palms over her cheeks, surprised to find them moist and cold. "Let's get the others out first." She lowered her voice. "No one has mentioned not finding someone, and by now everyone at the resort must know about the avalanche. He's either here alone or someone's waiting back in one of the guest rooms. We'll need to see if he has some ID."

Jack came over to stand beside her. "Even if we'd found him sooner, it wouldn't have changed anything. You know that, right?" He put an arm around her and squeezed her shoulders. "There wasn't enough time to clear the slopes before it hit, even if we'd started across right after you noticed the first movement."

"I know." She couldn't stop herself from leaning a little closer, and then glanced over at Anson. "Thank you for coming."

"Any possibility that anyone else could be under here?"

"I tried to keep count as the avalanche came down. I thought there were only seven people buried, but…" she motioned toward the victim "…this makes eight."

Anson nodded. "I'll go ask at the lobby to see if anyone is missing and then do one more sweep of the area." He paused. "I don't want to leave until we're sure everyone is out."

"Agreed," Mira said. "While you're at it, can you ask Security to start contacting the guests to make sure everyone is accounted for? My dad should be back by now."

"No problem."

"Thanks again."

As she watched Anson and his dog head down the slope, a shudder swept through her body. She was freezing cold, even with all her gear on.

Jack pulled her closer and eased her several yards to the right, away from the poor avalanche victim. Most of the other patients had either been transported or were in the process of being loaded onto stretchers. "You need to get back to the lodge."

"Not before everyone is out. It's part of my job—and it's the right thing to do." She straightened. "But you go ahead. Thanks. You're not having much of a vacation, are you?"

"That's okay. Wasn't my idea to take a vacation in the first place."

He'd mentioned that before. Who came to a ski resort against their will?

A horrible thought came to her. "Are you married?"

He pulled back, dropping his arm from her shoulders and meeting her eyes with a frown. "Are you serious? Have you forgotten that sleigh ride?"

She swallowed. No. Not for a second. "That doesn't always mean anything." Who knew that better than she did? Her dad hadn't respected his vows, and neither had her ex. She and Robert might not have been married but they'd been heading that way.

"It might not mean anything up here, but it does where I come from."

"Meaning?"

"Evidently people up here on the slopes play loose and easy with their marriage vows."

And how did he know...? Oh! Mrs. Botox.

"Those kinds of people live all over the world. Even in Texas."

"Well, I'm not one of them." His eyes, dark with some intense emotion, stared right through her for a second before he took a deep breath. "Sorry. That was uncalled for."

Yes, it had been. But she could see how he might have taken her words. "It's okay." Another shiver went through her. Her hands went into her pocket to find her gloves, only to remember that she'd ripped them off to do chest compressions earlier. They were still over on the other side of the slope.

She turned, thinking she was going to retrieve them, when Jack pulled his out of his pocket. "Put these on."

"Oh, but—"

"Do it." He touched his fingers to hers. "I'm not as cold as you are."

It was true. His hands weren't warm, by any stretch of the imagination, but next to her stiff fingers his were like a tropical paradise.

One she didn't dare think about right now.

"Okay." She slipped her hands into the thickly lined

fingers, smiling when Jack pulled her hat further down over her ears. "Thanks."

"No problem." He smiled back at her. "Lady, I have to tell you, you have a strange idea of a date."

"I wouldn't exactly call this a date." It may have started out that way, but it certainly hadn't ended the way she'd envisioned.

"Neither would I." His thumb slid along her cheek. "It's one thing after another when you're around."

"Believe me, I'd rather there were no such things as avalanches." Her eyes went to the shovel sticking up out of the snow near the last victim. The whole lodge would mourn the man as if he were one of their own. These guests, even though they knew the risks of winter sports, never expected it to happen to them. And as careful as her father was, Mother Nature could—and sometimes did—trample right over the resort's precautions. "I hate that this happened."

"I know." His arm went back around her.

It felt good. Comforting. She was used to being the only doctor around this place. It was nice to have someone to share this particular burden with. And she honestly wasn't sure she could have handled this on her own. The worst thing she'd encountered other than the odd ski injury had been a norovirus outbreak that had swept through the ski resort three years ago, making a third of the guests and staff sick before they'd finally been able to contain it.

"Thank you for your help."

"I'm glad I was here."

"Even if being here wasn't your idea?" She couldn't help tossing his earlier words back at him.

He was tugging her further away from the site when

two rescue workers arrived with a basket and some more digging equipment.

Now that most of the patients had been cleared from the area, the other skiers had also headed down, no doubt urged by the ski instructors to clear this part of the mountain until further notice.

Anson came by and gave her a half-wave and said her dad and some others were working on contacting the rest of the guests. He was fairly confident no one else was under the snow, so he was headed back to the station to check in and fill out a report.

As soon as he was gone, Jack turned to her. "It might not have been my idea to come but I'm beginning to think my coach might have known what he was talking about."

"And what was that?"

He hesitated, then finally said, "Long story."

"Fair enough." He didn't owe her any explanations. He was simply man number five. It was better if she didn't know anything about him—well, except for the marriage thing. She'd have to remind herself to verify the marital status of any other man she went out with. She'd looked for the obvious thing, like a ring, but hadn't bothered doing that with anyone else.

Then again, she hadn't expected to go out multiple times with the same man.

She frowned. Now was probably as good a time as any to make her escape and move forward, otherwise she would just end up in the same old rut. Attracted to a man who wasn't what she needed him to be. He'd said it himself. He hadn't wanted to come. Preferred the surf to the snow.

Definitely not compatible. If she hadn't been able to make it work with a man—make that *three* men—who were from the Silver Pass area, why would she even think about getting attached to someone who not only wasn't from here but had no interest in sticking around?

Before she could say anything, though, he reached over and gripped her hand. "Walk you down?"

"Thanks. I'd like that."

Okay, so she could put off this whole separation process until she got back to her room. She wasn't even going to worry about dinner. Then, with their date officially over, she could sleep knowing this little bump in the road had been successfully navigated. She could tell Ellory she was moving on.

Life would continue, and Jack—no matter how tempting it might be to linger for a while and let him throw that rare smile her way—would be in her rear-view mirror, his reflection growing smaller and smaller with each day that passed. Until, finally, he was gone. Back to his home team. Back to his life with his coach and his friends.

And out of her life, forever.

CHAPTER EIGHT

MIRA HAD DESERTED HIM.

With dinner behind them and the night closing in fast, Jack sat at the bar, wondering exactly how he'd gotten here. After the shock of the avalanche and subsequent rescue efforts had worn off, it would have been easy to just cancel their plans to eat at the restaurant and go back to their rooms. Alone.

And yet once they'd come off that slope and stood in the arched doorway of the lodge, the words had come out of his mouth of their own volition. "Are we still on for dinner?"

She hadn't paused, even for a second, before saying yes.

Jack wasn't sure why he wanted it so badly, but he did. Maybe he wasn't quite ready to be by himself. Seeing that person's death earlier today had shaken him. Would someone grieve for the victim the way he'd grieved for Paula?

He ordered his first drink of the trip—other than that spiked hot chocolate—from the bartender and took a healthy swallow.

His wife had helped so many people. Worked tirelessly for her young patients, even when hope had seemingly been lost, to make sure they'd been cared for and comfortable all the way to the end. And he'd taken that away from her—had taken it away from those she could have helped in the future. She had been brilliant in her field. One of the best. And now she was gone.

All because he'd wanted to play doctor with a damn sports team. Lining up their specialties side by side, he'd known which one gave more value to mankind. But none of that had mattered at the time. Because he'd wanted that job. Had wanted it badly. And now none of it meant anything.

He'd seen that same special spark that Paula had possessed in Mira today. She'd been up on that mountain when the avalanche had hit. No one had known if that snow was going to shift again or not. She could have simply called in the rescue teams and waited for them to get the survivors out before she'd begun treatment.

But she hadn't. She'd been one of the first on the scene, digging right alongside the relatives and friends of the victims. And the way she'd run toward him and that rescue worker, fire in her eyes as she'd yelled at them to pull the last man out of the snow, saying there was still hope.

Something his wife had said constantly. *There's always hope.*

Until, of course, there wasn't. Until a plane—a plane Jack had asked her to be on—had gone down in a ball of fire. Until hope had been snuffed out by reality.

Just like in Mira's eyes when she'd looked into that hole in the snow and seen the truth. That there had been no hope.

His brain headed down familiar dark paths. He took another sip of his drink. Relished the steady burn of the alcohol as it trickled down his throat and hit his gut.

Dinner had been good, helping him relax and forget all the reasons he should be avoiding Mira like the plague. She'd made him smile time and time again, her animated expressions changing with each subject. She was passionate and beautiful, and he'd decided he could watch her talk all evening.

Only now she was on the other side of the room, talking just as passionately to her friend, the blonde.

Ellory, wasn't it?

An argument? No, he didn't think so. It looked more like Mira was trying to get the other woman to agree with her, palms facing up, their faces close together. In fact, it resembled some of the huddles he'd seen during games, when players had planned their next move.

Except this was hardly a play on a football field.

Break! A quick hug and a smile and then they were done.

Sometime during dinner, as he'd watched her laugh, he'd had some very bad thoughts. He'd entertained them all the way up to the last few minutes when guilt had wormed its way through him, devouring everything in its path. It happened every time he let his guard down.

Mira glanced his way and her shoulders went back, as if she'd come to some kind of decision.

What the hell?

As quickly as she'd left she was back, standing in front of him, hands on her hips, eyes on his face.

"What?" he asked, setting his glass on the bar.

"Nothing." She stopped for a second and cleared her throat. "Just seeing if I can get up the nerve."

"The nerve to…?"

"Ask you if you want to get out of here."

The words were so unexpected they shoved the breath from his chest. He sat on his barstool like a lump for several seconds. Had he just walked into an alternate universe? One where his wildest imaginings suddenly became reality?

Whatever universe it was, his body decided it much preferred this one to the one he'd just been in, reacting to the innuendo with a slow unfurling of a certain flag.

He decided to make sure he wasn't mistaken before he let his thoughts run any further ahead.

"Get out of here and go where?"

"Your room. My room. Take your pick." She looked closer at his face, her brows puckering. "Unless you don't want to."

Nothing plainer than that. In fact, the man sitting on the next barstool looked at her so quickly that his head nearly flew off his neck. And the expression on his face? *Hey, buddy, if you're not going to take her up on it, then clear out.*

Like hell!

"My room." Better stick to his own territory. Only…

Damn. He hadn't brought anything with him. This whole vacation had been taken under duress, he certainly hadn't expected to have a woman invite him back to her room.

The guy on the barstool was still ogling Mira from behind. Jack sent him a scowl that told him to back off in no uncertain terms. Then he threw some bills onto the bar, got off his seat, and grabbed Mira by the hand. In the distance, her friend watched them.

So what?

He got as far as the hallway and then glanced down the length of the space to make sure they were alone. Then he moved in. Close. Chest to her breasts with just enough pressure to send a jolt of desire arcing through his gut.

His cheek slid along hers, scooping up her scent—

vanilla and snow—and absorbing the soft feel of her skin. He journeyed toward her ear. Arrived.

"Now, see, Mira, you have me at a disadvantage. I want nothing more than to drag you back to my room, but unless your gift shop carries…certain items…"

"I have no idea, but it doesn't matter." Her head went back, and she stared at him for a second. "Ellory thinks I need to sleep with you. Get whatever…" she motioned between the two of them "…this is out of my system."

Ellory. The friend.

So wasn't the only one who'd felt the sparks. Who'd experienced the chemical heat that sizzled any time they were together. "So, am I 'in' your system?"

"Definitely. She thinks it's why I can't move…" She shook her head. "I don't normally do flings, but I think I want to make an exception in your case. So if you're clean, I'm on the Pill."

On the Pill.

Because she'd been sleeping with that oaf of a ski instructor?

Not fair, Jack.

Another thought came to him. "Are you trying to make your ex jealous?"

He couldn't say for a certainty he would refuse to go with her, even if that were the case. He'd wanted this woman ever since she'd stood over him in the snow and offered him her hand.

Why? Why now?

He had no idea, unless it was because he was out of his comfort zone—away from his team. Maybe he was just tired of wallowing in a vat of grief and self-pity. Paula would be horrified to see what he'd become.

Mira shook her head. "My ex will remain my ex for

evermore. But if you're trying to get me out of the mood, it's working."

She started to slide out from beneath his body, and instinct had his hands going to the wall on either side of her, caging her in. "Sorry. Yes, I'm clean. And if you're looking for a fling, I'm your man." His lips found her jaw and skated along it. "I have to warn you, though. I wasn't expecting company, so my room might be a mess."

Tilting her head back as he made his way down the side of her neck, she murmured. "If you think I'm interested in looking at your…room, you're very much mistaken."

Part of his anatomy went haywire at the image of her reclining on his bed looking him over and putting her own special seal of approval on him. "I think I can find other things to occupy your thoughts."

She relaxed. "Think so?"

"Pretty sure."

He forced himself to stand upright, although all he wanted to do was take her mouth and make it his. But he could wait. He *would* wait.

Wrapping his fingers around her hand again, he started down the hallway toward the elevators. "Do you have to check on any of those patients from the avalanche?"

"They've all been taken to the hospital. The staff has my cell number, if they need to get in touch with me."

He got into the elevator and punched the button for the top floor. Mira's eyes widened. "You're in one of the penthouse suites?"

"My coach, remember? I didn't book the room."

She leaned against the wall. "Your coach has good taste. And a hefty bankroll."

He snagged her hips and dragged her against him. "They spared no expense."

"They must like you an awful lot," she murmured, looping her arms around his neck.

The last thing he wanted to do was talk about his coach, or how much they were or weren't willing to fork out to get him back up to snuff. "And what about you? Do you like me?"

A shadow went through her eyes before it was gone. "I wouldn't have asked you if I didn't."

At least they both knew where the other stood. Jack didn't have to worry about Mira getting hung up on him or deciding she wanted to take things to the next level, because he couldn't. Not now. Probably not ever. She wanted a fling. And he'd been thinking that it had been too long since he'd been with a woman. They were both on the same page. And after tonight they could turn that page and never revisit it.

Mira waited outside the door as Jack slid his keycard into the lock and listened for the familiar snick as it released. She'd been in these rooms before, of course, but never as a guest. She'd forgotten that pro football players made millions of dollars a year. But even if she'd remembered, she wouldn't have expected Jack to make as much.

Besides, after her talk with Ellory—where Mira had grilled her about whether or not she'd told Robert about their bet—she'd wondered if her friend was right. Whether a naughty romp with the man in question would solve her problems once and for all—or if that was a plan doomed to fail. She was attracted to Jack. Very attracted. Which is why she couldn't quite move on to the next guy.

So, Ellory's answer? Sleep with the man. Kind of a wash-that-man-right-out-of-your-hair move that would clear him from her system. It had worked for Ellory in the past, so it should be just as easy for her.

Jack pushed the door open, and she stepped into the large marble foyer. While the downstairs portion of the lodge was a study in rustic furnishings, this room went in the other direction, its sleek, modern touches hinting at wealth rather than shouting it from the rooftops. From the white plush carpet to the glimmering stainless-steel accents, the room reflected the snowy setting outside.

He shoved the door shut with his foot. "I thought you weren't interested in my room." The words had a smile behind them, but she jerked around to look at him anyway.

"I'd forgotten how nice the penthouse suites were." Where was that mess he'd mentioned? The room seemed as clean as a whistle.

He glanced around. "They are nice." Motioning toward the tiled wet bar on the other side of the living room, he asked, "Do you want a drink?"

Yes. She did. And now that she was here she was beginning to wonder what she was thinking. She couldn't believe she'd actually propositioned the man, something she'd never done in her life. But she hadn't been able to think of a way to casually head him in this direction, and she had no desire to hang around the bar, hoping he'd make a move. So she'd decided to pull an Ellory and take the bull by the horns.

And now that she had him? What exactly did she do with him? Tell him to strip naked and get to work?

A drink. She'd start with that. "I'd love one. Red wine, if there's one of those mini-bottles somewhere around."

"I'm afraid this room doesn't have a mini-anything. It's all big."

He was right on that front. Her eyes went to the man as he walked toward the bar. The room was huge, but

Jack's height and frame made it seem almost ordinary. And that butt she'd admired a week ago…

She swallowed, changing her mind about the wine. "Jack?"

"Mmm?" He walked behind the bar and retrieved two glasses from a stand beside the sink.

"Would you mind if I skipped the drink?" She twisted her hands in front of her, wishing she was better at this whole seduction gig.

He set the glasses down, and brown eyes bored into hers. "I was just thinking the same thing." He leaned his elbows on the polished wood surface. "Come here."

On legs that were suddenly shaking she made her way toward him, until she was on the other side of the counter. He crooked his finger. "Closer."

She licked her lips then leaned over the surface until she was within inches of him.

"Nice." One of his hands came up to cup the nape of her neck, fingers threading through her hair. He tugged her nearer until they were mouth to mouth. "Is this more along the lines of what you were thinking?"

"Yes," she whispered.

"Good." His mouth met hers with a sweet pressure that made her want to melt against him, made her wonder if she could leap across the barrier and grab handfuls of his shirt and haul him against her. But she didn't act on any of those thoughts. She stood there, leaning as close as she could get while his lips slid over hers time and time again. His teeth played with her lower lip, teasing it, until all she wanted was him hard against them, thrusting into her mouth like he'd done on the sleigh ride. Only tonight there was no Norm or Patsy to catch them in the act. It was just her and Jack. And this time she had no intention of stopping.

Her hands went up and caught his head when he started to move away from her mouth.

Uh-uh. That hadn't been nearly enough. She wanted him right there.

She eased him back to her mouth, and this time she opened, hoping to tempt him into sticking around for a while. With a low sound his hand tightened in her hair and the kiss morphed into something else. Harder. More demanding. His tongue pushed past her lips with a quick thrust that made her gasp. He filled her, head turning sideways so he could reach even deeper.

A moan worked its way up from inside her as he released the pressure, only to surge forward again. When he finally lifted his head she dragged in deep breaths, trying to clear her fuzzy brain.

"You're still too far away," he murmured. Taking her hand, he led her around the bar until she was at the spot he'd been standing seconds earlier. "Better."

He proceeded to drug her with several long, wet kisses that had her insides quivering with need. His hands slid down her sides, until he came to her waist, which he gripped. "When I say three, jump."

Her breathing still erratic, she somehow managed to spring up when he hit the number, finding herself perched on the glossy wood bar, looking down at him. When she frowned, wondering what he was doing, he backed up with a smile and then yanked his dark shirt up and over his head.

Ooh, she liked that. Her glance skated over his bare torso. Strong and muscular without being bulky, his tanned skin had obviously been kissed many times by the sun.

Surfer dude...football doc. That's right.

A smattering of dark hair started at his chest and

flowed downward, narrowing until it was just a slim, fascinating line that disappeared beneath the waistband of snug black jeans. When her eyes finally came back up, she found him watching her. Her teeth gnawed her bottom lip when he came forward, his warm palms landing on her thighs just above her knees and slowly smoothing along the surface of her legs. Her mouth went dry the higher he got, his thumbs grazing the sensitive area just inside her thighs.

Oh, man.

Then his hands were on her hips, and he jerked her forward until she was balanced on the very edge of the high bar, her thighs parting on either side of his chest. She felt open and exposed and the slow smile he gave her said that's exactly how he wanted her.

"Remind me to thank whoever put this bar in my room."

Since that was probably her dad, there was no way she was reminding him of anything.

He moved deeper between her legs and leaned over to plant a kiss on her stomach, sliding his hands beneath her shirt and pushing it up, until his lips grazed bare skin rather than her white tee shirt. His tongue dragged up her stomach, her muscles rippling in the wake of his touch.

Almost against her will, her eyes fluttered closed and her fingers went to his shoulders as he continued to kiss his way across her belly. When he reached the hip that lay just above the top edge of her jeans, he nipped at the bone, sending a quiver of electricity arcing right down to the parting of her legs. She ached for some type of pressure, but there was only air between her and his chest with no way of inching any closer. Not unless she wanted to fall off the bar. And there was no way she wanted to distract him from his current task.

His fingers went to the button on her jeans and had it open within a second, the zipper following soon afterwards. For once she was glad she'd put on feminine lacy panties and not her utilitarian black cotton undies.

As if reading her thoughts, his growled "Nice" hit her ears, making her smile.

The smile disappeared when he looked up the length of her body. "I'm going to need your help for a second. You lift, and I'll slide."

Why that raised a decadent picture, she had no idea, but the image of her hips coming up while he slid home swamped her brain, making it difficult to obey his command.

Lift. He said lift.

Bracing her hands on either side of her hips, she lifted up while Jack tugged her jeans down her thighs and then her legs as she returned to her seated position.

His fingers trailed around the top band of elastic on her panties and slid under the lace ties at the sides. "I am going to enjoy undoing these. But first let's take care of that shirt."

He stepped back, making her frown.

What?

Wasn't he going to help her with that as well? When his arms went over his chest she had her answer.

It was either put up or shut up. And she was definitely aiming for the "put up" side of the equation. As in…grabbing the bottom of her shirt, raising her arms and dragging it over her head. She then let it drop onto the floor behind the bar.

Her bra matched her panties, both peek-a-boo pieces of lingerie that did a whole lot more peeking than anything else. She found her courage from somewhere. "Bra?"

"Not yet." Stepping forward again, he planted his

hands on her knees and slowly pushed them apart until he was back between them.

Too late, she realized what he was planning when his lips pressed against the skin of her rib cage, just below her bra, and moved on a slowly winding path that headed south. He reached her belly button, dipping inside for a second, then the tip of his tongue toyed with the upper edge of her panties.

"Jack."

Plea? Or protest?

She wasn't sure. Only knew that he'd finagled things so she couldn't clamp her legs closed, and all the parts that mattered were well aware of that fact, pulsing with a heavy need she hadn't felt in a very long time.

His fingers came up and found the ends of the ties on either side of her underwear. "Do you want me to stop?"

If she said yes, it would be all over. He hadn't said it, but she knew herself well enough to know it was true. She'd be too embarrassed to continue. And in truth she didn't want him to quit. Wanted him to show her exactly what he wanted from her.

And she had a feeling she wouldn't be sorry.

"No. Please, don't stop."

His eyes closed for a beat or two, hiding those gorgeous brown irises. Then they opened back up. "I'm going to make you say those words again in a very short while."

She gulped as a wave of awareness swamped her just as he tugged those ties and released the knots. Her underwear fell away, the front and back panels dropping to the bar. Jack wrapped his arms around her butt and pulled her hard against his chest, until that center part connected with his bare skin.

"Ah." She wanted nothing more than to grind against

him in a frenzy but, as suddenly as he'd made contact, he pulled away again, the cool air flowing against her and making her squirm with need.

Lord. What was he doing to her?

"Take me to the bedroom." She was more than ready to have him right there, inside her, giving her the relief her body was starving for.

He kissed her stomach. "Soon." The warmth of his breath rolled across her skin. "Do you remember what I said up on that mountain?"

He wanted her to remember...*words*? At a time like this? With the heat his body was putting out? "No."

His hands were back at the tops of her thighs, thumbs pressing just enough to let her know he was there. "That's a shame. Because this would be such a great demonstration of that gentleman's rule."

Ladies first. That's what he'd said.

As his lips lowered to the top of her right thigh and kissed it, a shudder rolled across her. "That's not necessary. Let's just go to bed. I—I want to."

"Oh, sweetheart. So do I. More than you can possibly know." He kissed the inner surface, teeth nipping at the tender flesh. "But I can't. Not yet."

He pushed her legs wider as his lips ventured closer to a very dangerous area. "Intoxicating. Your scent. The taste of your skin." The words muttered against her sent fire rushing through her veins and anticipation clenching through her stomach. Then he was there, and the shock of his tongue making gentle inroads made her go completely still. She had to prop herself up on her elbows to keep from falling backwards at the rush of sensation as he slid up and around, avoiding that one tiny part that craved his attention more than anything.

"Please. Jack. Oh, God."

He pulled her closer, until everything came into contact with his mouth all at once and her legs draped over his shoulders as he finally gave her what she wanted. Her back arched, and she couldn't stop herself from using the soles of her feet to push closer to that incredible source of pleasure. He didn't disappoint, his lips surrounding her and sucking gently—tongue rubbing against her.

That was all it took. She grabbed a breath and then let go with a loud moan, pumping herself against him as her body flashed red-hot, the lights in the room fading to almost nothing. Again and again her inner walls clamped, finding nothing to grab onto, and yet the ecstasy was still stronger than anything she'd experienced in her life.

She lay there for a few seconds, mouth open, eyes closed, her lungs snatching for air and still feeling deprived.

When random thoughts finally started trickling back into her brain, she was stunned. Winded. Unnerved. Then she looked down to find his eyes on her, his mouth still poised between her legs.

She couldn't believe she'd let him do that to her. On a hotel-room bar, of all things. But she couldn't bring herself to regret it.

"You're bad," she said, unable to come up with a more sophisticated expression at the moment. "Very, very bad."

He laughed and stood, reaching behind her—to help her down, she thought. She was wrong. Snap went the clasp on her bra, and he eased her upright, removing the garment before he finally gave her a response.

"Sweetheart, you have no idea just how bad I can be."

CHAPTER NINE

HE SCRABBLED FRANTICALLY at the heavy lid, trying to pry it open. How could she breathe inside there?

She couldn't.

Putting the tips of his fingers beneath the smooth, shiny surface, he put all his force into opening it, breath whistling out through his teeth, muscles shaking with exertion as he strained upwards. His grip failed, hands slipping and throwing him back onto the plush carpet behind him. Soft music played in the background and people milled around, holding plates piled with food.

Why wasn't anyone helping him? Couldn't they see she was trapped?

He glanced around for something. Anything. His eyes fell on a crowbar that had been tossed up against the wall beside a dainty blue velvet couch. Crawling toward it, he grabbed it with both hands, the weight of it surprising him. He stood to his feet, dragging the metal bar behind him until he was in front of the box once again. The music got louder, and what had been soothing elevator music became a little more sinister in tone. Nothing that he could put his finger on exactly as it seemed to be the same tune.

Time was running out.

It was as if everyone else had finally noticed as well.

They gathered around him, plates in hand, as he swung the heavy crowbar up, like he would one of those carnival hammers, and somehow got it to hook under the lid. He swallowed, suddenly not so sure about what he was doing. But they were all watching now. Waiting. Including a familiar blonde near the back of the room.

Where had he seen her before?

He shrugged and turned back to his task. Taking a deep breath, he silently counted to three.

One...two...

Three!

He put his full weight onto the metal rod, pushing down, down, down, the splintering of wood telling him he was getting somewhere. With a groan the top released and popped up an inch or two before the crowbar fell out of the groove. But no matter, he'd broken whatever seal was holding it closed.

He dropped the tool beside him and once again placed his fingers beneath the lid and slowly lifted. The sheen of blue satin met his eyes, the color matching that of the sofa behind him. He pushed the top higher and saw the cool white skin of her cheek. Her nose. Her pale lips.

A shot of horror went through him as he finished opening the top of the box.

It wasn't Paula. And she wasn't sleeping.

Mira!

He let go of the lid, and it fell in a series of disjointed frames, like a stack of still shots ruffled with a thumb to form movement. Then it hit the lower half of the box with a craaack!

Jack jerked, his eyelids flying apart and meeting darkness. Panic swept through him. He reached next to him to see if Paula was still there. His fingers met warm flesh, and he let his head drop back to the pillow in relief.

Just a dream.

More thoughts sifted through. Memories of making love. Groaning as he'd touched each silky inch of her body. Trying to hold off the inevitable until it had become too much, and he hadn't been able to resist pouring himself into her. Holding her until his breathing had slowed.

He swallowed hard, his head turning to the left. But it hadn't been Paula.

It had been Mira last night.

It was still Mira this morning.

And he'd enjoyed himself far too much. Had laughed and played the wicked rogue to the very end.

Hell.

He threw his arm over his eyes and tried to figure exactly what had happened last night.

A fling.

Yes. She'd used that word. So had he, in his head.

The bed shifted as she moved. Sighed.

Jack couldn't resist turning his head again. It was morning, it had to be, but it was still some time before dawn, judging from the darkness that hovered around the edges of the curtains. His adjusting eyes caught the first glimpse of a bare shoulder peeking from beneath the thick duvet cover. Her back was to him, her arm curled up to rest on the pillow beside her face.

The face he'd just seen lying in a satin-lined coffin.

Damn. And his bottle of sleeping pills sat on the bedside table untouched. The "mess" he'd been worried about her seeing.

He swung his legs out of bed and sat on the edge of the mattress for several long seconds, trying to stamp out the images still flickering in his mind. To distract himself, he opened the drawer on the table and knocked the medicine inside it. No need to let Mira see them. She'd just ask questions.

Questions he couldn't answer.

Like why he'd put her in Paula's place. The dream was the same as always, but the face had changed.

It had to be the aftereffects of the avalanche. Of those people suffocating, and one of them dying. Mira had been there, so maybe that's why she'd been in the nightmare this time. His wife's coffin had been closed. In reality, there hadn't been a body to go in it as Paula had been incinerated along with most of the other passengers.

Or maybe Mira had been in his dream because his subconscious was telling him to slam the lid down on this particular relationship and to seal it tight. But they didn't have a relationship.

They had a fling.

Just the word had a calming effect on him.

He'd had fun. There was no crime in that.

So why did he feel like the lowest form of low?

Guilt, probably. A false sense of loyalty to a woman he'd loved and lost.

She'd want you to go on.

Yes, she would. But that's not what he wanted. He remembered all too well facing that polished coffin and wondering how he was going to pick himself up and go on living.

Never again.

Standing, he made his way to the bathroom, suddenly wishing they'd gone to her room instead. Then he could just quietly get dressed and let himself out. No awkward goodbyes. No wondering if you should say thank you or I'm sorry.

He took his time, brushing his teeth and showering, then toweling off, all the time rehearsing exactly what he was going to say when he opened that door. But all he could see was the way Mira's back had arched like a cat as she'd moaned.

Please, don't stop.

Yes, he'd made her say it again. And where male pride should be, there was a slight sense of something else. Shame?

No.

He wasn't sure what the emotion was, but he didn't like it. It felt like something was poised to break loose, like that snow on the mountain that had gotten heavier and heavier until it had finally thundered down that slope, wiping away anyone in its path.

And from what Jack could see, he was standing right in front of it. Only it wasn't snow. But something just as devastating.

Staring at himself in the mirror, he wrapped a towel around his waist, wishing he'd thought to bring in a fresh set of clothes. Getting dressed would send an obvious hint that the night was over and that it was time to make their way back to reality and their own separate beds.

Except that tiny images of the pleasure he'd given and received last night circled in his head, bringing with them a whole new set of ideas. Ones that whispered that this was only a fling, no need to fear. Just get back in there and do a little more flinging.

The more he thought about it the more he relaxed. Why not? He wanted her. Wanted to slide his hands over that lithe body and roll her beneath him again. She'd seemed to like it as much as he had. In fact, there was a sore spot on his shoulder he was pretty sure had been made by Mira's nails as they'd reached yet another pinnacle.

Yes. He wanted that. Wanted more of those scratches. More of those kisses.

It was okay. The dream had been nothing more than the stupid workings of his mind and that avalanche.

He undid the towel and let it drop to the floor, his body already anticipating what he wanted to do to her next.

Sweetheart, I hope you're ready.

He turned out the bathroom light so it wouldn't disturb her, then carefully opened the door. He was halfway across the room when he realized the bed seemed a little flatter than it had been. He frowned, moving closer. It looked different because it *was* different.

Mira was no longer there under the covers. His eyes skated around the room, going through the door to the living area and seeing just a silent hotel room.

No sound. No flash of movement.

He glanced at the floor next to the bed. No clothes. Although his were now folded and placed neatly on the seat of a chair on the other side of the room.

She was gone.

She'd done exactly what he would have done had he woken up in her room that morning. She'd crept out of bed and thrown on her clothes while he'd been in the bathroom. And then she'd turned tail and raced as fast as she could out of the door and out of his life.

Sleep with him, she'd said. *It'll do you both good,* she'd said.

Mira slammed her hairbrush down on the small vanity in her room and berated herself for running away like a coward. It would have been better to just lie there and pretend to be asleep, and then when Jack came back into the room give a big stretch as if she'd just woken up. She could have nonchalantly said she had to get dressed for work and say, "Thanks for everything."

Yeah, like propping her up on the bar and making her see stars.

In reality, she hadn't slept a wink once they'd made love a second time—in his bed this time. She'd lain awake for hours, totally blown away by what had happened between them. Rather than kick the attraction in the teeth and send it skidding down the road, it was now crouched in the left-hand corner of her mirror, grinning at her with that all-knowing smile. No matter how many times she blinked, it was still there.

Maybe because the smile belonged to the stuffed Cheshire cat Ellory had sent her for her birthday last year.

"Yeah. Keep grinning and it's under the bed for you."

When the smile remained where it was, she found the corners of her own mouth lifting. "Oh, Ellory. What have I done?"

But, of course, her friend wasn't there to tell her what she should do the morning after.

She wanted to see him again. Something she hadn't expected.

Gulping, she scrubbed her hand over her stomach. She was going to go and get all attached to him, she just knew it.

"Idiot."

She laid her head down on the dressing table and thought through all the options.

Option one: she could remain in her room for the next two weeks...or however long he was scheduled to be here.

Option two: she could wear a Gaga-ish mask and pretend she was musical royalty.

Option three: she could forget about this whole bet-slash-resolution thing.

But she knew Ellory would worry about her if she really did go and jump into a new relationship. Hell, she would be worried about herself, if it came to that. She had three failed relationships under her belt. *Serious* relationships. To jump into a new one almost on the heels of breaking her engagement to Robert…

Stupid.

Which brought her back to thinking up more options.

She yawned. Option four: she could fall asleep and hope she didn't wake up for a couple of weeks.

Or she could just be a grown-up and go up to him and say, "Hey. Thanks for last night. I had a lot of fun. See ya around."

Quick. To the Point. Truthful.

She liked it.

She dragged herself up off the chair and headed to the bed, crinkling her nose at Chessie, who was still grinning madly at her. She knocked him sideways.

There. Just grin into the pillow for a while.

She decided to jump in the shower and try to pull herself together. As soon as she stepped under the spray she knew it was the right thing to do. The warm water helped soothe her nerves. Maybe she really would take a nap. Everything looked worse when you were tired. Scrubbing herself down with a soapy loofah, she tried to put what had happened last night out of her mind.

If she could just get his scent off her body and out of her head…

From a distance she heard her cell ring.

Please, don't be Jack. Not right now.

Despite her thoughts, by the second ring she'd sluiced off the rest of the soap and stepped out of the shower, feet slipping for a second on the bare tile floor in her hurry to get to the phone.

Damn, damn, damn.

She picked up the thing and glanced at the readout, adding a fourth "damn" for good measure. Robert. Not Jack.

"Hello?"

"Mira, are you free?"

Oh, Lord. Now what? If he thought they were getting back together he was mistaken. "Why?"

"Number Five is up here with me, and he might need some help."

"Jack? What happened?" Her heart started crashing around in her chest, making her vision swim for a second or two. Here she was agonizing over what they'd done last night, and he was already up on the slopes first thing this morning.

"He's fine. But someone fell off the ski lift and…uh… Dr. Perry says she has multiple broken bones. Can you get up here? EMS has already been called, but it'll be a little while, there's evidently a lot of ice after the freeze we had yesterday, and they're having to deal with some accidents on the roads. Your guy wants to stabilize the guest and then get her someplace warmer."

"On my way. Which slope?" She probably already knew. Jack wouldn't risk his life on one of the bigger ones.

"Grade two." There was a pause. "Mira, we think she was a jumper. There were a couple of witnesses who saw her go over."

Her heart stuttered.

A jumper. Oh, God. Every couple of years someone decided life was too painful to bear and threw themselves off the lifts and onto the slopes in a suicide attempt. Normally it was onto one of the more advanced slopes, though, as the lifts servicing those areas went higher.

Her throat was so tight she wasn't sure she'd be able to respond. But when she opened her mouth, somehow the words were there. "Give me a few minutes. I'll keep my cell with me, so call if there's any change."

Throwing the phone onto the bed, she rushed around yanking her clothes on and then her snow pants and parka. Her coat still had a ripped spot on the sleeve—just like the shredded portion of her heart.

Please, let her be okay.

She searched around for her gloves for a minute or two, and then frowned at the unfamiliar pair she found in her pocket.

Jack's gloves. He'd given them to her after the avalanche yesterday.

Her throat tightened further.

Had that just been yesterday? It seemed like it had happened weeks ago.

In reality, there were plenty of accidents to go around at a ski resort, but not usually on a day when she'd gotten so little sleep. Although, with the adrenaline now coursing through her veins, she felt wide awake. Her hair was still wet, but it would have to stay that way for now. She hauled it back into a quick bun and secured a rubber band around it. She'd just pull a hat on and then her parka hood over the top of that. She could blow-dry it when she got back to her room later.

She knocked Chessie back upright. "Watch the room for me, okay?"

Five minutes later, she hurried out the door, telling the front desk where to reach her. She snapped on her skis. It would be faster to go up the lift and then ski down to their position. Slope number two. A little harder than the bunny slope but still an easy ride for beginners like Jack.

Sliding past those in line with an occasional murmured "Excuse me", along with the fact that there was a medical emergency on one of the slopes, she cut to the front and allowed the next chair to scoop her up and carry her on her way. Her eyes scanned the area. There. About halfway up there was a small crowd of about five people. The one at the center of the group, nearest the patient, was Jack, the sun glinting off the lighter strands of his hair.

Her heart squeezed again.

At least the injured woman had someone capable helping her. As a sports medicine doctor he'd have specialized in orthopedics and be well versed on serious breaks. There could be no better person attending that patient, and that included her.

Impatient to get down there, she had to wait another three or four minutes for the lift to reach the top of the slope. Then she was off and with a couple of pushes from her poles was heading down the mountain at a good clip, mentally playing through her mind how far she had to go before she reached the scene. Thankfully the trip down was a lot faster than the trip up. She turned her body and skis sideways and skidded to a halt next to the little group.

Robert nodded at her from the edge of the ring, where his job was to keep gawkers at bay. She'd really have to say something to him about using Number Five when referring to Jack. Yeah, yeah, she'd referred to him that way in her head as well, but that was so she could keep some emotional distance.

A lot of good that had done.

Right now, though, that was the least of her worries.

She knelt beside him, noting that he had several splints laid out and was currently binding one to the patient's arm. The girl— Oh, Lord, and that's all she was. A teenager. On her back, with her eyes open wide, she whimpered in pain as Jack worked on her. The sleeves on both her jacket and her sweater had been slashed up past her right elbow, revealing a bloody spot on her forearm that looked ominous.

Compound fracture. A hint of pearly bone protruded from the site.

Dragging in a shuddered breath, she murmured, "What have you got?"

He glanced up, and his lips tightened for a second then he said, "Stacy Painter, sixteen. Broken right radius, compound at the ulna, and two fractured femurs—both at the neck, from what I can guess, based on her leg position. And she has tenderness on her right side as well...possible fractured ribs."

She closed her eyes at the mention of the femur fractures. "At the neck" meant the bones had broken off at the ball where they went into the socket. And if those sections went too long without oxygen, it could mean a double hip replacement. In a teenage girl.

Now wasn't the time to think of that, though. They needed to have her ready to transport once the EMS crew arrived. "What do you want me to do?"

"I'm stabilizing the compound fracture and need to protect it. But I've got her radius and hips to deal with." He glanced up at her again. "We have to do this without any meds. Can you talk to her while I work?"

No pain meds. She knew that was protocol when they didn't know what a patient's other injuries might be, but it had to agonizing for Stacy to have Jack manipulate her bones. It was one of the worst parts of being a doctor. Once again, she found herself glad he was there.

She didn't argue about what he'd asked her to do. Didn't say she was a doctor too so she should be doing some of the work. She simply scooched over until she was by the girl's head and then leaned down. "Hi, Stacy. My name is Mira. Dr. Perry is going to get you all fixed up."

The girl blinked, a few tears breaking free and sliding down her cheeks. Then her eyes focused on Mira. "He—he said to call him Jack."

Mira glanced up to find that the man's eyes were on her. She pulled her attention back to the patient. "Is that so?" She forced a smile. "You're lucky. He doesn't let just anyone call him that."

In fact, some of us call him Number Five.

She pushed that little voice away and continued. "What happened?"

The girl's chin wobbled and another tear escaped. She wouldn't quite meet her eyes. "I—I fell. Off the ski lift."

Had she hesitated before using the word "fell" or was that her imagination?

There were witnesses.

Mira glanced up at the chairs going overhead—people in them were now staring at the scene below. It seemed like a long way down from here. The teen had to have tumbled a few feet once she hit, to have broken so many bones.

"Was the safety bar down on your seat?"

The girl winced as Jack touched her leg. "No. I—I forgot."

Another coincidence.

Oh, honey, what would drive you to do something like this?

She forced out her next words. "Do you know where your parents are?" Had anyone contacted them yet?

Stacy started to shake her head and then screamed, the sound ending on a group of sobs.

Jack had slid a long splint beneath her right leg and hip and was strapping it in place.

Sliding onto her side, so that her head was as close to Stacy's as possible and blocking the view of what Jack was doing, she said, "I know it's painful, honey. Dr...er, Jack is putting something called splints on your legs so they won't hurt as bad once the ambulance comes." Mira wanted to squeeze her hand, do something to comfort her, but she couldn't. The girl had bones broken in both arms. She settled for murmuring to her instead.

The girl closed her eyes for a few seconds and then opened them again, looking at Mira. "It was so stupid, you know?"

Jumping? Oh, God...

She was afraid to ask. Afraid the girl would clam up. So she settled for asking her earlier question again, while Jack secured her leg. "I know. Can you tell me where your parents are?"

"At home. I'm here with my cheerleading squad."

A cheerleader. It just kept getting worse. An injury like this could be life-changing for anyone, even more so for a high-school girl who needed strength and agility in order to do something she loved.

Down below, the sound of a siren came through.

Thank God. The EMS team was here sooner than she'd expected, despite the icy road conditions. She touched Jack's shoulder. He didn't look up from what he was doing but said, "I hear them. I want to get this other leg in place so they can take her right away."

He glanced up, his eyes meeting hers. Mira saw her own fear and horror reflected back in his gaze. "Last one. Can you keep her calm?" he asked.

"We'll be fine."

He nodded then pulled a second long splint toward the girl. Thank heavens her father kept a full array of those on the premises for times like this.

"Get ready." He took hold of the teen's leg to stabilize it.

"Ahhhh!" The agonized shriek tore right through Mira's insides, leaving her trembling. "It hurts," the girl sobbed. "It hurts so bad."

Mira touched her cheek. "I know, he's almost done." At least the pain brought with it a little good news. Stacy had feeling in her legs, so her spinal cord was intact. If she had landed differently she could be paralyzed or worse.

She glanced up to see if Robert was still there. He was. Watching over the proceedings with a brooding expression. No time to worry about that now. "Robert, can you go find one of the girls' chaperones—?"

"Th-there aren't any." Stacy bit her lip. "A friend got us some driver's licenses. We came on our own."

Another layer of shock pressed down on her chest. "*None* of your parents know you're here? How many of you are there?"

"Five." She turned her head away. "Th-they think we're at a training camp."

This was bad. Very bad. That meant there were no "permission to treat" forms on file. No adults to give verbal permission. "Are you all the same age?"

Stacy nodded. "We skipped school yesterday. We're planning to go back tomorrow. But m-my boyfriend called to break up with me a few hours ago." She closed her eyes again. "So stupid. I thought it would change things."

Change things? As in her boyfriend might decide he didn't want to break up with her if he heard she'd tried to jump from a ski-lift?

Although on the one hand that made no sense, at least

the girl seemed to acknowledge she shouldn't have done whatever it was.

She motioned to Jack to wait. He frowned, but stopped with the second splint still a few inches from the teen's leg.

"What's your phone number, honey?" They needed to get in touch with her parents...or someone. Soon.

Stacy gave it to her, and Mira wrote it in the snow with her gloved finger. "You aren't going to tell them about any of this, are you?"

Any of this. The girls' secret little trip to the mountains? Or Stacy's fall?

"They're going to be happy you're safe." It was the only answer she could give at the moment that wouldn't upset her. Because, yes, the parents needed to know, as did the authorities. Especially if she really had attempted suicide. Although Mira hoped she was reading the girl right and that it had been a bid for attention from her boyfriend. Either way, she needed counseling.

"Do you think so?"

"Yes." That was what was important right now.

She underlined the digits she'd written in the snow then fixed her attention on Robert. "Can you read that?"

He nodded.

"See if you can find the rest of her group. And get a hold of her parents."

"Okay." He hesitated. "After this, we need to talk."

"Just find her parents. Nothing else matters right now."

Out of the corner of her eye she saw Jack's hands tighten on the splint and wondered what he was thinking. What she'd said was true. Nothing else mattered right now, except for treating their patient. She took a deep breath and murmured to the girl, laying a hand on her forehead, "Jack has to finish securing your leg. Are you ready?"

The EMS guys were already trudging up the slope, one pulling a stretcher, while the other one carried a medical kit.

"Yes."

She nodded at Jack then looked at Stacy. "Keep your eyes on mine. It'll be over with in just a minute."

Behind her came the sound of something sliding on the snow. The splint as it went under her leg.

Stacy's head went back and she cried out, the hoarse scream rising along with the level of pain. Mira's eyes watered, despite the number of times she'd worked on injuries like this. But never on a minor who was up here all alone. Or one who'd decided being without her boyfriend had called for drastic—and very possibly permanent—measures. Mira smoothed the girl's hair as she settled into wrenching sobs once again.

She herself had made a drastic change, in the form of a resolution, because of what had happened with Robert. But never in her darkest moments had she thought of ending her life.

"Done." Jack's low word made her draw a relieved breath.

"The worst is over, Stacy." At least physically. Any other treatment would happen with pain medication at the hospital. But once her parents found out what the teen had done, the emotional pain would begin—along with healing, hopefully. The resort was required to report any suspected suicide attempts, which meant Stacy would receive a psychological evaluation at some point. She hoped the girl got the help she desperately needed.

The paramedics arrived, and Jack explained the situation while Mira stayed with the girl, talking to her.

Jack had hoped to get her down to the hotel where it was warm, but at least this way she'd only have to be moved once.

The rescue workers secured Stacy's neck in case there were other injuries and gently slid her from the snow onto the rescue stretcher. Up on skids, the lightweight plastic frame would stabilize her back and keep Stacy off the snow, while allowing it to be pulled rather than carried, like a traditional stretcher.

Mira snapped her skis back on and spoke in a low voice to Jack. "I need to go down and see about the other girls. I think we'll need to call in child services."

Jack nodded. "I'll go with her to the hospital." He moved over to Mira and slid his fingers beneath her chin. He had gloves on—he must have rented them, because she was wearing his. "And then I'm going to come knocking on your door. And you're going to tell me exactly why I have the number five attached to me wherever I go. And what it means."

With that he was gone. Back at Stacy's side, helping fill the workers in on what he'd done and what he suspected.

Leaving Mira to ski the rest of the way down the hill and wonder exactly how she was going to tell him that he was man number five in a long line of men. And hope he'd understand why she now had to move on to number six.

CHAPTER TEN

A RESOLUTION.

Jack wasn't sure he'd heard her correctly. "What kind of resolution?"

In Mira's hotel room, he listened as she told him about what she and the blonde had decided to do for their New Year's resolutions.

"So…" His jaw hardened to stone. After five hours of sitting at the hospital while Stacy's parents drove up from Aspen to be with her, this wasn't what he'd expected to hear. "Sleeping with me was just part of some…*hilarious* New Year's prank."

"Oh, it was no prank." Her eyes skipped away from his. "And what happened between us wasn't supposed to happen at all."

Seated on her bed, clutching some kind of weird stuffed animal, he felt like he'd been sucker-punched, landing in some crazy dream sequence. One that was almost worse than his periodic nightmares.

"So you're only planning on dating twenty-five men. Not sleeping with every single one of them."

"Correction. I wasn't going to sleep with *any* of them."

Jack wasn't sure if he should be pleased she'd made an exception in his case or insulted. "Maybe I would have been better off going with Mrs. Botox last week. It would have been a whole lot less complicated."

A flash of what might have been hurt swept through her eyes before she blinked it away. "Maybe you should have."

Hell. This was not how he'd wanted this talk to go down. But never in his wildest imaginings had he thought she'd gone out with him as part of some cockamamie scheme to date as many men as possible over the course of a year.

"Why did you decide on this for your resolution?"

"I was hurt. I didn't want to get involved with anyone after what happened with Robert."

"Your broken engagement."

She hesitated and then nodded.

"So you thought this was an acceptable alternative."

"No. It was a spur-of-the moment thing. Ellory and I have a tradition…" She shifted the animal on her lap. "Never mind. Anyway, she didn't think I could see it through to the end, thought I'd get stuck part way through."

"Really? It looks like you're doing pretty damn well to me." Good. Anger. At least that was an emotion he was well acquainted with. He grabbed it with both hands. "Exactly when were you planning on telling me about it?"

Mira's teeth came down on her lip.

Ah, so she hadn't planned on telling him at all. "Were you going to tell any of them?"

"No." The word came out as a whisper.

The thought of her parading around with three or four more men while he was still at the resort made his gut roll around inside him, although he wasn't sure why he cared. Probably just part of his male pride. As much as he didn't want to get involved with anyone on a permanent basis—in that, he and Mira were definitely alike—he also hadn't liked the way her ex had said he wanted to talk to her.

He wondered what the man thought about what Mira was doing. Robert evidently knew about it, had actually called him by a damned number rather than by his name.

And that just made his anger burn brighter. Hotter.

"So it was okay for your ex-fiancé to know and get a couple of good chuckles out of it. I'm surprised you didn't give each of us a hand stamp. A kind of one-day pass into your magic kingdom."

She stood, dropping the stuffed cat onto the bed. "It wasn't supposed to be like that. It wasn't a joke. At least, not to me. I was trying to avoid being hurt again. Trying not to repeat the same mistakes."

Isn't that what he'd done—avoided getting involved with anyone to keep from losing them? But he hadn't decided to go out with a million different women in order to achieve that goal. He'd avoided going out with any of them, for the most part.

"So how does your ex know about any of this?"

She shrugged. "I think he heard me talking to Ellory about it at the bar one day."

"He wants you back, you know."

"He doesn't. Not really. He only thinks he does now that he can't have me." Her chin went up. "Remember that lady who came on to you? She and Robert are well acquainted."

That made him blink. Her ex had been with that bimbo? "You know that for a fact?"

"I didn't see them going at it, if that's what you mean. One of the female instructors saw them making out in a supply shed. When I confronted him, he admitted to it. And then I found out there were others—some of them his students." Her eyes swam for a second before she forced back the remembered humiliation of breaking off their engagement amid the swirling rumors.

"Bastard."

"That goes without saying." She gave a hard smile. "But it's happened to me with more than one man. Since I seem incapable of telling the good guys from the bad, I figured it would be better if I stuck to 'shallow and meaningless' when it comes to dating. This year was supposed to show me how that's done."

It didn't make him feel any better that she lumped him into the shallow and meaningless category. "So, I'm man number five."

"Don't call yourself that."

"That's what you called me, isn't it? And your friend. And your ex."

"You're right. I'm sorry."

He picked up a hat on the table, the pink one she wore when out on the snow. "Are you going to date other men over the next couple of weeks? While I'm still here?"

"I don't know. It's not like I pick up a new guy every night."

No, but he doubted she had a lot of trouble attracting them. The woman was gorgeous. And smart. And her ex was an asshole above all others.

He suddenly knew what he was going to do.

"What if I asked you to stick to me for the remainder of my stay?" He wasn't sure why, but if she was going to have random dates with random men, then he wanted to be the guy she went out with more than once. More than twice.

"I'm not sure what you mean."

He set her hat down then moved toward her, sliding his hands along her cheeks and easing her face up. "I want you to date me. Just a group of outings, nothing serious. You can show me the sights—when you're not on duty, of course. I'll get the vacation my coach was looking for, and you'll get a man who's not interested in passing anything but the time."

The words tasted bitter on his tongue as they passed over it, as if he were asking her to be a paid escort or something. He wasn't.

But he couldn't promise her any more than that. They were from different worlds. His wife had left a thriving practice to be with him. He'd taken her not only from the children she'd treated in California but from every sick kid who might have come under her care in the future.

He would never ask that of anyone again.

"Why would you want to do that?" Mira asked.

"For exactly the reasons I mentioned."

"You're not mad about the whole number thing?"

He wouldn't go so far as to say that. "It's not what I expected but, then again, not much in this life is."

"Remind me how long you'll be here."

He calculated the days in his head. "I have to go back in a little less than two weeks." And why did his stay suddenly seem far too short?

Because the trip was working?

Or because he was an idiot?

She paused for several seconds and stared just beyond his face as if doing some heavy thinking. "These wouldn't be real dates. Just going around together and seeing the sights."

Letting go of her, he nodded. "If that's how you prefer to think of it, I'm okay with that." He caught her eye. "But you can't move on to number six until after I'm gone."

"Okay." She stepped closer and touched his arm. "For

what it's worth, I'm sorry. You weren't just a number last night."

The words went a long way toward soothing his bruised pride. "For what it's worth, neither were you."

And that was exactly what he was afraid of. His strange dream came back to him in all its horrifying detail. The fact that Mira's face had been the one he'd seen in that coffin seemed like a clear warning: *This is what could happen if you allow yourself to get too involved.*

Rational or not, it was the truth.

So what was he doing here, asking her to see him exclusively? Exactly what he'd said. It was time he poked his head back out into the world. Last night had at least shown him that much. He'd had a genuinely good time. And his reasons for sleeping with her hadn't been a whole lot purer than hers had been. He'd been upset by that death up on the slope, and so he'd turned to her in order to escape for a few hours. Wasn't that was she was doing? Trying to escape a painful situation?

He could act all holier than thou about her resolution, but the reality was right there in front of him.

"So. If we're going to do this, what would you like to see first?"

How about what was under those clothes?

He wasn't going to say it, even if it was what he was thinking. And he already knew what she looked like naked. It seemed that having her last night had not quenched his thirst. In fact, the memories of them together just served to make him feel even more parched. So he would just ignore the feeling and hope it went away.

"Well, I didn't get a chance to see the rest of the property, since I wasn't exactly concentrating during our sleigh ride."

She smiled. "I think I can remedy that."

"Another sleigh ride?" One brow hiked up. He didn't see how their ride would fare any better this time than it did last time.

"How about a ride without the sleigh?"

No way was he touching that one.

"If you're talking about on horseback, I don't know how to ride."

"Wow. You don't? You don't know how to ski. You don't know how to ride. Were you born in a monastery or something?" She stepped up close and tilted her head back. "Don't worry. While I do have some horses in mind, they don't have four legs."

"Really? Then what do they have?"

She smiled. "I have some things I need to get done today, and I want to check with my father on something, but if you're up for it I'll show you exactly what I mean first thing tomorrow morning.

Mira revved up the snowmobile. Owned by her dad, she'd often used it to get away from the crowds and go off by herself. There were a series of private trails that only she and the other employees knew about.

She and Robert had ridden around a couple of times, but he'd always been in the driver's seat when they'd been together. But this time she was the one in front. Jack didn't know how to ride one of these either. He was a warm-climate boy through and through.

"Put your helmet on and climb aboard!"

Looking the slightest bit dubious, Jack slid the helmet onto his head and fastened the strap before swinging a leg over the back of the vehicle. "You're sure you know how to drive this."

"I've done it my whole life."

He chuckled. "You are just full of surprises."

"Am I? You have no idea." She let go of the steering-wheel to fasten her own strap. "Ready? You're going to want to hang on tight."

His hands went to her waist as she eased them away from the equipment barn, skirting the ski-lift area. His grip reminded her of the way he'd lifted her onto that bar. She had to fight to banish the image from her mind and concentrate.

The two ski-lift attendants waved at her as she went by. Mira waved back. Maneuvering down a slight incline, she rode onto a section of the property that was partially wooded but which had a path carved out of it.

"Where are we going?" he asked, above the roar of the motor.

"I know a little place." She'd let her father know she'd be gone for the day—possibly until tomorrow, depending on how things went. And in the back of the snowmobile she'd packed a lunch, along with wine and a thick blanket. There was firewood at their destination, but it could still get pretty chilly. "Okay, I'm going to crank it up a bit."

Mira pressed the accelerator lever with her thumb and the track on the bottom of the vehicle picked up speed, grabbing onto the snow and propelling them forward. The destination she had in mind was about five miles away through some of the most gorgeous country known to man. Jack settled in closer, his body molding to hers from behind, legs pressed tight to hers. Was he doing that on purpose?

"This is similar to a Jet Ski," he yelled in her ear. "Except we push water through the engine to propel us forward."

"Never ridden on one."

"You'd like it."

Yeah, she probably would. Too bad he'd never teach her how to ride one. Or a surfboard, for that matter.

That's not in the cards, Mira. Just enjoy today.

Silence reigned between them for a few moments as they ate up some more terrain. She slowed to go around a tree and then accelerated once again, the tracks kicking up a blast of snow.

When she'd begun her yearlong journey to become footloose and fancy-free, she never dreamed she'd wind up riding on her dad's snowmobile with one of her dates. Or making out on a sleigh ride. Or working side by side to rescue avalanche victims.

Or helping a girl with emotional wounds much deeper than her own.

She and Jack worked well together. Which was probably why it was harder just to mosey on past him. During their confrontation yesterday he'd seemed offended that he was just a number on a list in her head, and he was right. She knew there might be a blip or two but hadn't expected to crash and burn quite so soon.

And that was the problem. She had no idea whether she should keep on trying to do something that seemed to be against her nature. Or if she should just forfeit her bet and agree with Ellory that this had been a royally bad idea.

She could pay up and be done.

With Jack's arms wrapped around her waist, it was easy to imagine just snuggling down in the here and now and enjoy their remaining time together.

His helmet bumped against hers once as she made another turn, re-emphasizing just how close he was. Maybe she should bypass the cabin and just keep driving around for the rest of the afternoon. She was enjoying have him next to her just a little too much.

But all too soon the small log building came into view.

Her parents' original home, and the place she'd been born.

Her dad had kept it to remind himself of where he'd come from. She could probably live out here, rather than at the hotel, but she preferred to visit the cabin periodically as a treat. She knew all too well how mundane the things in life could become if you weren't careful.

Like her and Robert's relationship? So it would seem. At least on his part.

Looking back, though, she wondered if that spark had really been there to begin with, or if she'd assumed that since they'd had so much in common their similarities would see them through.

Pulling up to the front door, she used the handbrake to stop. Jack hesitated and then let go of her and climbed off. She started to follow, swinging one leg over the front, then sat sideways on the seat instead, looking up at him while she tried to re-gather her composure.

"So how was your first snowmobile ride? Did you like it?"

He gave her sideways smile. "It was interesting."

She'd expected a little more enthusiasm than that. Then again, Jack seemed to have cornered the market on measured reactions. That's why his behavior in his hotel room had shocked her so much. Who would have known he had a bit of caveman wandering around inside him.

And on that note she'd better shut down this line of thought before it got her into trouble.

"Okay." She laughed. "We'll go with interesting." She stood up and opened a storage compartment in the back of the snowmobile and pulled out a small chest containing their lunch. Jack took it from her with a raised brow.

"I thought you might be hungry." She tugged the

blanket from the compartment as well, draping it over her arm.

"I might." He nodded toward the cabin. "I didn't know this was out here. Is it yours?"

"No. It belongs to the fam…to my dad."

"He doesn't rent it out?"

She paused. "He likes to come out here to stay every once in a while."

"He and your mother are divorced."

She headed for the cabin, peeling off her gloves and checking her pocket for the key to the front door. "They are." She and her dad had made their peace last week, but there were still some tender spots when it came to the reasons for her parents' divorce.

"Sorry." His voice came from behind her. "Is your mother still living?"

"Mmm-hmm. She lives in Aspen. How about your parents? Still living?"

"Yes. They live on the east coast of Florida."

She stuck the key in the lock and turned. "Let me guess. They live on the beach too?"

Jack laughed. "How did you know?"

"Surfer dude. Plenty of beach knowledge and almost no mountain knowledge. You had to have gotten it from somewhere."

He followed her into the house and looked around. "Wow. Not what I expected."

Mira peered at the interior of her parents' old home and tried to see it through his eyes. Rustic on the outside, the house was modest but modern. Hardwood floors ran throughout the cabin, and her dad had done most of the work inside himself, from the plank walls to the oak trim. There were so many memories attached to this place. Some of them good. Some of them not so good.

"Not quite as swanky as the lodge, is it?"

"It's not that." He moved over to the oversized fireplace. "Does this work?"

"Dad keeps the wood box in here filled with split logs. The bigger chunks are outside. You'd be surprised how well it warms the place. Do you want to start a fire while I take our lunch into the kitchen?"

Mira took the basket and headed for the space across the room. The cabin was built on an open concept, so the dining and kitchen areas were all visible from the living room. And as she set the box down and gazed across the space, she couldn't help but admire Jack's strong back as he gathered wood from the compartment behind the wall and knelt in front of the fireplace.

By the time he had the fire going, she'd unloaded lunch, which consisted of fried chicken, potato salad, baked beans and some cheese and crackers. All hearty picnic food that would do well on the cold trip over here. She got out a pan for the beans and set it on the stove. "Do you want me to heat up the chicken, or do you prefer it cold?"

"I'll like whatever you do." His voice came from right behind her, making her jump.

She spun around. "You scared me."

"Join the crowd. You scare me too, lady." Something about the way he said it made her think he wasn't talking about being startled but about something a little deeper.

No. No *deeper* allowed. She'd lectured herself on this very thing. They'd only known each other for less than two weeks, but she was already feeling much too close to this man. It had to be the sex. Women felt an emotional response to sleeping with a man, right, whereas men could just shrug it off? At least, that's what she'd always heard. But maybe that wasn't always the case.

Maybe Jack was struggling with some of the same issues she was.

She forced her voice to remain light. "Well, one thing that isn't scary is this lunch. Marie always makes a great fried chicken."

"Marie?"

"The chef at the lodge. She's been there ever since I was a teenager."

"You've lived here your whole life?" He unzipped his coat and moved around the bar, perching on one of the stools.

"My whole life. I lived with my mom for a year or two after the divorce but, yeah, I grew up here. Once I finished college and med school, I came back."

"Wow. I've always lived near the ocean, but my parents moved around quite a bit. My dad was in the service. He retired in Florida."

Mira put the burner on low and turned around to face him. "My friend Ellory—the one from the resolution— likes to travel as well. She's been all over the place. But she grew up here too, her mom worked at the lodge when she was little."

"You can't see yourself doing that someday? Traveling?"

The funny thing was, lately she'd been thinking about that very thing. About whether it was time for her to spread her wings and move away from her childhood home. Make her own memories somewhere else. Maybe she'd stayed for so long to make peace with her dad. Now that she had, something inside her was itching with discontent.

"I went to college and medical school away from here, obviously. I don't know. It's certainly something to consider, but I'm not to that point yet. Maybe I just need to find a reason."

His jaw got tight. "Make sure that reason has to do with you, Mira. Not someone else."

Was he speaking from personal experience? Had he resented moving around as a kid?

She turned to stir the beans, the heat from the burner as well as the fireplace beginning to warm her. Shrugging out of her coat, she laid it over the bar behind her, deciding to ask. "Was it hard, moving from place to place when you were young?"

"What? Oh…" He shook his head. "No, that was just part of normal life—it didn't bother me. Anyway, you were right. The fireplace does a great job."

He picked up her coat and moved away from the bar, hanging their outerwear on the hooks her father had installed next to the door. Then he poked at the fire with his back to her.

Frowning, Mira gave the beans another couple of stirs as steam began to rise from the pot.

Make sure that reason has to do with you. Not someone else.

If he hadn't been talking about moving around during his childhood, then what? Had he moved as an adult because of someone else? No, he was a sports medicine doctor. He'd obviously taken the job in Texas because he'd wanted to—because he'd loved football and his team—not because someone had made him. But his coach had made him go on this vacation in the first place. Why?

She reached up to one of the overhead cabinets and pulled out two plates and wineglasses, rinsing and drying them. She did the same with the silverware in the drawer before setting everything on round twig placemats on the bar. "I think we're about ready."

When Jack joined her, she helped dish everything up and poured them each a glass of wine. "That fire feels good. Thanks."

"You're welcome." He pushed the food around on his plate for a minute or two. "You asked about it being hard to move. That wasn't what I meant about making sure you did it for yourself and not someone else."

Mira tensed, wondering where he was going with this and not sure she really wanted to know. "Okay."

"Did I tell you I was married at one time?"

Her eyes widened. She'd asked whether he was married and when he'd said no, she'd just assumed he'd been single all his life. "No."

"I was. Paula was a pediatric oncologist with a thriving practice in California. She loved her patients. Her staff." He paused, staring at the handle of his fork as if it were suddenly fascinating. "Four years ago, I was approached by the Hawks and asked if I'd be their doctor. At the time I was working with a smaller team in California, so it would have been a big promotion for me. I asked Paula to go with me. Told her that with her skills she could open a practice anywhere in the U.S.—could keep helping sick kids, just like she did where she was."

Had the strain been too much, and they'd divorced over it? "Did she decide not to go?"

He shook his head. "Oh, she decided to go. But it would have been better if she hadn't."

"I don't understand."

Dropping his fork back onto his plate, he turned his stool to face her. "My wife got on the plane to fly out to Texas and never made it off." He took a deep breath. "It crashed in the Gulf of Mexico. Her body was never recovered."

CHAPTER ELEVEN

MIRA WAS SHOCKED.

He saw it in her face. But was she shocked at the fact that he'd been married or that his wife had died because of him?

Her fingers touched his. "God, Jack. I had no idea. I'm so sorry."

Yeah, well, so was he. Sorry he'd been so eager to climb up that career ladder. Sorry he'd dragged Paula with him as he'd gone up one step and then another without any thought as to how it would affect her career or the lives of her patients. Sorry that he never got to hold her and tell her that before she'd slipped away.

"I didn't tell you to gain your sympathy. I told you so you'd never make a decision you regretted."

She stared at him for several seconds, a bunch of emotions running over that beautiful face of hers. Then her mouth tipped to the side in a half-smile. "Too late. I've done plenty of things I've regretted."

"Like your ski instructor?"

Her brows went up, and her smile grew. "I'm sure you didn't mean that as in, 'Do you regret *doing* your ski instructor?' That does not sound good, Jack Perry."

Relief swept over him. She wasn't going to sit here and make him dissect his every regret or say that he shouldn't feel guilt over his wife's death. Or that he shouldn't take pills to sleep. She'd catalogued what he'd shared and was okay with moving past it. He was just as happy to keep the ball rolling in that direction.

"Well, how about this, then. Do you regret *doing* me?"

She drew imaginary circles on the wooden surface of the bar with her finger. "I think you have that event reversed, Doctor. I seem to remember *you* doing *me*."

"Is that so?" His body began to show a definite spark of interest in where this conversation was headed. "I think there was a little give-and-take going on there at the end."

"Your beans are getting cold," she said innocently, scooping up a bite of her own and popping it into her mouth.

He couldn't prevent a smile. "That's about the only thing getting cold." He'd indulge her. But now that she'd thrown open the door, he had no intention of slamming it shut again, agreement or no agreement.

Why not enjoy each other for the next week or so? There was nothing wrong with that, and as long as they were both okay with it...

So he dug into his own food with gusto. Putting off the inevitable would only make it that much sweeter. "What time do you have to be back?" He wanted to make sure he enjoyed every decadent second of their time together.

"Actually, I'm not due back until tomorrow, unless there's an emergency."

"I didn't pack clothes for an overnight stay."

Her lips pursed as she looked him over. "Who said you needed clothes?"

Okay, so there was no mistaking those words. "Did you bring me out here just for this?" Not that he'd mind. At all.

"No, but now that we're here I'm thinking it might not be a bad idea. Unless you'd rather go back to the lodge."

Oh, sure. He was just going to smile and say, "Thanks but, no, thanks." Not hardly. Not with this particular woman.

"Going back is not on my agenda. In fact, my schedule just became wide open."

"Good, because I'm thinking the thick blanket I brought would look pretty darn good in front of the fire."

He picked up his chicken. "I can think of something else that would look even better." He took a bite, still staring at her.

"Mmm. So can I." She blew out a breath. "Wow. I don't know if Ellory is rubbing off on me or if it's you. I'm not usually this forward."

He swallowed his food, chasing it down with a slug of wine. "I like it. It's a whole lot easier knowing where you stand than having to guess."

That was one of the things that had bothered him most about Paula's death. He'd never been entirely sure whether she'd wanted to move to Texas or if she'd been doing it just to please him. The heart of his guilt lay in that uncertainty. If she hadn't wanted to come and had just spoken up, he would have stayed in California. Gladly. Now he'd never know. He pushed back the thought.

Mira sipped at her own wine. "It's funny. I've always been a good girl. Quiet. Obedient. It's why I love Ellory so much. She's spontaneous and fearless. She always goes after what she wants, rarely letting anything stand in her way."

"And you do?"

"Sometimes." Her mouth twisted. "I think I work too

hard to meet other people's expectations of me. I forget who I am at times."

He set his glass down and touched a finger to her cheek. "I think you're the girl who's sitting at this bar right now. And the girl who worked so hard to rescue those people after the avalanche. There's more to you than you realize, Mira Dupris." His fingertip traveled along her jaw and then down her neck. "And you blow me away. Every time I look at you. Talk to you. I haven't been with many women since my wife's death. And never more than once, but with you…"

Taking a deep breath, he decided to go for broke. "But with you I find myself wanting a next time. And a next."

And maybe that revelation was where the healing finally began in earnest.

She gave a visible swallow then said, "I feel the same way. You were supposed to be just one more guy. But you're not."

He planted his hands on either side of her stool, gripping it tight and turning it toward him. Then he hauled it closer and leaned in. "I'm glad."

His mouth met hers and that familiar rush of heat washed over him, undiminished, just as strong as it had been the first time they'd kissed. That combination of sweet and sexy that went straight to his gut.

Hands touched the back of his neck and then curled around it as if afraid he was going to back away. Not likely. All he wanted was more.

Beneath her winter coat she'd worn a creamy turtleneck that, when he reached up to touch her, met his fingers with a buttery softness he wanted to lose himself in. Just like he wanted to lose himself in her. Skimming up her sides, he laid his palms on her back, luxuriating in the feel of her.

God, she just did it for him.

He didn't want to examine the whys right now, just wanted to enjoy being with her, absorb a little bit of that *joie de vivre* she had, just like a vampire.

Mira made a little sound in her throat, the kind that slid over a man like silk…that made him want to draw more of those sexy gasps and capture them inside his mouth.

"Hey," he whispered. "Let's break out that blanket."

She blinked at him with glazed eyes for a second before nodding and getting off the stool. She walked over to the sofa, and hell if his gaze didn't stick right to her ass, admiring every little twitch and jiggle it made as she moved.

Yeah, he had it bad.

He joined her, taking an edge of the blanket and spreading it in front of the fire. He couldn't wait to see the warm glow worship every inch of her skin. Because he planned to kneel at that particular altar himself for most of the night.

When he moved toward her, she shook her head, making him frown. Then he realized why, when she pulled the turtleneck over her head, revealing a peach bra that was so thin he could see the buds of her nipples pressed tight against the satiny fabric. Jack's mouth watered.

Her hands went to her back.

"Don't take it off," he murmured.

She bit her lip but did as he asked, leaving the garment in place. Her fingers toyed with the button on her jeans, glancing at him in question.

"Definitely."

His body hardened, a thumping going through his head as she undid her pants and slowly pushed them down her hips.

Her panties matched her bra, just like they had the last time they'd been together, but there were no ties on the sides this time. That was okay. There were plenty of ways to get those off her. Or not. Depending on how he felt when the time actually came.

Right now, his brain was tapping out *Hurry* in some kind of weird Morse code. He ignored it. No hurrying. Not tonight.

She stepped out of the jeans and kicked them to the side, before getting on her knees on the blanket. Crooking a finger at him, she motioned him closer. When he went to kneel in front of her, she gripped the knees of his jeans and hauled him closer, keeping him on his feet.

Did she know how close she was? How suggestive her position was?

"Your turn," she said. With that, she used both hands to open his button and then unzip his fly.

His turn to what? Get undressed?

He had his answer soon enough when she tugged his pants and briefs down to his knees, freeing him. He gave an internal curse. He was right. He was in line with a very warm and wet area, and his body was sending out all kinds of messages. But he wasn't going that route. Not without a clear sign from her.

Her hands went around him, and she glanced up at him. "Like I said, it's your turn. Come here."

It suddenly dawned on him. She was referring to their last encounter when he'd put her up on that bar and had his way with her.

She was about to turn the tables.

Sinking his fingers in her hair, he slowly closed his fist around the silky strands and edged her closer. That gorgeous mouth opened right on cue. So very, very close.

Hell.

"Do it." His muttered words were rough, surprising even him.

Mira closed the gap, the heat of her mouth engulfing him in a slow glide that had him shuddering with need. Hot flames licked at his body as her hands left his erection and went to the backs of his thighs, curling around them, hauling him even closer.

His vision went white, all sensation pooling at the points of contact between them, her tongue sliding over his length in a single smooth stroke that made him wonder if he was going to lose it right here. Right now.

No. That's not what he wanted.

When he went to step away, though, she followed him, forcing him to reach back and grip her wrists, tugging them away so he could put some space between them. The popping sound of lost suction created an agonizing mixture of triumph and despair inside him that he was in no hurry to erase. But he was in a hurry for something else.

Still holding her wrists, he hauled her to her feet, insides steaming with heat when she gazed up at him and licked her lips. "Not fair," she murmured. "I wasn't done yet."

"You were done all right." In another few seconds he would have been as well. He moved her wrists behind her back and held them there with one hand, while he palmed the back of her head with the other, holding her still so he could capture her mouth. His tongue plunged inside, a demonstration of what he had in store for her, and he used his hold on her wrists to press her abdomen against him, trapping himself between their bodies. It wasn't nearly enough, but he had to somehow slow this train wreck down.

He let go of her hands, sliding up to find the clasp on

her bra and releasing it. Then he stepped back yet again, taking the straps with him, allowing the silky garment to drop onto the blanket. Then he tugged his shirt over his head and finished losing the rest of his clothes.

Allowing his gaze to slide over her, he reveled in the toned limbs that came with skiing and working in the snow and ice, and the pale creamy skin that went so perfectly with a chilly climate. No tanning beds for this ice princess.

Only she wasn't made of ice. She was hot and smooth and made him ache like no one ever had before. He held out his arms, and she came into them willingly, her nipples pressing against him, her silk panties welcoming his hands as he slid beneath the back of them and cupped her bottom. Hell, he wanted to be inside her. Wanted to thrust and grunt all the way to completion, but part of his pleasure was watching her come apart beneath his hands. So he set about making that happen, allowing his lips and teeth to trail from her face to her neck and finally to the tips of her breasts until her low moan washed over him.

Yes.

This was what he wanted more than anything: to be what brought her to life and led her down that sensual path until she could no longer resist its pull.

His tongue scrubbed over her nipple, letting the sounds she made guide how long he visited, how much pressure he used. And the woman could take a lot, fingers thrust into his hair pressing him closer and urging him to be just a little rougher.

Jack's body let him know in no uncertain terms that it wanted in on the action, the ache ramping up to almost painful proportions. When she moaned again, his flesh jerked in a silent plea.

Soon.

Still beneath her panties, his hand slid from her butt around to the front and edged deeper, his fingers finding a familiar sweet heat…and damp readiness. He stroked over her, moving to kiss her mouth as those delectable little sounds increased in frequency.

Making his decision, he pulled free, wrapped one arm around her thighs and slid the other beneath her shoulders. He swept her off her feet and onto the blanket, following her down.

He kissed her hard and wet and long, feeling her arch against him.

Off came the panties. One knee went between her legs.

Anticipation roared through him as he slid a finger deep inside her, thumb going to that sensitive nub of flesh and stroking over it in gentle flicks that had him quivering with need.

"Jack." Her back arched again.

That was all the encouragement it took for him to slide his body into the gap between her thighs and surge forward. He found her, just as he'd expected. Hot and tight and slick with her own need.

He swallowed, knowing he'd waited too long. His body was tightly wound, full, ready to burst open at the slightest move.

"Hold on, sweetheart, it's going to be a bumpy ride."

Struggling to keep himself in check, he thrust again and again, concentrating on hitting that one vital spot at the top of her legs. Legs that wrapped around him, pulling him deeper and harder as she lifted her hips and plastered herself against him the second they made contact again. She ground and gasped and wiggled, eyes closing tight as that final wave of sensation swept toward them. It crashed over her first, the sudden tightening of her flesh around his unleashing a torrent inside him. He rode the crest a second or two longer before finally succumbing and tumbling headlong into the surf, allowing it to carry him all the way back to shore.

He lay there for several seconds, not sure if he was stunned into immobility or if he'd died and rocketed straight into heaven. All he knew was that there was no place he'd rather be than right here in this woman's arms.

And that fact terrified him. Paralyzed him.

Because one act had just cost him everything.

In rushing to the finish line, Jack had lost much more than the fight with his body. He'd also lost the battle with his heart.

Jack had been quiet the whole ride back to the lodge the next day. They'd gone to bed the previous night, where he'd held her, looping his arm around her as they'd slept. But he hadn't tried to make love to her again, unlike the previous time they'd been together.

She wasn't sure if she'd done something wrong or if it was just him.

Part of her was afraid she'd appeared too desperate and needy, grabbing at him and giving herself that last burst of pleasure. But it had been too late to stop by that point. And he'd seemed to like it at the time, groaning encouragement into her ear and increasing his pace.

But afterwards he'd seemed strange, rolling off her and staring at the ceiling for several long seconds. He'd recovered and pulled her to her feet, giving her a quick kiss on the mouth before offering to let her use the shower first.

First. Not together.

They'd eaten a canned dinner of stuff they'd found in the pantry, but the mood had been somber as they'd sat on the couch later, facing the fire, Jack's arm around her.

What had he been thinking?

If she'd said something, he'd responded, but emotionally he'd seemed to have withdrawn.

Today she'd treated a couple of patients, giving one teenager a lecture on helmet usage when he'd appeared with a lump on his forehead after falling on the slopes, and hugging a child who'd had a boo-boo on her finger—courtesy of a sharp pinch from a door. Neither were serious injuries.

Unlike the weird volley of emotions that soared through her chest one second and fell into the pit of her stomach the next, only to bounce up and start the cycle all over. It was exhausting.

She slumped in a chair in the dining room, picking at her salad. Ellory was off hiking by herself for the day. She'd left a note at the front desk that she'd check in with Mira later and that she hoped her outing with Number Five had been productive—and hot. She had a "feeling" about this one.

So did Mira. And it wasn't a good feeling.

In fact, it was as ominous as the weather forecast for the coming week. There was the threat of the first big storm of the season. Moisture was gathering to the southwest and there was a high-pressure system in the northeast that was preparing to send a frigid blast of air their way. When those two forces combined, things could get dicey over the next five days. At just over twelve thousand feet elevation, Silver Pass was almost sure to get a large portion of that snowfall, if it arrived. Already the resort was busy preparing behind the scenes while trying not to worry any of their guests. The storm could very well peter out. She'd met with her dad this morning for breakfast, but he'd been distracted about the preparations.

If only she could be just as diligent to prepare for any eventuality with Jack. But without even a vague forecast to go by, there was nothing she could do. Oh, she could tell him she was reneging on their deal, that she didn't want to see him any more for the duration of his stay. But what if she was overreacting?

A man's shoes came into view beside her table. Her heart leap-frogged over itself as she jerked her head up, only to land with a clunk when she realized it was Robert. Great, just what she needed.

"Mind if I join you?" he asked.

She motioned to the chair across from hers. "Help yourself."

He set his coffee on the table and then dropped into the seat. "We never did get a chance to talk."

"About what?" Lord, she really didn't want to rehash their whole breakup.

"Your dad came out to see me a few hours ago," he said. "Did you tell him about us?"

"Yes. Why? Did he say something?"

He shook his head, lips pursing. "No. He really just talked about how long to keep the slopes open, if this storm hits."

Leaning back, he ran a hand through wavy blond locks that had always reminded her of a Norse god. She could see why women were attracted to him. But he no longer did anything for her.

"Okay, I'm not sure I understand, then. Are you worried?"

"I just want to know exactly what you told him. Do I need to look for another job?"

Ah, so that's what he was worried about. With his snarky comments of late, maybe she should let him sweat for a while. But since she was finding out first hand how it felt to be kept in the dark about someone's intentions, she didn't wish that on anyone. Not even Robert.

"Whether or not you look for another job is up to you. If he asks for specifics, I just plan on telling him the truth, that we both realized it wasn't going to work and decided to break our engagement." She shrugged. "So as long as you keep doing your job, you should have nothing to worry about."

"Thank you." In a move that was not in character for the self-assured cocky man she knew, he covered her hand with his and gave it a squeeze before tucking a lock of hair behind her ear. "I know it doesn't mean anything, but I want you to know I'm sorry for how things went down. I should have had the courage to tell you up front that I wasn't ready to settle down."

You mean before you made out with that bimbo and several others? Yeah, you could have saved us both a whole lot of grief—and saved me from a clunker of a resolution.

One she no longer wanted to keep.

She didn't say any of that, though. "What's done is done. I recommend honesty the next time you get involved with someone."

His lips gave a rueful twist. "Understood." He hesitated. "If later on down the line—"

"If you're going to say what I think you are, then no. You're right. It wouldn't have worked."

"Is it because of that guy you've been hanging around?"

Mira swallowed, trying to divert her thoughts to something else. It didn't work. Jack's face popped into her mind—the way his eyes had darkened as he'd settled over her last night.

Lord. Robert was right. It was because of Jack. That's why she was so sure it could never work with him, even if she found out he hadn't been cheating.

She was in love with Number Five. Someone she knew beyond the shadow of a doubt would never cheat on the person he loved. He'd shown that in how he talked about his wife…the guilt he carried about how she died.

Mira just…knew.

Maybe she really could tell the good guys from the bad.

And she loved him—for that reason and so many more.

The knowledge was both exhilarating and devastating. He'd made it clear he wasn't looking for anything serious.

But with you, I find myself wanting a next time. And a next.

Jack's words from last night whispered through her mind, then rewound and played back all over again.

It certainly wasn't something she was going to admit to Robert, though.

"I'm not involved with anyone. Nor am I planning to be. I'm just not interested in giving us another chance."

He gazed at her for a second before giving a slow nod. "Okay. Let me know if you change your mind. I'll be around."

With that, he picked up his insulated drink carrier and walked away.

Right past Number Five, who was standing not three feet away, his own coffee cup in hand. His eyes were on them.

Oh, God. How much of their conversation had he just heard?

Enough, evidently, since he veered away and chose a table twenty feet away.

Oh, no, he didn't. If he wanted nothing to do with her, he was going to have to tell her flat out.

Leaving the remainder of her salad uneaten, she got

up and went over to his table and pulled out a chair. Unlike Robert, though, she didn't ask if she could sit. She just did.

"Hi," she said. For all her bravado, her heart was slipping around in her chest like a skier who'd just realized the run he was on was way above his skill level.

Jack's fingers tightened on his mug. "Hey. Hope I didn't run him off."

"You didn't." She licked her lips. "How are you?"

"That's the question of the year, isn't it?"

"I'm sorry?"

He blew out a rough breath. "Nothing."

After several beats went by, she decided to test the waters. "About yesterday—"

"Yeah, I was just coming to talk to you about that." Another pause. "You love it here, Mira, don't you?"

"Silver Pass? Yes, of course I do. I grew up here. Why?"

"No reason. Just curious."

That was a strange thing to be curious about. Besides, what did it have to do with yesterday?

Before she could turn back to that particular subject, Jack started in again.

"I don't know if you've seen the weather forecast, but I'm due back in Texas in a little over a week, just after that storm is supposed to hit. I don't want to take the chance on my flight being canceled if it's worse than predicted, so…"

He was leaving. Not in a week. But soon. Maybe even today.

"When are you going?"

"They're trying to book me on any flight they can get, so I figured I wouldn't have time to track you down and say goodbye. The reception desk told me you were in here, so I thought..." his jaw tightened "...now was as good a time as any."

As good a time as any? As if she were no more important than any other business acquaintance. She guessed that put her in her place. If he wanted to tell her exactly where she stood, he couldn't have chosen a better way to let her down easy.

Only it wasn't easy. But she wasn't going to drop to her knees and beg him not to go. He had a job back in Texas. She'd known that from the very beginning.

That was one thing living at a ski resort taught you, that people were not permanent fixtures. They came and they went. An endless cycle that could bring heartache, if you let it. Isn't that what she'd been trying to teach herself with her resolution? That she needed to let them wander through while keeping her heart away from those high-traffic areas?

God. And look how successful she'd been at that.

"Well, it's been fun. Thank you." She swallowed. "Have a good flight."

When she stood to go, he grabbed her wrist, fingers tight against her skin. "It was more than fun, and you know it. I just can't do...this."

This. *This?* What the hell "this" was he talking about?

She had no idea. But whatever it was, he didn't want it. Didn't want her.

Her chin went up. "I don't remember anyone asking you to."

There. Way to lob it right back at him, Mira.

Instead of pride, though, all she felt was sadness... and that same weird desperation she'd felt in his arms last night.

Number Five was leaving, and she hadn't even had to tell him to go.

She could try to convince him not to. Tell him how she felt. But did she really want to grasp at someone who...what was it that Robert had said? Oh, yes, who just "wasn't ready to settle down"—with her or with anyone.

Jack released her and the fingers of her other hand rubbed at the spot, trying to erase the memory of his touch. It didn't work, though. He'd branded himself on her. Not last night. Not that time in his hotel room. But that very first time their hands had gripped each other's in the snow.

And now she had to find a way—like he had—to un-curl her fingers and let him go.

CHAPTER TWELVE

"What do you mean, he's leaving early?"

Ellory's face was a study in disbelief as she stood in Mira's room, hands on her hips.

"There's talk of a winter storm blowing in, and he's afraid of getting stranded."

"Oh, he's afraid all right, but not of getting stranded. What happened?"

Mira went through the whole story, about how they'd gone to the lodge, how everything had seemed to be going really well, about how he'd talked about his wife's death.

"He told you about that?"

Mira nodded. "Why?"

"That's not something you tell someone you have no intention of ever seeing again. Why would he bother, unless he felt it was something you needed to know?"

Mira dropped onto the foot of her bed and grabbed her Cheshire cat. "He started acting funny right after we..." she rolled her hand around in the air "...you know."

"After you boinked like bunnies in front of the fire?"

"Elle!"

Her friend grinned and then sprawled next to her, poking the stuffed cat in its furry little belly. "You were supposed to teach her a thing or two about loosening up."

Oh, she'd been plenty loose. That was her problem. If she'd held on to her emotions just a little bit tighter, she could have avoided this whole mess.

That wasn't true, and she knew it.

"Okay," Ellory said. "Let's go down the list of things we know. One, his wife died in a plane crash. Two, he asked that you two see each other exclusively while he was here at the resort. Have I got it right so far?"

"Yes, but—"

"I'm thinking here." She put a finger to her lips and tapped. "Three, after he tells you about his wife, you get down to business and then he seems weird afterwards."

Mira nodded. "I thought I was being too forward."

"Get real, ninny. Men love that stuff. So what happened after that?"

Impatience flared to life. She'd wanted hugs and a sympathetic shoulder, not to write a dissertation on what had gone wrong. "What does it matter?"

"It matters."

Mira's brows went up. "Okay. Four. He asks me if I like it here in Silver Pass. Five. He says there's a storm coming…says he's leaving early." Her voice sped up as another wave of hurt rolled through her. "I reply that it's been fun, bye. He grabs me and says it was more than that, and that I know it, but he just can't do…" she drew quotes in the air "…*this*."

"This."

"Yeah, one minute he's asking me about Silver… Oh, my God." Wrapping her arms around her stomach, she let Chessie slide to the floor. "He can't ask me to leave. That's what it is."

"What?"

"Silver Pass. His wife died on the flight to Texas. She'd left her job to be with him."

Ellory picked up the cat and tossed it onto the pillows behind them. "He's afraid you'll die?"

"I don't think so. Or at least I hope he's not irrational enough to think it could happen twice. I think his guilt won't let him ask me to choose between him and the resort. He asked me if I loved Silver Pass. Right out of the blue, after he saw me talking to Robert. It didn't go along with anything we were talking about. I thought it was strange at the time, since he said he wanted to talk about what had happened at the cabin."

"I think you're right, Mirri." Her brows went up. "So what's stopping you?"

"From what? He's probably already left."

"So? It's not like you can't find Texas. It's freaking huge. Right there on every map."

Mira closed her eyes. Her friend was right. What was stopping her?

Fear.

Fear of rejection. Fear of what she'd find when she saw him. Fear...that he didn't love her.

And?

What more did she have to lose? She'd let him walk away—so he was gone already as far as that went. If she confronted him, and he said he didn't want to be with her, she hadn't lost anything more. Just a small chunk of her pride.

But she deserved to know how he felt once and for all.

"You're right. It's on the map." She reached over and grabbed her friend and squeezed her hard. "Thank you, Elle. Wish me luck."

"I already did that when you made your resolution." She laughed. "I sent out a little note to the universe, asking them to let *me* win our little bet. Which meant that Number Five—well, like Obi Wan Kenobi, he was my only hope."

Jack slid his sunglasses higher on his nose as he waited in line at the airport. It had taken more than one attempt to finally walk out of the door of the resort this morning, two weeks to the day from when he'd first set foot on that ski slope and seen Mira standing over him.

He'd left two things behind. One thing meant nothing. And one meant everything.

The nothing: his pills, which he'd flushed down the toilet the day after his and Mira's little trip to the cabin. He wouldn't be needing them any more. It was time to face his fears and his dreams.

The everything: Mira. He still couldn't believe he'd found the strength to walk away.

But he wasn't going to ask her to leave. The words had been on the tip of his tongue, but he'd bitten them back. The storm was just an excuse, but she didn't need to know that. It had come just in the nick of time, saving him from making the same mistake with another woman that he'd made with his wife.

If she wanted to stay in Silver Pass, he wasn't going to be the one who urged her to leave.

And what if Mira had asked him to stay, rather than the other way around? Would he have?

His mind toyed with that idea for a few minutes. Yeah. He probably would have. But he'd never given her the opportunity to do anything except say goodbye. He'd cut her off before she could even have her say.

And what if she'd wanted more? More of their days together? More of making love? More…of everything?

Hadn't she earned the right to be heard?

Yes. He sucked down a breath. And maybe he should do something about that.

Whether it had been a mistake to ask his wife to move for the sake of his job was a moot point. What was done was done—he couldn't go back and change it, no matter how much he might wish to.

But he could change how he went on from here. What if—instead of asking Mira to leave—he asked her if he could stay in Silver Pass? With her?

It would mean giving up his job with the Hawks, but he could practice medicine anywhere. It didn't even have to be with a sports team. In fact, he could imagine his services might be in high demand in any of the hospitals around a ski resort.

His heart hadn't been in his job for a while. The coach knew it, which was why he'd sent him on this vacation in the first place. To clear his head. To help him make a choice.

It had worked. What he wanted out of life had never been clearer to him than it was right now.

Decision made, he tore the plane ticket in half and then in half again, continuing the process until the stack was too thick to rip any further. Then he stuffed all the pieces inside his coat pocket and got out of line, his pace quickening as he caught sight of the exit across the concourse.

"Jack!" A familiar voice came from somewhere behind him.

The sound stopped him in his tracks.

In slow motion, he turned. But he didn't see anything other than folks hurrying to the security check-in area. It must have been his imagination. Then a hand waved from the line he'd just vacated.

Mira. What was she doing here?

He stood there for a second, before making his way back to the line. She met him halfway.

"What's going on?" he asked, taking in the hair she'd tugged back in a ponytail, her lightweight jacket. Much too light for the mountains.

She held out a slip of paper. "I have a plane ticket to Texas. On your flight, in fact. If you want me."

He blinked, staring at her hand, her words not registering for a second or two.

She'd chosen to come with him. Of her own volition. Just like he'd chosen to stay here in Silver Pass.

Jack laughed—the first really free chuckle he'd allowed himself in almost four years.

"What's so funny?" she demanded.

He pulled the torn pieces of his ticket from his pocket. "This."

"I don't understand."

"You just bought a ticket. And I just shredded one."

Shock flashed through her eyes. "You did? Why?"

"Because I don't want to leave. Not yet."

"But the storm... Your job—"

"Can all wait," he said. "I needed to come back and find you." He blew out a breath, not sure where to start. "When I went to the restaurant two days ago I had everything planned out in my head. What I was going to say. What I was going to do. How hard I was going to kiss you."

"You were?"

He nodded. Oh, how he'd screwed up his courage, only to have it desert him at the last minute. "And then I saw you there with Robert. Heard him try to win you back and realized you could have so much more if you found someone from Silver Pass. If you spent your life loving a man who shared your life, your passions...your location."

"But—"

"Wait." He set his bag down and slung an arm around her shoulders, his heart growing lighter by the second. This was what he should have done at the restaurant. Especially after seeing her beautiful face standing in the line of passengers behind him. "As I was in that line, I started thinking. Why couldn't *I* be that man?"

"What?"

"I love you, Mira. I know nothing about the mountains, and I don't know how to ski or how to ride a snowboard or even a snowmobile. But I swear I'll be true and that I'll spend the rest of life learning about all those things. If you'll have me."

Mira stared up at him for a minute and then turned toward him, burying her face in his chest, her shoulders shaking.

What the hell?

She'd bought a ticket. Surely she couldn't be that blind that she hadn't read the signs…figured out how he felt. But then again, he wasn't sure about her feelings either, just assumed that buying a ticket to Texas meant she cared about him. "What's wrong?"

She leaned back, her eyes streaming, swiping away the tears with her palm. Her body still shook. It was then he realized she wasn't crying. She was laughing.

"Wh-what's wrong?" she asked between gasps. "I was going to say the exact same thing. I even ordered a surfboard to be sent to the team's address—guess they'll be surprised when that package is delivered, huh?"

"You ordered a surfboard?"

She sucked down a deep breath. "I did. I love you too. And I *want* to be where you are, Jack. You're not forcing me to leave. I *want* to." Her teeth came down on her lip. "Although I have a confession to make."

His chest tightened. "What's that?"

"I'm deathly afraid of sharks. Think you can still teach me how to surf?"

He smiled and planted a hard kiss on her mouth, forcing himself not to linger more than a minute or two. "I think that's something we should discuss in detail. Back at the lodge. Because I suddenly have a very urgent need."

"Anything I can help with?"

He kissed her again. "Actually, you're the only one who can."

Three hours later they were snuggled together under the covers in her room, perspiration still drying on her skin. Jack lay behind her, his body pressed tight to hers, thumb brushing back and forth over her bare hip. A shiver went through her.

God, she loved this man. No matter where the future took them, she wanted to be right in the middle of it.

"Does this mean you're not moving on to guy number six any time soon?" The low gravelly tones slid across her temple, carrying more than a hint of possessiveness.

"Mmm. I'll think about it."

The hand caressing her hip dropped a quick slap to her butt.

"Oww. Okay. No more men." She blinked as the stinging in her backside morphed into a wave of heat that washed over her. "Although your reaction to that *was* kind of hot."

Something came to life against the swell of her bottom.

"Woman, you are going to be the death of me."

She rolled onto her other side. "What about the storm? Are you sure you don't need to go back? I'll go with you."

She touched his face. "Because I want to. Not because I have to. My dad is getting married in a few months, and I've already talked to him about finding a replacement for me."

"I still have a few things to work out in my head, and you need to know what you're getting into. I've struggled over the last four years."

"It's okay. We have plenty of time to figure things out. It doesn't even matter where we end up."

He drew her closer. "For now, I just want to ride out the storm here at the lodge. With you."

"Emphasis on the riding part, I hope."

"Mira!" He gave a half-strangled laugh that lit her up inside.

She snuggled back against him. "I guess this means I owe Ellory a hundred bucks. She bet I wouldn't make it past man number five without falling for him."

Jack turned her over and took her mouth in a long kiss that had her clinging to him, breathless for more. "A hundred bucks, huh? Not sure I'm worth that kind of money."

She reached beneath the covers and found him, already hard and ready.

"Well, then," she said. "I guess you'd better start earning your keep."

She stroked him once and then again, relishing the low groan of pleasure he gave at her touch.

"Mmm...I think I could get used to this." He rolled her beneath him and parted her legs. "How long do you think it'll take me to pay off that debt?"

She arched into him, her own need beginning to rise out of control. "How does forever sound?"

* * * * *

BREAKING HER
NO-DATING RULE

BY
AMALIE BERLIN

MILLS
BOON

Published in Great Britain 2015
by Mills & Boon, an imprint of Harlequin (UK) Limited,
Eton House, 18-24 Paradise Road, Richmond, Surrey, TW9 1SR

© 2015 Darcy Gafeira

ISBN: 978-0-263-24681-0

Harlequin (UK) Limited's policy is to use papers that are natural,
renewable and recyclable products and made from wood grown in
sustainable forests. The logging and manufacturing processes conform
to the legal environmental regulations of the country of origin.

Printed and bound in Spain
by CPI, Barcelona

Dear Reader

I have failed in every single New Year's resolution I've ever set for myself. In fact I pretty much pick the most extreme resolutions possible and set myself up to fail. Because, like my heroine, I'm kind of flaky. My resolutions usually go like this:

I want to lose weight…

Day One: I RESOLVE TO GIVE UP SUGAR FOR EVER.

Day Four: Where's my chocolate?!

This year I might actually keep my resolution—or get pretty close to it. I won't know if I succeed until December 31st, since it's a year-long career goal and I still have time to pull it off. We'll have to see who wins—the flake in me or the over-achiever.

It's fitting that in the first year I have a shot at holding a resolution I also got to work with Tina Beckett (a complete joy for me) and write linked books about besties who go to opposite extremes in setting their New Year's resolutions… and set *them* up to fail spectacularly instead of myself for a change. Of course I don't want to spoil the ending, but they fail in the best way possible.

I hope you enjoy reading my half of the *New Year's Resolutions!* duet, and encourage you to grab Tina's book—HOW TO FIND A MAN IN FIVE DATES—for Miranda and Jack's story. And I wish you resolutions that work out for the best—succeed or fail.

Amalie

Dedication

To Tina Beckett—a great friend, fantastic writer, and an awesome lady to work with! It's been a blast!

To Laurie Johnson—for giving me the chance to collaborate with a writer I adore, and letting me slip a hippy chick into a book :) You rock.

There's never been a day when there haven't been stories in **Amalie Berlin**'s head. When she was a child they were called daydreams, and she was supposed to stop having them and pay attention. Now when someone interrupts her daydreams to ask, 'What are you doing?' she delights in answering, 'I'm working!'

Amalie lives in Southern Ohio with her family and a passel of critters. When *not* working, she reads, watches movies, geeks out over documentaries and randomly decides to learn antiquated skills. In case of zombie apocalypse she'll still have bread, lacy underthings, granulated sugar, and always something new to read.

Recent titles by Amalie Berlin:

RETURN OF DR IRRESISTIBLE
UNCOVERING HER SECRETS
CRAVING HER ROUGH DIAMOND DOC

**These books are also available in eBook format
from www.millsandboon.co.uk**

PROLOGUE

"I KNOW THAT you want to manage this situation yourself, but you do have to relax at some point. Let me and the universe carry the load for a few days."

The fact that most of the resort had been abandoned at the first hint of the approaching storm gave Ellory Star more confidence than she might've otherwise had in what would be an intense situation at best. Only a handful of staff remained—enough to keep the resort running— and a handful of guests trying to get in as much time on the powder as they could before the clouds rolled in. But it wasn't like Mira was leaving the premises. She'd be around for catastrophe, her safety net.

"Enjoy your post-coital vacation, spend time with Mr. Forever, Number Five. I promise not to refer to him any more in any way that highlights the fact that I totally won the New Year's resolution war this year." Ellory leaned over the bar in Jack's suite, where she and Mira were chatting, tidied a stack of napkins emblazoned with the lodge logo, and pretended not to be feeling smug about how totally right she was.

Mira—her sister by everything except genetics and actual family ties—was the concierge doctor for the ski lodge where Ellory was now living and working, and her best friend since they'd set eyes on one another as toddlers, when Ellory's mother had brought her to work at the lodge Mira's family owned. She was the brilliant one, and rational, dependable, smart, and a lot of other good-sounding words that everybody would use to describe Mira and only Mira would ever use to label her.

"You haven't won until you figure out your quest. Your project. The thing you're working on."

A project Ellory hadn't explained. "I should've just bet you I could go without a man longer than you could keep serial dating. Though I haven't seen any contenders for sexy fun since I've been home. So the resolution is safe."

But that wouldn't have served the point of her making the resolution to begin with. Besides, her inability to articulate exactly what was wrong was part of the problem she needed to figure out. She skated through life, largely flying on instinct and ignoring anything that hurt her to the point that she wasn't even sure what hurt her any more. For the past year she'd been running from some pain she couldn't name—because ignoring the reasons for pain didn't mean she didn't feel it. It just meant she felt it blindly.

Her quest had led her home, and left her with the understanding that she had something to work on. Banishing men from her life kept her from sublimating with sex, kept her from distracting herself. She'd spent a decade distracting herself with a string of different boyfriends, and she wasn't any closer to finding enlightenment…or just plain old happiness…than she had been when she'd left home, determined to give her life meaning.

Before things got too deep, before Mira picked up on the melancholy lurking in Ellory's soul, she shifted the subject back to one she knew Mira couldn't resist. "So, I'm going to have to come up with a new nickname for

Jack. I could make some 'playing doctor' references, but that's too obvious."

Jack's timely arrival through the suite door was her cue. "Hey, *Loooove* Doctor," she called, and then shook her head. "Nah, that's not it. I'll keep working on it. Somewhere else now that we've got everything hashed out." She winked at Mira and brushed past Mr. Mira on the way to the door.

Before she stepped out she turned to say something, and interrupted kissing. "Man, I was going to say that I was totally wrong about the resolution—that it just wasn't that Jack was lucky to be the fifth dude but that I believed he was the one…and would have been if he'd been number twenty-five or number five. Now I just want to give you a safe-sex talk!"

When they both laughed at her she smiled and cooed at them both while closing the door, "Oh, Number Five, you'll always be number *one* to me!"

The door clicked before she could get pelted with bar paraphernalia for her pretend Mira-sex-talk.

The universe did like her. Occasionally.

CHAPTER ONE

ELLORY STAR HAD never been a sentinel before, and there were good reasons for that.

But this was where her mission to find herself had led. From the hot, life-laden forests of Peru to Colorado in the winter. To cold legs and a head full of static, hair that stuck to everything, and, of course, to trying to find other people. Correction, she wasn't even out doing the heavy lifting on the finding. She was just waiting for other people to find people.

The universe had a wicked sense of humor.

A tight cluster of yellow headlights flickered in the far left of her field of vision and soon grew strong enough to cut through the gray-blue haze of hard-falling snow.

The rescue team was back!

She turned from the frosty glass inset in the polished brass doors of the Silver Pass Lodge to face the ragtag group of employees she'd managed to round up after the mass exodus. Most lodge employees had families they wanted to get to before the blizzard hit, and nearly all the patrons had left too—the ones who hadn't left were the ones the rescue team was returning with. She hoped.

"Okay, guys, do the things we talked about," she said—the most order-like order she'd ever given.

Usually, she was the last person to be put in charge

of anything, and that was how Ellory liked it. She had less chance of letting people down if they didn't expect anything from her. It probably highlighted some flaw in her character that the only time she was willing to take on any kind of serious responsibility was when her primary objective was guarding her best friend's sexy rendezvous time.

Ellory—gatekeeper to the love shack.

She who kept non-emergency situations from disturbing the resort doctor while she got her wild thing on with Jack, aka Number Five.

Pure. Accomplishment.

She watched long enough to see the first staff member break into motion, placing another log on the already blazing fire and opening the damper so the lobby fireplace would roar to life.

Later she could feel guilty for the amount of carbon she was responsible for putting into the atmosphere today. Right now, her heart couldn't find a balance between the well-being of people around her and the well-being of the planet.

Some lifestyle choices were harder to live with than others.

Those returning would be cold at the very least, and Ellory prayed that was the worst of their afflictions. Cold she could remedy with fire, hot beverages, hot water, and blankets hot from the clothes dryer—even if all those warm things further widened her expanding carbon footprint and left her feeling like a sasquatch. A big, hypocritical, sooty-footed, carbon-belching sasquatch.

And those kinds of thoughts were not helping. She had no room for negativity today. She had a job, she had a plan, she'd see it through and not let anyone down—especially the only one with any faith in her.

One of them should be having wild monkey sex with someone, and as she wasn't having any she'd defend Mira's love shack to the last possible minute. Be the stand-in Mira today, and do the very best she could for as long as she could. At least until she knew exactly what Mira would have to deal with when it got to be too much for *her* to handle.

When she looked back at the headlights, they'd grown close enough for her to count. Six sets, same number as had gone out. Good sign.

She fastened the coat she wore, crammed a knit cap on her head and pushed her hands into her mittens. Her clothes might be ridiculous since she hadn't yet augmented her wardrobe with Colorado winter wear, and her bottom half might freeze when she went out to meet the team, but at least the places where she kept her important bits—organs, brain—would be warm.

As the snowmobiles rolled to a stop in front of the ornate doors, she took a last deep breath of warm air and pushed out into the raging winter. Wind whipped her gauzy, free-flowing skirt around her legs and made it hard to keep her eyes open. With one hand shielding them from the blast of snowy, frigid air, she counted: ten people, one dog.

Should have been eleven.

Another quick count confirmed that all the six rescuers in orange had made it back, which meant one of the lodge's patrons was still lost in this storm that was forecast to only get worse.

Oh, no.

She'd have to disturb Mira.

People were already climbing off the snowmobiles, rescuers in their orange suits helping more fashionably dressed and slower-moving guests from the machines.

"How can I help?" she called over the wind, approaching the group.

The large man paused in his task of releasing a big snowy black dog from the cage on the back of his snowmobile, turned and pointed at Ellory. *"Get inside now!"*

Real yelling? Okay... Maybe it was just to get over the wind.

He unlatched the cage and his canine friend bounded out. The sugar-frosted dog didn't need to be told where to go. Ellory made it to the outer doors behind the massive canine and opened it for him, then held it for people.

It wasn't technically a blizzard yet. It was snowing hard, yes, and blowing harder, and of course she was cold, but she wouldn't freeze to death in the next couple of minutes while she helped in some fashion. And she needed to help. Even if all she could think to do was hold the door.

As the man approached, he lifted his goggles and sent a baleful stare at her, stormier than the weather. With one smooth motion he grabbed Ellory's elbow and thrust her ahead of him into the breezeway, "That wasn't a suggestion. Get inside now. You're not dressed for the weather."

"I didn't offer to make snow angels with anyone," she joked, looking over her shoulder at the angry man as he steered her inside.

Stumbling, she pulled her elbow free and pushed through, intent on getting some space between them.

Good grief. Up close, and without fabric covering the bottom of his face or the goggles concealing his eyes, the fact that he was working some kind of rugged handsome look canceled the effect of winter and made her feel like she was dipped in peppermint wherever she touched him.

Ellory didn't get those kind of excited feelings for anyone ever, not without really working at it. Must be the cold. And now that she was inside, she had things to do besides tingle and lust after Ole Yeller.

A specific list of things, in fact, to look for when checking these people out.

As the group gathered around the fireplace and the hats and goggles came off, she got a good look at how beaten down they all were. Exhausted. Weak. All of them, both the rescuers and the rescued. But those who didn't do this for a living, the ones who'd been helpless and still had a missing friend, looked blank. It was the same shell-shocked expression she'd seen on the faces of victims of natural disasters—earthquakes, mudslides, and floods. Being lost in a snowstorm probably counted...

Her people stood around, waiting for her. Follower to leader for one day—no wonder they didn't know what to do. She was supposed to be leading them. Her list of things had *hypothermia* at the very top as the most important situation to remedy.

"Okay, guys, we need to help everyone get out of their snow suits and boots. Get the hot blankets on them. And hot beverages. Hot cocoa..." she corrected. Everyone liked cocoa, and it was loaded with calories they no doubt needed after their harrowing day.

While the employees did as she asked, Ellory backtracked to the Angry Dog Man. He seemed much more leader-like than she felt, so he got the questions.

In hushed tones, she asked, "Where is the other one?"

He frowned, his left hand lifting to his right shoulder to grip and squeeze through the thick coat he wore. "The other one tried to get back to the lodge when these four wanted to stay put."

"Where were they?"

"South Mine."

Ellory winced. The terrain around the mines was left

rugged on purpose in the hope of discouraging exploration by guests. The mines weren't safe, and signs announced that, but they could serve as shelter in a pinch. A very dangerous pinch.

"Did you see a trail or any sign of him?" Mira would want to know everything, so she tried to anticipate questions.

"There is a trail, but it's the one that they followed in. If he's wise and we're lucky, he'll follow it back. There's still a chance that he'll make it back to the lodge while we're out looking for him. If he does, I need you to call on the radio and let me know. It was impossible to take the snowmobiles directly along that trail, but we're going to go back out and look. We'll take a quick peek in the mines between here and there, and hit South Mine again in case he went back to where they all were."

"After the storm?"

"No." He looked back and called to the group, all of whom had dove into the drinks and stew to fortify themselves. "Ten minutes and then we're going back out."

"You can't!" Ellory said, much louder than she'd intended. She tried again, quieter, calmer than she felt. "The storm is going to get really bad."

"We have some time." His voice had a gravelly sound that sent warm sparks over her ears, almost like a touch. That kind of voice would sound crazy sexy in whispers, hot breath on her ear... Raspy and...

"I'm sorry, what did you say? I think I misheard you." Or hadn't heard him at all. God, she had to do better than this.

"Are you a doctor?" he repeated.

"No." It was time for him to figure out she wasn't important, or capable of handling this.

"Where's Dr. Dupris?"

She noticed him looking back at the people in front of the fire, all out of their suits now, which meant time for step two.

Ellory spun and headed for the guests, expecting him to follow. "She's here, but I'm like triage or something. I have a list of things to wake her up for. And we have water heated in case there were any frostbite cases. Also I read that heating the feet would help get the body temperatures up fast. Actually, I have the saunas roaring too if that would help. I just wasn't sure whether or not that would be a bad thing or a good thing, and it wasn't in the books. Do you know?" She didn't stop, just threw the question out and then went on.

Since the staff had handled her warming requests, she headed for the smallest member of the party, a petite, pixie-like woman who wasn't drinking her cocoa…and who held her hands above her lap as if they were hurting.

His stride longer, he overtook her and scooped up a stethoscope as he passed the tray of first-aid and examination supplies she'd laid out and slung the thing around his neck. Catching it caused a brief flash of pain on his handsome features. He ignored the pain, but Ellory noticed. That was her real job: Physio and massage therapy. Just not today.

He wasn't the concern right now. He'd been mostly warm when out there in it, though his cheeks looked chapped from the winter winds…

She reached down to gently lift one of the woman's arms to get a better look at her fingers. "What's your name, honey?"

"Chelsea," she answered, teeth chattering. "My fingers and toes burn. Like they're on fire."

"Socks off, everyone. Time to check extremities." Chelsea's fingertips were really red. Ellory didn't want to touch them, but she didn't really know enough about medicine not to investigate fully. Maybe frostbite started with redness?

Gingerly, she wrapped her hands over Chelsea's fingertips, causing the freezing woman to gasp in pain but confirming that they were indeed hot. This wasn't frostbite. Though that was probably going to be the next stage. "I'm sorry," she whispered, and let go of the hands, her gaze drifting down to where Angry Leader had knelt at Chelsea's feet, which he now examined. Her toes were exactly the opposite in color from her fingertips: an unnatural, disturbing, somewhat corpse-like white.

That might be a good reason to call Mira...

"Is that—?" She hadn't got the question out before he nodded and looked Chelsea in the eye.

"My name is Dr. Graves. Anson, if you prefer. I'll even tell you my middle name later if you need some more names to cuss me with... This isn't going to be pleasant. We have to warm your feet fast," Anson said, his raspy voice much gentler with the woman. "You have the beginning stages of frostbite."

Chelsea's gaze sharpened and she blurted out, "Are my toes going to fall off?" She sounded so stricken every head in the lobby turned toward her.

Ellory's heart skipped.

Anson looked grim and his wind-burned cheeks lost some of their color, but he shook his head. "It's going to feel like it. It will hurt like probably no one but you can imagine right now, but that's how you get to keep them." He didn't sugarcoat it, not even a hint of the usual *discomfort* nonsense doctors liked to say.

Chelsea nodded, her eyes welling.

Anson looked at Ellory again. "Get her pants off. How hot is the water?"

"One hundred and ten on the burners." Ellory answered. That she knew.

He looked surprised they'd been using a thermometer on it. "A little too hot. Add a small amount of cold water to it to get it to one hundred and five and then pour. It's got to be between one hundred and one hundred and five degrees Fahrenheit all the time. Dip out water, pour more in, or swap out the containers to keep it within range. I know that's going to be hard to do in buckets, but it needs to be done as exactingly as possible for a full half-hour." Anson said this to Ellory, who nodded and relayed the orders to her kitchen helpers, then helped Chelsea out of the bottom half of her suit.

By the time Chelsea was down to her thermals, the water had been sufficiently cooled and poured into a large rubber container. Ellory pushed the cotton cuffs to Chelsea's knees and guided the woman's feet into the water.

It hurt. She could tell by the way Chelsea's lower lip quivered, though admirably she didn't cry out.

With all the time Ellory had spent in disaster zones, witnessing human suffering, she should have built up some kind of callus to it by now, but it tore at her heart all the same. "I'm so sorry this has happened to you… We'll get you something for the pain."

"My fiancé is still out there," she whispered, clarifying in those simple words what hurt worse right now.

Ellory put one arm around Chelsea's shoulders, giving her a squeeze. "Let's get your insides warmed up and see if we can beat the shivering." She took the cocoa Chelsea hadn't been drinking and held it to her lips. "We'll help you with this until your fingers stop smarting and you can do it yourself, okay?"

"*Ohh*…chocolate," Chelsea said.

"That's pretty much how I feel about chocolate too." Ellory lifted the cup to the woman's mouth. "Sometimes it's the only thing that makes the stuff we have to go through bearable. Though I do feel like I should apologize for not making it from better ingredients." A nervous laugh bubbled up. "You didn't do anything wrong, that's not why I'm making you drink preservative juice." She was doing that thing again, where she lost control of her mouth because she was nervous.

Chelsea looked at her strangely. "Preservative juice?"

She named the popular brand of cocoa everyone knew, then added, "I'm sure it's fine. I'm just…" What could she say to explain that? "I'm big on organic."

"Ahh." Chelsea nodded, relaxing back in her chair.

Great bedside manner. Most of her patients worked with her for a long stretch of time so they got to know her quirks and oddities, and only had to suffer her help with exercise and a program that their physiotherapist designed. All Ellory did was help them through it and massage away pain, she didn't need to be trusted to make decisions.

Ellory added in what she hoped was a more agreeable tone, "Ignore me. It's a throwback to childhood."

"You were big on organic in childhood?" Anson asked from down where he crouched, examining the feet of another patient. Which meant he was listening, and probably losing faith in her with every word that tumbled out of her mouth.

"Yes. In a manner of speaking."

His eyes were focused on the patient, but it still felt like he was staring at her. "Which is?"

The only way out of this conversation was to pretend it wasn't happening.

Stop. Talking.

Handing Chelsea's cup to another staff member, she said, "Please assist Chelsea with her cocoa. I should assist Dr. Graves." The man needed a different last name. Which she wouldn't bring up. She probably already sounded like an incompetent idiot to them.

She caught up with him kneeling before the last of the rescued, checking extremities.

As she stepped to his side he looked up, locking eyes with her in a way that said he knew she'd heard him and that he wasn't going to press the matter.

Message delivered, he got back to work and the potency of his stare dissipated. "Get all their feet into the water. But Chelsea's the only one you have to keep in the temperature range."

"What about the sauna?" She rolled with his return to business. As out of her depth as she felt, she did want to do a good job, take good care of them all.

"Maybe later, or if they don't get warm enough to stop shivering soon, but I'd rather you not put them into the stress of a sauna until a doctor is on hand should things get hairy."

Ellory nodded.

"I'm going to check on my crew. And Max."

Hearing his name, the fuzzy black dog currently stretched in front of the fire popped up and looked at Anson.

"Or maybe I'll get him some water first..." He called to the rescuers to check their feet and while they peeled off boots he took care of himself and the big bushy dog.

Ellory organized the helpers with instructions on the water, her shoulders growing tighter and tighter every time she looked through the door or the windows at the worsening storm. After assigning two people to Chelsea and getting them another round of hot blankets, she finally went to find Anson.

And Max—maybe the dog would listen to her concerns.

CHAPTER TWO

"WHAT IF YOU'RE not back in half an hour, when they come out of the warm water? And isn't that weird, a doctor moonlighting as a rescuer?" She'd always considered Mira to be an unusual doctor—fabulous and outdoorsy— so Anson seemed like an anomaly. He had the bossy bit down, at least. But he could be safe and inside during this weather, or out driving his four wheel drive and... smoking cigars. Whatever people did in four wheeled drives, she wasn't sure.

"Dry them gently and wrap them in loose gauze." He answered that first, then added, "I don't moonlight. I work in the ER six months of the year, and the rescue team is my life during ski season."

His admission surprised her. Adrenaline junkie? Extreme sports wackadoo? Both those fit the idea of returning to the outdoors in this weather. Once more, her gaze was pulled to the glass doors. The snow, already heavy before they'd returned, had picked up even worse since. "Are you sure it wouldn't be better for you all to wait until the storm passes?"

The sharpness that came to his green eyes shut down that thought process completely. Right. He didn't say anything. He didn't need to.

Anson turned to his crew instead. "Five minutes."

He pulled a plastic baggie from his pocket and extracted some kind of jerky to give to the big shaggy dog.

One of the group asked, "Where are we going?"

"Blue Mine and South Mine," Anson answered, then looked at Ellory. "Why are you not dressed for the weather?"

"I haven't bought clothes for being home yet, and all the winters in the past decade, I guess, have been in warm places. Before New Year's Eve I was in Peru. It's summer there right now. I wasn't sure if I was going to stay, so I didn't want to buy clothes I might not wear very long. It's wasteful."

He shook his head. "Rent a snow suit when you're going to be out in the elements...what's your name?"

"Ellory. And I have one." It's the one thing she did have, but it was old, hopelessly out of fashion and not nearly as well suited to the winter as the suits these people wore because she didn't wear manufactured materials. So it was bulky, and kind of itchy. And she left it at her parents' after every New Year...so it was musty from storage and...

She didn't need to share that with Anson. He was covered in layers of modern insulating materials, and while she could understand it and tried not to be jealous of his warmth and mobility, he wouldn't understand if she explained. Not that his opinion should matter. "I wasn't going out to stay in the weather earlier, just to meet you all. And I have thermal underwear under this."

Like he would think well of her if she'd been wearing wool and a parka in her short jaunt into the weather to meet them. She was a flake. That's how normal people viewed her. So today she was a flake who didn't dress properly. What else was new?

"Go put it on."

Ellory didn't know how to respond to a direct order like that. And she really didn't like it that the bossiness made her tingle again... Wrong time, wrong place, wrong feelings.

She wanted to blame them on her nerves too, like being nervous amplified all her other emotions, but she couldn't even lie to herself on that. Ruggedly handsome wasn't a look the man was going for—he just had it. Some combination of good genes, lifestyle and that voice gave it to him. She tried to ignore that, and the squirmy feeling in her belly she got when his mossy hazel eyes focused on her.

"Anson." She went with his name, in an attempt to reclaim some power. "It's not just blowing more, it's falling thicker. If you guys get all...frozen and stuff, then you aren't going to help find—"

"There's still time." He cut her off. Again.

Rude. Curt. Terse. That should make him less attractive. That should definitely make him feel like less of a threat to her stupid resolution...

He had flaws. The bossy thing, which shouldn't be hot. What else? He probably wasn't even half as strapping and impressive as his winter wear made him seem. It was just the illusion of beefy manliness from the cardinal rule of winter: loose layers kept you warmer. It somehow amplified the squareness of his jaw and the scruff that confirmed the dark color of the hair currently hidden by his knit cap.

Her heart rate accelerated and her hands waffled at her side. This was not going the way she'd pictured it while waiting and watching through the windows. She didn't anticipate having to try and convince someone not to go back out in the storm, and for some reason she knew he wouldn't care that she was more afraid for the crew than for the missing man.

She could just lock the door and keep everyone safe inside. Except she hated confrontation, and if he told her to give him the key in that bossy gravel voice of his, she'd give it to him. And possibly her undies too.

She could really think of a good way to distract him. It definitely violated her Stupid Resolution parameters, but it was in the name of humanity and keeping people safe. Surely that was a good reason for an exception.

Through all this stupidity, the only communication Ellory managed was skittish hand motions that made her jangle from the stacks of thin silver bangles she loved. Sentinels probably didn't jingle.

He glanced down at her hand and then back up, impatient brows lifting, urging her to say something else. Only Ellory didn't know what else to say.

Winter was his job after all. And, really, she'd spent most of the past lots of years in places where her weather awareness had mostly consisted of putting on sunscreen and seeking high ground during the rainy season. She probably wasn't the best judge of snow stuff.

When she failed to form any other words he started talking instead. Instructions. Things she'd already learned from studying Mira's medical books when reading up on treatment for frostbite and hypothermia. But it was good to hear it from someone who really knew something about it. Anything about it.

He even gave her additional explanations about signs of distress, outside the cold temperature illness symptoms she'd read about—other stuff to look for that would require Mira immediately, and he capped off the instructions with a long, measuring look. "If you're not up to the task, tell me now. I'll get Dr. Dupris down here."

"I'm up to the task." She was, she just wished she wasn't. "Are you? Your shoulder is hurt. I've seen you roll your arm in the socket at least three times since you came inside and you've been rubbing it too."

He closed the bag of dog treats and stuffed it into his pocket. "I'm all right. We'll call if we get stuck. And we've got survival gear on the ATVs."

Movement behind her made her aware that the team had all moved toward the door, ready to go wherever Fearless Leader told them to. They all either ignored what she'd been saying about the danger of going out in the crazy falling snow or were busy building an imaginary snow fort of denial.

Anson held the door and looked at the dog. "Max." One word and his furry companion scampered right out behind them.

It would be okay. People who risked their lives for others had to build up good karma. The team would make it back, and maybe their karma would extend to the still missing skier. Until then she'd do her best—manage the lobby/exposure clinic, keep the fire stoked and the water heated and flowing, and keep those who'd been out in it warm and safe.

After the team returned, and when the head count was official, then she'd get Mira.

Anson Graves's snowmobile crept through the falling white flakes. Theoretically, there should be another couple of hours of daylight left, but between the dense clouds and miles of sky darkened by falling snow it felt more like twilight. Zero visibility. He was half-afraid he'd find the missing man by accidentally running him over.

A trip that normally took fifteen minutes was taking forever.

Anson knew only too well how much longer it would seem for the man who was stuck in the cold, counting his own heartbeats and every painful breath, wondering how many more he'd have before the wind froze him from the inside and winter claimed him.

That's what he'd done.

The blonde at the lodge hadn't been wrong, he'd just wanted her to be wrong. At least half an hour had passed since they'd started the trek to the third-closest abandoned silver mine, and they weren't even halfway there yet. She should be getting Chelsea's feet out of the water and bandaging them by now. He'd forgotten to tell her not to let Chelsea walk…though maybe she wouldn't try.

If they hadn't had to take the long way they'd be there by now. But this was the safest route with the snow drifting the way it was.

If the wind would just stop…

The wet, blasting snow built a crust on his goggles, his eyes the only places not actively painful and cold from the wind. He shook his head, trying to clear the visor, but had to use his hand to scrape it off. He didn't even want to see what was becoming of Max in the back. Snow stuck to his fur like nothing Anson had ever seen.

The only thing he felt good about right now was leaving the four rescues with the hippie chick. Her choice of attire showed a distinct lack of common sense, but she'd picked up on his shoulder bothering him. She was perceptive and paying attention. And he'd seen her hug his frostbite patient. She cared. They'd be safe with her, especially considering the detailed instructions he'd given. She'd be watching them with an eagle eye for any slight changes. Getting Dupris should an emergency arise would be a simple enough task for anyone.

His stomach suddenly churned hard, a split second before he felt an unnatural shifting of the snow beneath him.

He reacted automatically, cutting sharply up the slope, and didn't stop until the ground felt firm beneath him. Damned sliding snowdrifts.

He'd only reacted in time because he'd been waiting for it to happen. After his harrowing experience, snow had become an obsession to him—learning the different kinds of snow, what made it slide, what made blizzards, all that. And since he'd bought Max and had him trained, he'd probably spent more time on the snow than anywhere else in his life. His instinct was honed to it, and he knew to listen to his gut.

Especially when he couldn't see the terrain well enough to judge with his eyes...

But he couldn't trust that his crew would have the same ability, especially with how tired they already were.

Conditions had just officially gotten too bad to continue.

His team had stopped when he'd pulled his maneuver—quickly enough to see how he'd survived it before they tried to follow—but he didn't want them to try it. They'd follow where he led, but he couldn't have any more lives on his conscience.

Grabbing the flashlight off his belt, he clicked it on, assuring that they'd see the motion even if they couldn't clearly see any other details, and gave it a swirl before pointing back in the direction from which they'd come.

Retreat.

He waited until they had all turned around and then started up the slope in a gentle arc to bring up the rear. Not ideal. The best formation had him at the front—taking the dangers first—but at least from this vantage he'd be able to see if anyone fell behind or started having difficulty.

He felt shifting against the cage at his back. Max huddled behind Anson, strategically placing himself to get the least of the cold wind that blasted around his owner, even as the machine crept along.

If it were just him, he'd stay out on the mountain, looking until it was impossible to do anything else, but there were five other human lives under his protection, not to mention his hard-working, life-saving dog.

"I'm sorry, man," he said to the wind.

They had to go back.

He'd have to tell the others they couldn't reach the mine. Yet.

They hadn't gotten far enough to find anyone or signs. Those they'd rescued earlier would just have to understand.

His gut twisted. He'd lost people to avalanches, recently even. But he'd never lost someone to a storm and not found them alive.

Worse, he'd have to lie to those people who'd been through so much. Say he was certain they would pick up the trail again as soon as the snow and wind let up. But the only thing he was certain of was the fear and guilt tearing through him—colder than the Colorado cyclone buffeting them about the mountainside.

Just as Anson had expected, Ellory was doing the job she'd been assigned. She'd been fast out the door when they'd first arrived, but not when they returned.

As quickly as they could, the team shut down their machines, climbed off, and hurried inside. They hadn't been out in the weather that long compared to their hours of searching for the group, but the wind speeds were now enough that the awning over the front doors sounded like thunder as it rippled in the wind. That, coupled with exhaustion, made it impossible to keep warm.

He stepped through the ornate doors to the comforting heat and the smell of burning wood. The fireplace in the lobby still burned actual wood, something that had surprised him when he'd returned to Silver Pass. It was good. Wood fire dried out the air and cut through the damp better than anything but a shower. Anson loved the crackling and the temperatures for those times, like now, when he just couldn't get warm enough. The dancing flames. The red coals. The warm golden light, so hopeful… Hopefulness he wished he felt.

Max looked up at him, made eye contact, and then headed for the fireplace at a trot. He always did that and Anson still didn't know whether it was him asking for permission to do something, or he was just giving Anson a heads-up that he was going.

His crew hit the hot beverages first, the fastest way to heat up your core, leaving Anson to check on his patients and deliver the news.

Ellory had positioned his frostbite patient close to the fire, having transferred her to a fancy brass wheelchair that matched the décor—the lodge kept a few on hand for the really bad skiers—and now sat at Chelsea's feet, gently patting them dry. She'd kept them in the hot water bath longer than he'd told her to. Not great. The tissue was fragile and being waterlogged wouldn't do her any favors.

A hot plate sat on the floor about a foot away, which was new. Somewhere closer to keep the water hot for the footbath.

She was taking that temperature range very seriously at least. Probably keeping it better than the whirlpool baths at the hospital.

"Chelsea's toes are pink now," Ellory called, on seeing him. It almost helped. "Well, almost all the way pink. A couple of her small toes have a bit of yellow going on. We had a little trouble with the water temperature at first, but once we moved the hot plate closer, it got easier to keep it in the range."

"It's not hurting as bad now," Chelsea added in quiet tones, swiveling in her chair to look the lobby over.

She was looking for her fiancé, as they all were, but she was the one who'd be hurt the most if the man didn't make it back.

Anson stepped around and crouched to look at her toes. "No blisters have formed yet, so that's good. You'll likely get a couple of blisters soon, when they start swelling. But we're going to take good care of you, and when the storm passes we'll get you to a hospital."

"What about Jude?" Chelsea asked, letting him know what she was interested in talking about but not whether she'd heard him at all. Someone would have to repeat the information to her later.

Anson straightened so he could address the group. "The storm has gotten to the point where it's impossible for us to continue searching. I want to be clear: this is just a suspension of the search, not the end of it. I'm sorry we haven't found your fiancé yet."

"Jude." Chelsea repeated the name of the missing skier, stopping Anson with one hand on his arm.

"Jude," he repeated, his pulse kicking up a little higher. He knew why it was important to her, but saying the man's name made it harder to maintain the distance he needed to be smart about this. "Just because we have to postpone going back out to look for Jude, it doesn't mean it's time to give up hope. So don't get ahead of us, okay? You'd be surprised what someone can survive. Those mines are a pretty good shelter. There are also some rocky overhangs between here and where we found you. And some of those might actually be better."

"How could they be better? You're closer to the snow," one of the rescued asked.

He contemplated how much to actually tell them about his experience with this kind of situation. *I know these things, I killed someone with snow once* wouldn't inspire anyone to trust him. This had to be about them, not about his fear or guilt. "Small spaces hold the warmth your body makes better, and the wind can't get into it as fully as it does in the mines, which have a bigger entrance and room for the wind to move around inside. He might still show up here before we get out to him, but as soon as the storm lets up we'll get back out there. It's not time to give up hope." He repeated that, trying to convince himself.

It was time to bandage Chelsea's toes…and hopefully him moving on would make them take the hint not to ask more questions. He didn't have any answers or much of a mind left for coming up with more empty words of comfort. He was too busy trying to ignore the similarities between this storm and *his* storm.

Pulling off his cap and gloves, he squatted beside Ellory at Chelsea's feet, struggling to hold his calm for everyone else. "Do you have some gloves for me to use?"

Ellory ducked into the bag of supplies she'd packed and fished out the box of gloves. One look at them confirmed they wouldn't do. Small. He could squeeze into a medium at a pinch, but large were better. "All right, this job has been passed to you."

To his surprise, she didn't argue at all, just grabbed a couple gloves from the box and put them on. Crouched so close he was enveloped in a cloud of something fruity and floral. The woman looked like summer, and she smelled like spring. Warm. And distracting. He scooted to the side to give her room.

"What is the job?" she asked, looking at Chelsea's toes and maneuvering herself so she could gently cradle the patient's heel in her lap.

He handed the gauze to her and began ripping strips of tape and tacking them to the wheelchair, where she could get to them. "Part of the healing process is just keeping the site dry and loosely bandaged." He gave short, quick instructions, and left her to it.

She unrolled the gauze carefully and began wrapping. He watched, ready to correct her, but she did it as he would've: a couple of passes between the two toes to keep them separate, controlling the moisture level better, and then loosely around the two together.

No matter how out of her depth she looked, she was anything but incompetent. There might even be some kind of medical training there. The cloud of floral scent stole up his dry, burning sinuses and almost made his mouth water like a dog's.

Awesome priorities. Reveling in attraction to some woman while the lost man was freezing. Maybe dying. He definitely didn't have the warm comfort of a fireplace and a wench-shaped blonde to take his mind off his failure to get back to the lodge safely, didn't even know his friends had been saved, so he suffered that additional torment—worry for them in addition to himself.

An inferno of shame ignited in his belly.

Hide it.

At the very least he owed them all a confident appearance. Calm. Strength. Determination.

Meltdowns were something to have alone—a luxury that would have to wait until he was no longer needed.

CHAPTER THREE

ELLORY HAD READ about frostbite treatment so she could anticipate Dr. Graves's needs for that, but she had no idea what his other needs were. She'd kind of pegged the search and rescue team as attracting the kind of adrenaline fiends in it for the thrill, but Anson looked almost as devastated by returning empty-handed as Chelsea had.

With the bandage applied, she switched off the hot plate, scooted it out of the way and stood. What came next? She didn't know, but certainly there would be something she would need to do, and being on her feet would help her react that much faster.

"They still hurt, I know," Anson said to the woman, looking at the toes now hidden by the gauze, the patch of yellow skin surrounded by angry redness hidden. "But most of this might not even be frostbite. The yellow area is, but the good news is that we got to it in good time and it's very unlikely to leave any lasting damage. I won't be able to tell for a couple of days if it's frostbite or the lesser version, which you all have on your fingers and toes... frostnip. We're going to treat yours as if you have frostbite, just to be safe. I'll see what kind of antibiotics Dr. Dupris has in her inventory, and some pain medication."

Good news. She'd take whatever kind of win they could get.

Anson asked the standard allergy questions, got whatever info he needed, and nodded once to Ellory—a kind of *do it* nod. She had been promoted: triage to assistant, or nurse...or whatever that position was.

"I can check with Mira. Which antibiotic do you need?" If she had to, she could no doubt find in Mira's books which kind of antibiotic was good for skin infections, but she'd rather he tell her. She wasn't a doctor. Not by a long stretch. But she knew enough to know that antibiotics were a tricky lot—some worked for everything, some worked best for specific things, and these days a frightening amount were resistant to stuff they used to be awesome at fighting.

"I'm sure she's got some of the broad-spectrum ones, but I don't know how well the drug cabinet is stocked for anything obscure." For some reason she wanted him to think well of her, and she felt more competent even saying the words "broad spectrum." Like proving to him she wasn't a complete idiot was important. Probably something to do with the lecture she'd gotten about her clothes...

She didn't even know the man, had never seen him before today, but as he spoke she became aware of something else: there was a rawness about him she couldn't name. Something in that raspy timbre that resonated feelings primal and violent.

He rattled off a few medication names that sounded like gibberish to her, and she didn't ask him to repeat himself, just hoped she could remember them when she came face-to-face with a wall of gibberish-sounding drug names.

Then she'd come back here and keep an eye on the good doctor with the terrible name, because alarm bells were ringing in her head.

Chelsea suffered the whole situation with more dignity than Ellory could've mustered, and directed the conversation back to what she really wanted to talk about. "If I got frostbite in the mine and I wasn't in the snow, Jude's going to have it for sure, isn't he?"

"Nothing is ever certain." Ellory said it too quickly. It sounded like a platitude. She shook her head and tried again with better words. "You can't compare your situation to his for a couple of reasons: women don't hold heat as well as men do, and your boots are different. Even if they are the same brand, the fit will be different. If his have more room inside than yours they'll hold heat better. If he's taken shelter in a smaller space than you did, like Anson...Dr. Anson...was saying, he could just be warmer..."

Anson pulled out the footrests on the wheelchair and carefully positioned Chelsea's feet on the metal tray. "Find a pillow for her."

Ellory knew he was speaking to her, even though he didn't look at her. She hurried to the main desk and the office behind, where she knew she'd find some. When she presented him with two slender pillows from the office, he put one under Chelsea's feet and rose. "Would you like the other pillow to sit on?"

"Yes." She made as if to rise and Anson put his hands out to stop her. "No walking. No standing. When you need to go to the bathroom, someone's going to have to go with you. Right now, I've got you. Luckily, you weigh about as much as a can of beans..." He caught her under the arms and lifted. Ellory slid the pillow beneath and then stood back as he returned Chelsea to her seat, lifting a brow pointedly at him when she saw his shoulder catch again and a wave she could actually name cross his handsome features: pain. His shoulder definitely hurt.

She really had to stop thinking about how hot he was. It wasn't helping at all. It wasn't breaking her resolution to think that the untouchable doctor rescue guy was hot, but it might lead her to other thoughts. It also wasn't her fault that his eyes looked like moss growing on the north side of a tree…deep, earthy green blending to brown. Was that hazel or still green if she looked…?

He was staring at her. It took a couple of nervous heartbeats for her to realize that it wasn't because he was a mind-reader.

Oh, yeah, she'd made the *Ahh, your shoulder does hurt* face at him. Because it did. He'd made the pain face, she'd made the *ahh* face, and now he was making the scowl face.

He didn't know she was sexually harassing him in her mind.

While she was trying to decide what she was supposed to be thinking, the man pivoted and walked straight through the archway leading to the rest of the resort.

Where was he going?

Crap.

She should have gone after the medicine by now.

He was going to disturb Mira, maybe make her leave the love nest and come down here.

"I'll be back in a few minutes, Chelsea," she babbled, and rushed after him in a flurry of flowing skirts and jingling bracelets, but she was too late to see which direction he'd headed. The elevators all sat on the bottom floor, where she was.

The man was a ninja. A cranky, frosty ninja.

Ducking into the stairwell, Ellory tilted her head to listen, hoping he wasn't outside earshot. The plush carpeting that blanketed the hallways and stairs made it hard to tell which way he'd gone. "Anson?" Tentative call unanswered, she stepped back into the hallway.

Okay, so he didn't go upstairs by any means, he wasn't heading for Mira and Jack's suite.

Mira's office? He did want antibiotics for Chelsea. She turned to the right, the shorter hallway, gathered her skirts to her knees so they'd stop the damned swirling, and ran. No yelling. Yelling disturbed people. And every single person in the lodge, except for maybe the two upstairs sheltered from all this information overload in their love nest, were disturbed enough with the current situation.

One turn and then another, she reached the final hallway just in time to see Anson reach the end and turn toward the wall outside the clinic.

Before she could call out to him, he reared back and slammed his fist through the drywall.

The loud slam and cracking sound stunned her into staring for a couple of seconds. Long enough for the pain to reach his brain and make him pull his hand out of the hole while the other gripped his poor shoulder. If it hadn't hurt before he'd done that…

"You broke the wall," she muttered as she trotted forward, no longer running. She was not at all sure how to respond to this masculine and aggressive display. She didn't know anyone who hit walls when they were upset. Generally, she kept company with people who avoided violence. "I have the keys to Mira's office, we can get whatever you need for Chelsea. I've been keeping an inventory of supplies."

He finally turned to look at her and she saw it again—he wasn't just upset. She saw desolate, blind torture in his hollow eyes. It robbed her of any ability to speak.

Whatever she'd thought earlier about his motivation

behind taking this kind of work, she was now certain: It had nothing to do with being an adrenaline junkie or any kind of fixation on the dream of being the big hero. This mattered to him. This *hurt* him.

She did the only thing she could, reached out and touched him. Tried to ground him here with her.

Contact of her palm with his stubble-roughened cheek sharpened his gaze, bringing him back from wherever he'd gone.

"Don't worry about the wall. We'll fix it. Everything will be okay." She whispered words meant to soothe him.

It took him a few seconds, but his brows relaxed and he nodded, looking down at the bloody knuckles on his hand and then at the wall. "That was pretty stupid. She's going to give me hell, isn't she?" He mustered a smile while simultaneously pulling his head back from her hand.

He didn't want her touching him… Okay. It's not like they really knew one another, and some people just didn't like to be touched.

It wasn't about her. It wasn't judgment on her.

Ellory pulled her thoughts away from the vulnerable nerve he'd accidentally struck and played along, faking a grin with her tease. "You have no idea. She's going to make you cry like a baby."

His smile was equally slight, but it was a start. And it reminded her of where she should make him focus. Sobering, she reached for his hand but didn't touch him, a request, open palms. "Can I see it?"

Okay, that might've been a test.

She'd been rejected more times in her life than any person ought to be—it wasn't anything new to her—but the second she'd found out that he was a doctor he'd become her partner in dealing with this and keeping Mira out of it. She needed him to actually connect with her and be her partner in it. And a good person didn't abandon her partner when he was hurting.

When he placed his large, bloody-knuckled hand in hers, her relief was so keen she had to fight the urge to squeeze and wind her fingers in his. He didn't shun her. Recoiling was about something else. He didn't find her lacking.

Nice skin, and considering she hadn't had any male contact since she'd come back from Peru it wasn't surprising that she wanted to relish the contact a little bit.

She forced herself to examine his knuckles before he caught on, paying careful attention to the cracked and rapidly swelling skin. "Can you move your fingers for me?"

He made a small sound as he got his fingers going, but his fingers moved smoothly at the knuckle, despite the swelling. "Well, we both know that it's an old wives' tale that you can't move something that's broken. Can't know for sure that it's not, but it looks good. Sorry, have to do this…"

Still holding his injured hand for support, she stroked her fingers over the abused skin, just firmly enough to feel the structure. She knew it hurt, he stopped breathing until she stopped touching it. "Don't think it's broken. Everything feels intact. Could be some hairline fracture, though. Guess we'll have to take a wait-and-see approach on this, along with poor Chelsea's toes."

Breathing resumed, and he pulled his hand back, nodding. "I don't think it's broken either, but I'm a fan of X-ray…"

"Come on. Let's get this cleaned up, then we'll get Chelsea's medicine into her, and I'll go and tell Mira what's going on so she can join the fun later. While the storm is here, you two will keep watch over our patient guests in shifts so she can have time with Jack and you can have some rest. Welcome to your first rotation at Silver Pass Blizzard Clinic, Dr. Graves."

"Time with Jack?" he asked, as she turned toward the door.

Ellory fished the keys from her coat pocket, unlocked the door and stepped inside, flipping on one set of lights as she went. "The past six months have been really hard for Mira, not that she'd admit it to anyone. Her fiancé was a louse. They broke up and the universe rewarded her for choosing to take care of herself."

"Jack from the avalanche, or do you mean her reward is having to do jack-all?"

Ellory peered at him. "Have you never heard the name Jack before?"

"I have and I've met a guest called Jack. But it's also a noun or an adjective." He followed her into the clinic. "Your manner of speaking is unusual. I'm looking for landmarks."

She decided not to comment on that—he didn't seem like a big talker and she had jobs before her. She talked strangely. She dressed wrong. Blah-blah-blah.

"I've been making notes of the supplies I took to the lobby. We'll just write down whatever we need, I'll go tell Mira and you can get the medicine for Chelsea. We should probably start charts for everyone too, but since your hand looks like hell, you tell me what you want it to say and I'll do the writing."

Anson followed her, enjoying the floral wake. The tropical scent reminded him she'd said something about Peru earlier. "Were you on a medical mission before you came here?"

She unlocked the drug cabinet and opened the doors, then flipped on a light above it and pointed at the bottles to direct his attention. "Medical mission? Oh, no. You mean in Peru. No, I was at a…" She looked sidelong at him, her expression growing wary. "I was at an ayahuasca retreat."

The word was familiar somehow, but between the pain in his hand, the pain in his shoulder and the headache he'd been nursing since he'd decided to turn the group around he couldn't place it. "I know I should know what that is, but it's eluding me."

"It's a place you go to have…" She stumbled along, clearly hedging and not really wanting to tell him.

People who avoided a direct answer had something to hide, either because it embarrassed them or they expected disapproval. Which was when he remembered what ayahuasca was. "Ayahuasca is a hallucinogen, isn't it?"

Her sigh confirmed it. "It's not like LSD or hard drugs. It's a herbal and natural way of expanding your consciousness. I went there for a spirit quest under the care of a shaman—someone who knows about use of the plant and how to make the decoction properly. Someone who could help me understand everything I needed to know beforehand. And before you say anything, I'm not a drug user. I don't smoke anything. I only drink alcohol once a year—champagne on New Year's with Mirry. And nothing else remotely dodgy the rest of the year." As she spoke, her volume increased, along with the tension between her brows. "My body is a freaking temple, Judgy McGravedigger."

Anson lifted both hands, trying to put the brakes on the situation before she got really angry. Obviously he'd hit a nerve, she'd gone from quiet and somewhat babbly to angry because he'd called it a hallucinogen. "I'm not judging, but I am curious. And I agree your body is a temple."

Smooth.

When she turned back to her task he focused on the cabinet again and the array of medicines, and changed the subject. "Well stocked."

She went with it and didn't comment on his completely unacceptable remark about her body. "Mirry's a planner. She likes to be prepared for anything. She's always been good like that, never lets anyone down." A clipboard hung inside the cabinet, but where he'd expected to see an inventory sheet had been clipped a single piece of notebook paper, a list of supplies in a scrolling, extravagant script. She picked it up and began writing again.

Mirry? Always been?

Ellory wasn't a nurse…

Sister? "Are you Ellory Dupris?" Anson put the two names together as he plucked one bottle of antibiotics from the shelf and set it on her clipboard so she could get a good look at the spelling and dose of medication.

"Ellory Du…? Oh, no. My name is Ellory Star."

She scribbled down the medicine then put the bottle into a little plastic basket. "You look for any other medicines, I'm going to get the supplies to clean your knuckles up." Before she headed away she turned back to him with a little pinch between her brows. "I'm sorry I made fun of your name. It wasn't nice. But in my defense it's kind of a terrible name. You should change it. Pick something more positive."

Pick something? "You picked Star, didn't you?"

"Yep."

Okay… He'd think about that later. "You do work here, though."

"Licensed massage therapist, which is my primary

occupation, I guess. I've completed training and passed boards to be a physiotherapy assistant in Texas, but I haven't done any office work on it or taken boards here. The closest I came was a mission where the leader had back trouble and I helped her with the daily exercises her actual treatment prescribed…helped her handle being out in the field," she answered, fishing a badge from under her sweater and answering the question that he'd been working toward.

Anticipating. She really was perceptive. And the occupations fit. But then again, she could've said artist, pagan priestess, or tambourine player and he would've believed her. So, a massage therapist who called the owner's daughter and resort doctor 'Mirry.'

He plucked another medication from the cabinet, the mildest prescription-level pain medicine Mirry…Dr. Dupris…had in stock, and put it on the clipboard. "I put another medicine there for pain for Chelsea. Frostbite pain is monstrous."

Shrugging out of his coat, he pushed his sleeves up and stepped over to the sink to wash his hands, paying special attention to the puffy and bloody knuckles. He gave his fingers a few more slow flexes. Burning. Tenderness. But no bone pain. He knew about bone pain, just as he knew about frostbite pain. So she was right, even without having that information at her disposal. Good eye.

"Oh, my God, that's all you…"

He turned away from the sink, hand still under the water. "What's all me?"

"I was hoping that the coat was puffier than it seems to be."

He briefly considered not asking her for clarification, but he needed all the information he could get to keep up in conversation with this woman. "Why were you hoping my coat was puffy?"

"You're seriously beefy. Shoulders a mile wide, muscled. It's going to make working on you hard. I was hoping that some of that was your gear, your coat... I've got pretty strong hands and upper body, but you're going to be a tough case." She'd put a tray on the table, an array of antiseptics, gauze, tapes and ointments on it, and then went to write the medicine on her special clipboard.

"No, I won't. I don't need to be worked on." He didn't mention the compliment. Best ignore that attraction she'd all but said was mutual.

"How's it feeling?"

Good. She wasn't going to push the subject. "Nothing broken but the wall and my self-control. Bruised. Some abrasions..." He dried his hands on paper towels and wandered toward the table. "Maybe a mild sprain." He'd hit the wall hard.

"After you give the medicine to Chelsea, I want you on my table."

"Ellory, I don't need it."

"Suffering for no reason doesn't make you tough, it makes you stupid." She made a noise he could only consider a verbal shrug, "Your shoulder needs working on. If you want that thing to heal up so you can get back out there to find Jude when the snow lets up, let me help you."

He should've seen that coming. Her vocation was one hundred percent hands on, and from what he could tell by having observed her, she was on a mission to take care of the world.

The idea had some appealing qualities. Not the least of which the prospect of having her hands on his body... She might be dressed like a crazy person, considering the season and latitude, and conversing with her might be like running a linguistic obstacle course, but strangely neither of those things made her unappealing. And neither did the revelation about her spirit quest.

But he didn't really deserve comfort, and it was possible that his shoulder would calm down on its own in a little while.

"Maybe later. I should stick around the lobby. Keep a watch on them and the weather."

"Have you seen the radar? The storm is going to be with us for a while, hours and hours. We'll leave one of the radios with your people in the lobby and they can call us if…" The lights flickered, stopping her flow of words and her hands. When the power steadied and stayed on, she continued, "We're going to lose electricity."

"Maybe. We should see about making preparations, on the off chance…"

"It's not an off chance, Anson. It happens in every bad storm that hits the pass. Summer. Winter. Doesn't matter what kind of storm. It's not the whole town, but the lines to the lodge are dodgy, always breaking or going out for some reason. Tree limbs. High winds. Accumulation of heavy snow or ice…"

"I thought you were just in Peru."

"And before that Haiti. And before that the Central African Republic. Before that Costa Rica. But I was born and raised in Silver Pass. I needed to come home after my retreat, and Mira offered me a place to work. I have a history with the lodge. I know what I'm talking about. Nothing ever changes here. The power *will* go out."

"What does a massage therapist do in those places?"

"Dig ditches. Build dams. Distribute food, clothing, or whatever the mission is. And I help at the end of the day when people are worn out and hurting from all the manual labor." She disappeared into the office, and after some mucking around in there came out with a file folder, some forms, and another clipboard. "And there have been a few projects where I ended up with the same project leader, and I think she took me along as much to help keep her on her feet as to help with the actual project."

She left him to clean and dress his hand and made some notes in Chelsea's chart.

She'd grown up at the lodge, which explained why she was on such intimate terms with the owners. "You knew Dr. Dupris growing up?"

"Yes, and before you dig further she's my best friend. I love her more than anyone else in the whole world and if I'm upsetting you by making you help with the skiers, or making you let me help you, you're just going to have to get over it. She's having some much-needed downtime, and I'm going to take care of her people. Right now you're one of them, Dr. Graves. So suck it up, get the medicine into Chelsea and meet me at the massage therapy room. It's three doors down. There's a sign." She locked the drug cabinet and then turned and tossed her keys to him.

He instinctively caught them with his right hand, and regretted it. The combination of flying metal hitting his throbbing palm and the quick jerk of his arm tweaking his shoulder doubled the pain whammy that followed.

"Fine." Not fine. Annoyed. But as annoying as it was, she had a point, and if she could help, he'd make use of her.

"Lock the door when you leave. And turn off the lights. No wasting fossil fuels."

At least she didn't gloat.

CHAPTER FOUR

WHEN ELLORY KNOCKED on Mira's door, she wondered if she would be interrupting something she didn't want to interrupt.

Not usually one to be shy about sex, Ellory could only blame her squeamishness on the fact that being around Anson was making her think naughty thoughts, and now she was acutely aware that she wasn't allowed to follow through with them.

She hadn't specifically said her resolution not to date included no hook-ups, but she was trying to break that cycle as she'd spent her adult life sublimating her desire for love with lots of sex. Safe, sterile sex. So in the spirit of the resolution it had to include hooking up with handsome, inexplicably surly, dog-owning doctors—because Anson and his mile-wide shoulders were the best Fling Contender in Silver Pass.

She scrambled out of the stairwell on the top floor, already avoiding the elevators so she didn't get trapped when the power went off, and jogged down the corridor to Mira's Stately Pleasure Dome.

In the plus column, Anson would never want to date her, so her Stupid Resolution wasn't in danger. He'd already remarked on finding her strange—unsurprising as most people who didn't move in her circles found her odd. Add to that him now thinking she was someone who would use the spirit quest as a reason to go to the rainforest and take drugs...

But none of that came close to touching the biggest block: the anguish she'd seen in his eyes earlier didn't leave room for much thought of carousing.

Even if sex was a really good way to generate heat when the power cut out during a raging blizzard.

Also? Sheer entertainment value. Something else she'd ignore from here on.

None of that helped her figure out how to talk to Mira without being afraid that she was interrupting something special. More special than any sex Ellory had ever had... another reason she was weirded out about it.

Mira had found love. Real love... It wouldn't just be sex Ellory interrupted, it'd be making love—which was probably sacred.

Or, as she'd like to think of it, making wild, reality-shattering love so potent it could mess with physics, the future, the past, and maybe illuminate all those dark places in her heart where negative thoughts and bad feelings liked to hide.

She'd been looking hard for that for the past decade, but it was elusive.

She stopped in front of the carved white door of Number Five's fancy suite and did the unthinkable: She knocked. "I'm sorry, Mirry, I have to talk to you."

The sound of stumbling and doors closing preceded the door opening, and her decidedly disheveled best friend appeared in the frame. "Hey. Is everything okay?"

Bedhead. That glazed look that came with passion that's been unexpectedly shut down. She'd definitely interrupted love...

"I'm so sorry. I just want to keep you informed about

what is going on, and there's some stuff. But I want you to know that I'm handling it, and Anson too. I'm not handling Anson…well, I am a little. But not in a sexy way. I'm still being faithful to my resolution." Ellory stopped talking. That's not what she was supposed to talk about. "The blizzard."

Mira, gaze sharpening with understanding, unsuccessfully tried to hide a smile smug enough that Ellory knew she'd be getting teased to hell and back if Mira weren't likely in a hurry to get back to Jack. "Good to know you're handling Anson. What about the blizzard?"

"We've got missing people. Person. One. The others, the rescue team got back. They were suffering moderate hypothermia but we've got them warmed up and are keeping a close eye on all four of them. One of them has either stage one or stage two frostbite on her toes, Anson said. Did you know he's a doctor too? He's been treating her. We went and got medicine from the clinic, and I've written down—"

"I'll get dressed…"

"No!" Ellory grabbed her arm to keep her from getting away. "It's okay, really. We're doing great…except for the missing man, and you can't help with that right now. One of the guests who was with the rescued group tried to get back to the lodge on his own, and he didn't make it back before the storm, or yet, and they weren't able to locate him before the storm got too dangerous and the visibility too bad. It's impossible to go out right now. I knew you'd want to know, but there's nothing you can do about it right now. Later or tomorrow, if you want to come check on everyone, that'd be great. Anson is tired. I'd feel bad making him do like a seventy-two-hour shift or something."

"Where are they?"

"Still in the lobby in front of the blazing fire, but we're relocating them to the fireplace suites. The lights flickered so I figure we're going to lose the power and then the central heat will go…so I'm corralling everyone into the fireplace suites, employees too. Doubling up occupancy and stuff. Everything is as under control as it can be, there's nothing else you could do. Well, unless you know how to fix drywall."

"What happened to the drywall?" Mira, unlike everyone else in her world, didn't have any trouble keeping up with Ellory's mind—which could be counted on to bear off in another direction without warning during pretty much every conversation. But especially those fraught with emotion and where something unpredictable loomed.

"Anson punched it. There's a hole…"

"This isn't sounding all that under control, Elle."

"I know it sounds all kinds of chaotic, but that's because I'm condensing hours and hours into a few minutes. He's sorry about the drywall, but he's very upset and worried about Jude."

Mira nodded slowly, taking it all in. She didn't even have to ask who Jude was, she just kept up. "The lost skier…"

"I brought you this." Ellory fished a spare radio from her pocket and handed it over. "I know you'll want to be contacted super-fast if there is an emergency. They're all tuned to the lodge emergency channel, and they'll be spread out among the patient rooms and rescuers, so anyone in need of help can get it fast when the power goes out."

Ellory's faith in Mira was boundless, and generally that faith extended to the confidence Mira would mirror her own faith. Not many people did that. No one, actu-

ally. Not right now, at least. But for a few seconds while
Mira considered the radio in her hands, Ellory's faith wavered. "I can do it, Mira. I won't let you down. I promise."

"I know. I know you can. I was just thinking about
whether I'm taking advantage…"

Relief warmed her and she relaxed, a smile returning.
"You're not taking advantage of anyone, except maybe
Jack." Ellory shook her head, covering her friend's hand
as she teased. "And don't worry about the hole in the wall.
I'll get Anson all patched up and then I'll make sure that
he fixes the wall or gets billed for putting his fist through
it when everything is up and running. And speaking of
running, I need to. I have him on my table."

"Anson?"

"He hurt his shoulder."

"With the wall…"

"Well, it was hurt before that. But he made it worse
with the wall." Ellory smiled and gathered up her skirts.
"Don't worry, I'm just going to work on his shoulder. Not
breaking my Stupid Resolution! You're still losing this
year, Dupris!" And since the wing was deserted and she
wanted Jack to hear, Ellory bellowed, "But that's okay,
your Karmic Love-Jackpot Sex Machine Jack sounds like
a good consolation prize!" She backed down the hallway,
smiling as Mira's cheeks went pink.

Karmic Love-Jackpot Sex Machine was a much better nickname than Number Five, even if it took forever
to say. Any man should be proud to bear that title.

Anson unlocked the door to the massage room and
stepped inside, flipping on the lights. It was warm in
there. Warmer than anywhere else he'd been in the lodge,
except rooms that had *steam* in the name.

He pulled the top of his snow suit off again and let

it pool at his waist, then took a seat while waiting. Like everywhere else, it was a deeply comfortable room, with plush chairs, stacks of fresh towels, a line of oil bottles and lotions…and the lingering scent of sandalwood and eucalyptus. A hedonist paradise.

Luxury. Comfort. And he was getting a massage when he should be out looking for the lost skier… No, nothing at all wrong with that.

Ellory had a point about him being in top shape for when the snow let up, but he was wound so tight it'd be a miracle if she could get him to relax at all.

He even felt guilty about wanting to relax a little. His rational mind knew how big this storm was, that if they were lucky it would be over in a day, and that he couldn't spend all the time until then on watch for a break. There'd be no break until it was over. Resting and taking care of the patients until then was the correct course of action.

He'd be doing something, but he wanted to do something more active.

And doing anything kept him from having too much time to think about what the man was going through while *he* was warm, safe, and…resting.

He stood and headed for a shelf with candles. Light the candles, save time.

He also lit a stick of incense propped in a holder, because that probably had some kind of peace-making mojo she would insist he needed.

When he stumbled over a remote control, he turned on music from a well-hidden stereo system.

By the time he'd gotten everything powered up, the door opened and Ellory walked in, pulling back her long, wavy, sun-kissed locks as she did, and twisting them into some kind of knot at the nape of her neck.

"So you do want a massage." She smiled. "Got the candles going for mood lighting, the incense, the music…"

"I was helping. Speeding things up." And now he was making excuses. He shut up.

"Yes, you were helping, but I'm pretty sure there's only one lightning-fast method of instantly relaxing." She closed the door, locked it, set her radio on the counter and began stripping. Off came the coat. Then her sweater… which left her wearing a small white T-shirt that had risen up enough to give him a view of the curve of smooth hip to waist before her arms came back down and she was once more covered. "And while that was completely inappropriate, it was payback for earlier. Don't worry, we're not doing that."

Despite seeing him at less than his best, and witnessing him put his fist through the wall—which he really wasn't proud of—the little eco-princess was flirting with him. He smiled, felt it, thought better of it and stopped. No wonder the woman liked to go to tropical places. Golden, shapely, and not at all what the media would classify a beach body…in the best way.

"Why are you getting undressed, then?"

It might have been years since he had a massage from anyone other than a lover, but he was sure that the only person who got naked was the one getting ministered to.

"I don't want to get oil on my clothes." She tossed the sweater onto the couch. "I'll keep my skirt on and the thermals beneath, but the sweater's sleeves are baggy and tend to drag. Oil would ruin it." A brief pause and she gestured to the opposite corner of the room. "There's a changing room through there, just strip down and wrap a towel around your waist. Underpants on or off, up to you. And I'll get…"

What she was saying registered and he shook his head,

moving to sit in a chair, "I don't need to change. It's just my shoulder."

"Okay. Take off your shirt, then. And your shoes. You're the only one who didn't have your toes checked when you came in."

"I don't need my toes checked," he muttered, that directive enough to pull him out of the fantastic place his mind was going. Perfect little beach body didn't need to gawk at his ugly feet. But now that he'd seen what was beneath the baggy sweater, he wanted to see what was beneath the flowing skirts.

"Shirt," Ellory repeated, done arguing with him for now. She'd work on his shoulder, get him to relax, and then get him on the table. She couldn't fix his shoulder without having full access to his back. It was all connected. Not that she was going to bring that up with him right now. He was a doctor, he knew full well how anatomy and muscles worked together. He was just being a pain in the butt, and there was no reasoning with a pain in the butt. Logic didn't win in an emotional kerfuffle and after seeing his display of testosterone earlier she could definitely say he was having an emotional kerfuffle he didn't want to talk about.

Out of the corner of her eye she could see him complying. Arms up, material moving… She didn't look yet. He may have lit incense, and there might be enough essential oils in this room to gag an apothecary, but with his suit open and body heat escaping, all Ellory could smell was Eau d'Yummy Masculinity.

All she needed was to start undressing him with her eyes. That would lead to her undressing him with her hands, and then her Stupid Resolution would be shot.

Distract him. She should talk about something.

"So, you ever been south of the equator?" And that

sounded like another come on. Because he'd turned her hormones on.

"No, and I've never done drugs with a shaman either."

"It's not like that."

Eucalyptus. That was a manly smell, and it would overpower the warm, salty awesomeness pouring off him. She snatched up the bottle of oil, a couple of towels and headed his way. "Do you want to lie on the table?"

"No."

She rolled her eyes, and didn't even try to hide it from him. He countered with a brow lift. "You can reach my shoulder from here." He did slide forward in the chair so he was sitting at the front edge at least.

In an effort to save his snow suit from the oil, she shook out two towels, draping one over his lap and tucking the other into the wad of insulated material at his waist, then stepped between his legs and reached for the oil.

"The skin on your shoulder isn't bruised, unless it's such a deep bruise that it hasn't come out yet. Is that the case?"

"Doubt it."

"Okay, how did you injure it?"

"Lifting Max. He is good at his job but he doesn't have the greatest problem-solving skills. Got stuck, couldn't jump out..."

"So you picked up a huge dog that probably weighs more than me." She rolled her eyes again. "Next time, just get his front feet or something. Picking up half a dog is less likely to injure you than going whole dog."

"He's my dog. I don't like to see him scared or in pain. I'm a little sore, it's no big deal. I'd do it over again."

"Fine. Anyway, it doesn't look like it's more than muscle strain." She drizzled the oil on and spread it around, carefully avoiding looking at his face. Looking a man in the eye was like challenging him, and she wanted him to feel comfortable, not put on the spot. Besides, if he was feeling as vulnerable about this Jude situation as she knew he was, then he wouldn't want her seeing it. "What should we talk about?"

Anson shook his head minutely, but didn't answer right away. Not until she'd started working her thumbs into the corded muscle on his shoulder. "Your spirit quest." He grunted the words.

Ellory didn't particularly want to talk about that either, but a small amount of explanation could keep him from thinking she'd just gone down there for some excuse to 'do drugs with a shaman.'

"I needed to try and figure something out, and I believe we're our own best healers. Your mind and your heart can heal you if you let them. I didn't want to see a psychiatrist and tell her things I already know, and have her give me some pharmaceutical that might do more harm than good, a pill to dull and pollute. I wanted to get through it on my own."

"Did you?" he asked, and did honestly sound interested. She didn't hear the censure she'd expected. And to his credit he hadn't yet asked what her issue was, maintaining some respectful distance from that subject.

"Not all the way. But I figured out that I needed to come home to get right. It gave me a starting point, and it also filled me with wonder for the universe… It's amazing that the earth gives us plants that allow for this kind of experience. I wish I understood better, but there's too much going on when you drink it. The shaman said it detaches your consciousness from your body, which sounds all woo-woo and like astral projection——something I'm not sure I buy. But I'm glad I went, despite having more questions than answers. Sometimes the biggest part of solving a problem is figuring out what the right question even is."

A soft pained sound escaped when her thumbs hit a particularly knotted area. He tried to cover it with words. "Did you go alone?"

"No. I went with my last boyfriend." She tried to ignore how final that sounded, like the last one she'd ever have and from here on out was a lifetime of loneliness. "He wanted to learn to hold those kinds of rituals so he could lead people in their own quests up here in the States, some retreat in Nevada he wants to work at. But I don't feel like his heart was in it for the right reasons. He was after money, not to help people. That's no kind of cause. So I left him there and came home. Been trying to work on my quest alone since I got back." She paused long enough for him to look up at her, establish fleeting eye contact, and asked, "Do you want to talk about Jude?"

Anson frowned. "There's nothing to say. He's still out there, and I'm getting a massage…"

"So you think you're letting him down."

"Of course I let him down." The admission came through gritted teeth, which either meant her thumbs were causing enough pain to make him grit his teeth or the situation was.

She stopped the deep kneading there and stepped forward until his head touched her chest. "Rest against me, I'm going to rub down your back, stretch those muscles out some. That will make it easier to work on your shoulder."

"That plan has me pushing my face into your breasts." He tilted his head back to look up at her as he said it, but his teeth stopped clenching, which she could only consider progress.

"Consider that a bonus." She smiled, "But if you ask for a happy ending when your shoulder is feeling better, I may punch you somewhere you wouldn't want me to punch you."

He smirked. "That could be anywhere. I'm not a fan of being punched."

"Just of punching. Which is how I know you're feeling worse than you let on."

He leaned forward, burying his face in the valley of her cleavage, and sighed. Still not wanting to talk about it.

"No motor-boating while you're down there either," she said, trying to draw him out of it a little. And it was easy to flirt with him. She hadn't seen a real smile from him yet and it surprised her how badly she wanted to.

Her teasing was rewarded with a little chuckle she felt a rumble through her chest to her belly, and his arms relaxed, elbows on his knees, his hands lightly cupping the outsides of her thighs. The innocent touch set off a wash of good tingles more powerful than his face on her chest. She'd long considered the back of the thighs an erogenous zone...

The tension in his spine lessened. Better. An even better sign that she'd be able to get him to smile later, when she could see it.

Another drizzle of oil and she pressed her thumbs into the muscle knotting the back of his neck, and stroked down along his spine, making little tight circles with the pads of her thumbs when she encountered a knottier area on his spine.

"How are you working on your quest?"

He still avoided the too-personal question, but kept her talking.

"Meditation. Exercise. Aromatherapy."

He laughed for real this time.

She was going to choke him. "Oh, hush, Doctor Man. You know that smell is one of the most powerful memory triggers?"

"So you're trying to recover a memory?" he asked, the chuckle fading from his voice.

"I don't know," she whispered, now that he'd started circling the subject she didn't really want to talk about. But lying was equally distasteful to her. She thought for a bit and tried to tell the truth while not exposing her tender underbelly. "This will probably sound all depressing, and I'm not depressed—I just haven't really been happy for a long time. Not truly happy or content. Doesn't matter what I do, even the highs I've gotten from volunteering and doing good things don't do much or last very long any more. It's started to feel like penance, and I don't know why." Which was part of it, but it still left her feeling vulnerable. She'd been hiding this from everyone.

Anson leaned back again, putting enough space between them to look her in the eyes.

Exposed. She felt exposed the way he looked at her, and aware of an unpleasant cold feeling in her chest. She looked away. "You want realigning."

Anson couldn't read her expression, but he knew a thing or two about living a penance-filled existence. There was such vulnerability to her honesty that it hit something inside him and made him want to help, to fix whatever was making her unhappy. She put on a good show. Had she not said those words to him, he might never have guessed.

"I need realigning," he repeated, no longer sure he was speaking of his spine.

"Right here." She pressed on the muscle that had seriously bunched up just below his shoulder blades, the pain proving her point. "T7 and T8 vertebrae. I can fix it if you get on the table."

She wanted to help him, and he'd let her. Maybe it would help her feel better too. "Fine, but I'm leaving the thermals on."

Her smile reappeared, though now he didn't know how real it was and how much was for show, even though he believed she wanted to help. She stepped back, pulling the towels with her and giving him room to move around. A pause to remove his boots, then he stretched out face down on the padded vinyl table.

Before he could protest she swung one leg over his waist and he was caught by warm thighs and an overwhelming desire to roll over. Her small hands pressed into the muscle on either side of his spine, walking up and down a few steps until the vertebrae reseated with a loud crack.

Task done, she patted his back, climbed down, and left him thankful she couldn't see what the intimate position had done to him.

It wasn't Ellory's practice to molest people she had on her table, but the feel of his solid heat between her legs made her breathless. She grit her teeth to keep her mouth shut, struggling to control the rapid breathing from the surge of hormones.

No matter that he'd spent the better part of ten minutes with his face pillowed on her breasts, he didn't seem bothered by her straddling, as she was. Although she wanted to talk to him about the situation that had put his hand going through a wall, maybe talking should wait... She continued working, tried to ignore the glide of the firm male flesh beneath her hands, and focused on the task.

By the time his arm was moving easily in the socket,

the muscles worked to pliancy, he'd fallen asleep. She heard the slow, rhythmic breathing and ducked under the table to where his face perched in the padded donut-shaped headrest.

This happened a lot. Get someone to relax deeply enough, they fell asleep. And that was when they weren't exhausted and worried from all the hours spent in the horrid climate and stressful conditions. He needed sleep so she wouldn't wake him until he was needed.

Moving to the end of the bed, she pulled his socks off and swapped the oil for some lotion to rub into his tired feet, which was when she noticed them. Missing toes, two on one foot and one on another. He had no pinky toes. Her heart skipped.

Frostbite pain is monstrous.

His words came back to her, brought tears with them that closed her throat. He knew that pain. No wonder…

She slowly bent his leg at the knee so she could see the top of his foot, and get a better look at the damage.

The scar extended far up the top of his foot, stretched out, pale and thin. An old scar. A very old scar, considering how far growth had caused it to migrate from his toes.

He'd been a child when it had happened.

CHAPTER FIVE

ANSON FELT SOMETHING touching his feet and snapped awake. Lifting and turning to look over his shoulder at the woman at his feet was harder, his movements sluggish and stiff. "God, what did you do to me?"

"Relaxed you." Ellory laid his leg back on the table and kept one hand on his foot. He wished she'd move away from them. "Your muscles will be a little slow to respond for a few minutes. You should drink a lot of water today too."

"Water?"

"Toxins."

He shook his head, not awake enough to run the mental obstacle course yet. Instead, he concentrated on lifting up and rolling over until he was sitting on the table.

"Toxins in your muscles get released with deep tissue massage. You should drink lots of water, flush them out. Or tomorrow you might have some mild flu-like symptoms."

"I thought the massage was supposed to make me feel better."

"How's your shoulder?"

Frowning, he tentatively lifted his arm and rolled it around in the socket to check. No catch. Sore still, but no catch meant no shooting pains, which was better than it had been.

He didn't answer her. Waking on the table he'd had no intention of climbing onto had left him feeling disgruntled and angry. And, pushy thing that she was, she'd had to get at his feet even though he'd told her they were fine...

"Frostbite pain is monstrous?" She pointed at the missing toes and looked up at his face.

He nodded. "You don't have to take care of my feet, you know. You can see there's no frostbite there."

"The scar has stretched and moved back from the toes."

He nodded again. She was already getting there. He'd just see how far she could take the logical path without his assistance.

"How old were you? Still in elementary school, I'd say. Unless you still had really tiny feet in high school and they only recently exploded like peppermint in your herb garden."

Anson assumed that meant peppermint grew fast. The fastest way to get her to get off this subject was probably to answer her. "Yes." It was an answer.

And judging by the way her eyes grew damp, it was enough of one.

How the hell had this gotten so out of his control?

"Socks," she said suddenly, and sniffed, then popped into the changing room for a moment. When she returned it was with thick cotton socks, which she pulled apart, threading her thumbs into the toe of one and beginning to work it onto his right foot. "Your feet wanted different socks, and you shouldn't neglect your feet in this weather. Doubt you have any to change into. I usually put these on my patients when they have achy feet and want a wintergreen treatment. Thick warm socks while the rest of your body pains are getting worked on, it's nice."

Anson let her get one sock on, since she'd already started and he was moving with decided sluggishness, and then moved his feet out of her reach and held his hand out for the other sock. "You don't have to take care of me, Ellory."

"You're sad. I don't want you putting your fist through anything else."

"I'm not going to. I'm not sad. The fist through the wall did what I needed."

"Which was?"

"Pressure release. And it helped."

"Your anger maybe, but not your hand or your shoulder. And it didn't make you feel better about being inside and warm while Jude is out there. If you need to talk about it, you can talk. We're in this together, and you're helping me with our patient guests, so I want to help you too. Plus…" She stepped away from him and grabbed the sweater she'd discarded earlier, not finishing her sentence.

"Plus?"

"I don't know." She pulled the sweater down over her head, untangled her hair from the knot she'd twisted it into, and let it fall around her shoulders. "This."

Before he could figure out what she was up to, she'd stepped over to the table, wrapped her arms around his middle and squeezed. She cared, just as she had cared for Chelsea. But it felt good, gentle and warm, and gave him an overwhelming desire to bury his nose in the hair atop her head.

He resisted by tugging her back just enough that she looked up at him. The look in her eyes was anything but pity. Suddenly, all he wanted was to taste her. For a few seconds the world receded—he gave in to instinct and covered her mouth with his own. A small surprised sound tickled against his lips, but she tilted her head at the first brush of his tongue against her lips, opening her mouth to him.

Her scent might've been floral, but her mouth was sweet and fruity, just the barest hint of tartness that made him think of berries. Ripe, juicy, and summer-sweet.

And this was winter.

The disparity seeped through the subconscious need to consume her, and he lifted his head, reluctantly breaking the kiss.

Her dark brown eyes were even more heated than her pink cheeks looked. Those lush lips parted, as moist and inviting as her quick, shallow breaths.

"No, no…" Ellory whimpered, when she realized he was backing away. Every inch of her screamed for more. One kiss would not violate her Stupid Resolution.

Neither would two kisses.

And if he kissed her again now it could still count as one.

Her hands slid up his torso until scruffy beard tickled her palms and she could urge his mouth back to hers.

His tongue stroked into her mouth and she let go of his cheeks and wound her arms around his neck, sagging closer, resting against him, chest to chest.

Strong arms came around her, catching her when every thrust of his tongue made her knees threaten to buckle.

A kiss more intoxicating than a keg.

"This is not good," he whispered against her lips, just as she was about to start tearing his clothes off.

She was confident enough to call him on that one. "Liar. It's better than good."

So much better it was impossible for her brain to begin comparing it to every other kiss in history, none of which had ever made her come close to losing control.

"Okay, not a good idea," he corrected, his voice holding a needy rasp that made her wonder how it'd feel against her ear with sexy whispers.

Which was definitely in the vicinity of violating her Stupid Resolution. "Yeah, maybe."

"Why are you still hugging me?"

She tilted her head and laid it on his good shoulder. "Because you need it. You're in pain and you're a good man. You're worried about…" She jerked her head back and looked up at him again, realization forming due to her mouth running wild again. Ruining everything.

"What?"

"You have a cause." She snatched her arms back and took two big steps back from the table.

"No, I don't."

"You're trying to make the world a better place," Ellory clarified, the realization making her exceedingly cranky.

"I am?"

"Yes, you rescue people from the winter! You have a driving goal! You have a mission in life!" Her stomach hurt. The man was definitely a danger to her Stupid Resolution, and her stupid quest and her stupid everything…

"You are such a strange little thing…"

He didn't get it!

"You're my type!" She pointed a finger at him. "And I'm not supposed to be dating!"

"I haven't asked you out, sweetheart."

And he didn't get it so much that he was joking around.

* * *

Ellory's cheeks had flamed to life when she'd surged away from the table, like she had just discovered she'd been kissing a big hairy spider. "This isn't 1957. Women can ask men out."

His joking eased her enough that some of the wariness left her eyes. She just seemed unreasonably irritated by the fact that he spent half the year helping people who got in trouble in the snow. Especially considering her activities prior to coming to this little special wintery haven had all been aimed at helping people.

He shouldn't rile her up more. He should put a lid on this situation, say whatever it was that would make her relax. But she'd hugged him, she'd rubbed his feet, and then she'd kissed him back... She was so insistent on taking care of everyone, it was kind of nice to see that she had an unreasonable side.

Donning his best flirting smile, he popped his brows up a couple times. "Are you asking me out, Ellory?"

"You're not listening! I can't date you. I have a resolution!"

"You have a resolution, and I'm jeopardizing it by having a cause—which I really don't think I have."

"Yes, you do. And, *yes*. That's... Well, no..." She took a breath, her mouth screwing up in a way he was probably not supposed to find cute. "Having a cause is my type, but that's not the only part of my type." A few seconds passed as she looked to the side, brows pulled together, thinking, thinking... "Never mind. It's just that you're very good looking, and you smell like sex and chocolate...and Sunday morning. And now you have a mission to help others. For a second all that messed up my brain."

He could sympathize—his brain felt equally scrambled. The difference was, he liked it. And he *really* shouldn't. Also, her description of his scent was probably the most outlandish and fantastic compliment he'd ever been given. That overt honesty charmed him as much as her manner of speaking amused him. He shouldn't be feeling this good. His job was unfinished and someone was out there waiting for the cavalry...

Remembering that took the spirit out of it for him.

"But the last piece is that you're like...a normal man."

"And you like weird men who want to be shamans." He filled in.

"I like men who would like me. And you aren't the kind of man who'd like me," she explained, and her declaration grew stronger with every version she repeated. "I'm not your type. So we would never date. You'd never date someone like me. So it's okay. It's okay! Everything is okay. Sorry. I don't process information quietly very well. It's kind of got to be out loud or it doesn't happen. I don't know why. Because I'm strange! Oh, thank all the gods."

Anson opened his mouth to ask what she was going on to decide that she was not his type but a hurried request for help crackled through the radio, a voice he recognized.

He grabbed the radio, "Go ahead, Duncan." The most experienced EMT on the team, Duncan led it during the warm months, but stepped aside in the winter when Anson was around with his miracle dog.

One of the rescued was having trouble breathing. He got the room number where the patients had all been relocated, pulled his snow suit on—it was the only clothing he had with him—stuffed his feet into his shoes and took off out the door. While he talked, Ellory blew out the candles, turned off the lights and grabbed her keys.

Anson made a note to rile her up again later when the power went out…that could serve as hours of entertainment. Ask a question, make a statement, and then just watch her start spitting out random words that would eventually make sense.

Conventional wisdom did say that to learn to speak a foreign language fast, submersion was the key.

The regular fireplace suites were all situated in the same place on the floor plan for each level of the lodge, blocks of four stacked up for several floors.

The patient guests had been split into two groups and settled in side-by-side suites on the second floor—the closest to ground level, which was taken with communal and recreation areas, like the clinic and therapy rooms. With the frostbite to her toes and Anson's ban on Chelsea walking, she couldn't go anywhere without a wheelchair or being carried, so it made sense to locate them close to the ground in the event that the power went out and there were no elevators working. Easier to carry or roll her up one set of stairs than five.

Anson said the gibberish names of two different medicines as they passed the office, and where to look, then left her as he took the stairs to get to the person in distress.

She hadn't written down the medicines. She'd have to do that. This inventory thing could get out of hand fast, and she couldn't let Mira down. His kiss had done a brain scramble on her. So much for resolutions. She hadn't even thought to protest when he'd gone all smoochy on her.

She was officially a weak-willed kiss pushover.

A kiss pushover who was obviously being given more responsibility than she should be.

Ellory had never been an important part of any medical team in a medical crisis before. The knowledge that the rest of Anson's crew was there helped her keep her cool, but her heart still pounded. If she failed to live up to people's expectations now, someone could die.

One of the orange-clad rescuers stood in the hallway, meeting her with an open door, which she rushed through. Anson was already at the window with Duncan and one of the patient guests, who was clinging to the windowsill, his head hanging out into the storm. Snow blew in around him, but even above the roar of the wind she could tell how labored his breathing was.

The group rescued consisted of two males and two females, one other couple, and with Chelsea's missing fiancé Jude still out in the wind, Chelsea was sharing the suite with Nate, brother to the other woman, and odd man out.

"He insists the cold air is easier to breathe," Duncan said, briefing Ellory on what was going on. They'd moved a chair to the sliding window so he could sit and breathe…but in Ellory's estimation it wasn't helping.

"Looks like that thing that happened with me last year," Duncan said, more to Anson than to her now.

How many years had Anson been doing this?

"Damage done to the respiratory system from the cold," Anson filled in, looking at Ellory's stash of medicines and supplies and then pointing to the inhaler she carried. "Pop the seals and shake it hard."

He listened to Nate's lungs again, leading him through breaths that were supposed to be deep but which ended up rasping and wheezing loudly.

"Had you been sick before you got here, Nate?" Anson

asked, the concern in his eyes enough to worry Ellory. She prepped and shook the inhaler harder and faster.

When the man chose to nod rather than speak, she had a clue about how serious the situation was.

Questions flew about allergies, Nate answering with shakes and nods of his head. He couldn't do anything but try to breathe.

Did he have any allergies? Yes. Food? No. Medicine? Yes.

In less than a minute Anson had gotten enough info to feel safe about giving the man the inhaler. He'd also started preparing some kind of injection.

"Nate, Duncan is going to pull you back into the room. I want you to breathe out as much as you can, Ellory is going to puff the inhaler by your mouth and you breathe it in deeply."

Anson looked between her and Duncan, making sure they knew their jobs. She liked it that he didn't repeat himself, didn't give them any extra instructions, just trusted them to handle things. It might not be the right call for every situation, but even she could handle an inhaler.

On the count of three, they all stepped in. While Duncan supported most of Nate's weight, Ellory watched him breathe out, holding his gaze. When he'd gotten out as much as he could, she gave him two puffs of the inhaler as he struggled to breathe in. Anson pushed Nate's sleeve up and injected something into the man's triceps, which he then rubbed to disperse.

His skin was very pale, maybe even a little bit blue— another skin color she could add to the shades that terrified her, right after the shade of Chelsea's poor toes.

Anson flipped the cap closed and handed the needle to Ellory, turned Nate's chair and helped settle him back into it...still near the window but not with his head hanging out.

Long terrible seconds ticked as Anson listened to his chest again, coaching him through the breaths as they slowly began to come easier.

She found herself breathing deeply, trying to breathe for the poor man, and noticed Anson doing the same thing. A quick look around the room confirmed it. They all breathed slowly, deeply, in unison, five other sets of lungs trying to do the work of one who struggled to breathe. All worried. All invested. All hoping it helped somehow. She felt part of something good, like she did on her missions, and it was probably silly since all she'd done was be the gofer and puff an inhaler. Still, it felt good.

As Nate's breathing stabilized, everyone else's returned to normal... And that was what she had trouble letting go of. Not the drama and the fear of his fight for air but how for a few seconds all anyone had cared about was helping make Nate's world better. It didn't matter what kind of lifestyle these people led, they were still people. She didn't even have to wonder what her father would've wanted to happen in those seconds. He wouldn't have batted an eyelid if Nate had died. One less consumer, one less parasite devouring the planet while giving nothing back... She could almost hear the tirade.

Anson closed the window and came around, hand held out to Ellory. She put her hand in his, not thinking about what he wanted. It seemed like the natural thing to do. The warm squeeze of one hand, the other relieving her of the inhaler, cleared up what he wanted. Quickly, she let go of the medicine and Anson, and stepped back from the group.

"Respiratory infection?" she heard him ask Nate, who nodded. "If you're not completely over them, it's not a good idea to go out and exert yourself in the cold. Remember that."

CHAPTER SIX

FOR THE NEXT half-hour Ellory watched Anson listen to the lungs of the other patient guests, and then he made his crew breathe for him as well. He gave the same speech at least four times. Prolonged exposure to severe cold could damage nose, sinus, throat, and lungs when someone was healthy, let alone when they were getting over an infection or illness that had damaged them—as had been the case with Nate. She did very little but follow, watch, and listen.

Well, that and look the man over.

She wanted to kiss him again.

The world was coming apart at the seams, winter and wind and random acts of crazy nature, someone stuck out in it, someone's heart breaking, friends in anguish, and Ellory herself caught in a full-on lust-o-thon with the man who'd taken charge of keeping everyone alive.

The only thing saving her had been the dog. He'd joined their tour of rooms as soon as they'd stumbled over him, and now he kept her company.

She spent most of the time crouched beside the big black fuzzball, petting him and whispering to keep herself occupied. Noting the changes in the rooms. She hadn't been in the fireplace suites in a long time. They'd been remodeled since she'd last been there. They were a blend of the new and the old, modern classy mixed with the comforting classics. But everything was secondary to the fireplaces.

Max was fascinated with her opinion on the décor and the superiority of the lobby fireplace to the ones in these rooms. They were top of the line, the logs looked every bit the real thing, and the hidden burners fed by gas and flames that wound through the wood…but it wasn't the same.

He agreed, wood definitely was better. "You're right. I should probably do some research and find out which one is the worst for the environment. But if we're using a hominess scale rather than the Scoville scale—or is that just about how hot peppers are?"

Real fire and all, but it didn't smell the same. And it didn't talk to you, make comforting noises when the lights went out and the only thing to listen to was the wind.

Anson was saying something…talking treatment. More drugs, no doubt.

"What about the saunas?" Ellory snapped back into the conversation, standing in a room with just Anson, her buddy Max, and the last two members of his crew.

All of them looked at her.

"Steam is good for soothing the respiratory system." She shifted to one foot, half-afraid the people in the room were going to give her hell for even suggesting something natural compared to whatever came from a pharmacy and had the backing of the FDA. "It'd bring in moisture to what's been dried out. And we could put some therapeutic oils into the mist. Maybe some eucalyptus and rosemary…stuff that's anti-inflammatory and good for decongestion?"

Anson smiled at her but shook his head—nicely contradicting himself. "It's not a bad idea, the steam and oils actually sound quite good if you've got the quality oils for it. But moving them into the sauna might put more stress on their systems than would be beneficial. It can dehydrate and they're all probably more than a little dehydrated as it is." He looked at the other two. "Are we pushing liquids?"

A small conversation occurred about drinks and Ellory cut back in.

"We could just do it in a bowl and tent a towel over, a breathing treatment without getting everyone awkwardly naked together in the sauna. And I have good oils. Nothing synthetic, of course."

The lights flickering again had everyone looking up, breath held to see if they went out for good.

"Unless the power goes out and we can't effectively heat water," she muttered, more to herself than anyone else, and suddenly felt chilled by the prospect.

The power would go out. It wasn't even a question of whether or not it would happen, just when. With a little shiver she wrapped her arms around herself and rubbed her upper arms through the coat, which just wasn't pulling its weight heat-wise. Though to be fair, it was probably impossible to keep her body temperature as high as she was used to having it with the clothing she had to choose from.

When the lights firmed up and stayed on, Anson continued his organization. "Get your helpers to start heating more water, and go find something warmer to wear. You're going to need it when the lights go out."

"I'm wearing the warmest clothes I have. I promise."

Anson rubbed his forehead, his words coming in short, clipped phrases. "Get everything set up. Water heated. Oils measured. My guys will run the treatments. Then meet me in the corridor. Be quick. I want to get this done before the power goes."

When had he gotten cranky? With the way things had turned out with Nate and the others, she'd have expected his mood to have improved, but in the last five minutes it somehow plummeted. Her clothes worried him that much? The loss of power?

"Enough for your crew and you?"

"Yes. Not me, but the crew."

"No one listened to your lungs," Ellory pointed out, feeling suddenly cranky herself. He hadn't let anyone look at his feet earlier, granted there hadn't been any *new* frostbite damage to look at, but he also had a problem he hadn't wanted them to see. Was he hiding something else by not letting anyone listen?

"Ellory." He waved a hand, cutting off her train of thought as well as the lecture that had been brewing, "See to it and meet me in the corridor when you're done."

With that, he was gone. And Max went with him.

Of course, Anson just stood in the hall and waited for her, like looming was his favorite pastime. Like she wasn't going to hurry, or maybe she was going to dilly-dally.

Ellory looked at him every time she passed, hurrying to and fro to gather the necessary ingredients for the steam bowls. Big metal bowls. Big fluffy towels. Eucalyptus, rosemary and lavender oils.

She couldn't read his scowl, he could be worrying about the power, but no doubt there was something else—something she'd done, the way his brooding and gorgeous eyes tracked her.

She hurried through her prep, counting drops into empty bowls, left instructions for the amount of boiling water to be added, then hurried to meet him before he had an aneurysm. "So, what's the plan?"

She could think of a good plan. A fun plan. A plan guaranteed to make him relax. A plan involving more kissing. A naked plan! But that would be a violation of her Stupid Resolution.

"To get you properly dressed," Anson answered. Of course he couldn't say Undressed—she'd told him about her Stupid Resolution.

"I told you, this is all I have to wear."

"What about Mira? Doesn't she have anything you could borrow?"

"Mira?" she said. "She's lean, toned and svelte. Have you looked at me, Anson?"

He took her hand and tugged her toward the stairwell. "I've looked plenty when you were ditching the sweater and wearing that…snug T-shirt." It sounded like he had some mix of pleasure and irritation at the memory, but at least she didn't have to actually say she was curvy like a mountain path, he got it. Mira's acceptable clothing wouldn't fit her.

"Where are we going?"

"Your room." He paused. "Where is your room?"

Bossy Man wouldn't be put off this until he saw it with his own eyes. "Fine. But you're not going to find anything more suitable." She tugged him toward the stairs up. "I'm not in the usual staff rooms. I have a guest room because I came late in the season and the staff rooms were already full."

She took the stairs at a jog, letting go of his hand so she could gather her skirts and avoid tripping and falling on her face. His shoulder was hurt. If she fell, no one was carrying her to safety.

Most of the employees being local was the reason there

were so few of the staff on hand for this little adventure. The only ones here were actually living in the staff quarters—those folks stayed even when Mother Nature and Old Man Winter got into a spat.

And she was Mira's best friend, which meant she also probably got a nicer room than she might've otherwise—Mira knew how her living spaces always ended up. It just didn't bother her.

Over the last couple of hours she'd not only decided she wanted a vacation from her Stupid Resolution, she'd come to the conclusion that it was a good idea. Like eating a little bit of chocolate once in a while when dieting helped avoid going nuts one day and chewing your way through the donut counter at the bakery. Moderation was always a good thing, right?

She stopped just outside her door. If she took him in there, he'd know just how big a mess she'd become since coming home, and sex would really be off the table. "Anson, my room is messy. You could just trust me, you know."

"I can handle messy." He held out his free hand for her key card.

She could just say no. Put her foot down.

Make it seem like she was hiding something really nefarious in the room...

Or she could let him in and get it over with.

Since she'd come home her habits had grown out of control. But it wasn't until this second that she realized how out of control she'd become again. Until faced with the prospect of wanting to make a good impression, of having someone look into this intimate glimpse of her life, and the judgments that she knew would follow.

If nothing else, this trip into her obsessively green

existence would help her keep her Stupid Resolution. Find the bright side. Embrace optimism.

Be cranky later.

Find some company that sold environmentally friendly vibrators… That should've been her first purchase when she'd come up with this Stupid Resolution.

With a sigh she grabbed her badge, which pulled double duty as her room key, unlocked the door and stepped inside before turning to look at him. She stopped him following by putting her hand to his chest. "I don't have that many clothes. I could just bring them out to you here."

Anson looked her in the eye, and she looked away. Scared. Was she afraid to be alone with him in the room now? Not something Anson often experienced. People trusted him—which he could argue wasn't the smartest option given his track record—but it still bothered him that she looked afraid. "I'm not going to hurt you, Ellory. My hand hurts, my shoulder hurts…we're locked in here during a blizzard. It'd be extremely stupid for me to try something ugly right now."

She nodded, but the glance over her shoulder cleared it up for him. "When I said it was messy, I meant that I'm…I'm working on a problem I have."

"Your spirit quest?"

"Actually, no. That's something else. I think." She looked nervous again, then groaned. "God, how many problems do I have? I thought I'd gotten over this one! I was fine when I was away, but I come home and then I fall right back into a decades-old pattern that I hate."

Anson reached over and flicked on the lights, illuminating the room behind her, then steered her inside.

He had gone to college, so he'd lived with slovenly

people before. When someone warned him their living space was messy, he usually had an idea what to expect.

That's not what he saw when he stepped into Ellory's room.

There were no clothes on the floor, no empty cups lying about or any real disorder that he could see.

But it was messy.

There were trays on the floor all around the room with different kinds of tiny plants growing in them. "What are those?"

"Sprouts. Please don't step on them," she muttered, stepping around to the closet to wrench the door open, apparently in a hurry now to get this over with.

"I thought you didn't know if you were going to stay? You're already sprouting plants for…a garden?"

He followed her toward the closet, which required some careful stepping: She also had those rickety wooden drying racks located anywhere the air blew into the room from the central heating.

Her hands went up in unison, shrugging to the ceiling. "Eating. They're mostly alfalfa sprouts. I eat them a lot. They're great in salads and sandwiches and Mira likes them so I grow enough for both of us."

"I see." He wanted to ask why, the contradiction between the at times flighty but always proficient way she'd handled herself and the situation so far would've made him want to help even if he hadn't been undressing her with his eyes earlier. But it was another distraction. "Clothes?"

She reached into the closet and pulled out skirt after skirt after gauzy skirt, then wadded up something that looked even sheerer than what she was wearing…and threw it behind her.

"What was that?"

"Nothing!"

And yet her voice seemed to say, *I have candy I'm hiding behind my back that I took without asking.*

The whole thing took a comical turn and Anson found himself unable to keep from smiling at her. Definitely the type of woman every horny man wanted to play strip poker with—hot, and with an astounding lack of guile. "You know, I could reach around you and get it."

She grunted and held her hands up in front of her, which did not deter him at all.

"You don't need to see it."

"Is it a nightie?" He had no business asking that, but the bright peach blush warming her golden skin made him want to tease her more. And possibly convince her to model it.

"It's a belly-dancing outfit."

There was no way to contain the laugh that confession pulled from him. It was the last thing he'd expected her to say. "Do you have a tambourine in here too?"

"It's good exercise, and you can do it anywhere. And it's fun! And it doesn't require special equipment…"

"Just outfits."

"I made them so that doesn't count."

This flighty eco-princess thing was serious business to her. And the mix of sweet, eccentric and vulnerable worked for her. Ellory was definitely one of a kind—a bright spot in the storm.

"You're the first man I have ever met who thought it was funny that I belly-dance."

"I might change my mind if you want to belly-dance for me." He forgot all about the reason for dragging her off to her room. Now all he could think of was: the hot blonde hippie chick was also a belly-dancer.

It was like hitting the idiot frat boy lottery.

He really didn't deserve to see her belly-dance.

And that really wasn't going to stop him from trying.

"I'm sure you could convince me that it's not funny. I have a very open mind. And I like art."

The humor of the situation finally got through to her and she laughed then shoved at his good shoulder. "You don't deserve to see it."

That struck a nerve, and his stomach felt hollow for the space of a couple of heartbeats before he realized that she didn't know what misery he'd caused in his life, so she had to have some meaning he didn't get. "Why not?"

"Because you think I'm an idiot." Her sing-song manner of telling him off made him feel guiltier.

Except that was one thing he was not guilty of. "I don't think you're an idiot."

"Then you think I'm a liar."

"No, I don't."

"You just dragged me up here to make sure that I didn't have anything more appropriate to wear after I told you several times that I was already making the best of things. So you have to think I'm either an idiot or a liar." She closed the closet door and crawled onto the bed again, her only route around him now that he'd blocked her from the closet and the rest of the room was some kind of cross between greenhouse and launderette.

"I don't think either of those things. I left you in charge of my patients, I trusted you to take care of them, and I completely approve of your breathing treatments. You also helped my shoulder, so I think you're probably very good at your job."

"Then why? If you wanted to come to my bedroom, God, Anson, all you would've had to do was say, Hey, want to get naked together? I've got this penis and I'm not doing anything with it right now. Want to see if it's a good fit!?"

Her terrible lines made him laugh again. "You do have the best pick-up lines I've ever heard." And would never in his life use, even if someone paid him and guaranteed that they would work. "You were right, though. I don't deserve to see you in that belly-dancing outfit…or to have any of the thoughts I'm having."

"Why not?" She tilted her head as she looked up at him, an intensity to her expression that made him want to tell her the truth.

"Because Jude is out there. I left him out there."

"So you punishing yourself makes him warmer?"

He knew how ridiculous it sounded, so he shrugged. It was the noncommittal kind of answer that usually got people to drop something when he didn't want to talk further.

"You know, I may not have much to show for what I've done with my life so far—I don't have land, a house, a car. I don't even have a winter freakin' wardrobe." She hooked a finger in his belt loop, which kept him from stepping away, kept him focused on her.

"No. You're unconventional and not at all materialistic. I respect that."

"That's not what I'm getting at. I've been places. And I've seen suffering…" She stopped and swallowed, those expressive brown eyes letting him know she relived those bad memories when she recalled them. "I've learned that the people who survive, they're the ones who remember pretty quickly how to find joy in life. The others might keep living for a little while, but if they give in to the tragedy that has hit them, part of their soul dies. And soon enough they die too. Your body can't continue without your soul."

"I've heard the sayings. A burden shared is a burdened halved. All that. They're nice ideas…but do you expect me to go and tell those people jokes and make them laugh?"

"God, no. The last thing they needs is to think you're not taking this seriously. You have other resources, though. If you take joy where you can find it, that doesn't diminish your worry about Jude, or the unfounded guilt you're feeling because he's out there and you're not. It's okay for you to smile, and even if I protest about you teasing me about my belly-dancing, it's a good thing. And not only do you need it, but it's like an alternate fuel source. Good feelings can keep you going so you can actually get out there and look as long and hard as you need to in order to find him. You need it."

"Like I need hugs?" It was hard not to agree with her when she was standing right there, somehow making him feel better.

She nodded, and when he smiled rewarded him by lifting her sweater and the other layers she wore beneath it. His gaze dropped to the soft little tummy and he watched her slowly roll through the abs, activating one at a time to produce an undulating wave that…wasn't even a little bit funny but still made him feel good.

CHAPTER SEVEN

THE TOP OF his snow suit was still open, and while the branded insulated clothing she tried ever so hard not to covet might keep him warm, where it stood open down the front heat poured off him. She could probably go outside in her ridiculous clothes and survive the terrible winter if she cuddled up with the man.

For a second she remembered that the cold had hurt him, though. He wasn't invulnerable. In fact, she was increasingly certain that he was more vulnerable than he could even admit to himself.

She dropped her sweater and stepped forward, taking the opening given to slip her arms inside the suit with him and wrap them around his waist. Just one more hug. One more squeeze. One more pressing together of two bodies in need. He wouldn't mind...

It took Ellory tilting her head back and chancing a look up at him to make sure he didn't actually mind, though. His arms had come round her.

What she saw on his face made her belly flutter and her heart race—terrified and excited. He had that look, the one that split time equally between her eyes and her mouth. The man was going to kiss her again, thank all things holy. She wasn't out on this ledge by herself, the idea appealed to him too.

He had been to her room, had seen the disarray that went with her everywhere, had had a glimpse of the chaos she was currently swimming through, and he *still* wanted to kiss her.

Maybe.

He might be looking at her mouth but he was taking his sweet time about it.

Another look from eyes to mouth, and now the kind of frown someone only used when they were either concentrating or...

"If you have to try this hard to psych yourself up to kiss me, then forget it!" She let go, pulled her arms from the warmth inside his suit and made to step around him—using his belt loops again, though this time to keep from falling since he had her blocked in.

Before she got her first foot placed, his hands were in her hair, catching her head as he leaned down and covered her mouth with his own. His fingers, which had just a hint of roughness, massaged the back of her neck and sent goose bumps racing down her arms, neck and chest.

The first kiss had been good. An appetizer, a bite snuck from dessert before the main course. But this meeting of the mouths sent a tremor racing even more potent than the first streaking through her. If she bathed in champagne, Ellory couldn't imagine a more potent eruption of tingles dancing over her skin.

Instinctively, her fingers curled into the loops she'd snagged and she pulled closer, using him as an anchor.

She didn't even have the will to make excuses regarding her abandoned resolution. All she knew was the heady pleasure of soft lips contrasting with the light scrape of stubble, the strong arms that had wound around her, and heat.

He tasted even better than he smelled—better than

anything she'd ever had in her mouth. Sex and chocolate, yes, sinful and decadent. But there was no hint of the indolence of Sunday morning now. Some time in the first heartbeats after his lips had touched hers, an urgency had taken them both.

His tongue stroked against hers, deep in her mouth, and her belly clenched. Desire licked through her, so strong it was all she could do not to tear the suit off him, get her hands back on that firm, glorious male flesh.

Firm and demanding, his hand slid under her sweater, seeking skin, fingers splaying across the small of her back. He felt it too.

She was ready to rip her clothes off, his clothes off... permanently swear off clothes! All she knew was that she'd never had a kiss bring her to life before. Make her forget her problems. More importantly, she'd never had a kiss turn her on without her actively trying to get turned on by it...and picturing kissing her daydream man in her head.

She opened her eyes, hoping to see that intention mirrored back at her, but the room was completely dark.

The power had gone out.

"Told you," she whispered, pulling his head back down so that she could punctuate the words with a soft little kiss. "Lights went out, or I went blind."

He chuckled against her mouth, even though he knew he had to stop this. After one more kiss... Sliding his hand out from beneath her sweater—where it had no business being anyway—he wrapped his arms fully around her, crushing her soft body to him, soaking up every sensation, every piece of information he could before he gave up kissing her...

She wanted him as much as he wanted her, but she

was a distraction…and a comfort he didn't deserve. It was unjust, at least right now. Maybe after the storm passed, after they had found the man and returned him to his loved ones alive…maybe he could pick up this raging attraction again. After he earned it.

He lifted his head, swallowed, and slid his hands on her shoulders so he could put her away from him a little bit. "How are we going to get out of here without stepping on your garden?"

His reason for coming to her room had been… "And the snow suit!" He cleared his throat, glad she couldn't see him yet. And that he didn't have to see her. The passion he'd glimpsed on her face the first time he'd given in to temptation and kissed her was almost too much to bear. The power being out now was a blessing. "Where's the snow suit?"

"Under the bed." She sighed the answer and crawled onto the bed at his side. "Stay there until I get the light." Apparently she'd picked up on his shifting mood. Which would make things easier.

Some clatter followed, and then the sound of cranking as she wound the eco-friendly lantern and cast the room in blue LED light. "Go sit down, I'll get it out. I'll bring it to the fireplace suites with us, but I am not wearing it unless we lose the fireplaces. It's really itchy and bulky and ugly."

Anson stepped over a few of the shallow sprout trays, made his way to a chair and sat to watch her crawl under the bed and carefully drag out a canvas duffel bag, somehow managing to keep from upsetting anything in this kooky ecosystem she'd built in her room.

When she righted herself, her cheeks glowed once more. He'd have said it was exertion that had caused it if she looked at him anywhere but the eyes.

Embarrassed.

That hadn't been his intention, though considering the way he'd dragged her to her room and questioned her ability to dress herself...okay, maybe he could understand the feeling. "It can't be that bad."

She shrugged and dragged it toward the door.

Rising from the safety of his chair, Anson took two big steps over the Ellory obstacle course until he stood in front of her, making her pause in her exit, and once more wrapping himself in that fruity floral cloud, and grabbed the massive duffel bag at their feet. "I'll carry it."

After dropping off Ellory's duffel in the suite next door, Anson entered the one saved for him and Max and found the big furry Newfoundland lying by the fire some thoughtful person had already lit, trying to keep ahead of the cold. His faithful companion stood and ran to meet him, tail wagging.

"So this is where you've been." He talked to his dog a lot. After he crouched and gave the big lover a good scratch, he found his way to the sofa and sat, leaving Max to return to the fire. As great as he was in the snow, he loved a fireplace.

Anson couldn't blame him, but after the trip to Ellory's room he knew one thing for certain—she gave out more heat than gas logs.

And he had no right to that heat.

On his last round to check on the rescued, Chelsea had shown him a picture of Jude. An engagement photo. Two smiling people with the future shining in their eyes...and he hadn't had the heart to ask her anything else about her missing fiancé.

He didn't need more motivation to want to find the man. So much of this situation echoed his own wintery nightmare. What he wouldn't have given for the fire in those days when he'd been so cold he hadn't wanted to move at all. The gaps between his snow suit and his skin had allowed the heat to build in pockets, and those pockets left the second he'd moved and the material had pulled tight.

All his hope had filled these small spaces, and all it had taken had been a muscle twitch to dispel it. Right now Jude was holding onto a thread of hope growing thinner and more brittle with every frigid breath he'd drawn since this morning.

A knock at the door brought him back to the present. Max lifted his big shaggy head and looked at the door. A couple of sniffs of the air and the search dog's big tail began beating the carpet.

No calls had come through on the radio, so it wasn't an emergency. He'd like to ignore it. Go to sleep. God, he was tired…

Anson peeled himself from the sofa and made his way to the door. Max beat him there.

"I see how it is." He ruffled Max's ears and pushed him back so the door could swing open.

Ellory stood behind a stack of sprout trays, arms straining to carry them. Her warm brown eyes met his over the spring-green shoots, and she smiled. He couldn't see her smile, but he saw the apples of her cheeks bunch and merriment in her eyes.

She kicked the duffel bag he recognized, and the stuffed thing flopped through his doorway to land on his feet. Heavy. Big. It took up as much room as at least two of his suits. Max sniffed the hell out of it.

"I need to bunk with you," she said, the strain from carrying the trays down several flights of stairs and long corridors showing in her voice.

Anson grabbed the bag and hurled it further into the room, then grabbed the edges of the bottom tray to relieve her of her portable garden.

"No. Your shoulder is hurt. Just move." She refused to let go, but since the way had been cleared she stepped forward to come in.

"No," he repeated back to her, and lifted, forcing her to let go. Once they were in the room, he placed the trays on the counter. Which was when he noticed two other bags swinging from her shoulder. She didn't travel light...

She closed the door and dropped her bags.

"Let me guess," he said, looking at the sprouts. "You're here because you changed your mind about that belly dance."

"Nope." Ellory looked the tiniest bit guilty then. "I can't bring myself to have a wasteful fire all to myself. And no one else would understand if I brought the sprouts and crashed in their pad. They'll be ruined if I leave them in my unheated room. I don't really know anyone else well enough to include them in...this. And...well, you kissed me. You like me. I like you." Max barked at her. She hadn't paid him any attention yet, and he wasn't having it.

"And I like you too, Maxie." She caught his front paws in the chest and roughed up his ears with the kind of affection usually reserved for someone's own pet. "I'm sorry I left you out. Go and tell Anson you want me to sleep over! Go tell him!" She pointed at Anson and Max dutifully ran to him, tail wagging hard enough to clear a table, tongue lolling out of his mouth. Happy panting.

"What about your resolution?"

"I'm not asking you to marry me, Anson. I'm not even asking you to curl my toes and make me forget that my enviro-OCD is out of control again, or whatever else is wrong with me that made me think coming home would fix it." Edging around the sofa, she dropped her other bags on the floor and took a seat there in front of the fire. "I just want to share space. And maybe I'd like to spend some time around a wild man who puts his fist through walls…and his dog."

As soon as she said the word "dog" Max came and flopped down on her, then rolled so he was on his back and his head propped on her thigh, all but demanding belly rubs. Anson briefly considered doing the same thing to her other thigh, but having it known that his dog had better moves than he did was just too much for his ego to handle today.

"Max clearly wants you to stay." Anson wanted her to stay too, he just wasn't into admitting that right now.

"We should move the bed over by the fire." Ellory didn't sit yet, but Anson did.

"It's not that cold in here. For people dressed better. You should put on your suit."

During the hour since Anson had kissed her lips and made her feel like she was drowning in champagne Ellory had devised a plan.

Or, well, she'd *un*-devised part of her plan. The whole point of her resolution had been to remove distraction and give herself the attention she'd normally pay to a relationship, so she could work on herself. Figure out what was wrong with her. Figure out what she wanted to do with her life. Traveling was getting old. She wanted to settle down, but she didn't want to lose her ideals in order to build a life.

Tearing off Anson's clothes and dragging him to bed wouldn't change any of that. It wouldn't solve her problems. It wouldn't make them worse. If anything, it made her more acutely aware of the fact that they were waiting for her. And they would still be waiting for her when the skies cleared and the power came back on, and Anson was no longer stranded here with her.

"Or we could go to bed and be warm under the blankets. I brought my quilt, it's really warm and snuggly." Temptation lit his eyes, but was chased out by that deep scowl she'd come to loathe. "Or you could go to sleep by yourself and I will go spend time with Mira and the patient guests. She's come down, by the way. You've got some free time to sleep if you want it. You look like you need it, and if you aren't into chasing away demons for the next few hours in the manner we'd both enjoy, then you should sleep."

She thought a second and added before he could protest, "Better now than when the storm clears and you have to go back out after Jude."

"No argument here." He untied his boots, kicked them off and stripped out of the suit as he walked to the bed.

Ellory watched until he was under the blankets in his thermals, at which point Max gave up his spot by the fire and went to curl up on Anson's feet on top of the fluffy duvet.

After she spent some time making sure everyone got fed, she'd get some sleep too.

On the couch. She'd already made enough moves on the man. The next move was his.

Ellory awoke after a long night of lumpy sleep on the couch, burrowed beneath her quilt with her head propped on one of the cushions and Max panting in her face.

"Good that you woke up. I think Max was about to wash your face. With his tongue," Anson said from where he sat, using her duffel stuffed with the snow suit from hell like a beanbag chair in front of the fire.

The dog's tongue was exactly the last thing she wanted on her face this morning. But after the way the night had gone, and the fact that she was sleeping on the couch when she'd much rather have been sleeping beside big warm Anson...well, Ellory didn't wake up feeling chipper.

Rolling over so she faced the couch back, she pulled the quilt over her head to block out the smell of dog mouth and ignored both of them.

When the power had gone out, Mira couldn't be kept out of things any more, so in theory Ellory didn't have anything to do this morning. No duties to perform, nothing to organize. And as guilty as it made her feel to be glad about that, she figured she'd probably handled things as well as she could for as long as she could. Two straight days of organizing and keeping everything under control was too much responsibility and decision-making for her.

Besides that, yesterday had felt like it had been weeks long.

And today still felt like yesterday, however that worked out.

The smell of food filtered through the quilt now that Max wasn't breathing on her face. Eggs. He was making eggs somehow. Could you cook with gas logs?

She closed her eyes tighter and tried to ignore the scent.

Her stomach growled.

"The storm is still going." Anson spoke again, apparently not satisfied with her attempt to cocoon herself away from all contact. "But the kitchen staff brought up breakfast. Scrambled eggs and toast."

So he hadn't cooked.

But someone else had. Someone she wasn't mad at. Someone whose food she could eat.

She was mad at Anson? The realization startled her enough to bring her up out of her quilt.

She took inventory. A frown, but nothing teary going on in the eye department. A desire to hide out, sleep some more and guilt him over his great sleep... A martyr complex about her own sleep, which had been anything but restful.

She *was* mad at Anson.

Weird. She rarely ever got mad at anyone. So rarely she couldn't remember the last time she'd gotten angry about anything. When someone disappointed her, she usually just got sad, and then moved on.

No matter that she'd playfully threatened to punch him yesterday, she had never engaged in any sort of violence. But now? She might be able to do something aggressive. Like throw something at him. Pelt him with scrambled eggs.

Well, she just wouldn't think about him. Do whatever needed doing. Ignore him.

Mira probably needed help anyway, and she'd have to sleep at some point...so maybe Ellory wasn't off the hook anyhow.

She crawled out from beneath the quilt, stood and shook it out, then carefully folded it before draping over the back of the couch.

"Not speaking to me today?"

No. Not speaking to him today. She pretended he was talking to the dog and went about getting her stuff together. She dug a fresh skirt from her bag, and then another... As they weren't as substantial as yesterday's barely substantial skirt, she pulled them on over the unflattering long thermal underwear she'd been wearing since yesterday. She hadn't brought any clothes-drying racks with her, naturally. And there was no hot shower. No sunshine. Because winter sucked, and winter in Colorado sucked even more.

She pulled on a fresh sweater, yanked from out of her collar the braid she'd worked her long hair into before sleeping, and went to wash up.

However they'd been cooked, she'd eat the damned eggs. Whatever realizations she might've come to last night seemed much harder to follow through with this morning. It took concentrated effort not to wonder where the eggs were sourced—or any of the other ingredients.

They were probably from chickens full of hormones, just like she'd felt she was since the grave doctor had grumbled into her life: full of hormones.

Sighing, she grabbed a handful of sprouts from the bin from the third-day ready-to-eats, rinsed them and sat at the table, her back to Anson.

This would teach her not to prepare ahead of time for these types of situations. With the predictable nature of the power to the lodge, she should have been making and storing granola bars and trail mix, dehydrating fruit—just doing something besides growing sprouts...

Max came around and rested his chin on her knee, giving her big sad eyes.

Okay, half of a sandwich for her and half for Max. She pulled the sprouts off his half and handed it to the dog, who took the sandwich and ran off to eat it.

"He has already eaten."

Well, he'd just eat more.

Ellory took a bite of her sandwich in silence.

"Did I do something to tick you off?"

Yes. Probably. She just wasn't sure what it was.

Maybe it was the rejection. Or the double kiss and run. Or the couch.

"I'll take the couch tonight." He pulled out the other chair at the table and sat where she couldn't ignore him as effectively.

She finished with her current bite before even trying to answer. It'd be the height of irony to be killed by foods that she usually avoided because they were bad for you. "Don't bother. I'll find another room." There, she was even proud that she managed to speak in a completely level and natural-sounding voice.

Anson gave a low whistle, leaning back in his chair until it tilted on the back legs, and linked his hands behind his head. "You really are mad."

CHAPTER EIGHT

MAX CAME BACK for more and Anson set himself back upright, snapped his fingers and pointed to the fire, and the dog obediently went to lie down.

Ellory took a big bite of her terrible sandwich and considered giving the rest to the dog.

"Did something happen that I'm not aware of?"

"Probably."

"Did I talk in my sleep?"

"I don't know, I didn't spend the whole night watching you sleep," she snapped, getting more and more worked up as he pumped her for information—obviously not feeling the same courtesy to refrain from badgering her that she extended to him. "I might be struggling with my compulsiveness about my carbon footprint and about what I eat, but I'm not a psychopath, a sociopath, or any other path that I can't think of right now."

"Did you have a bad dream?"

Not deterred.

Why was he not deterred? Did people yell at him all the time? Was this how he liked to communicate?! "I don't know. I don't think so. I don't think I slept enough to dream anything of significance." Ellory pushed the plate away and went to get more sprouts. Eating the sprouts didn't feel like punishment.

"The couch is uncomfortable." He offered another incorrect guess.

"More comfortable than the ground," she muttered between fresh, crunchy bites.

"What does that mean?"

"It means I sleep on the ground all the time. So if I can learn to do that, I should be able to sleep on a cushy couch in front of a fire. Well, a fake fire. The hissing sound it makes...and this place smells like gas to me all the time, even though I know the gas can't be leaking—the fire would burn it up."

"So the gas kept you awake?"

Like he could fix that if she confirmed it bothered her. Ellory thought about doing what she liked to do—go silent and brood or punch things—but talking about the fireplace was better than talking about the real problems. "Yes. And some other stuff."

"What stuff?"

"I really don't want to talk to you about it. You've seen enough bad things about me, and to give you credit you're handling it better than most normal people would."

"I haven't seen any bad stuff about you," Anson said softly, shrugging. "You keep saying that I'm normal. The insinuation being you're not normal."

"Yep, that's the insinuation." She stopped there, shrugged and shook her head. The only word that came to her was even more negative than usual. Broken. She felt broken, and with no idea how to fix herself. No idea how to learn to be content...

"Quirky. Free-spirited," he filled in when she didn't finish the thought.

Ellory grunted, stuffed some more sprouts into her mouth and resisted the urge to throw them at him. She might not have anything remotely natural to eat if she gave in to the urge to smash them in his face. "Stop sucking up."

"Something must have changed in the night."

But somehow, as they talked, she got less irritated with him. Even though she didn't want to tell him anything. Which was when it became clear. "I came home for a reason, because I have to figure out what is wrong with me and fix it. Instead, I had some kind of compulsive relapse, and I told you about it! I told you more than I've told anyone else about it. I haven't told anyone what's going on with me. I told Mira that I needed to spend time working on myself, but not why. But I've been open and all that with you. I hoped that you would open up to me too. But you didn't. You won't even admit that you are upset about anything. I can't help you if you won't even talk to me at all."

Anson righted the angle of his chair and linked his hands on the table, his eyes staying fixed on her even if she couldn't read them right now. "What makes you think you can be of any help to me? Or that I need help in the first place?"

"Please," she intoned, running a little water into a cup so she could water her sprouts and at least be busy doing something while he gave her the third degree. "I'm on a quest too, even if I'm not currently 'doing drugs with a shaman in the jungle.' I can recognize a fellow traveler when I see one. You have the look. You're searching for something…"

"The only thing I'm looking for is for the storm to pass so I can actually go out and search for that man."

She said the man's name even if she knew how it made Anson react. "Jude." Immature of her to say it, but she couldn't help herself.

"Yes, Jude." He bit the name at her, his voice finally

rising from the calm, detached doctor voice he'd been using on her. "And I will be fine again once I can go out there and find him."

"Fine. You're fine. You're perfect and great. You punch the wall every time it storms." She poured the rest of the water into the sink and ate another pinch of sprouts for good measure.

"Do you feel better?"

"No, of course I don't feel better! You can't make me *un*-mad at you by basically saying I'm dumb for being concerned about you." She shook her head, eyes rolling. He was just being obtuse on purpose, she knew he was smarter than this.

Max stood up in front the fire. Now that voices had been thoroughly raised, he was becoming upset. Ellory watched him rise up to sniff Anson's face, and when satisfied he was okay come to sniff her. "Down." She lowered her voice and petted his head then shoved him gently but firmly to the floor.

When she spoke again, she kept her voice level, for the sake of the dog. "For the record, I'm not mad about the couch, it was a symptom. Not mad about the food. Not the weather. Not the hole in the wall. I'm mad that I shared something with you that I haven't shared with anyone—even my best friend. I thought that we were bonded or something after yesterday. But I felt lonelier last night than I think I ever have while in the same room with someone. So, yes, I'm not feeling my sunny self. I'm disgruntled and I'm going to find somewhere else to stay. I shouldn't have invited myself to begin with. I'll be back for my stuff."

She stepped behind the chair she'd been sitting in and scooted it back under the table—keeping things as tidy as she could was the only way to deal with the amount of clutter she traveled with. Then she slung on her coat, dug into her bag for clean socks and her boots, and left barefooted. She'd put her shoes on in the hallway, or somewhere else she couldn't feel him watching her, glowering at her. Somewhere Max didn't follow her around, looking worried.

So he didn't want to sleep with her. So what? Lots of men didn't want to sleep her. And he didn't want to talk about how he felt about Jude or how he'd lost his toes. That was his personal business. Her focusing on his emotional well-being was probably just her using him as an excuse not to focus on her own emotional well-being anyway. And a danger to her Stupid Resolution. The heart of her resolution was about fixing herself…and there was no difference in the level of distraction between dating a man and fixing him.

She didn't want to tell him anything about her past, though, which was stranger than anything else. She was like an open book, or she tried to be. People asked her questions, she answered them. She didn't lie. She didn't conceal. Not usually. She had flaws and she embraced them or tried to change them, but she didn't hide them. Until now. Until this problem.

She hadn't been lying to Anson when she'd said she wanted to be content, she wanted to be happy. She just didn't know what exactly was standing in her way.

All she did know after this morning was that she needed to talk about it. As much as she didn't want to give her best friend something heavy to carry when she was supposed to be enjoying new love bliss with Sex Machine, she had to tell Mira as much as she knew.

She could only hope that putting the words together would give her access to the information her conscious mind had trouble getting at.

* * *

Ellory made her way through the circuit of rooms, knocking on doors, checking on staff, and worked her way back to the patient guests' rooms, with Chelsea's room her last stop. Mira was there, the two of them in front of the fire, talking in low tones to avoid waking Nate.

She snagged a chair from the table and as quietly as she could moved it over to where the two women sat, forcing as much chipper as would be appropriate, and making her greetings in whispers, then added to Mira, "Your relief is awake, so you can go off duty and get some rest again. Where's Jack?"

"I can stay a little longer." Mira gave her a long look, no doubt picking up on her fake chipper. "Jack has already gone back up to the suite, you just missed him."

"I wasn't really looking for him," Ellory admitted, "Just thought you might like to get back to him." And then she focused on Chelsea. "How are you this morning? Is there anything I can do for you?"

The small woman shook her head. "I'm hanging tough, as Jude likes to say. Dr. Dupris and I were talking about how we knew we were in love."

"Oh." Another conversation that she couldn't really participate in, though at least this time it wasn't because she was being excluded.

She just didn't have anything to add. She had never been in love and she'd never claimed to have been in love, but who kept track of that kind of thing? Would Mira put it together? Should she be ashamed of that? Was that something she should admit?

Now she'd found something else she didn't want to tell anyone. All this hiding had to stop.

The other two repeated their tales for her. The way his voice could make her heart flutter, the way her belly flipped when he looked at her, spending the whole weekend in bed together and refusing to even answer the phone and be apart for a minute… Stories full of smiles and epiphanies, details burned into their memories.

Having shown her the way to tell this particular kind of story, Chelsea fixed her with a hopeful smile, expecting a similar one.

Ellory could only shrug. "I don't have a story like that."

When both women looked a little sorry for her, she added, "I have sexy stories, but this is probably not the time for those. I also have lots of feel-good stories about weighing malnourished children when they were finally starting to put on weight. I can tell you about the sounds of the rain forest at night and stories about food I stopped asking for details on…because it might involve bugs. They're good stories, just not the 'I knew I loved him when' sort."

Mira was a wonderful doctor, she knew just when to push and when to hold the line, and although the smile she gave Ellory said she would get it out of her at some point, she gave her a pass because of the people around.

Mira tried to change the subject, and Ellory wanted to let her, but she had joined their conversation for a reason and it seemed like as good a moment as any.

"Mir, I haven't been entirely honest with you, hiding something…which is probably making it worse."

Mira glanced at Chelsea and then looked back at Ellory. "Do you want to go somewhere else to talk?"

There was a suggestion in her tone, and Ellory realized only then that it might give Chelsea a bad impression. "Chelsea's already seen some of it," Ellory murmured, and then looked to see if the woman wanted them to go somewhere else.

"What did I see?"

"I apologized for the cocoa," Ellory said softly, then refocused on Mira. "You know how a few years ago my attempts to…be environmentally responsible got a little…out of control?"

Mira nodded, a thoughtful frown on her features. She summed it up in one word. "Preservatives?"

She meant the cocoa. Ellory nodded. "And, well, the sprouts. The clothes washing in the bathtub and drying on racks in my room, never using the lights or…well, the electricity in any way I have control over…"

"Is that why you wanted to come home?"

Mira sounded confused, which Ellory couldn't blame her for. She ran on instinct more than anything else, probably because she had such a hard time identifying what she actually felt at any particular time, let alone being able to explain it.

"That was the spirit quest."

"Right." She nodded, and like a good friend and doctor she asked questions, gathered information to make a treatment plan. "How long has it been bad?"

"Mostly since I came back. I didn't know exactly what I was working on at the time of my spirit quest. I just was looking for…contentment, and an indication of what I was supposed to be doing with my life. The only answer I got was that I needed to go home…so home I came."

A knock at the door preceded Anson and Max strolling in, there to check in, no doubt. Her stomach bottomed out, and she looked everywhere but at his eyes.

"I just wanted you to know, in case I've been extra… eccentric lately." She focused back on the two women, and Max came to nose at her hand until she petted him. "But we can talk later. I'm sure Dr. Graves wants to… do his rounds."

* * *

With everyone in a holding pattern until the storm let up and no emergencies currently happening, Anson and Max had nothing to do. Except wonder about Ellory. And why she'd fled upon his arrival. How could she be that mad at him?

"Actually, if you don't need me, I have something to discuss with—" Anson didn't get through the statement before Mira waved him off.

Time to put an end to this quarrel, whatever it was.

By the time he got Max out the door, Ellory was nowhere in sight. He hit the stairs on the chance that she'd gone back to do that moving she'd threatened him with.

How had she gotten so wrapped up in his life—in his mind—in twenty-four hours?

When he'd lain down last night, it hadn't been with the intention of hurting her, or making her sleep on the couch. Hell, he hadn't even meant to sleep so long, just a nap to recharge. But his body had had other ideas.

He and Max caught up with her and followed a few steps behind, all the way to their shared suite and in behind her. She went for her bags first.

"Put those down." Anson gestured to the couch. "We don't want you going anywhere, Max and I. You want to talk. Let's talk."

"Is this some kind of trick? Don't think I won't move just because you make it sound like Max needs me." She blotted her eyes with her sleeve, turning her face away from him as she did. Crying? What had escalated things to crying level?

"No trick." He closed the door behind him and decided to give her a moment to breathe. "Let's move the mattress in front of the fire, like you wanted." Physical things were easier to take care of, and the action gave him time to think.

Moving the couch and furniture out of the way was easy enough. By the time he'd moved to the bed she'd joined him, and together they lugged the unwieldy thing to the cleared spot in front of the fire.

Max thought it had been put there for him, naturally, and ran over to lie down in the middle.

"No, Max. Go lie down." Anson ushered the big dog off the bed, then bent to unfasten his boots so he could shed the snow suit and be a little more comfortable on the floor bed. It also gave him an excuse to get under the quilt with her once she'd settled with it. "What were you three talking about?"

"I already talked a bunch."

"Okay. Me first." He pulled her against his side and anchored an arm around her waist. "When I was ten I was lost on the big mountain for several days with my mother during a storm," he said without preamble, since it seemed like the easiest way to start this story.

She looked up at him, her eyes going unfocused beneath frowning golden brows. Not really looking at him—that was the look of someone searching her memory. Did she remember hearing the story? Had he become a tale told to frighten local children into right outdoor behavior? It was something he never talked about, so the idea had never occurred to him.

"Did you hear about that?"

She shook her head. "Maybe...I'm not sure."

His relief surprised him.

"We crawled under a ledge to get out of the snow. The ledge wasn't small, but it was very close to the ground. Too close for us to do much besides lie there on our backs and wait for the storm to pass. It took a long time. By the time it was past I was drifting in and out of consciousness. My mother…she died."

Ellory looked down to where his legs disappeared beneath the blankets and with one hand she found his closest foot. By chance it happened to be the one with the most damage. The one she'd been looking at in the massage room before he'd kissed her.

He felt her hand curl around the remaining toes and squeeze, but she didn't say anything. She just rubbed his disfigured foot, which he'd really rather she not touch at all—he didn't like anyone touching his feet.

Before he could stop her, she'd snagged the top edge of the sock and pulled it down and off his foot. Anson had to work not to say anything or stop her. Not that she was going to say or do something cruel, but he just didn't like how exposed it made him feel to open up about this stuff, to let someone see the mark of his shame.

She wouldn't know that part. He hadn't told her everything.

"You touch everyone," he said as her hand curled over the decades-old scar.

"Yes. I touch everyone." She finally spoke as she caressed his foot and leaned her head on his shoulder. "People need to be touched in order to be healthy. Touching heals and…" She started to say something else but stopped short.

He'd finally started to understand most of what she said without asking for clarification, but when she left off thoughts entirely, he still needed help. "And what?"

The woman was like an exotic creature he had no chance of understanding if he didn't ask all the questions that other people would leave alone.

"That's how I express love."

That sounded like a declaration. Only it couldn't be,

they barely knew one another. And she touched everyone. Compassion. She meant compassion.

"I can't imagine how alone they're all feeling right now, even if they're in it together. Especially Chelsea. The man she loves is still out there because he wanted to save her. I want her to know that I feel for her and that there are people here who want to help her through this if she wants the help," Ellory murmured, but she didn't sound like herself. "Sometimes it's harder for someone to hear words than just to offer your touch and presence for them."

Like she was touching him now. It was still all about how he was doing, making him feel connected to someone and better, whether or not he deserved her compassion.

"It's good. I had teachers in school who made a point of telling some...well, a good number of the students to touch their patients."

"All book, no heart?"

"Something like that."

She may be all heart. Based on their fight earlier, he knew she wasn't just sad for him and the patients. She was struggling too. He held back telling her more, and pretended it was in case he should need to barter the information with her later, because he really needed to know why she was crying. "Why were you crying earlier?"

Her eyes warmed again, giving Ellory warning that tears were imminent. She laughed. "So annoying, you can just mention tears and they spring right back up." A sniff and she swiped her eyes again, mentally cursing her lack of control.

"Only when you've stopped crying because you're avoiding what upset you." The gentleness in his voice helped. At least it pushed away the embarrassment she felt as the result of tearing up.

"Mira and Chelsea were talking about being in love," Ellory began, trying to find words that fit what she felt so she'd actually know what she was thinking. "These moments of insight when they knew they were in love..."

Anson's arm came around her again and gave a squeeze—encouragement to talk, not that she needed encouragement, she just needed words. It was sweet anyway.

"Started thinking about someone you lost?"

If only that were the case...

"No. I realized I never loved any of the men I have been with. Not one of them. I never had that realization of love." She couldn't look at him. The confession sounded terrible enough to her without seeing disgust or something worse in his mossy green eyes. "Which is horrible, I know. And makes me sound like a—"

He shushed her. "It doesn't make you sound like anything."

"Not something bad? Because you'd think I would've loved some of them, they were all perfect for me in some way. We were..." She started to claim they were just alike, but the words sounded false. "We had a lot of the same ideas and beliefs. And they were always doing something good. And they taught me..."

Anson let her work through things at her own pace. She tended to work through things out loud, and he suffered her pauses with patience she only recognized when she'd fallen into her thoughts long enough to make him prompt her. "Elle?"

"I know why I've fallen apart since I came home."

He could hear the disgust in her voice, and it was all

Anson could do to keep from dragging the information from her.

"What did they teach you?"

"They taught me their habits. We usually lived someplace where simplicity was the only option, and I just did whatever they did. If they had fruit salad in the morning, that became my routine too."

The sigh that came from her was so forlorn his first instinct was to change the subject. Don't make her dig that deep—he hadn't dug that deep for her earlier. The difference was he knew how he felt, he knew what had happened, he knew what he'd done. He'd examined it all so many times the memories barely made him feel anything any more—except shame.

But it was clear her process was one of discovery. Not something to be shut down. Clean out the wound so it can heal.

"Whose habits are you following now?"

"My father's. And they keep invading what I do. Like when I was apologizing for the cocoa. That was a habit he gave me."

"How so?"

"When I failed to follow the rules in some fashion, his favorite punishment was a diet of junk food. Because if I behaved like the rest of the parasites on earth, I should eat what they did so at least I'd not live very long. Some kids got grounded, I got fast food, the greasier and more processed the better."

Anson felt his mouth fall open. The psychological warfare of that made it horrifying. Other kids would rejoice to eat candy and snack foods, but if she'd been raised believing that they would kill her—and that her father wanted to her to die young because she didn't live up to his expectations... That was a special kind of twisted.

"There are a bunch of ways to live the kind of life I need to live, but I come here and I fall into this pattern of extremes. It's ridiculous that the place I love more than anywhere on this earth turns me into a basket case. I want to stay, but I don't know how I can if I can't get control of this. Figure out how else to be. Relax my rules. Or actually just figure out what *my rules* really are. Right now, central heat feels like a gateway drug! It's not even something I can control here, but it's like some slippery slope that's going to make me give up my beliefs or compromise my ideals. So I push to the other extreme, as hard as I can, and..."

Her words died, but he knew it for what it was now: where her epiphanies dried up. She burrowed closer to him and he tightened his arm, for once uncertain of what to do, or even to say to help her.

Max finally picked up on the tension in the room and invited himself to the bed with them, where he could plop his big heavy head onto where their knees met.

Ellory took it as a request to be petted, and obliged him, comforting the dog who wanted to comfort her. It was exactly what they were doing—a cycle of comforting and no one fixing anything.

"Change one thing you're doing," Anson said, the only solution he could come up with that didn't involve putting his fist through something living and infinitely more deserving than the drywall.

"What thing?"

"I don't know. The sprouts. Get rid of the sprouts." It was the first thought that came to him.

"But I like the sprouts."

A gust of wind rattled the window, timely and a reminder. "Get a new snow suit, one you'll actually wear." There was a ski shop downstairs. She could do that immediately, which would give him some peace of mind.

"We're not dating, but how is that any different than me just adopting your habits?"

"It's not just my habit. My habit is an orange reflective snow suit. A regular suit is the habit of everyone who hits the slopes during a Colorado winter." He strenuously avoided using the word 'normal.' She didn't need those kinds of comparisons right now. "You get a suit so you'll be better protected, and you'll be changing something small. And I'll do something for you in return. I'll do... spirit quest stuff. Just no drugs."

"Ugh, stop calling it a drug. It's a natural decoction," she grunted, pulling back so she could look him in the eye. "You'll do spirit quest stuff if I get a new snow suit?"

"That's what I said." It might not solve anything, but it was something that they could do that might let her feel like she was helping him too, which balanced the margins. She didn't need to know his margins could never actually be balanced.

"You could also look for a job once the storm passes. I know a few centers I could recommend you to."

"I don't know if I want to work at a center. Regimented schedules are hard for me."

"Okay. Then make some plan. Come up with what your ideal situation would be if you decided to stick around." He wanted her to stick around, God help him.

She laid her head back down on his shoulder and resumed stroking Max's snout so he'd stop making big sad eyes at them both. "What are you going to do for upholding your end?"

"You tell me. Where do we start?"

"Meditation."

The rest of the day passed at a lazy pace. No emergencies dragged them out of their meditation, and Anson only really left when it was time for him to make another round to check on everyone. Just because no one was in a state of life-threatening duress it didn't mean he slacked off on his duties. They all ate together, and Ellory managed to make something that didn't send her into an OCD tailspin. Mira provided a key and Anson helped her pick out a snow suit from the shop—not too big but big enough to hold in some heat—and set his mind at ease.

When watching the fire got old, they spent time in front of the window, watching the snow swirl and blow.

And he held her hand. All the time. When they were alone in the room, Anson held her hand. She always had known that touch healed, reminded you that you were part of something bigger, a way to share strength. She'd always believed those things, even if she didn't feel it as deeply as she wanted to.

But as they sat by the fire, saying nothing, his support flowed into her and carried away the loneliness she'd been feeling since…always.

As night came, Ellory felt content for the first time in a long time. It probably wouldn't last. Maybe not even the night, but it was a start—like glimpsing the end of your journey while still on the mountaintop, with days of hard travel still to make.

With their thermals still on, they stretched out for the night, Anson's big body behind her, matching her bend for bend, his arm around her waist. "Wake me up if you have bad dreams," she said over her shoulder, then settled down to the smile-inducing feeling of his nose burrowing into her hair.

"I should get it out of the way. Braid it."

"Don't you dare," he mumbled, his arms tightening.

CHAPTER NINE

ANSON LET HIS eyes close and tried to make his body relax. She felt too good, she smelled too good—especially in this position, where he got the sweet, natural scent of her beneath the long sun-kissed honey locks he'd like to wrap himself up in.

So he'd managed to avoid kissing her today, which didn't mean much considering where they'd ended up anyway. People who weren't already feeling intimate didn't cuddle. Two people who just happened to be sharing a bed and who didn't want more than that…they lay with as big a gap as they could between them.

"This is a joke," Ellory muttered, pulling thoughts right out of his mind. "I can't sleep like this. If you don't want me, if you don't want to want me, or whatever, then I should sleep on the couch."

"You're not sleeping on the couch." And, by God, neither was he. Anson sighed into her hair, keeping his arms around her.

Ellory looked over her shoulder at him. "You know what I would be doing right now if we *were* dating and you were being this big of a brat?"

"I'm not being a brat."

She snorted and then beneath his hands he felt her

tummy do that roll thing again, which pushed his thoughts further down that path they should not travel.

"You're the brat."

She rolled her tummy again. "Did you know there are a whole bunch of ways to move your tummy and your hips? It's about controlling muscles, not just the abs but accentuating the movement of the hips and the curve from waist to hip."

"You're playing dirty."

"I haven't even begun to play dirty." She laughed and then did something with her hips that rubbed that firm round little tush against his groin. In an instant he was hard, and just like that he stopped caring whether or not he deserved her attention and the amazing womanly body pressed against him. He had it. If Fate was making a mistake, then Fate would be to blame.

Except…

"I don't have condoms."

"I do!" She scrambled out of his reach and leaned off the mattress, one hand on the floor so the other could reach her bag and drag it over. The position gave him the best view of her backside, and before this second he'd have never said thermal underwear was sexy.

"Your thermals are too snug. They're supposed to be loose to keep you warm…"

"Shhh." She flung condoms at him, and then started peeling those thermals off, starting with the top.

The room was fairly warm, but as the shirt whisked over her head, he could see that she was a little chilled. The shirt landed on the floor and she was about to strip right out of everything else, her thumbs in the waistband of her leggings, when he grabbed her by the hips and dragged her back to him on the bed.

"I get to take those off." After he kissed her. After

he got to explore the gorgeous flesh he'd already been granted the pleasure of.

As he slid her beneath him, Ellory reached for the hem of his shirt, pulling it over his head. While her confidence might be hit or miss in other areas of her life, one thing she'd never had a compunction about was nudity—her own body or the nude bodies of others. With the kind of life she led, there were a great many communal activities, and her actual between-missions job was massaging frequently naked bodies...

Since the minute Anson had yelled at her and dragged her inside from the cold, she'd been trying not to think naughty thoughts about him. Seemed like forever had passed since then. She might not have the most accurate concept of time, but she was pretty sure that her massage of his shoulder and back had lasted three whole years. And in the intervening years since she'd had him on her table—yesterday—she'd missed the sight of him.

As soon as the thermal top was off, she did what she'd been itching to do since the start and ran her hands over his chest, lightly scratching her fingernails through the whorls of dark hair that danced over his glorious torso.

"You're beautiful." She hadn't meant to say that, but the smile he gave her made her glad it had slipped out... so glad she almost said it again. Instead, what came out was, "Let's take off your pants!"

Anson laughed again and pinned her hands above her head, levering himself over until his deliciously manly chest and belly flattened to her own.

But one kiss, and the playfulness was gone. The third kiss was the charm. In the space of a single heartbeat her thoughts turned as chaotic as her body became needy.

Heat.

Hunger.

And on the horizon the likelihood of hurt. Nothing good could come of this. It was not dating. It wasn't a relationship. It wasn't anything except the moment.

Forbidden fruit, the allure of what could never be.

His tongue dipped into her mouth and he let go of her hands so he could lean off her again and remove her bottoms, every inch of flesh exposed burning with awareness.

Under any other circumstances she couldn't have him and he would never want her. But right now he needed someone to lighten his load and she needed to feel connected to someone—that's what they'd be to each other.

Being the leader meant keeping up appearances to those who looked to him for something. All Ellory could think to look to him for right now was some relief. And maybe being able to save him from something, since she couldn't freaking figure out how to save her own damned self.

She was just the life raft.

And that was okay because under any other circumstances she wouldn't...well, she probably just wouldn't want to want him. The idea of actually not wanting him was so far removed from what she felt right now that she couldn't even really picture it.

He kissed and licked his way down her chest, with detours to kiss and suck. When his teeth scraped her nipple she thought she'd come apart, the growing tension the only thing that held her broken pieces together.

Even knowing this man was a recipe for betraying herself and her way of life. A gorgeous man with a cause, and standing. And who knew what else? His lifestyle was a complete unknown. He could be the picture of everything she'd hate. But with the way he made her feel she had to consider that he'd still be someone she'd change herself for. Her mother had changed for the love of her father. Even as a child, Ellory had understood that.

She'd tried to change and make her father love her too—but he still didn't. He never could, just like Anson never could. She'd never been able to fit into her father's world, and she couldn't fit into Anson's. The best she could manage was a short stay in this twilight zone version of it. The lodge was a deserted island, a bubble away from the rest of the world.

So he wasn't really a violation of her resolution. This wasn't dating. It was sex.

The desire she felt for him might leave her feeling like a virgin on the cusp, but it was still just sex. Just sex. Much-needed sex, sure, but still… Just. Sex.

As he kissed and licked his way over her belly to her breasts, the extreme appetite she'd developed for him took over. Lifting her legs, she hooked her big toes into the waistband of his thermal pants and dragged them down, causing his erection to spring free.

Her toe tracked over a scar on his thigh, which she registered…something to ask about later, when stopping wouldn't kill her.

Everywhere his mouth touched her skin became heated. Something she'd never experienced with her past lovers—this need. She ached to the point that the whole thing was becoming unpleasant.

One hand shot to the side, where she thought he'd dropped the foil packages, and half felt, half banged around on the floor. "Condom…condom." She panted the word. When he lifted to look at her, there was a question in his eyes.

"I don't doubt you'll remember. And this isn't a date. And neither of us thinks so, right?" And with her brain functioning at half-power she added, "I'm not supposed to have babies."

He reached for one of the condoms she'd pelted him with, bit into the foil, placed it over the head of his shaft and unrolled it with one stroking fist. The bruised knuckles even thrilled her. There was something incredibly erotic about watching his muscled arm complete that motion, and she was never so happy to have massaged someone in her life—gods only knew how this would go if his shoulder still hurt like it had.

His hands fell onto the mattress at either side of her and he lowered himself until they were pressed together again, his sheathed heat between her legs, though he made no move to enter her yet. "Why aren't you supposed to have babies?" The words were an effort for him to speak, every one carrying an edge of tension and urgency.

Had she told him that? "Uh. Well…because I'm not supposed to be alive."

She grabbed his head and tugged his mouth back to hers, needing his kisses like she needed air. He pulled back long enough to look at her, a question on his handsome, scruffy, three-day bearded face, but to her relief he didn't ask. Instead, he reached between them and glided the head of his erection over the little nub begging for his attention, and then drove into her with a single thrust.

She arched, lifting her hips from the bed, pushing against him in such blatant wantonness she kind of shocked herself, but he wasn't moving yet—just holding her, pinned by his big body and the frowning concentration in his eyes.

"Don't look like that," she muttered, wiggling her hips again to try and spur him on. "What's wrong?"

"You will explain yourself to me after we're done." He gritted the words through clenched teeth.

Ellory groaned then slid her hands down his back to squeeze his clenched butt as he held himself motionless inside her.

"Say it."

"No." Already flushed and wanting, the heat that stole over her face now was of a very different sort: anger. She was mad at him again. "This is cruel."

"Say you will explain it when we're done or we're done now."

"No."

He began pulling away. The madman meant it!

"*Fine*," she growled, now really wanting to hit him. "I'll tell you but this is blackmail."

The savage smile he gave her made her want to hit him even more, but he pressed forward, filling her again and then establishing a rhythm she was too thankful for to remember to be angry.

Bracing her feet against the bed, she lifted her hips to push at him and he took the hint, rolling with her, letting her be on top. There would be no more withholding anything from her if she was in control.

She'd just stay sitting up, it was a little bit of distance because he was a big hunky jerk and he didn't deserve the full-length loving.

But within a few measly heartbeats she'd leaned down to kiss him again, and his arms locked back around her waist, chaining her to him so tightly that she could feel the instant their heartbeats synchronized. Not every beat, but as they moved it became obvious to her that they were meant to be there together—two heartbeats that overlapped for short intervals that gradually became one thunderous, unified hammering as they built to a climax so fierce and pure she could have cried.

Ellory believed in fate, and that sometimes things were meant to be. She and Anson, here in this moment, was bigger than her pitiful needs, desires, or resolutions. Their hearts beat together.

She could only pray hers kept beating when they came apart again.

The curtains had been drawn before they'd gone to sleep, the extra layer of wind protection also keeping it mostly dark in the room.

So it wasn't the light that woke Ellory. It was the foreign sound of the fireplace clicking off. That hadn't happened since they'd moved into the suite. The wind had been blowing hard enough that the thermostat in the fireplace fought constantly with the wind to keep the room warm.

But not Ellory. She had a big warm man behind her, wrapping her in heat, and a big warm dog on her feet, keeping them warm.

Max lifted his head to look at the fireplace, which gave her an opening. She rolled to face the sleeping doctor, who had at some point put his shirt back on. She found the hem and slid her hands inside over the firm male flesh and the crisp tickle of hair against her palms.

Anson awoke to the feeling of Ellory pushing his shirt up. His chest was bare by the time his mind cleared and he lifted his arms enough to let her push the warm material over his head.

"I need skin. Why did you put these back on?" she grumbled, her voice just a little bit raspy from sleep. Sexy.

Just like that, he woke up.

She nudged him until he rolled to his back and she rolled with him, straddling his hips in a position that reminded him of last night's activities and made his body respond—intentions forming.

Wiggling around a little, when she was satisfied with the bare chest-to-chest position, her head turned to press her cheek into his shoulder and her nose up under his chin. "Just so you know, we can have morning sex and it still doesn't mean we're dating. We're still not dating, we're just comforting each other."

"So your resolution is intact?"

"Mmm-hmm."

He grinned, his hands stroking over her bare back, having not really had the time to luxuriate in her body when they'd been together before.

The sound of silence cut through the sexy haze settling over his brain. No hissing from the fireplace.

No wind.

No wind!

Light reflected up onto the ceiling in a pink band above the curtains.

"The storm…" He rolled her off him immediately and stood up to look out the window. Deep snow, at least five feet, had been dumped on them, but it was calm now and reflected the soft pink hue of sunrise.

Ellory joined him at the window, pulling her thermals back on. He didn't look, he was still waiting for his body to catch up with his brain and give up on the idea of sex so soon after it had become ready for it.

"It's over?" she asked.

"We can go back out."

Ellory looked toward the brand-new snowsuit laid out like a deflated person-shaped balloon on the sofa. She'd already purchased the thing, not wearing it would be even more wasteful than wearing it. Plus, if she wanted to go out with the team and help look for Jude—which she really did—she'd have to put it on.

While Anson was on the radio, waking everyone up, Ellory got dressed in her new gear.

"You have to eat something before you go out there."

"The kitchen staff are going to make breakfast now," he said, turning to look at her by the door. "Where are you going?"

"I was going to talk to Mira for a minute before we go out." She said the words casually, hoping he wouldn't pick up on her meaning until she was actually out with him and he couldn't…

"You're not going."

Do that…

"I want to go." He should know how badly she wanted to go considering her getting dressed in the new—and worrisomely awesome—snow suit. "I want to help."

"I know you do." He sighed, scrubbing a hand over his face. "But Mira is going to need your help. Chelsea isn't going to want to leave, but with the snow past, you can get her and Nate to the hospital. Have Mira call for a chopper or maybe another crew to come up. Do they have a snow coach or something here? Multi-passenger? Preferably enclosed. I'd rather keep Nate out of the cold wind as much as possible and Chelsea can't wear her boots while her toes are swollen."

Ellory frowned. "Mira's a doctor too, you know. She can handle this stuff. Plus she knows how things work here and I don't. If I come with you, I can maybe get places you couldn't. I'm smaller."

"How big is Jude?"

Okay, she didn't know how big Jude was. He could be Anson-sized for all she knew. "Probably bigger than me."

"It's dangerous out there. I don't want to have to worry about you too."

"If I stay with you—"

"Ellory? I'm not having your life on my hands too. That's how it is out there. I have to find the one who is lost and keep my crew and Max safe. That's seven lives on my shoulders. I'm not adding to that weight with one more person who won't be of any help and who I don't need."

She flinched and hurried out the door before he could say something else negative. No, she didn't know what she could do, but it was doing something. An extra pair of eyes would be helpful. When she was just here, just waiting for them to return, it had been bad enough when she hadn't even known him.

Even when someone was as on the ball as Mira was, it took time to ready the snow carriage to transport patients down the mountain. If they waited until tomorrow the workmen would've had time to inspect the cables leading from the resort down to the town, but just jumping into an aerial carriage and hoping for the best would've been colossally stupid after the couple days they'd had.

Since Mira was doing the organizing, she waited with Chelsea. "How are you doing?" She dragged a chair up to Chelsea's wheelchair and sat, offering a hand should the woman need some support.

"Bad," she admitted, and then took Ellory's hand. "I know that I need to go to the hospital, and Nate needs to go too—we probably all need checking over, but I want to stay. Even with the power situation as it is, I just want to be here for the instant that they find him."

Her hand felt dry and tight, still chapped and rough from her time in the storm. Spotting a bottle of lotion across the room, Ellory stood and went to get it. She made a conscious decision not to check the chemicals, poured some into her hands and set about rubbing it into Chelsea's hands, working the muscles as she went.

"I pray that they find him today, but if they don't, we'll make sure you get regular updates."

"Regular updates?" Mira said from behind her, having entered quietly. "Absolutely. I've got my cell and I will call your hospital room several times a day to keep you up to date." She gestured to what Ellory was doing and asked, "Almost done?"

"Yes, just rubbing the lotion in. Are we ready to go?"

"They're out plowing the lot now and someone shoveled a path to the snow carriage, so we can go as soon as we're ready."

Anson had a plan, but he didn't have a good feeling about it. Normally, out on the mountainside, doing his job, he felt peace. There was purpose to it, the extreme focus and need to push himself cleared his mind of anything else. Even the cold air he breathed exhilarated him.

Today every breath burned, both going in and out. Which was how he knew it was in his head and not him coming down with whatever Nate had been ignoring for his ski vacation.

There was no thrill from zipping around the mountainside on his snowmobile, though he usually loved it. Snowmobiles triggered avalanches easily, and because the day before the snow front had arrived had been sunny and warmer than usual, it had weakened the snow supporting the thick, deadly mantle they were all riding around on. Even without them making any mistakes or pushing any limits, that layer of snow could slip at any time.

Six people on his crew meant he had enough to split up in to three teams and work on the buddy system, driving far enough apart that if the ground started to slip it was less likely that both searchers would be swept away in the snow, and all were wearing locator beacons in case the worst happened. Even Max had one on his collar.

Anson looked behind him in the mirror again and caught sight of his buddy, and then Max's big head filling up the rear view, panting in that way that looked like a smile.

Having the Newfoundland with an insanely talented nose made their searching easier.

Anson stopped outside South Mine, got one of Jude's shirts from a plastic bag he carried, and opened Max's cage. By the time his search buddy reached him, Max was already snuffling the shirt and taking off for the mine. Both rescuers grabbed their lights and followed him inside, but the dog didn't stay.

Jude wasn't in there.

He sniffed in a circle in the entrance, and then headed back outside to sniff the air, looking for an air trail to follow.

The wind was blowing from the northwest—the direction of the lodge—and Max got nothing. No excited yips that would indicate he'd found a trail.

Anson pulled his radio off his belt and called it in. "Search team one at South Mine. It's clear."

The radio crackled and it became immediately clear that Ellory was still considering herself part of the search, even if he hadn't let her come out.

"What does that mean? Where are you going now? Did Max pick up which way to go from there?"

She didn't even know how to use a radio properly.

"No, he didn't. Would've been hard considering the storm, hard winds and deep snow."

"Oh."

He heard the disappointment in her tone. And since he'd already disappointed her once today he added, "If he found a scent, it would probably mean Jude was outside in the snow, and that would be bad news. The other teams are going by foot through the woods to try and pick up his trail where we couldn't search. And to hit the cave between. We're going northeast."

"But that's away from the lodge."

"I know. I'll call when we've reached the next stop."

He ended the communication and stashed his radio again, getting Max back into his cage to go.

He'd probably given her false hope. If the other two teams didn't find Jude where the snowmobiles had been unable to travel, it was unlikely they'd find him alive. Everything else was outside the direction he should have traveled, which was why they were heading off in the wrong direction.

That's where he and his mother had gotten lost: Down the wrong side of the mountain.

CHAPTER TEN

Twilight had ended thirty-seven minutes ago, which meant it was officially dark. So dark Ellory could probably see the Milky Way if she looked long enough.

They were supposed to stop searching when it got dark. It was a rule. The other two teams that made up Anson's crew had returned to the lodge, but he and Marks? Still. Not. Back.

Ellory didn't need to ask why they weren't back yet. Anson was pushing it to the last possible moment in order to find the missing skier. Or past the last possible minute...

Because they hadn't found even a trace of Jude. Yet. Yet, yet, yet. She mentally scolded herself for her pessimistic thinking. As angry as she'd gotten while waiting for them to return—and being mad at Anson again just underscored the fact that they were incompatible—she knew Anson would be beating himself up more than she could ever stand to do.

With the snow that had fallen the risk of avalanche was incredibly high. The teams had managed to trigger two different small slides today without getting trapped in them, which was why they didn't bring in a helicopter for air searching yet. They'd been lucky that the slides had happened in areas where there weren't caves or mines where Jude could be hiding.

Headlights bouncing off the blue night-time snow told Ellory they were back, and no one else would have to say boo to him about being out there after dark. She was going to confront his handsome and well-toned ass, and she didn't even like the idea of it.

In her new suit—which she loved even more after a couple weeks of Colorado winter in equatorial clothing, she stayed inside the breezeway leading to the lobby, opening the outer doors from the inside when Max got there, and then again when the bipeds caught up.

"It's dark," she said to Anson, who stepped past her and into the lobby, making a beeline for the fire she'd kept stoked for them. "You are supposed to be here before it's dark. When it's still light out. To travel safely... *more* safely. Two slides! Two in one day."

She put a bowl of warmed water down on the floor for the dog then grabbed two big mugs of cocoa she'd been keeping warm and forced them on both men. "Drink this. And say you will be back earlier tomorrow."

Anson took the cocoa thankfully and drank it down fast enough that she once again felt compelled to apologize for giving him food with preservatives in it. Maybe they'd preserve him longer if he got trapped in a freaking slide tomorrow. "We checked in."

Sure, but after dark, and the only way that would've comforted her was if he'd also kept up a steady stream of running chatter on the radio while they'd been driving back, so she'd know from second to second that he'd still been alive. "Not recently."

"Elle, I can't talk and drive at the same time. It's treacherous out there."

"Yes. Yes, it is." She puffed and took a seat, making

herself calm down before she actually did yell at him. He looked haggard, worse than he had that first time she'd seen him, and he'd been grappling with the idea that he had lost his first person on the mountain overnight. And put his fist through the wall.

"Tomorrow more crews with their own dogs will be here. Mira called up everyone she could think of when we were getting Chelsea and Nate down to the hospital. We passed power crews working on the poles and the power should be back on tonight or tomorrow," she informed him. "Two of her toes had sprung big blisters this morning, so they've confirmed that she has stage-two frostbite on two of her toes. But they've got a treatment plan and said it's very unlikely that she'll lose them."

He nodded, still grim but happier to hear some good news. Because the window where they could hope to find Jude alive was rapidly diminishing. She couldn't even think about what that would do to him.

"The original rooms in the lodge, the first ones built, still have water heaters that run on natural gas. Mira showed me today and we all had baths. You can have a hot shower to warm up. I'll take you to the rooms. But the rooms are pretty cold. No fireplaces there so dry, dress and get back to your real room so you don't get pneumonia or something."

She led them to the rooms they'd been using, steering Anson toward one and leaving Marks for the other, pointing out that fresh towels had been put on the bed for him. And repeating her warning that he not dawdle.

"Are you okay?" she said to Anson, as they and the dog stepped into the room. She'd lit candles in there earlier. They'd been burning since the first staff member had gone to shower, so the room was not nearly as chilly as she'd expected. Max hopped onto the bed and lay down.

Anson sighed and shook his head. The admission surprised her. "I don't think he's alive. And what a coward I am. I didn't want to come back here and have to tell Chelsea. The others... I know they're all close. I can tell the other two..."

"They all went down together. No one wanted to wait here."

"Because I can't find him?"

Ellory stepped over and helped him with his suit, knowing how stiff and useless your fingers got when you'd been in the cold too long. "No, because they want to be with Chelsea and Nate. And Mira and I both promised them that we would contact them if the situation changed, and Mira is taking lead on contacting them several times a day anyway, just so they expect to get updates and all that. Waiting is murder."

"You have no idea."

She wanted to ask, but the wound seemed too raw right now. Instead, she just continued helping him undress. And once he was in the shower she undressed too and joined him under the spray. It was dark so she couldn't see what he was feeling by looking at his face. The best she could do was distract and comfort him.

If she was honest, that wasn't all it was. She needed a little comfort too.

By the end of the second day of searching the power had come back on, returning them to the twentieth century, but the broadband was still out, making rejoining the twenty-first century still a goal. Anson and Ellory remained in the fireplace suite they'd been using for the extra heat the gas logs provided. And she didn't feel at all bad about the carbon—not because she was adopting the habit of her current boyfriend, he wasn't her boyfriend, but he needed the heat. He needed it, and that was enough to keep her from focusing on the negative.

By the end of the fifth day, no matter what she tried she couldn't get him warm when he came in.

The hearty and thick lentil stew she'd made didn't warm him.

The showers he took were so hot they left him a vigorous shade of pink, but still didn't manage to cut through the ice that had settled in his core. When he stepped out of the steamy shower or bath he got cold again.

Worst of all—the sex failed to heat him up too.

Bleak, fast, and over too soon, Ellory felt blistered by the haunted look in his eyes, even at climax. She'd have sworn he didn't want her there with him at all if every night he didn't wrap himself around her on the mattress that still rested before the perpetually burning fire, and burrow beneath the thick duvet and her quilt.

Even when the heat he surrounded himself with made him sweaty and miserable, he still shook when he slept. He still said he was cold.

The sex was supposed to help him sleep, but it didn't. He remained stiff behind her, except for the constant low rumble of shaking that seemed to come from his chest and shoulders.

They both avoided mentioning the elephant in the room: everyone's worry about how long they would be able to search for Jude, and when would it be called off or considered pointless?

Putting the thought out of her mind, she rolled to face him, her hand coming to cup his cheek and force his eyes to open. "You have to relax."

"I'm trying." He licked his lips. "I know I should be sleeping so I can be my best tomorrow, but I just really want to get back out there right now. I'm not even sleepy."

"Do you want a massage?"

He shook his head.

She didn't offer sex again, it hadn't worked the first time and with his head as screwed up as it was right now he didn't need to venture into anything adventurous and kinky in search of relaxation.

"Meditate with me."

"Elle, I can't concentrate right now."

"You don't have to concentrate." She pulled away from him, though it took effort—he didn't want to let go. "I'm not going far." The words were ones she might've said to comfort a child. Grabbing the quilt from on top of the duvet, she shook it out. "Sit, legs crossed."

His arms loosened.

To his credit, Anson didn't sigh. He didn't roll his eyes. He sat up and did as she asked.

Ellory wrapped the quilt around his back to keep him warm and then climbed onto his lap, wrapping her legs around his.

"Is this some kind of sex meditation?" he asked, wrapping his arms around her waist as she settled against him. The tremor he was unable to stop made it feel vaguely like cuddling a big manly vibrator.

A shake of her head. "No. It's much simpler than that." She combed her fingers through the hair at his temples and kept his face facing forward. "All I want you to do is look me in the eyes. Watch the light of the fire, and just be. You don't have to do anything. I don't expect anything from you. It's not so hard to look at me, is it?"

"It's incredibly easy to look at you," he breathed back, but his brows were still pinched, like he was concentrating. "But how is this meditating?"

"It's supposed to make you feel safe...and connected. Do you feel safe?"

He gave her one of those smiles that contradicted his pinched brows.

"How about connected?"

"I feel connected."

That one she believed, but he needed to relax his brow if he had any hope of this working. She pressed one thumb between his brows and gave that muscle a firm rub until it relaxed, ran him through some breathing techniques and then settled her arms around his shoulders.

Her neck relaxed a little, causing her head to tilt to one side, and stared deep into deep green and hazel eyes, saddened at the bleakness there.

He mirrored the action, keeping their eyes aligned.

She kept her voice gentle, wanting nothing more than to soothe. "We're sharing energy. It's like physics. Entangled particles. We will just sit and be together, share breath, share heat, share touch. You will look into me, and I will look into you. And when our particles are good and entangled, no matter where you are on the mountain, doing this terrible job that needs to be done, you can share my peace and hope when your well has run dry, and I can share your burden."

He swallowed, but he didn't argue. She half expected him to declare the exercise stupid and pointless, but surprisingly his arms relaxed until they were more looped around her than holding her.

If there was one thing Ellory knew how to do, it was relax. She could cast off her conscious mind with astonishing ease, having learned long ago how to escape into her imagination.

Pulse and respiration slowed, relaxation extending from her body to her eyes. The focus went past the firelight dancing in his mossy eyes, and images started to emerge. First blurry, then crisp. A home in green fields, babies with eyes like the forest, and fuzzy black puppies. She saw the green fading from his eyes, the dark fringe of his lashes turn sparse and grey, and love that grew strong.

She saw everything she'd always said she never wanted, and knew it for what it was: the biggest lie of her life. The bond she felt with him, the aching need, that was love. She loved him. This was that moment that Mira and Chelsea had been describing, where her heart swelled and… She remembered she couldn't have that future. She couldn't have him, but she couldn't even begin to understand how she would ever be strong enough to walk away from it.

Anson shook her.

Something cold and wet splashed on her chest, and she realized she was crying. Her breath came in broken hiccups and she let go of his shoulders. "I can't do this." Her having some kind of a breakdown wasn't the purge he needed to start healing. It was hers. How many purges did she have to have to reach the bottom?

"Why? What just happened?" His voice firmed with intention, focus, and he kept his arms locked around her waist. "What are you afraid I'm going to see?"

"I don't know." She pulled back hard, and turned to crawl off him and away. Just get away.

He let her go, sounding bewildered but not following. "You do know. What's wrong?"

"I don't know," she repeated, and only stopped once she reached the farthest corner of the mattress, her back to him, on her knees, struggling to calm herself.

This was supposed to be for him. Metaphorical, a way of releasing tension, not anything real. If this was how he felt…

She gulped the air, smelling the sharp ping of the natural gas from the fireplace and focusing on that smell, using it to clear her head. This was supposed to be about him, not about her...

"Talk. You said you put things together in words. Talk." His words came from right behind her, and his arms came around her waist again, pulling her back to his chest and then into his lap as he sat. "You're not going anywhere. You said we're having a spirit quest, so if you really believe that then you either know something you don't want to know, or you just figured something out. Tell me."

She had to say something, and blurted out the first words that came to her mind. "You find people who are lost..."

"I find people who are lost," he confirmed, and waited for her say more. Think it through.

But right now it wasn't about making connections. That one statement unlocked so much more. So much she didn't even really want to think about, let alone put into words. Or what she could even tell him without freaking him out.

That she knew she loved him?

That she knew she wanted him?

That she'd change every part of who she was just for the chance to be with him?

That she wasn't even supposed to be alive, so how could she be with him?

She wasn't supposed to be able to have a family and make more people, more consumers, add to overpopulation. She couldn't settle down, stop going out into the world on her missions to try and make her accidental life a happy accident instead of being the waste her father had always said she would be.

As she felt the firm heat against her back she realized he'd stopped shaking. At least she'd managed that...

She'd never loved any man because she'd always dated men she wasn't especially attracted to—the ones who wouldn't tempt her—and if they were from the places she frequented they understood her lifestyle.

She couldn't even let herself think about the possibility of having her own family. It was wrong. It confirmed every bad thing her father had said about her. It made him right, and it hurt too much. Daydreaming gave her hope, but it was false.

But somehow Anson had slipped past her defenses and she wanted to change, be someone that he could love. Become someone real.

She had to say something, and she couldn't lie to him.

Instead, she whispered the only thing she could. "I don't want to tell you."

He didn't say anything right away, just held her and nuzzled into her hair until she relaxed against him.

"Is it too hard to say?"

"I don't want you to know."

He stilled. "You don't trust me?"

"You find people who are lost," she repeated, not knowing what else to say, "but you can't find me, Anson. There's nothing to find."

The sigh that preceded his words said as much as his tone. "There damned well is someone to find."

"I don't want to hurt you."

"Is this about what you said the other night? I forgot about that. You aren't supposed to be alive?"

She went quiet again, trying to sort through it. But the epiphanies that had given her the bum's rush dried up with her gaze fixed on the wall. His heart beat against her back slow and steady while hers hammered so hard her lungs felt they would bruise.

"My father and mother didn't ever want to have children. The world is overpopulated, and people who are trying to change should lead by showing the way. They shouldn't have kids because it helps offset all the people who have lots of kids and all that."

"Why did they?"

"Accident. Mom got pregnant and her conscience wouldn't let her have an abortion. So I'm this black mark on Dad's record. I make him a hypocrite."

"He said that to you?" Anson asked, the incredulity in his voice making her look back at him.

"Honesty is the best policy."

"It's not the best policy when it makes your kids feel... I don't even... I can't even think of what you..."

"I'm fine. I just I don't want to mess up. I need to do better than they did. Not ever get pregnant, or have the strength to do what has to be done if I do. I shouldn't have the opportunity to make more lives to burden the planet with, or burden the planet in any other way either. So I try..."

He flipped her around so she landed on the mattress on her back. He leaned over her, his expression thunderous. "You're not a burden on the planet. If your parents actually said that..."

"Oh, not my mom. She never... Just my dad. He has very strong morals."

Anson might've put his fist through the wall once or twice in his life, but he didn't take out his aggression on people. Ellory's father? He'd make an exception for that man, if he ever met him. "What did you think of when you ran away from me just now?"

"Nothing. Nothing important."

"You tell me right now."

"It's not important. I know why I was supposed to come back here now. That's what is important."

She reached for his face, trying to distract him or soothe him, when she was the one who needed soothing. He pulled her hands away from his face and laid them on her chest, holding them there, holding her beneath him. "You want to know why you're not happy? That's why. No one can be happy under that weight. That lie."

"I was supposed to come back here and find you."

"So I could tell you that what they told you was bull?"

"No. Stop thinking about that. It's not important. What's important is that you're lost too. You find people, but you're lost. Someone else has to find you."

CHAPTER ELEVEN

ANSON KEPT HER pinned beneath him so she couldn't get away—it felt like that kind of a situation, where one wrong move and she'd be gone from him. "You can't be okay with this. It's not an okay situation. You can talk to me."

"You can talk to me too. I've told you so much about myself, but I know very little about you. It has upset you, even though that's silly, so now you want to talk about it. But there's other stuff that upsets you and you never talk about that stuff. I've told you, like…everything about me. If you can't tell me anything, then whatever connection… whatever is going on between us is just a joke."

He didn't want to talk about that stuff. He wanted to talk about this stuff. This *I'm supposed to not be alive* stuff. "If I tell you that stuff, will you talk about this too?"

She looked at him for several long seconds and then nodded. "If you tell me about the important things, about how you feel about Jude and why it's so personal, and I want to know about your toes…and your mom—were you with her when she died? You tell me that so I don't have to keep trying to badger it out of you, and I will tell you what you want to know. You can't just try to shut me up with kissing or some other method. If you keep bottling things up, eventually you're going to put your fist through another wall."

"That was before we were together."

"It was when you needed someone to talk to and refused to talk to anyone."

Anson sighed and leaned off her, pulling her with him as he rolled onto his back. He liked this position. His arms could go around her and her hair was loose, not lain on or pinned down in any fashion—he could touch it without accidental pulling and he found that soothing.

She did warm him, and he finally noticed the tremor he'd been feeling in his guts had stopped.

Being with her—fed by her, held by her, loved by her—were all comforts, but being challenged by her, being worried about her, was what turned up his internal furnace and finally warmed him.

Telling her the whole truth would make her feel differently about him. Maybe not negative—not telling her was doing that already—but would she take his guilt on? She'd said as much before she'd started inexplicably crying.

"Me not telling you that stuff, how I got stranded on the mountain, it's not that I think you wouldn't understand. I know you would understand, you're probably the most empathic person I've ever met..."

"Then why? It hurts me that you won't tell me. And, more importantly, it hurts you."

"That's not more important." He bit the words out, then stopped and took a breath. He didn't want to yell at her, upset her more. It was his frustration talking. And the fact that he needed to know why she'd started crying, what dark thing she'd thought about herself. She couldn't carry that darkness, it *would* hurt her. Change her. "What makes you think I don't deserve the burden I carry?"

"You're a good man."

He shook his head, and she must have felt it because she lifted her head from his chest and looked up. He kept his eyes on the ceiling, though, not looking her in the eye might be the only way he could get through this.

"You're a freaking hero!"

"I killed my mother."

She went utterly still in his arms, even to the point she stopped breathing. He felt her heartbeat increasing beneath where his palm flattened against her back, keeping her close.

"I don't believe you."

But her behavior said she did believe him. He gave her a little shake and she started breathing again, though more shallowly and faster than normal.

He had to tell her now. And he couldn't look at her when he told her. Rolling again, he managed to get her on her side and lie behind her, where he could once more bury his face in her hair. It was soft, and her scent comforting.

"We were on our yearly ski trip. I was ten."

"Where?"

"Here." He answered the question then continued. "A storm was coming. We, my mom and I, had stayed out until the snow started coming down too hard. She said it was time to go down, go back inside. I said one more run... And before she could grab me I took off down the back side of the pass. If I was going to get in trouble for disobeying, then I was going to get the most mileage out of that punishment I could. That side of the pass, the steep side...no one had let me go down every time I'd tried. They all said it was too advanced for me."

"Did you fall?"

"Of course I did. It *was* too advanced for me. I gave

it a good run, made it about two-thirds of the way down before I wiped out on a rock while going too fast. Fell. Slid the rest of the way down the slope. Broke my leg. Thigh. Femur."

"Where your scar is?"

He'd seen her examining it before, she'd touched him everywhere, but he'd been pretty good about distracting her when she'd been working up to the question. "Yes."

He waited for her to absorb that. She thought through things out loud usually, and no way was he going to do this again. Do it once, do it right, put it out of his mind. That meant letting her have questions as they went.

"Did she find you?"

"She caught up to me when I was on my back, facing downhill, screaming. We were completely alone— if someone had been around they would've heard the screaming."

She started squirming, trying to turn herself around. He didn't want to look her in the eye right now. "Be still." He squeezed then pressed a kiss into the crook of her neck. And then another. And then behind the ear. Sex between them was explosive enough that he could put an end to this conversation for now, continue kissing her, work her up... She'd give up talking but then he'd just have to deal with it again another day, and he wanted answers right now too.

"So what happened? A broken femur can't bear any weight. Was it a straight break? You must have hit... It was here at the pass? I don't remember hearing about this."

"I'm a few years older than you. I was ten. So you were..."

"Six."

"Most six-year-olds don't keep up with the news."

She nodded and sighed. "So it was that big boulder toward the bottom of the insane slope...the one that juts out and is all sharp? I used to think it was a tooth that the mountain had. Mountain tooth."

"That's the one," he confirmed. "Tooth works. And, yes, I couldn't put any weight on it. She wasn't a large woman, so the best we could do was me pushing with one leg while she pulled me. The storm was really picking up, the sky got so dark it could've been night, but she managed to find a tight overhang, a ledge close to the ground. She crawled in then dragged me in after her."

Her fingers twined with his, showing the support he'd known she'd show him. It was easier to accept the support from her hands than to see it in her eyes.

"The first night was the worst. So cold. We couldn't even really huddle together for warmth because of how shallow the space was. My leg hurt so bad. She fished a toy from my backpack and used it like a puppet, told me stories...

"We thought the storm would break in the morning. I was losing consciousness in spells that day, so it was a better day for me. I try not to think about what it was like for her."

She managed to roll over when his arms relaxed, taking advantage of that small window before he could stop her. Her hand pulled free of his and she used it to brush his hair back from his face, her palm soft, and in that moment he knew she loved him. Which meant he had to tell her what he'd caused so she could know what she was getting into. If he told her he loved her before telling that, it'd color and corrupt her thoughts.

"From there, the story is what I've managed to cobble together from what other people have told me and what I remember. When the storm stopped on the third day I was completely out. I don't remember that night or morning at all. I imagine she tried to wake me. I didn't actually wake up until several days later in the hospital, which was a couple of days after my final surgery. There was one to repair my thigh, the pins needed to set the bone and remove some tissue that had died. And the second one was to remove toes that had succumbed to frostbite. Only one on the healthy leg, but the broken one got it worse. Probably because of restricted blood flow to the area."

"I didn't put that together. I saw the scars…"

"I know." Part of being loved by Ellory meant she touched him everywhere. She hadn't simply stroked her fingers over that scar, she'd kissed it on multiple occasions. She just hadn't known it was all connected.

"How did they find you?"

"She'd tucked her outer jacket over my legs to try and keep them warm…"

"Femur breaks are terrible…"

"Yes. And lots of blood pooled. She was a doctor too, an ER doctor, so she would've known how dire my situation was becoming. After doing what she could to keep me warm, she crawled out and tried to make it up and over the mountain."

"Did they find her?"

"Yes. She'd frozen before she reached the top. Being three days without food and water…she just wasn't strong enough to make it. They followed her trail back to find me."

She combed his hair again and pulled him down until his head was on her chest and she could continue the petting. He should argue with her about it. He didn't deserve her comfort. If he had to relive it while finding Jude… who had left his friends to try and get help, just like his mother had done…he deserved to feel miserable.

"What you're feeling now? Everyone goes through it. It's the bottom."

"Rock bottom?"

"When you're on a quest, you have to purge all the bad stuff before you can start to heal."

Healing. She was so sweet. He wouldn't heal, and he didn't want to. He deserved whatever punishment his mind, or the universe, as she liked to say, deigned to dish out. There could never be redemption for what he'd done. There just was no way to make up for it. His mother was gone. She'd always be gone. His father had lost the woman he loved, and it was *his* fault.

It was his weakness that kept him from pulling away from her. Just another sin, a mark of his cowardice. The search was pulling him back into the void he'd suffered in his darkest days during recovery, and Ellory was his lifeline. If she was pulling away from him, he had to keep her with him. At least until he found Jude and could afford the time it would take to lose his damned mind properly.

"What are you thinking?"

"That I need this," Anson muttered. He shouldn't, but if she knew…maybe she'd stick with him a little longer.

"This? Do you mean to feel bad?"

"No. I mean this." He slid his hand over her skin until it settled over her breast, and the soft firmness that instantly changed, the nipple growing hard to poke the hollow of his palm.

Before she could ask anything else, he pulled her under him, slid an arm under her neck and kissed her. He could lose himself in her—his only way to keep from thinking. Burying himself in her was his only form of meditation, her soft body, her tender heart, and the brief, blessed oblivions she could give him.

"You owe me words, Ellory Star."

"I know," she whispered, still touching his face. "Can we save it for tomorrow? I'd really like it if you would just kiss me right now."

Day fourteen of searching since the storm had passed.

Nothing had been the same since that night—except in every physical way.

Another long hot shower, though she didn't join him wasting the water any more. Their showers got longer and longer—more and more wasteful—when she was with him. And she wanted to ignore that little voice that insisted she was making herself into whatever she needed to be to fit into his lifestyle. But she didn't really know what his lifestyle was—in her mind it was the worst it could be for her. Becoming the antithesis of all the things she'd believed in her whole life…even if it would make life easier and keep her from being this obsessive crazy person, it felt like exchanging one set of bad habits for another.

At least if she listened to that annoying little voice right now, she could feel confident that she wouldn't be manufacturing more guilt for herself later when she finally did figure out what she was supposed to do with herself, how she was supposed to find a way out from beneath the crushing guilt, and find contentment. It was all hard enough without having to think about the things she'd been conditioned to do. Habits, even while tiring and tiresome, were easier than the uncertainty.

Another hot and hearty meal to cut the chill and fortify him. He ate too fast, so did she—it was simply nutrition, tasteless no matter how she tried to make it good, and they both needed to get back to that mattress, their only comfort.

She'd tried to explain to him that her father's distance

and disapproval had driven her to live the best life she could, and that while she could see why it upset him, she thought she'd turned it into something positive. Or she'd always thought that until now. She'd tried to explain it until they both were so frustrated with one another they stopped talking altogether.

She didn't know what to say or how to help him. She wanted to help, and she'd made early attempts to try and tell him he couldn't live his life with that kind of blackness in his heart without it consuming him. He'd nodded, repeated it back to her, and disregarded her advice.

As soon as they found Jude, Ellory was going to break it off. It would be an acceptable time then. She wouldn't be abandoning him when he needed the support she absolutely knew he did need. But afterwards…breaking up was just what had to happen.

It already hurt so bad to be with him that she was trying to soothe herself when they went to bed as much as she was trying to soothe him.

Those all-too-brief moments of bliss when they were together carried her through the next day. Well, almost through. Like a drug, the more she had of him, the quicker the effect wore off until she needed more. She'd had friends who had gone down dark paths—had watched them spiral down, and when lucky, their recovery.

It was the only mental comparison she could make. Withdrawal. How bad would it be to recover from his touch? Would she have any chance of staying on the wagon if she stayed in town where she had access to her drug of choice?

She should start looking now for a new mission. Some exotic new location, people she could actually help and feel good about herself again. Somewhere she didn't have to work so hard to figure out how to live... If she were in some remote village away from all modern conveniences—where they struggled to provide running water— she'd live simply and have no way to be a planetary burden.

They were just finishing dinner when someone knocked at the door.

Mira?

"Graves?" A low man's voice called.

"It's Frank." Anson stood up and answered the door. "Are we going back out?"

Frank Powell was his supervisor, and he had taken over managing the search operation once roads up to the lodge had been cleared enough to get additional search teams in.

Wishful thinking. Ellory saw it on his face the moment she joined them. They weren't going back out.

Frank stepped inside and closed the door. "No, not tonight," he answered first, and then dipped his head to her. "Evenin', Ellory." They'd met many times in the past two weeks as she'd made it part of her job description to bring food to the base of operations they'd set up in one of the conference rooms.

Her visits had never been wholly selfless. With all the tooling they did about the mountains on the snowmobiles, she was in a constant state of anxiety that a slide would happen and bury them all. Showing up with food or drinks gave her an excuse to be there and hear any information, and sometimes to just hear Anson's voice come through on the radio and know that he was okay. Or as okay as he could be.

She was about to offer food when the older gentleman turned to Anson. "I wanted to come tell you in person—

word's officially come down that the search for Wyndham is being reclassified as a recovery mission."

They'd been waiting for this moment, but her heart still sank. She may have only been a few feet away from Anson but hurried over to him and slipped her hand into his.

"There's still a chance," he said, for once not accepting her comforting touch. His hand pulled free and he scrubbed it over his face, trying to wipe off the lie he'd just uttered. They all knew better. Jude could've never survived two weeks in the cold without food or water. He couldn't have survived one week, and probably not even a few days. He was gone, and had been for probably the whole time they'd been searching.

Frank knew his words for what they were—grief. Grief for a man he had never met. Grief for a man he felt like he'd let down. Grief for himself... His normally booming voice was gentle, gentler than Ellory would've ever thought he could make it. "You know that's not true, son."

Anson stepped away from both of them, and Max, sensing the discord in the air, stood up where he was in front of the fire and went straight to Anson's side, ducking his nose and pushing forward until Anson's hand cupped his head.

Anson took the request and petted his trusty companion. Which was good. At least he was touching and taking comfort from someone who loved him.

"Most of the outside teams are leaving and we're reworking our plan," Frank continued. "You and Max should be on duty where you can help the living. I want you to take a couple of days to rest and then report for regular duty."

Anson folded his arms and shook his head. "No. We

need to see this through, Max and I. We're not off the search team." The dog moved in front of Anson and sat, a silent and calm sentinel doing what sentinels did. Protective instinct. Ellory couldn't blame him. Hers were running on high too. She just couldn't pull off the calm sentinel routine like Max did. She'd have said something if she knew what to say.

Was she supposed to back him up? The search was killing him, but not searching? She had no idea how that would affect him.

The next day, while Anson was disobeying orders, Ellory did what any sensible kind of almost-girlfriend would do when confronted with a man in pain: she dug around for information about him on the internet. Found his father's name and that he was a doctor still practicing in San Francisco. Found his mother in an article talking about the rescue, and a memoriam set up to remember her by her old hospital.

None of it was particularly insightful, though she did find one gem: an old photo attached to the rescue article showing exactly where Anson had been found, the place they'd hidden and where his mother's trail had led the rescuers back to. And she found something else: a young Frank to one side, caught in mid-gesture as he'd crouched and pointed into the dark space.

God bless Frank and whoever had taken the picture. They might as well have left a road map for her.

CHAPTER TWELVE

SINCE HER DISCOVERIES had come early in the morning, by noon Ellory had rented a snowmobile and set off on one of the lesser-used trails of Silver Pass. Thanks to the article and the photo she'd found, she was pretty sure she knew right where Anson and his mother had weathered the storm. Maybe there was some trace of the time they'd spent there. His toy? Marks on the stone…something. Even just a simple understanding of what it was like to be in there would be a start.

Even Ellory knew she was grasping at straws, but aside from grilling Frank—which would no doubt be the next step if she didn't find anything in the overhang—it was the only idea she had that might help her help *him*.

The slope Anson had crashed on in his childhood wasn't marked for guests to find easily these days, and she really didn't know if that had always been the case or if it was something that Mr. Dupris had done after the accident. It was maintained and usable—if you knew what you were doing and how to get there. But all signs led to other slopes.

She knew she'd found it when she started seeing the warning signs.

Stopping the snowmobile at the top of the slope, Ellory

surveyed the way down, trying to decide whether there was a safe route to the bottom or not.

With the machine idling in low gear, she heard some short staccato sound echoing through the pass.

She killed the engine and immediately realized what it was: frantic barking. Max…it was Max. But the echo made it impossible to follow.

If Max was barking like that, then something was really wrong. Anson should be calming him down.

Her heart skipped. If Anson wasn't calming him down…

This rugged part of the pass was the most remote, the most dangerous… Her instinct told her that down the crazy run was the direction to go.

The cold air suddenly felt suffocating. Adjusting the face mask and goggles, she started the machine again and took a chance with the machine in the trees. If she went slowly, she could make it down that way. And it couldn't get out of control and end up rolling too far if there were trees in the way. She'd just crash into one, and hopefully not be going that fast when it happened.

Now wasn't the time to stop trusting her gut.

As carefully as she could with any speed, Ellory wove between the trees in a wide zigzag down the slope. The further down she went, the louder the barking got.

About halfway down she realized the barking was getting quieter again.

She'd passed them.

She turned the beast hard toward the cleared slope and worked her way to the tree line.

About a hundred yards up the slope she saw a snowdrift and the black dog in stark relief against it. He was barking at the snow between periods of frantic digging.

Avalanche dog.

She scrambled off the machine and up the slope as hard and fast as she could. *"Anson!"*

When Max saw her, he barked more frantically and ran to meet her, grabbing her sleeve and half dragging her toward the snow she clawed her way up and over.

If he was in there…as long as the barking had been going on… God, she knew someone died in avalanches every couple years. They'd already lost one in a slip this season.

Rounding the drift to where Max dragged her, she saw a hole dug into the bank and Anson's head. Max had got to his head.

"Anson!" She strangled on his name, a barely controlled sob almost choking her.

His head turned and he looked at her. Alive. Alive and awake. No neck injury…he could move his neck.

"We'll get you out." She began pushing the snow off the mound holding him down. Max joined in again, digging beside her.

"It wasn't a real slide…there was a weird cornice…"

She didn't have time to look around and figure out what the hell he was talking about. The only thing she could think of was getting through the heavy wet volume of snow and pulling him free.

"How long?"

"I don't know." He sounded tired. She knew he was tired.

Her goggles fogged from the tears streaming from her eyes, so she tore them off and used the cup like a shovel. She should have had a shovel…

"Tell me what you're feeling."

"The snow is heavy," he said, but as she dug through

several feet and lessened the load on his chest, he began to breathe more easily.

When his hands were free, he held them up to her. "Pull."

Taking both his hands, she leaned back as hard as she could, putting all her weight into the pull. Max pulled too, grabbing Anson's hood and giving quick powerful tugs that made her worry about his spine.

He slid free enough to use his legs, and soon he was out with her and Ellory grabbed for his hands, tearing through the buckles to get his gloves off and inspect his fingers. Red. Still red.

She fell at his feet, and shoved his still wobbly body back into the snow so she could rip one of his boots off. The foot with the most toes had red toes. She checked the other. Two red toes, red feet.

"I'm okay," he said, but he still didn't sound okay. She didn't believe him, not one bit. But she couldn't leave him with his boots off, so she shook the sock to make sure no snow had gotten on it, and helped get his boots back on before she even tried to look him in the eye.

"We're going to the hospital." She looked up now, at the cornice that had fallen on him. "Is your snowmobile under there?"

He nodded. The fact that he wasn't arguing with her about going to the hospital actually did worry her.

"Max will just have to walk with us. I have one, down the slope a way. We'll go slowly."

"How did you know to come?"

"I heard Max."

"You were out already?"

"I was…looking. For something." She wasn't going to tell him precisely what she'd been looking for, and she wasn't going to ask why Anson had gone looking for Jude on this slope. She had the idea that they were headed in the same direction, but neither of them was emotionally ready to talk about it yet.

He moved stiffly and slowly, but when she took his arm again to get it over her shoulder, she realized he was shaking again. Really shaking. The kind of intense shivering the body did to warm itself. Hypothermia...and more than a mild case.

"It's not far." She held him as best she could and they wove a sliding path for the machine, Max keeping pace with them.

When she got him on the machine, she dug into the back and pulled out an insulated jug of hot tea. "It's ginseng and honey for energy." She didn't drink the preservative-laden cocoa, and was trying to get herself back to the habits that had had to be abandoned when things had gotten hairy during the blizzard. "It will warm you some."

Anson took the tea and drank. First a few sips, then more deeply.

When it was half-gone he handed it back. She capped it back up and stowed it in the back compartment.

Max looked around for his cage...but since it was on the buried ATV she said, "Come, Max." Hoping he'd follow them.

"Track," Anson said, wrapping his arms around her middle. The tea helped a little. He wasn't shaking so hard now that she thought he would lose his seat on the machine.

Even so, as a precaution she took a moment and cross-buckled the straps on his gloves, securing them together with his arms around her waist, in case Anson passed out while they rode. The last thing he needed was to fall off and add head trauma to his hypothermia...

Max barked once, she repeated the command, "Track, Max. Track." And then fired her rental to life and started back the long way she'd come.

Too many hurdles had been thrown at her in the past month, she couldn't keep up or even keep track of what she was supposed to be worrying about from moment to moment. Jude. Anson's emotional state. Her carbon footprint. Whether the dog would keep up with them. And now whether Anson had frostbite. Again. Never mind how she was going to cope when she had to go…

She and the universe were going to have to have a long talk after this was over.

Anson had never actually been covered by snow before, not to that extent. Had the situation been any different, had it not been for Max, had Ellory not been mysteriously out on the mountain on a machine she hated…

He'd have to ask her about that later.

Right now, sitting in the examination room at his emergency department, waiting for X-ray results to be read, he was glad he'd banished her to the waiting room.

If he had, in fact, broken ribs, as he suspected he had, then she couldn't know. She'd try to use it to keep him off the mountain, and that couldn't happen.

Technically, the doctor checking him out—a colleague he worked with during his six months of the year when he wasn't on winter duty—was supposed to report his injury to Frank, who would then suspend him from duty. But Anson had gotten hurt while on his own time, since he'd been ordered off the search and had been actively disobeying. And he could ride around the mountains on his snowmobile without much physical exertion. When he found Jude, he'd just have to call for someone else to recover the body.

He owed it to Chelsea and the rest of the group to find the man. He'd looked her in the eye and told her he'd bring Jude home. He'd bring the man home. And on the way out, when this exam was over, he'd stop by Chelsea's room to let her know he wasn't giving up.

Twenty minutes later, having been given a lecture he could've done without, Anson had been zipped back into his suit and in a wheelchair, being wheeled back out to the waiting area. Hospital policy, blah-blah-blah. He could walk, but considering he was getting by without being officially reported to superiors he decided not to push his luck.

Ellory stood as soon as he was wheeled out and came over to take over the pushing. "Are you ready to go?"

"I want to see Chelsea first. But I have to ride there in this chair...stay in it until I have officially left the hospital after being seen."

She wheeled him through the sliding doors toward the elevators. "I know where it is."

"How do you know where it is?"

"I checked while you were being treated. I had a couple of hours to do it." She waited until they were alone in the elevator to ask him more questions. "What did they say is wrong?"

"They said I'm all right. It wasn't the best thing in the world to have happen, and I'm very sore, but it's not going to kill me. They said to make sure and force a cough once an hour, which is what I expected."

"Why?"

"Because when your ribs are hurt, you don't want to breathe deeply. That can cause some people to get pneumonia. But if you keep coughing regularly, it keeps your lungs clear."

The elevator dinged and she pushed him out and to the left, not mentioning to him that she'd actually gone to check in on Chelsea once while waiting for him and going nuts with worry about him. Mira was watching Max, so Ellory hadn't even had her furry support system with her to distract her for her wait. Rescue dogs, while service animals, aren't in the same class as personal service dogs—like seeing-eye dogs—who can go anywhere.

She didn't even feel bad about not telling him that she'd gone to see Chelsea. He wasn't telling her everything, and he'd not let her go into the examination room with him. Because this wasn't a relationship. This wasn't a relationship. This wasn't a relationship.

Maybe repeating the words again and again would make them finally sink in. She was not his girlfriend. He didn't love her, he couldn't love her. It was never going to happen. This was not a relationship.

As she pushed him into Chelsea's room the woman sat up in her bed, eyes wide and round as she looked at him.

"You look like hell," she informed him. "Looks like this search is wearing everyone to the bone. Maybe you should let someone else do the searching for a while."

He shook his head then commandeered the wheels of his chair to wheel right up to Chelsea's bed, where he could reach over and take his patient's hand. "I'm all right. Max the wonder dog and Ellory got me out of my little accident."

"What happened?"

"On the back side of the pass there's a place about midway down the slope, a geographical oddity where there's flat ground beneath a short, slanted overhang…short in terms of mountains. I stopped the snowmobile there because it was flat and Max needed to water some trees… It was a dumb place to stop. The mantel slid and dumped snow on me, knocking me down but not sweeping me away. It wasn't enough for that. Not even a proper avalanche, more like all the five feet thick blanket of snow off a big slanted roof dropping on you unexpectedly."

"You were lucky," Chelsea said, her expression soft. Ellory wished she could see inside Anson's head and read the emotions there as easily as she could read Chelsea's. She felt guilty that he was still out there.

Anson shook his head. "Max dug the snow out before I suffocated and then barked loud enough for Ellory to find us."

Ellory didn't know what to do or say. He wouldn't want her comfort here in front of people, and she didn't really know what to say or do for him right now to help.

Chelsea settled her gaze on Anson, still in his chair. "When the storm passed your crew were the only ones who could search for Jude, but they came to visit the other day, and told me how there was no way he could have survived in the snow this long. That it was turning into a recovery mission."

Something else Ellory didn't know was how Chelsea managed to speak so steadily. Now that Ellory knew what it meant to love a man, and remembering the panic she'd felt when she'd realized Anson was under the snow...

"It doesn't matter if you find him today or in two weeks now. It's not worth dying over. They said I'll be here for a few more weeks at least, maybe even until spring arrives and the snow melts... If there's no chance that he's alive..." Chelsea's throat finally closed, stopping her words.

There was absolutely nothing she could do or say to help either of them. She opened her mouth to say something, though she had no idea what would help, when a knock behind her had her turning and stepping away from the door.

Sheriff, a deputy, and Frank.

Her stomach bottomed out. The presence of three officials together…

They must have found him.

"Jude Wyndham has been found."

Anson heard the voice, heard the words, and carefully turned the wheelchair he'd been confined to so he could face the doorway and whoever had walked into Chelsea's hospital room.

Sheriff Leonard. Deputy Gates. Frank.

"Where was he?" Anson asked, even though he knew that they'd come to tell Chelsea. One look at her face confirmed for Anson that she wasn't able to ask the questions she'd later need the answers to.

"Montana."

Montana. He searched his mind for the name of different peaks and valleys in the area, and came up with nothing. "Where is that? I don't think I'm familiar…"

He noticed Frank looking at him. Frank, his boss, who didn't know he'd been hurt today. Not like it mattered now that Jude had been found.

Frank kept the censure Anson knew he was due out of his voice and his words at least. "The state."

"Montana," Anson repeated, and then again, this time in unison with Chelsea and Ellory, "Montana?"

"How did he get so far away?" Ellory asked.

He couldn't have walked that far during the storm or after without someone noticing. Only an idiot wouldn't walk west or east to get out of the mountains if he was lost. The area was developed well enough that he'd have stumbled over a road and gotten help before he made it all the freaking way to Montana.

"I don't understand. How did he get to Montana?" Chelsea repeated the sentiment.

"By car. He and a woman were picked up in a bank, trying to cash a stolen check they'd tried and failed to cash in Canada," Sheriff Leonard said.

"A woman?" Chelsea asked, her voice rising in pitch.

"Maybe we should speak about this further in private," the sheriff said gently to Chelsea, but Anson didn't need further explanation. He got it.

A look at Ellory confirmed that she was still as confused as Chelsea was.

"Elle?" He said her name softly, getting her attention. "Let's leave them to speak with Chelsea." He tilted his head toward the wheelchair handles, silently asking her to push him out of the room.

She stepped behind him, and after giving Chelsea's hand a supportive squeeze wheeled Anson out of the room. Once out of earshot of those still inside the room she stopped and crouched beside him to whisper, "What were they trying to say to her?"

"That he was never lost in the pass." He said the words gently. "The stolen check he and some woman were trying to cash? They were probably Chelsea's."

"He planned it? He abandoned them out there in the cold and...stole from them and left?" Her voice rose, much as Chelsea's had done. Not only was she shocked that someone would do that, she was angry. Anson could recognize the emotion, even if right now he was surprised to find he didn't share it. He didn't actually feel anything.

"Looks like it. Let's get out of here." He nodded in the way they'd come.

"They could've died..." She continued to speak quietly

as she pushed him out of the hospital and on to Mira's car, which she'd borrowed to bring him to the hospital, listing the man's offenses as they occurred to her.

She left him sitting at the patient pick-up and drop-off area to get the car, and Anson took his chance to cough and clear his lungs. It hurt. And she'd insist on staying with him tonight to take care of him if she knew what was going on with him.

A half an hour later, following Anson's directions, she pulled off the highway onto a one-lane road that had recently been plowed. "What do I do if we meet someone?"

"We won't meet anyone. My house is the only one out here," Anson mumbled, "but I have a service to come plow the lane for the big snows."

The road wound through trees on either side, thick enough that Ellory wasn't sure whether or not there was a ledge anywhere in sight. She drove slowly, afraid of sliding into a ravine in the dark.

It didn't take long to break through the trees to a blanket of barely disturbed whiteness. The lane, which she now realized was more of a long driveway, sloped down and back up, following a gently undulating terrain toward a very small house.

Really small.

"Anson, is part of your house underground?"

"No. It's a micro-house. I thought you'd be familiar with them."

"Of course I am. I guess I just thought…with the size of your dog…" Teeny-tiny environmentally friendly house? Who was this guy?

"Does Max even fit in there?"

It had been a really tough day, but this discovery was a bright spot.

"He stays mostly in the living room. Sometimes I think it's a glorified doghouse, like when it rains and he gets that wet-dog smell. The bedroom is in the loft, which you get to by ladder. That took some getting used to for him. We lived in an apartment when I first got him, he got used to sleeping with me…and then suddenly he couldn't even get near me when I slept. I think that's why he's been so possessive about sleeping with us…"

He didn't go on at length about much, but the man did love his dog.

He opened his door and climbed out, so she did the same, intent on seeing him safely inside and getting a gander at the interior.

On the tiny porch stoop he fished his keys out of his pocket and let himself in, disabled the alarm, and then looked back at her. "I saw the weather while we were at the hospital. You should probably head back to the lodge now. It's going to get bad again in a little while."

Before she'd even gotten her toe over the threshold he'd slammed down the unwelcome mat? "You aren't coming with me?"

"I really just want to sleep. In my bed."

They may have found Jude, he may not have been on the mountain in need of rescue and all that, but there was an unpleasant sort of hanging feeling left over. At least if they had found him dead, there would've been resolution, a completed task, a way of honoring his promise and all that.

This way? It was just over. It was just done, and as calm as he acted he couldn't be okay with the way things were.

"Are you feeling like punching the wall?"

"No," he said softly.

"What about Max?" And what about her? Was this

the end? Now that there was no finding that monster on the mountain, it was just a switch he could flip and be done with her?

He didn't answer as immediately. "He could stay with you tonight if you don't mind, and I'll pick him up in the morning."

Stay with her. Somewhere he wasn't.

"I could stay." She tried again, and barely cared that she sounded pathetic, even to her own ears. "Mira could watch Max. I know she wouldn't mind."

His eyes were tired, his shoulders not nearly as broad and weight-bearing as they usually appeared. Much too quiet.

"You want me to go." The words were out of her mouth before she actually thought about saying them. "I don't feel good about it. About leaving you here without anyone, even Max."

"It's not that I want you gone, but I'm tired. The idea of crawling into bed and sleeping a day or twelve appeals."

He'd slept with her every night for more than two weeks, but now that Jude had been found...alive...

"Are we supposed to be glad he's alive?" she asked finally. "Because I don't think I am. I've never wished anyone dead or anything, but before, when we were looking for a guy who'd tried to be a hero and save his loved ones, I so wanted him to be found alive. Now I just want to go to Montana and drown him in his own jail toilet."

Anson nodded, though his expression remained sedate. Too sedate. It was worse than when she'd been trying to get him to talk about how Jude being lost affected him. At least then he'd had some kind of emotional expression. He'd put his fist through the freaking wall, so she had at least known he'd been upset, even if he'd denied it. Now, though, now he just seemed numb. And numb scared her.

Whatever he was feeling had to have been worse than what she was feeling. He'd been the one out there searching, reliving losing his mother, overwhelmed by guilt... But he wasn't going to share it with her.

Everything he said, including the stuff only said by his body, let her know he wanted space. Who was she to deny him?

Ellory covered the short space that separated them and leaned up to kiss him.

He tangled his hand in her hair and kept her close, even if he didn't hold her like she wanted...his kiss warm and full of feeling even if she hadn't been able to see it when she'd looked at him, or heard it in his voice.

Maybe she was just reading too much into things. He could just really need some sleep. Maybe tomorrow he'd feel like talking.

CHAPTER THIRTEEN

ANSON WASN'T SITTING about in his underwear, refusing to shower, drinking too much beer, and punching his walls full of holes.

And that was the best thing he could say about his response to the news about Jude.

Jude.

Judas. Was that the man's name? He was going to have to look it up. At some point.

Max, on the other hand? Pretty much doing half of that list. It was next to impossible to get him off his fireside doggy bed. He didn't eat, not even his beloved jerky treats. There had been exactly zero hours of play since their return home. And he got really disgruntled when Anson forced him to go outside.

It looked like mourning to Anson, and probably because his new person was gone. Ellory. He hadn't seen Ellory in several days, and Max hadn't seen her either.

With a sigh Anson peeled himself off the couch and retrieved the phone. He'd call her, let the dog talk to her or hear her voice, and maybe that would help.

She answered just as the call was about to shuffle off somewhere else—the front desk? Voicemail? Anson had no clue where unanswered calls went at the lodge.

When he heard her voice come down the line his chest

squeezed, which set off a coughing fit before he'd managed to say a word.

"Anson?"

He cleared his throat. "Ellory. Sorry."

On hearing her name, Max got up from the bed and nearly knocked Anson over. "Max wants to talk to you on the phone."

"Max wants to talk to me." He heard it in her voice—she might as well have called him the bastard they both knew him to be.

The massive Newfoundland standing on his hind legs and putting weight on Anson's upper body got him moving toward the point. "If you wouldn't mind. He's been really depressed. Won't eat or anything." He pushed the dog off him and walked to the couch. At least there Max could crawl up on the seat beside him and maybe not break his cracked ribs the rest of the way.

He punched the speaker button and laid the phone on the coffee table. "You're on speaker."

"Hi, Maxie-Max," Ellory crooned, and the dog's tail went wagging with enough force Anson thought his legs might bruise. The big furry head tilted in that confused and interested way he had and he looked up at the loft, then behind him, smelling the air. But he couldn't find Ellory.

"Want a jerky, Max? Tell your big dumb jerky-face who loves you very much. I'm sure he'll give you a jerky. Jerky? Jerky?"

Every time she said "jerky," the dog got more and more excited while she left Anson abundantly clear on exactly what kind of jerky she was talking about: not the kind his dog lived for.

"Just a second," Anson said. "Keep talking, I'll get the stuff."

He stood and walked into the kitchen, leaving Ellory to psych up his dog into eating.

When he came back, she was saying "jerky" so fast and so frequently that the word had stopped sounding like a word. But Max still took the piece when Anson offered it to him.

"He's eating," he yelled, to get over the sound of her silly jerky song. Then he picked up the phone and switched off the speaker. "Thank you."

Asking how she was would be the right thing to do, she'd been upset about Judas too. But asking her that would certainly open the door for her to ask him, and he just had no answers to give her on that score.

Ellory made her way back through her bedroom obstacle course to sit on the bed. After the storm the lodge had started filling up again. She could be working right now if she wanted to. Guests had returned to the lodge and the slopes as soon as the slopes had been prepared and the power had come back on.

By now someone would've overworked an ill-used muscle or joint. Injured themselves...something. But she just didn't have the desire. She was exhausted from worrying, trying not to worry, trying to pretend she didn't care, etcetera—so she didn't worry Mira or work herself up into such a state about Anson that she made herself crazy.

"I'm just a symptom," she said into the phone, after silence had reigned for entirely too long.

Anson spoke with caution, because this whole business was awkward. "A symptom of what?"

"He doesn't miss me so much as he has a big chapter of his life unfinished."

"Finding Jude?"

Ellory nodded, then actually spoke out loud because this wasn't video conferencing… "He spent weeks of his life looking for someone who never got found. He needs closure." And she did too.

And just like that she knew what she had to do. She'd never gotten to her destination that day. Only the universe knew whether or not she'd find anything of his time in the tiny cave. Maybe getting to find someone where he'd lost his mother would help him move on too.

"There isn't going to be any closure about that. Though I think they are extraditing him to the area, so maybe we could go and find him at the jail."

"He needs to find someone. Anyone will do. I'm going out on the mountain in my old crappy snow suit that doesn't keep very warm compared to what my beautiful new suit does."

"Elle…"

She ignored the warning in his voice. "I'm going back to where you got trapped. Take Max there and come and find me. When he finds me, he'll feel better."

And maybe he would too.

Before he could say anything, she hung up, dropped her phone, and crawled under her bed to retrieve the snow suit from hell.

On the plus side, if she froze to death out there, when they found her, everyone would get a good laugh out of how ridiculous she looked.

If it weren't for the fact that he was generally against killing people…

Anson's snowmobile was still buried on the slope where he was going to find Ellory, which meant he had to go slowly enough on the rented thing for Max to keep up.

Unlike the weather that had plagued them for the

past several weeks, the day was bright, sunny and warm enough that the snow held high in the trees was dripping and dropping off, forcing him to take the long way around to where he knew to begin the search.

When they got near the area where Max and Ellory had pulled him from the snow, Max took off and left him speeding in something other than the safest manner in order to keep up with him.

On the other side of the big mound of snow sat another empty snowmobile.

Max sniffed it and then ran back to Anson, to and from until he'd gotten the machine throttled down and had climbed off. Footprints led down the mountain, the snow being still deep enough in this area that she'd left deep leg prints in the snow.

And if she was in the old-fashioned snowsuit, it would not be water-resistant, so she'd be cold. Anywhere her body touched snow would be wet, and that wetness would sink in toward her body fast.

"Dammit, Ellory," he muttered to himself, and led Max to her abandoned snowmobile, tapping the seat twice and giving the command "Find."

Max didn't even smell the seat—it wasn't like he couldn't follow the tracks she'd left. He tore off down the mountain after her, barking and so excited that Anson felt bad for having kept the big guy away from her.

It had taken Ellory an hour of digging in order to make an opening in the snow big enough to crawl through into Anson's tiny cave. She got about halfway in before her suit caught on a jagged piece of rock hanging down. Ellory felt it rip as she backed up, deepened the hole with a couple more shovels of snow, and finally made it inside.

He hadn't been kidding when he'd said it had been a tight fit.

With how long it had taken her to get to the area and make it inside, she half expected that he'd get there just before her feet disappeared inside and drag her out.

She looked toward the light. Feet inside.

Very dark.

Rolling to her side, she got a small flashlight out of her pocket and flicked it on to shine around the creepy interior.

Now that she was there, she felt the strangest feeling of peace—like she was right where she was supposed to be, when she was supposed to be there. Though she really had no idea why, aside from providing Anson the closure he and Max both needed.

Closure. So final. She shivered.

With effort, she shifted to a slightly taller area of the overhang and managed to roll over. That left the area she'd dug out open for Max or Anson, or anyone else who decided to come crawling inside.

If she had been Anson's mother, when they'd crawled in here she'd have put her son on that side of the cave. It was smaller, would've kept him from moving around too much with his broken femur.

She shone the light around, looking for anything he might've left behind...some evidence of having been there...but she didn't see his toy or his backpack. She didn't even see any marks on the rocks where he might've passed the time.

But she did see a dark little cubbyhole opening in the rocks.

And something shiny sparkled in the dirt beneath the hole.

Rolling back to her cold belly, she crawled over to

that side again and stuck her mittened hand into the cubbyhole.

It went deep, all the way to her elbow before her hand touched bottom. Weird.

She patted around, trying to decide if that was maybe a place that air had come in and had maybe made Anson colder during his wait. There was no outlet she could feel, and with the snow blanketing everything outside no air came through either.

When she began working her arm back out of the hole, something bumped into her knuckle and she cried in alarm and jerked her hand out. A few seconds of listening confirmed it—no sound of movement came from the dark and suddenly dangerous-seeming cubbyhole.

What had it felt like? Animal? No… If it had been an animal, it would've bitten her. She looked at her mitten. Intact. No pain in the hand in it.

Dead animal? Felt way too solid for that. When she didn't hear any movement, she took a deep breath and shoved her hand back inside. This time her hand curled over the object immediately and she extracted her arm from the hole.

She fished a toy from my backpack and used it like a puppet…told me stories.

Ellory looked at the plastic army man in his camouflage fatigues and black flat-top haircut and really wanted to cry this time.

He had peeling paint on his legs and back, but his molded plastic face was pristine.

The sound of barking cut through the air, letting her know Max was on his way to find and save her. She stuffed the doll into her suit, and then looked around. Where had that shiny thing gone…?

She flashed the light around in the area she'd seen it,

didn't find it, and then started roughing up the dirt in the area as well. Silver Pass wasn't just called that because of the silvery white snow that fell in great quantities. And she'd discovered a tiny silver nugget once…

By the time her flashlight caught the reflection again, she'd almost worked up enough dirt into the air to send a dust bunny into asthmatic convulsions.

A delicate silver chain. She lifted it out of the dirt and her breath caught as the chain grew taut and a good-sized oval pendant hopped free from the earth.

Correction: oval locket.

Giving it a quick wipe, she pulled one mitten off and found the seam with her thumbnail, popping the catch.

The picture inside had been through however many seasons of snow and ice. The colors had faded. Her throat burned.

She knew the eyes looking out from the picture.

Anson caught up just in time to see Max's fluffy tail disappear under the overhang of rocks where he'd known Ellory would be.

"You found me!" he heard her say, her voice animated. "Good boy!" And then, a moment later, "Anson?"

"What?" He folded his arms, not in the mood for this.

"Can you call him back out? It's hard to crawl around in here."

He shook his head, feeling an epic eye-roll coming on. "Come, Max. Out!"

Many long seconds passed before his oversized dog crawled back out, wagging his tail so hard he could have cleared land with it. Completely happy.

"You too. Come, Ellory. Out!"

He saw padded black boots first. The dog might've

been able to squirm around and crawl out head first, but Ellory didn't have the room in there to do it.

The further out she got, the less angry he became. Her snowsuit, if it could be called that, looked like a quilt. An actual quilt...but canvas, and possibly made from army surplus duffel bags, and maybe even circus tents? And the best part: some kind of purple and yellow checkered canvas.

She came up butt first, and when she turned around it was all Anson could do not to laugh. On her head? A knitted cap in of many colors—as if if it had been made using a little bit of every yarn in the store, and topped with a puffy ball. He had to remind himself he was mad at her for going in there.

"I can see why you don't often wear that snowsuit." He laughed a little, the sound would not be contained. "Must be hard to bear the envy of all around you when the skiers get a look at that magnificent creation."

She ignored him, though her cheeks looked quite pink by this point beneath the smears of dirt she'd undoubtedly picked up in the tight little cave.

Instead, she crouched and petted Max again, making much of him in a way that made Anson feel a little lonely, truth be told. She hadn't tried to hug him, though, to be fair, her arms were so padded it didn't look like she could put them all the way down. Wrapping them around anything bigger than Max would be a feat.

"Elle?" he prompted, when she'd avoided looking at him for long enough that it became apparent she was procrastinating. "Did you think that me finding you here would help or something?"

"Did it?"

"My mom is still gone. Max can be distracted and

move on from a...really awful experience by giving him a win...but..."

"But you're smarter than that," she said, squeezing the dog one more time and then standing up. "When I devised this plan I pictured you crawling inside, finding your toy...and I hoped it might help you."

"My toy?"

"The army man your mom used as a puppet to act out stories for you."

He'd never told her it was an army man. "Did you find...? Was the toy in there?"

She smiled and unzipped her crazy snowsuit, reached inside and pulled out his army hero action figure. Something in his gut twisted as she held the toy out to him and he felt the light plastic weight of it in his hand for the first time in twenty-five years.

"Sargent Stan." He said the toy's name and then stepped back to a bank of snow and sat, not feeling like his legs could support him suddenly. "Why would you even think to do this?"

She followed and knelt before him, pulled off her dirty mittens and stuffed them into the open monstrosity she wore so she could clean Sgt. Stan's face with her fingernail. "I know you already know what I'm going to tell you, but I think you still need to hear it."

He looked up from the doll at those warm brown eyes and nodded, not trusting himself to speak.

"You can't find something on the mountain that you didn't lose on the mountain."

It was like talking to her in the first hours they'd met. He knew she was saying something that she felt was important, but he needed some landmarks to try and run this linguistic obstacle course. He nodded, slowly, hoping she'd elaborate.

"I internet-stalked you."

He nodded again, still waiting.

"Your mom was an emergency room doctor."

"Yes." He could understand that statement.

"And so are you."

He nodded.

She added, "And you save people from the fate that befell her when she…saved you."

Max sensed his growing discomfort and came to sniff at his face. Anson leaned back and gently shoved the dog's head to his lap to pet.

Ellory added, "You lost her on the mountain. But you didn't. She died here, but she was found, and because she was found, you were found. She had a funeral."

All he could do was nod.

"She's not here, Anson. Because you didn't lose her on the mountain. Not really. But Sargent Stan…" She repeated the toy's name and then laid her hand on Max's head to pet him too. "You did lose him here. And now you have him back, and the memory of your mom doing whatever she could to make you feel better…"

Her voice strangled at the end and she looked away long enough to swipe her cheeks. When she looked back he saw her tears had streaked the dirt and muddied her up a little. Any other woman he knew would stop and clean her face at this point, but Ellory didn't and he suddenly knew why: dirt was natural. Like the material of her insane outfit. Natural and real, like she was.

"I went there to find that because I feel like he's your totem. And because I really do think that Max needed to find someone…"

"He did." Anson murmured, not sure how he felt about all this. Or what she meant by totem, but all he could see was his mother's hand holding Sgt. Stan. He wished he could remember what she'd said…

"I found something else. Something I didn't expect. You didn't tell me…"

She slipped one hand into her pocket and when she pulled it out it was closed around something.

"I told you the whole story…all that I know, at least." He kept his eyes off the toy, it was too emotionally charged and he was barely keeping himself together. And he was afraid to look at whatever was in her hand.

"Then it's another piece to cobble together," she whispered, and opened her hand and held it out to him.

Dirt-covered and tarnished, his mother's locket rested in her little hand.

He couldn't move. And when he didn't reach out for it Ellory popped the thing open with her fingernail and showed him the portrait he knew was inside: the one of him and Mom when he'd been a spaghetti-sauce-covered monster toddler, and she'd pressed her cheek to his for a close-up picture all the same. All smiles.

"You have her eyes."

He nodded, and swallowed, finally reaching for the piece of jewelry.

"She left her totem to protect you. Before she left. The rescuers probably just didn't see it." She paused and then added, "You can't control what other people do, that's what I learned from this Jude mess. You can't control anyone but yourself—whether they do something awful like Jude, or whether they're true heroes like your mom. All you can control is how you respond. I get why you're a doctor and why you and Max risk your lives for others." She stood and backed away from him, focusing on getting her dirty mittens back on, so he almost missed it when she whispered, "She'd be proud of you."

His mother would be proud of him, something he had heard from other people in his life, but had never believed. But when Ellory said it…he did believe it. And he suddenly wished he had something he could say to her that would help. He'd been so focused on Jude and Chelsea, on how the search had made him feel, he had neglected tending her in the way she tended him… She was still hurting. He'd done nothing to diminish it.

"I wouldn't try to clean it too much," she said, breaking through his thoughts. "The picture is fragile, and any chemicals that would remove the tarnish would probably ruin the photo. Plus…"

"Dirt is natural?" he asked, teasing a little.

"It is, but I was going to say…maybe there's still a trace of her. Even a particle. Maybe even protected by the tarnish." And then she shrugged, and turned toward the tree line and slogged off through the snow. "Which is also natural. Tarnish… Or you could ignore me."

"Doubtful." He closed the locket, unzipped his suit and stashed the precious cargo in an interior pocket. "Where are you going?" He zipped back up and stood to follow her.

"Lodge." She reached the trees and turned up the hill, using them like posts to help pull herself up through the snow. "It's cold."

And she was wearing the world's most ridiculous snowsuit. "Is it wet?" he asked, hurrying to catch up to her so he could link elbows and they could pull up the steep slope together.

"Yep. It doesn't hold water out as well as…" She looked at his face and stopped speaking, probably noticing how displeased he was with this little tidbit. Out in the cold, freezing for his benefit…

He let the silence go on between them for a few minutes before asking, "Are your feet cold?"

"My feet are fairly warm. Not wet, three pairs of wool socks. Boots two sizes too big."

When they'd made it far enough up the slope to reach the snowmobiles, she pulled away from him and climbed on hers. She waved a mittened hand at him and called, "Take care of yourself and Max," then turned around and zoomed across the slope, heading back for the lodge and leaving Anson to try and catch his breath.

His chest ached, though not from exertion or even from his cracked ribs.

Her farewell had sounded an awful lot like goodbye.

CHAPTER FOURTEEN

"SHE LEFT."

Anson stood in the doorway of Miranda Dupris's office, staring at the woman. "What do you mean, she left?"

"I mean she isn't here any more. She doesn't work at the lodge any more. I told her we'd be happy to have her here for the whole year, guests don't just get hurt when skiing, but you and I both know that as much as she loved being here, she has her code and that code requires space." She paused and looked at him. "As well as no central heating. She's been making small changes, but she's still very against central heating."

Okay, so it had taken him a couple of weeks to figure his life out, what he wanted versus what he did. But he hadn't expected her to run away in the meantime. Winter wasn't even over yet. "Did she go back to Peru?"

She could be anywhere!

Mira shook her head.

"Do you know how to contact her?"

"Of course I do."

Best friend, guardian at the gate, torturing the guy who'd hurt her best friend. Right. He deserved that. "Will you call her, please?" He tried some honey, because what he really wanted to do was hose the woman down in vinegar. And shake her.

"What do you want to say to her?"

Definitely shake her. Except if he was going to be part of Ellory's life, he couldn't go shaking her best friend. And they obviously stuck together. Tight.

"I don't need to be vetted before you'll let me talk to her. Trust me."

"You hurt her," Mira said, and then sat down at her desk, hands linked as she fixed him with an unrelenting stare.

Anson sighed, closed the door and went to sit down. If he had to jump through hoops to reach Ellory, it was his own damned fault. "I did."

"You don't understand, you made her break her resolution and then you hurt her on top of that."

"I understand. Believe me." He had to say something to convince her. "I don't know if she will want to take me back, but I have to talk to her even if it's just to tell her one thing. And if I have to go all the way to Patagonia to do it, I will go all the way to Patagonia."

Mira said nothing, just watched him.

"I love her, Mira."

"Is that what you want to say?"

"That, and I want to tell her something about her father."

She sat up straighter, brows surging to her hairline. "Did you go see him?"

"Yes, I did," Anson answered, then frowned, "After I told him what I'd come to tell him, he refused to tell me where she was. I didn't expect him to know, I just wanted to highlight this fact in a completely obnoxious manner."

An hour later, after he'd relayed a blow-by-blow account of his meeting with Ellory's parents, Anson left with a Main Street address in hand and the urge to shake Mira again.

He'd spent the whole time thinking Ellory had left the country, and she was just in town.

A brass bell at the top of the main door rang and Ellory popped her head round the corner from the back room. "We're not open for business yet," she called, but all other words died in her throat. Anson stood in the doorway wearing actual clothes, nothing orange in sight.

Jeans that fit his muscled frame well. A worn leather jacket hung open, revealing a flannel button-down over a navy thermal top.

He'd shaved.

His hair was combed back and not hidden beneath a knit cap.

And he had a plant with him.

Max, his perpetual companion, didn't stand on ceremony and obviously didn't feel any of the awkwardness the humans felt. He danced around the counter in that happy wagging-tail way of his to greet her.

Ellory greeted Max before he destroyed the place with his big swinging tail.

"Max," Anson grunted, "You're stealing the show, buddy. Go lie down." He snapped his fingers and pointed to the fire, which was enough. The big black Newfoundland all but pranced over and flopped onto the old worn wood floor of the building Ellory had leased from Mira.

Her heart in her throat, Ellory looked back at the man, and only then realized she should say something. "Thank you. For the…the…spa-warming gift."

"I wanted to get flowers but apparently you can't buy flowers that are locally sourced in winter." He approached the counter and thrust the potted fern at her.

She took the pot, careful not to accidentally touch the man, and set it on the counter. "It's really nice. Reminds me of the rainforest. Besides, cut flowers just die anyway. Nice of you to bring it by."

"I actually don't have any clue if the plant is a viable substitute... You're supposed to bring flowers when you apologize to the woman you love."

No preamble. He just laid it out there so boldly that her mind went blank.

"You can't control what other people do, right? That's what you said. You can't control what other people do... or think or anything. Just you, how you react."

"Right," she whispered, her hands starting to shake. The blasted bracelets jangled, and he noticed.

Before she could hide her hands, Anson reached out and took both of them, his thumbs on top to stroke the backs of her hands. "I visited your father."

"Oh, no... Did you hit him?"

"No. I wanted to, but he's a miserable old cuss, and nothing I can do will ever change that." He said the words slowly, like she hadn't already come to that conclusion on the mountain.

"I know that now. And I hate to say it, but Jude taught me that lesson."

He nodded, seeking her gaze and holding it for the space of several heartbeats. She loved his eyes...

"That's why you left us? So I could figure everything out? It wasn't because you stopped loving us?"

Us. She knew he meant him and Max, not the two of them as a couple, but it was still cute how he was hiding in language a little bit.

"I never said I loved you." Having her hands in his gave her the confidence to torment him a little. It had been at least twelve years since she'd seen him on the mountain... a couple of weeks ago. Twelve really long years.

"Yes, you did."

"No, I didn't. I definitely never said that."

He shook his head, looking at her like she was crazy. "You did too."

"I never ever said that to anyone but my parents and Mira. Never. Not once."

"Well, I heard you say it." He let go of her hands suddenly and reached across the counter, his hands folding over her shoulders to pull her toward him as he leaned in to meet her. No working up to it, no flirting and coyness, he just kissed her like a starving man, like it was all he could do to keep from dragging her across the counter into his arms.

She did it for him. Ellory's arms stole around his shoulders and she hooked one knee on the counter to climb over. Warm hands slid to her waist and he helped drag her to the front with him, and right onto the floor, only deepening the kiss when he got her well and truly plastered against him.

By the time he came up for air the worried look she'd seen in his eyes was gone, and he smiled. "And there you said it again."

"Did not." She grabbed his head and pulled him back down, not caring at all whoever happened to walk by the big glass windows on the old general store she was converting, and that they might see them making out.

Though she was really glad that she'd taken several days to clean and restore the hardwood floors with lemons and beeswax. Which reminded her...kissing and making out hadn't been their problem. They were really good at that.

"Say it," he grumbled. "I know you love me. You might as well admit it."

Ellory sighed and then nodded. "I love you. But that doesn't mean we're compatible."

He snorted softly. "Are you and Mira compatible?"

"Of course we are."

"You're totally different. And you still fit together. You and I? We're not that different, and we fit together. I can prove it."

"You cannot prove it."

"Things you'd do to improve the house and property—greenhouse, doghouse, solar panels everywhere, and a thermal well into the earth to get the heat without a drop of carbon in the atmosphere. How am I doing?"

She laughed up at him. "Proud that you figured that out? It's pretty obvious."

"I'm a smart guy, what can I say?"

"I can't really tell you if I like your little house or not. You never let me inside, smart guy."

"Okay, yes, I have made some mistakes. But you will love it, as much as you love me and Max."

"But I still never said that."

"Everything about you says it. Mira said you moved out of the lodge. Where are you living?"

She pointed up at the ceiling.

"Above the shop?"

A nod. "Spa."

"Is it furnished?"

"Mmm it has a futon…and a fridge. And a pot-bellied stove."

Because she hated central heating.

"What made you decide to stay?"

"What I realized in your cave." She started to look a little nervous then, and chewed her lip which made him want to kiss her some more.

"About my mom?"

"Sort of." She started wriggling to get out from under

him, but Anson knew better than to let her get away again.

"Look at me. I just told you I love you. What can you possibly be afraid of?"

"You don't know how successful I've been with wrangling my compulsions."

"Tell me."

"I'm about half as obnoxious as I was." Ellory said, shrugging. "It's not going to happen overnight, and I don't want to just become whatever you want me to be. I want to be what I want to be, and I need some time to figure that out."

"Okay. If you want to wait, I can wait." He leaned down and brushed his lips against hers. "So is this a grocery?"

"Do you see fresh fruit? It's a spa, maybe a wellness center. There will be some natural remedies available, oils and decoctions for different common ailments—like muscle soreness, and the respiratory flush we used on our patient guests. And some other natural stuff. Like deodorants without propylene glycol and other bad chemicals. Meditation, yoga, and primarily treatments."

"Treatments?"

"Massage therapy…remember? And with Mira's old contacts there are a few serious ski competitors who will likely be bringing their physio orders here."

"How have the epiphanies affected your stance on children?"

She opened her mouth to say something and then shut it again, her shoulders creeping up.

"You don't know?"

"I didn't want to think about it," she confirmed, though with less energy than she'd spoken with up to that point.

It was better than her saying outright she wasn't

allowed to have them because she wasn't supposed to be alive to breed a bunch of new people into existence. "Afraid it's too far off your new paradigm?"

"New paradigm?" she repeated, and then shook her head. "No. More afraid I might turn mean, like my father. What if my child, no matter how well I try to raise it, turns into the world's biggest polluter and consumer?"

"We won't let that happen." He'd slipped that "we" casually in there and watched her smile return before adding, "So long as you don't make them wear that snow-suit."

"You haven't asked me to marry you yet." She laughed, getting Max's attention.

Anson shoved the big furball back before they both got licked on the mouth. "I'm working up to it!" When Max would not be dissuaded from licking them, Anson stood and pulled her up from the floor, then set her on the counter where he could kiss her safely and add, "But, it's going to be a lot easier to ask now that you've already said yes."

She laughed against his lips. "I did not!"

"Yes, you did. I heard you. Plain as day."

Flinging her arms around his neck, she kissed him again and then peeked around him toward the entrance. "We have to lock the door. Because it's definitely time I give you the tour of my futon." With a bounce in her step she scampered to the door and then back to take him by the hand. "Just so you know, it's a naked futon tour. We like to keep things natural around here…"

EPILOGUE

"No champagne."

Ellory Graves drank once a year. Once! But not this year. She looked at her new husband, who had spoken the words, and made a face at him as he shooed off the waiter carrying a tray laden with sparkling flutes of bubbling liquid amber yum-yum. They'd been married since Thanksgiving. True to his word, he'd waited until she was ready for the ring, which happened to be a few months after she'd been ready to make a baby...

"I brought a sparkling apple cider."

He flagged down another waiter, leaving Ellory to slowly spin on her bar stool, hand resting on her rounding belly that had finally reached the point where none of her shirts seemed long enough.

Mira was a few months further along than she was. Ellory had decided she could have one baby and not ruin the planet. And since every child needs a sibling...and Mira was making a baby...

"I'm almost afraid to make any resolutions this year," Mira said. "Like nothing can live up to the last year, so stop making them while we're ahead!"

"No way. We need a goal. I need a goal. Can we hold the resolution to midway through the year when the babies are out and we need to lose weight? Because you're looking mighty round, Mirry."

Jack stepped around his wife and laid a hand protectively on her belly. "Don't listen to her. You're perfect."

"Shut it, Sex Machine. I am trying to get out of doing work for the first half of the year!" Ellory laughed, leaning against Anson. It still felt surreal to her—the most negative and contrary resolutions they'd ever made had turned into blessings bigger than either could have imagined.

The universe really had a wicked sense of humor.

Although, if making negative resolutions was the way to ensure big changes in your life, she was done with that. Her life was perfect. No changes welcome!

"I'm going to learn how to turn flax into linen," Ellory said, snagging the sparkling cider and waiting for Mira to lift her glass. Nice and innocuous.

The countdown had started. She felt pressure on her back, spinning her stool so she faced him. "Leave the lady alone," Anson said, his lips right at her ear. "She's got her first New Year's kiss with her husband to attend to." He waited a beat, tilting his head to catch her eye, then added, "*Hint.*"

He regularly made her laugh, and she knew their child's life would be full of love and laughter. Neither of them would allow anything into their lives that threatened that contented bubble of happiness they'd wrapped around their home.

Graves wasn't even a bad last name in the right context. A love they'd both go to their graves to protect? Good context, and Anson had the perfect example of it.

When the crowd hit one, he swooped in and delivered a kiss full of promise and acceptance. Her favorite pastime.

And it was even good for the environment.

* * * * *

MILLS & BOON®

Want to get more from Mills & Boon?

Here's what's available to you if you join the exclusive **Mills & Boon eBook Club** today:

✦ *Convenience – choose your books each month*

✦ *Exclusive – receive your books a month before anywhere else*

✦ *Flexibility – change your subscription at any time*

✦ *Variety – gain access to eBook-only series*

✦ *Value – subscriptions from just £1.99 a month*

So visit **www.millsandboon.co.uk/esubs** today to be a part of this exclusive eBook Club!

MILLS & BOON®

Need more New Year reading?

We've got just the thing for you!
We're giving you 10% off your next eBook or
paperback book purchase on the Mills & Boon
website. So hurry, visit the website today and type
SAVE10 in at the checkout for your exclusive

10% DISCOUNT

www.millsandboon.co.uk/save10

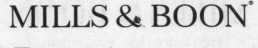

THE ULTIMATE IN ROMANTIC MEDICAL DRAMA

A sneak peek at next month's titles...

In stores from 6th February 2015:

- **A Date with Her Valentine Doc** – Melanie Milburne
  and **It Happened in Paris...** – Robin Gianna

- **The Sheikh Doctor's Bride** – Meredith Webber
  and **Temptation in Paradise** – Joanna Neil

- **A Baby to Heal Their Hearts** – Kate Hardy
- **The Surgeon's Baby Secret** – Amber McKenzie

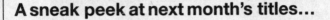

Available at WHSmith, Tesco, Asda, Eason, Amazon and Apple

Just can't wait?
Buy our books online a month before they hit the shops!
visit www.millsandboon.co.uk

These books are also available in eBook format!

0115/03

MILLS & BOON®

Why shop at millsandboon.co.uk?

Each year, thousands of romance readers find their perfect read at millsandboon.co.uk. That's because we're passionate about bringing you the very best romantic fiction. Here are some of the advantages of shopping at www.millsandboon.co.uk:

- **Get new books first**—you'll be able to buy your favourite books one month before they hit the shops

- **Get exclusive discounts**—you'll also be able to buy our specially created monthly collections, with up to 50% off the RRP

- **Find your favourite authors**—latest news, interviews and new releases for all your favourite authors and series on our website, plus ideas for what to try next

- **Join in**—once you've bought your favourite books, don't forget to register with us to rate, review and join in the discussions

Visit **www.millsandboon.co.uk**
for all this and more today!

ТОВ.
Р.Б.
от
М.Р.